Shoot the Lights Out

A Gametime Series

Stephanie Sinkfield

This book is dedicated to my daddy, Thomas Sherman "Shorty" Brown. May your spirit live on for generations to come!

"Whatever you do, don't stink up the gym. Just go out there and shoot the lights out!"

Thomas "Shorty" Brown

Acknowledgements

I never thought I would get to a place where I would start and then complete my first novel. This was seriously a labor of love. In 2011 I lost my father and it shattered my world. Lord knows I should have gone to counseling but instead I started writing in a little journal I kept in my purse. That journal became a note pad and then my IPad and the story just kept on coming. This book is more to me than just some fictional characters. Yes, it's fiction but so many components of my father are here. Things he said, advice he gave and just the pure essence of him. He was a force to be reckoned with whose spirit will live on for generations.

There are so many people I need to thank. First I want to thank writers like Judy Blume, Terry McMillan, Alice Walker, Alex Haley, Ntozake Shange, Langston Hughes, Carl Weber and Lolita Files for being such prolific word smiths who have fed my intellectual need to read during my lifetime. Reading your books and poetry made me so proud to be who I am and made me believe I could write.

I also want to thank my mother Ellen (Janie) Brown who loves me so mightily and introduced the gift of believing in God and reading to me as a baby. My oldest sisters Shelbie Hugle and Kimberly Gibson-Harris who have always encouraged me and told me I could do anything in this world. Special shout outs to my head editor in charge Dody Riggs and my unofficial editors and dear family and friends Ursula Richardson-Bizzle, Melinda Bone, Andrea Hobson, Rodney Hugle, Beverly Muse, Rich Milner, and Patricia Smith for reading this story at its roughest and being my biggest fans and encouragers while giving me honest feedback. Thanks Antonio Tate at Visually Appetizing and Karlene Claridy at Claridy Communications for helping me bring this book to life! I also want to thank my Gen Y babies Ashlee Harris and Caressa Epps for having my back and keeping me current, my Alpha Kappa Alpha sisters, and all of my friends who told this little engine she could!

Last, I want to thank my gorgeous husband Gerald for just loving me and supporting me through this journey. He is my anchor and has been through so much in the last ten years. You are my hero. Without your prayers, support and patience I would not have brought this to fruition. You complete me!

I hope you enjoy my first book in the Gametime Series. Write to me at www.insinkpress.com and give me your reviews.

I'm Coming Home

I never thought I would be coming home for something like this. When we're kids, we always think that our parents are going to live forever. Heck, when we're kids we think *we* are going to live forever! The funny thing is, when the people closest to you die, it brings your own mortality into focus.

That's why coming home is so hard this time. I know I should not have left, but that's what the Holy Spirit told me to do. "Go home," is what He said. Nothing is harder than watching the first man you ever loved die. So now I am coming home to help my mom, sister, and brother (if he can get out of the halfway house) bury my father. The pillar of the community, the consummate basketball coach, the faithful husband, the loving father, the best advice-giver in the world. Home to bury a man that just a few months ago was so full of life.

I hate cancer. It has ravaged both sides of my family. And when it literally hits home—that's right, my dad died at home, in his man cave right in front of his 64-inch TV—it really sucks. So that's why in less than two days I'm on my way back to Nashville, which is halfway across the country from my home in Seattle, to bury my father. At least I had four hours to contemplate all the drama I am sure to find when I get to my parents' house. From what I've heard from my older sister Serena, Aunt Lucy, my dad's only sister, is headed home on the Greyhound bus. Meanwhile, all my dad's players are sulking around the house. My brother Leo is still at the halfway house…we haven't told Leo yet. Thank God he has no access to Facebook or Twitter, but I have got to hurry because within a few hours the entire city will know what has happened. We can only pray that Leo doesn't relapse before we can put Daddy in the ground.

I guess you can say I'm a lot like my dad. Honest to a fault, a sinister sense of humor, loyal to my family and friends, street smart and practical. Which is why I had to get here so fast. I have got to stop my mom and Serena from going overboard on Dad's funeral or, as we say in the South, his "home going" service. And who the hell ever heard of a wake? We sit around for hours while people we don't know come in to look at him, tell us how sorry they are and that he is better off in heaven, and that even if he wanted to he wouldn't come back. That's bullshit as far as I am concerned. Who wants to die? As much as I believe in heaven, I don't think I have ever heard anyone under the age of 100 say they were ready to die.

As I was saying before, the Holy Spirit told me to go home. At first I didn't believe it, but it was as clear as a bell. He said it: "Go home!" (Assuming it was a he...) So, using the ruse of having to check in with my coach and teammates during our conditioning, I hop my ass back on a plane, fly four hours across two time zones, and three bags of peanuts later I'm back in Seattle. I swear I had just gotten off my flight and into a cab headed to my condo downtown when I got the call from Serena, who calmly told me, "Daddy's gone." I said sinister sense of humor, right? Only Daddy would wait four hours until I could get home to take his last breath. My mom, Ella, kept saying over the last week that Daddy was waiting on someone to come or someone to leave. So he waited for me to get safely back to Seattle, for my sister Serena to walk upstairs, and for my mom to flip over into a deep sleep, and then he slipped away.

If my cell phone doesn't stop beeping I am going to hurl it across the airport. Social media is a mother. I have received more condolences over Facebook than I can imagine. How about we have a stay-at-home funeral? We can broadcast it via You Tube, then everyone can stay at home and watch it and put their comments on Facebook and Twitter. I may be 28 years old, but I still believe in good old fashioned letters, phone calls, and face-to-face contact. Which brings me to the reason I am currently not dating? Who in the hell wants to hold a conversation in 60 wrds o lss ovr txt? I met a guy right before Thanksgiving who sent me a text on Thanksgiving Day asking if he could stuff my turkey! I promptly replied "Hell no!" and deleted his name and number from my phone.

I am walking down the concourse in the Nashville airport behind some twit who is walking slow and talking loud on her phone. While they are busy outlawing texting while driving they should also prohibit walking and talking on the cell phone. This chick looks to be about twice my age and three times my size. I often wonder why the slow walkers don't walk their asses to the edge of the hallway so we fast walkers can have the middle of the floor. All of a sudden she stops abruptly and I plow right into her. I forgot to tell you, I am 5 feet 11 inches, and at the age of 28 I am still a little clumsy, except on a basketball court. As I am flying over her suitcase and onto the floor, I see what looks like a mob scene to my immediate right. I realize that all of those people are gathered around to watch me pick my long-legged self up off the floor. I hear snickering, some laughter, and a few clicks of cameras. I know right then that not only will my dad's funeral be posted on You Tube but also my airport fall. I hate social media!

I know this sounds like some make-believe movie stuff, but out of that sea of people come about four feet of the longest legs I have ever seen. Keep in mind that this sister is still on the floor so my view is vertical. And what a view it is! As my eyes continue to travel upward, I start singing in my head, "The leg bone connected to the knee bone, the knee bone connected to the thigh bone..." Well, you know the rest of the song. He just kept going and going, and finally my eyes connected with chocolate brown skin, a wide chest, a broad neck, a whole lot of pearly white teeth with some silver braces wrapped around them, a long, slightly crooked nose, toffee brown eyes, and thick eyelashes surround by some really cute black-rimmed eyeglasses. And his head is as bald and smooth as the day he was born. Did I mention that the brother is 6 foot 4 and about 250...no, about 240 pounds? His legs look like big brown tree trunks and his stomach appears to be a 12 pack. Then I realize that my new fan is Adaris (BKA Dair) Singleton. Yes, the star tight end of the Tennessee Trailblazers, Nashville's NFL team. His profile reads like the *Who's Who* of football. Pop Warner superstar, all conference in high school track, basketball, and football. Recruited by all—yes, all—Southeastern Conference schools for track and football and a few for basketball. He played football for two years as an Auburn War Eagle, where he was only the third tight end ever to win the coveted Heisman Trophy. He was drafted in the first round his junior year and has played for the Cowboys, Jets, and now the Trailblazers.

How do I know this? Well, the question should be, how don't I know about Nashville's sweetheart. He is a walking talking billboard. The only Scarlet A on his resume is that he had a child at age 16 by his then high school sweetheart. Said sweetheart became his baby momma and then she left town and also left him with the baby because she wanted to be a superstar. The heifer should have stayed with "The Dair"—she would have been the brightest star in the sky.

Speaking of stars, I think I am seeing a few. As I sit there acting like Steven A. Smith, the self-appointed king of the ESPN sports stats, I realize that I am still sitting on the floor. So I get my clumsy butt up, give The Dair a dazzling smile, and run down the concourse toward the baggage area. Well, I run about 20 feet before I realize that the TSA folks are starting to whisper into their walkie talkies as if I were a terrorist, so I put on my "I'm sexy and I know it" Naomi Campbell strut and walk the rest of the way to the baggage claim area to get my suitcase.

After I wheel my huge orange suitcase out of the baggage area, I go as quickly as I can to catch a cab. I didn't want my sister Serena or my mom to come and pick me up. They already have enough going on with trying to handle the mortician, family members, friends, and basketball players.

What happened is, about a year ago Theodore "Shorty" Donovan—BKA my dad—went to the doctor for a normal checkup and the doctor noticed that he had an unusual growth on his leg. Now Shorty was only mildly concerned, but Ella (my mother) was extremely so. After having a battery of tests, ultrasounds, x-rays, and MRIs, the doctor diagnosed my dad with a sarcoma in his right thigh, a cancer most commonly found in athletes or ex-athletes. Just to fill you in on the infamous Shorty Donovan, he is/was (I forgot I should now mention him in past tense) a basketball superstar in Nashville who integrated Middle Tennessee State University in the late '60s as one of the first African-American college basketball players. He went on to play some semi-professional basketball, had some odd jobs, and then came back to Nashville to coach at Seymour High School where he was the HCIC (head coach in charge) for 25 years. Why the nickname Shorty? Because at one time he was the shortest boy in the 'hood. He went on to be about six feet tall, but in my eyes and those of all of his players over the last 25 years he was a giant. I'm not bragging about my dad or anything, but he was a force to be reckoned with. He could teach, motivate, or bully his boys into being the best at everything. During his tenure he won 13 state championships, turned out more than 45 all-state players, over 75 percent of his players went on to college and more than 50 percent of those on basketball scholarships also graduated. At the ripe old age of 63 he was just as effective as he was the day he started. And boy could he cuss. He could have taught a course in cussology. I mean, who puts the words "shit" and "ass" together to make "shittinass"?

To play for the great "Coach D" was a tribute to the patience of parents. They knew that by the time he finished with their child the boy would be a first-class student, athlete, and gentleman, but also that his vocabulary would be peppered with a few shittinasses. And my dad gave the best advice. Most of the time you had no clue what he was talking about, but he was so old school '70s cool with it that you somehow figured it out.

I'm in a cab on the way to my parents' house and I decide I'm going to "long handle spoon" a few people in my family. Long handle spoon means that you keep someone at a safe distance until you can figure out what they want. What I have learned in my 28 years of life is that EVERYONE wants something. For example, because my dad has been coaching for so long, I can guess that every wannabe coach who ever coveted his position is either lurking somewhere around our house or calling the principal's house to put in a bid for his job. I can also guess that we have some family members just waiting in the wings to see what they can get from my mother now that my dad is gone.

My mom Ella is beauty personified. My dad always said that his mother could never figure out how he got together with the most beautiful girl at Pearl High. I have heard several variations of the story, my dad's exaggerated version and the truthful story told by Ella. You see, my mom is from a huge family. She has 15 siblings who range from age 50 to 80. When my mom and dad were growing up there were only a few schools you could attend if you were of a brown paper bag hue or darker. My dad was a few years older than my mom, so he had been at Pearl for a few years before she came on the scene. Since she was a freshman when my dad was a junior, he decided he would give her a year to mature before he pounced. Well, pounce he did, and right after my mother graduated from high school they were married, and soon after that my sister was born. I often tell my sister that she was the mistake, but that is only when I am a little jealous because she is the spitting image of my mother. They both have caramel brown skin, big brown doe eyes, long eyelashes that don't even need mascara, these big pretty teeth, and they are built like a brick house. Oh, they also have the prettiest legs that they often show off in short little skirts and dresses. And they both rock this awesome short spiky haircut, which draws more attention to their eyes. Both of them have grace and manners that would rival Emily Post. And, of course, Ella is a God-fearing woman. So much so that she prayed my dad back to church about five years ago. Daddy always believed in God but hated the pomp and circumstance of church. He said that if you wanted to find the biggest crooks, abusers, and drug users, you only had to open the doors of the church and the mfs would just start spilling out.

Thirty-seven years later my mother Ella is not only dealing with the death of her beloved husband but also with the stress of having a son in a half-way house and of getting ready to entertain the countless family members, friends, and students who are swarming around our house at this very moment. Ella is trying to figure out where in the hell to put all the buckets of Kentucky Fried Chicken and the eight spiral hams. Serena sends me a text: *"El s psd she dnt no whr to pt the 10 bkts of kfc and 8 hms."* I text her back: *"Put a note on the dr tht sys no mo chkn and hm pls but we cld use sm more vegges or u cld jst bring $$$$!"* I always have the best sense of humor at the worst times.

Back to Coach. After finding out he had this football-size sarcoma, he decided he didn't want to do anything about it. Well, at least not until Ella stepped in and asked the doctor quite simply what the protocol was for getting this sarcoma out of his leg. The doctor recommended eight weeks of radiation, an eight hour surgery to remove the tumor, followed by chemotherapy to keep the cancer from spreading. She also mentioned that removing said tumor would leave a gaping hole in his leg that could be covered up by a simple skin graft from either his back and or his other leg, and that after the surgery he would walk with crutches or a cane. So Ella prayed over the doctor, the nurses, my daddy, his leg, and the bed he was lying on while Dad had a huddle with the orthopedic oncologist, the plastic surgeon, and the radiologist to tell them how to do their damn jobs, and the decision was made to get started on treatment right after Christmas. To use Coach's words, "Merry damn Christmas to him," and off to the races we went.

Radiation started in January, surgeries in March, April, and May, and recovery time until August. In October we found out that the cancer had spread to Coach's lungs. Two rounds of chemo later, Daddy decided that he had had enough. We took Coach home on Friday and he went on to heaven the following Thursday. In classic Shorty Donovan style, he defied even the doctor's prognosis that he had two weeks to two months to live. The son of a biscuit eater always told us that he did not want to suffer or be a burden to Ella and his girls. He knew that "the boy" wasn't going to be any good so he didn't mention him. He didn't prolong his agony. As I said, he waited until we were all out of the way and then slipped off as quietly as he could. No fanfare, no fireworks, no last testimonies.

While traveling to my folks' house in a cab with the taxi driver from hell that smells like five-day-old Fritos, I think about why my dad was so silent in his last days. He was silent because there was nothing else to say. No more advice to give, no more plays to call for his team, no more loving words to my mother, and no more cussing at my brother Leo. Then I realize how much he said to and did for so many people for the last 63 years. He helped my mom raise their children, and he taught all three of us how to be stellar athletes and good people. He coached thousands of kids and contributed to their successes on and off the court, and he left a legacy that was unparalleled. He said everything there was to say for 63 years.

Wait a minute—did I just see a brand new black Aston Martin Vanquish flash before my eyes!

"Dair, Dair! Do you have any comments on your new head football coach?"

"No comment guys. You know I don't talk out of school."

"Dair, I think that was Jackie Donovan from the WNBA we just caught on camera tripping over that lady's suitcase. What do you have to say regarding the death of her father, Nashville's own Coach D?"

"The only comment I have is that the press needs to respect the family and let them mourn and grieve in private. That said, let me get out of this airport so I can check on my family."

"Is it true that your son Adaris Jr. plays for Coach D?"

"Once again, no comment. I need to get out of here."

My name is Adaris Singleton. My friends and the paparazzi call me Dair—my friends because they can, the "razzi" because they think they can. I think I just saw Coach D's daughter bust her ass on the floor. I have only seen her on TV, but based on what I just saw she is beautiful. Long legs, onion booty, wide hips, beautiful brown paper bag skin, brown eyes, a big forehead, high cheekbones that look like she has some Native American blood in her genes, and eyes that tilt upward just a little. Her hair was in a tight pony tail so I couldn't see much of it, but I can tell she has a lot of it. She wasn't skinny either, which is good 'cuz I like a woman with a little junk in her trunk. I didn't get a chance to introduce myself. For some reason she gave me a cheesy smile and then ran down the concourse. I am sure she's in a hurry to get home to her family, which brings me back to why I am here in the airport.

I just flew in from Connecticut, where I was speaking with some executives from ESPN about a sports analyst position. I've been in the NFL for 12 years, played for three teams, and it's time for me to retire. ESPN has been courting me to join their team in anticipation of my retirement. They keep telling me I have the looks, the smarts, and the presence to be a player for ESPN.

People don't realize how stupid football is. It's not just a contact sport, it's a collision sport, much like Russian roulette. You know there is a bullet somewhere but you just don't know when the thing is going to come out and hit you. Lately, every time I go out for a pass I wonder if it's my last. And because I am starting to feel that way, I know it's time to retire. It's time for me to do something with the engineering degree it took me six years to earn. I also have to admit that with all the football players who have committed suicide after suffering head injuries, I am looking at retirement more seriously.

Most athletes learn quickly to deal with the aches, pains, and injuries that come with the sport. We hide behind the pain and play through it in order to feed our need for notoriety, money, and fame. Over the last 12 years I have had it all. But I know that every great athlete reaches a point in their career when they need to walk away, and that is what I plan to do when this season is done. The operative word being to walk away and not be carted off in a wheelchair.

It's also time for me to spend more time with my son Adaris Jr., or AJ. Fortunately I have earned millions of dollars playing in the NFL and invested much of it to make me more money. Even if I never work another day, I could live several lifetimes and still leave a legacy for my son and his son. I take to heart what the Bible says about leaving an inheritance for our children's children.

My mother, Katherine, has been helping me raise AJ for the last 16 years, but I know these are the years when I need to be more present in his life. I love that boy, but he is young, talented, and cocky enough to give anyone fits, which is why I just cut short my meeting with ESPN so I could get back to Nashville. AJ was moved up to the varsity basketball squad at Seymour High School, where the famous Coach Donovan reigned for well over 20 years. Coach D hosted my son AJ at his summer camps for the last three years, before he became ill, and AJ was really excited about joining his team this year.

When Coach Donovan got sick and we were told that his chances of returning to coach were slim to none, I started to see AJ's attitude change. His coach, mentor, and friend has now passed on, and I need to be here to help him get through the next few days.

It's also time for me to get ready for training camp. I have decided to give the Trailblazers one more year to see if we can get a Super Bowl ring. Not many people get to return to the town where they were born and raised to finish out their career. I know God brought me home for a reason, and I can't wait to see what the year brings me. Speaking of which, I never got a chance to meet Coach D's daughter Jacqueline, called Jack by her dad, but I heard a lot about her when I talked with Coach during the summer camps. Heck, at first I thought Jack was his son. I used to hear Coach yell at his players, "My Jack can out run, out jump, or out shoot all of you chumps out of the gym any day." I realized last year that his Jack was Jacqueline Donovan of the Seattle Stars. If I had known that a few years ago I would have invited myself to his house when she was home. Not only is she beautiful, I heard she is really smart. Oh well, I need to head to the house to check on AJ—good thing I left my Aston Martin parked here at the airport.

As I continue the not so pleasant drive with Mr. Frito to my folk's home, I decide to check my phone. I have 12 text messages and 22 unheard voice messages. "

> *"Hey girl, I just got the message about your dad. I want you to know that I am on the next plane burning as soon as you finalize the funeral arrangements. I can only stay for a few days but I am coming back during my spring break. I also have tentative hotel arrangements. Ok, love you. Text or call me when you get a moment."*

That's Dr. Maxine Hilton, JD, attorney extraordinaire. She got her law degree, practiced for a few years in Florida, and then decided she wanted to teach and went back to get her PhD. We met in college and became sisters in Alpha Kappa Alpha Sorority, Inc. That's Max. Always pragmatic, practical, and to the point. She is a master of the King's English, but she does tend to mess up colloquialisms from time to time. "Next plane burning"…I just may need her if I catch a case in the next few days.

> *"Hey niece. It's me, Lu. I know I sound a little out of it, but I had to drink me a few beers to calm my nerves. Damn, I can't believe my brother is gone. You know I loved my brother. I am getting on the bus in about two hours. I'm going to get Pookie to pick me up and bring me over your way when I get there.*

Tell Ella I am on my way and that I got the $200 that you wired me to come home. Love you niece."

My Aunt Lucy. My dad was like a father to her and they were extremely close. She has had a rough life. Their parents fought all the time and, since she was so much younger than Dad, she had to endure all of their arguments. Daddy used to say sports were his escape, but as a girl in those times she had none…Who the heck is Pookie?

"Good morning Jack. I just got the message that your dad passed away. Listen, I want you to know that while we would love you to be here helping us get our rookies in shape, you need to be home taking care of your family right now. Let's talk soon so we can decide what to do about your final season. You know I want you to stay in Seattle to work in our front office when you officially retire but…we'll talk. Take care of yourself Jack."

That's Coach Tricks, my coach. I love that man. He is just as rough as my dad but he has taken care of me for the six years I've been in the league.

"Hey honey, it's me, Maurice. I just left your mom and dad's house checking on Ms. Ella. I knew you would want me to be there. You know Coach D was like a father to me. Remember your best guy friend is right here if you need me. Call me when your plane lands."

That's Maurice, BKA Cornell. He has been my best guy friend since the seventh grade. I can always count on him to be in the right place at the right time. I can also count on him to get the word out to all of our high school crew, the old fashioned way, by using Ma Bell. He is a Renaissance man or, in today's terminology, a metrosexual. But don't let the suaveness fool you

"Jackie, where are you? I know you said you were flying out asap, but you didn't call me when you got to the airport. You know mom is worried about you. She always said you were just like Daddy. You know how to get lost on people so you can suffer in silence. Oh damn, someone just brought another bucket of chicken into this house! Daddy just died five hours ago and they are already bringing food in here. Gotta go! I've got to find someplace to put all this stuff before your nephew and Daddy's basketball team eats another piece of chicken!"

That's Serena, my oldest sister. She is six years older and lives in Chicago with her husband Micah and my nephew Jordan.

> *"Hey Babe. I just heard about Coach. You know I would be there if I could but I can't get off work. Not that you probably care. Since all that stuff went down last Valentine's Day you haven't taken any of my calls. You know I love you girl. And I love your family. Text me when you get home so I know you made it safely. Oh, and this is my new phone number so lock it in your phone."*

Delete. That mickeyfickey (from time to time I try to stop cussing) has the nerve to call me and offer his condolences. As always, it's all about him. I need to do me, I need more space, what-ever! I found out he needed more space because he had to fit in about three other women. I may be a lot of things, but I aint goin be yo chick on the side. And what job? He is like Tommy from Martin Lawrence, always talking about going to work but I never saw a paycheck. He was fine as wine, but fine don't bring home the bacon. Daddy never liked him anyway. Note to self...listen to your daddy!

> *"Hey Jackie. I talked to your mom this morning. She seems to be doing ok. If I can get a ride down there I will come and check on everybody. 'Cause you know I don't drive in the dark. Hey, do you know when they are going to have the funeral? I need to give my boss at least a 48 hour notice to get off work. Oh, and who has the body? People keep calling me to find out what is going on. I have been trying to call the house but no one is answering the phone. Since I am the president of the Pearl High Alumni Association it's my job to get the information out asap. Call me girl!"*

That was my mom's sister Leslie. She drives me nuts. Who would call you the day someone dies to find out when he is being buried? And who doesn't drive in the dark? We often refer to her as Mary J, as in, What's the 411? She always knows who died, when they died, how they died, and where they died. I find it funny that Mom and Serena aren't answering the phone.

> *"Hey girl, it's me, Keeva. I know you won't get this message until you land but call me when you can. You know Uncle Shorty was like a father to me and I miss him already. I am headed to the house in the next few hours. I am trying to wrap*

up a few things at the office so I can be free for as long as you
need me. I love you."

That was my first cousin Keeva Hudson-McGhee. Yes, you can tell by the three names that she is a lady of the 21st century. She is more like a sister than a cousin. She has been there helping us the whole time. I don't know what I would do without her.

After hearing Keeva's message I don't have the energy to check any others. They can be checked later—or the folks can just head over to the house with more chicken. It is time, as my dad would say, to get my mind right and prepare for the next few days.

I close my eyes and whisper a quick prayer to God to give me the strength to endure what will surely be the hardest time of my life.

The Men All Paused

When I spoke with my mother before I got on the plane, she told me I needed to call my brother Leo to tell him about Daddy passing away. Leo and I are four years apart. As a child I didn't realize that Leo wasn't really my brother but my first cousin. You remember my crazy Aunt Lu. Well, Leo actually belongs to Lu, who has been "on vacation" for most of her life. When I was little my mom and dad would tell me Aunt Lu was on vacation, and I actually thought "vacation" meant a trip to someplace exotic where you had drinks with those nasty cherries and pretty little umbrellas. When I asked, "How long is she going to be gone this time?" they would say, "For a while." I didn't realize until I was about 10 that "vacation" actually meant Aunt Lu was locked up, which brings me back to Leo. I thought that Leo was my natural brother, as he lived with us, went to school with us, did everything else with us. Sometimes he would go visit Aunt Lu while Serena and I stayed home, and I finally told my dad I didn't think it was fair that Leo got to spend weeks at Aunt Lu's house but we never got to go. He proceeded to tell me I was too young to think, but finally he told me that Leo was Lu's child and that he and my mom had had legal custody of him since he was six years old.

One thing I noticed while growing up is that no matter how many whippings Leo got, he still dared to do things Serena and I would never do. And yes, my mom and dad believed that if they spared the rod they spoiled the child. We girls didn't get many whippings because my dad's voice was enough to stop us dead in our tracks. When I heard my dad yell "HEY!" I knew the beatings would soon begin if I didn't straighten up. My mother was better with the choke holds. If you acted up, especially in church, you were bound to get jerked up by the collar really quick. And no, they did not believe in time outs. Wait a minute, yes they did. I often heard, "Hey, time out, you know better. I am about to whip your ass if you don't stop that." So I guess before I got whipped I took a time out.

Leo always had a bit of an edge. During his teenage years he got into trouble for smoking marijuana and cutting class. Once he turned 18 my parents decided to let Leo do what he wanted to do when he wanted to do it, but not in their house. In my dad's words, "You aint going to pimp us anymore. We love you but you need to get the F out." So, he got the F out and started getting worse and worse. The last charge against Leo was possession of drugs, which is a Class E federal crime, because it was his second time. The judge gave him four years in jail and a $2,500 fine, but since Leo isn't a hardened criminal he served two years in federal prison and was released for good behavior into a halfway house here in Nashville, called the Happy House. Tell me, who would refer to a raggedy place with 20 ex-convicts living four to a room as a happy place? I guess it's better than being in a place with 5,000 people and living in a 10X10 jail cell.

My dad loved Leo like a son. It hurt him terribly to see him go through so much turmoil. But Dad always said, "All your mom and I can do is raise you right and teach you how to make good decisions. Choices are yours. You will make some good ones and some bad ones. I just pray that you can recover from the bad decisions."

So, here goes.

"Happy House!"

"Hello, may I speak with Leo Donovan please?"

"Who dis?"

"Dis is his sister Jackie and I have an emergency. Who dis?" I figured I might as well ask, since we were getting acquainted.

"This is Red. It aint visitation time yet so he can't take any calls."

As I sit in the cab smelling Mr. Frito, I put on my best Caucasian voice and say, "Is there anyone I can talk to in order to request expediting the timetable for speaking to the alleged convict regarding an immediate issue?"

"Huh…hold up, let me let you talk to the probation officer."

Why do people always put the most unintelligent person on the damn phone?!

"This is Bill, how may I help you?"

"Hello, my name is Jackie Donovan and my brother is Leo Donovan. Is there any way I can speak with him. Our father passed away this morning and I need to notify him."

"Sure Ms. Donovan. Let me get him on a line in one of the back rooms so he can have some privacy. My sympathy to you and your family."

"Yo sis. What's up? I haven't heard from you in a while. While I got you on the phone can you three way Queesha for me? I need to tell her to come down here and put some money on my card."

"Leo, I need to talk to you about something more important right now. Daddy passed away this morning."

"Pops did what? Ma said the doctor said he had a minute!"

"He passed away this morning. The doctor couldn't really predict how much time he had left Leo. Mom said he was so peaceful and not in any pain when he passed away."

As I sit there and hear heavy breathing, crying, and mumbling, I wonder how I am going to make it through the next minutes, hours, and days. I wonder if our dad passing away is going to set Leo back even more. I wonder how my mom is going to live by herself after being with my dad for over 37 years. I wonder how his basketball team and his students will adjust to another teacher and coach. But most of all I wonder how I can get off the damn phone with Leo! After a few minutes of listening to Leo talk and snot, I tell him that we haven't made arrangements yet but as soon as we do I will call his probation officer to see if we can get him a furlough for a few days so he can come home. Before I get off the phone I also let him know that Lu is on her way home and I will have her call him when she gets off the Greyhound.

I have been the messenger since Daddy got sick. Although he was one of the toughest people I know, he didn't deal with the thought of being sick very well. He dealt with the sickness itself well, but I really think he felt that the less he talked about it the better off he would be mentally. Life for my dad was always about how your mind focused. He would tell me before each surgery, each round of radiation, and each round of chemo, "It's Gametime. It's time to get my mind right and I'm going to shoot the lights out." And I would watch as he put his mind and body in a place where he could withstand the pain and discomfort of his illness.

So Daddy would leave it up to me to tell our closest family members and friends what was going on with him during each step of the treatment. Although Dad shared so much of his knowledge of basketball and life with his players and confidants, he was an extremely private person. In his darkest hours he always had a smile or an encouraging word for those of us who dared to feel sorry for ourselves, or for him. Ironically, most people didn't know he was as sick as he was until the last few days of his life.

That is why I called Leo. That is why I sat on the phone while he cried and cussed about losing the only man he ever knew as his father. As the cab driver swerves around the corner about three blocks from what will now be referred to as my mother's house, I know it's Gametime. It's time to put away all of the tears I have shed over the last year because I subconsciously knew I was losing my dad. It's time for me to be the rock that I know my dad would want me to be. It's time to smile for the countless people who knew my dad as they offer up awkward condolences and empty sentiments: "Just call me if you need anything." It's time for me to help my mom figure out how to live the rest of her life without her husband, lover, friend, and confidant. It's time to help my sister Serena figure out how she can be what she now needs to be in our family hierarchy. It's time for me to help Leo get over the regret of being a huge disappointment to our family. But most of all it's time for me to remember all the things my father taught me about how to survive this thing called life. It's gametime!

Mr. Frito pulls onto the street where my parents live and I realize some things you can't prepare for. My parents live at the end of a cul de sac in a small quiet neighborhood in a plantation style (I could never figure out why Ella would want to go back to the slavery days) three-story house with six bedrooms, five and a half bathrooms, and a porch big enough to fit about 25 people. I yell for Mr. Frito to "stop!" which sends me spiraling full force into the Plexiglas thingy that separates riders from the front seat. I sit there and whisper a prayer to God for the strength I am going to need to get through these next few hours until it's late enough to ask people to go home…well, after they finish off the eight buckets of KFC and at least four of the hams. Then I decide to call my cousin Keeva because I always call her when I need some encouragement or a kick in the butt.

"Hello."

"Hey Keeva, it's me, Jackie."

"Hey girl, I wanted to wait for your plane to land before I called you again. How are things going?

"Girl, I just pulled up at the house and there are over 25 cars lining the street, another five in the driveway, and there are so many people standing on the porch that it looks like the house has slanted a little to the left."

"Damn, I am on my way down there in about 30 minutes. Someone needs to help Aunt Ella clear that mother out!"

Leave it to Keeva to do exactly what I have been thinking. She is five feet tall and about 120 pounds soaking wet. She is known as a LSLH, or a light skin, long hair chick. Because she is light skinned, has long hair, cat eyes that are a color somewhere between gray and brown, and a body to die for, she acts like she is 6 foot 10. My mother Ella and her mother Jean were sisters. When Jean died, Keeva and I became even closer. Although my mom knows she can never replace her sister, she is a surrogate mother to Keeva. While my dad was sick, Keeva spent a lot of time helping my mother and father, since both Serena and I live out of town. I don't know what I would do without her, and in about 30 minutes I will get to see her in action. She has this way of walking into a room with all five feet of her loveliness and, with a twitch of her slanted eyes, letting you know real quick that she is the boss. "See you in a few minutes girl."

I pay Mr. Frito, get out of the car, and get my suitcase. Some of the first people I run into are some of my dad's players. It's funny how teenagers separate themselves quickly from the adults. In fact, they're in the driveway dribbling a basketball, throwing a football, and hitting tennis balls. "Hey guys, what's up?" I say, trying to sound cool.

The captain of the team, Josh Stevens, BKA Scoop, hollers back, "Hey Ms. Jackie. Sorry to be blocking the driveway, but it's crunk up in there! And yo, folks are bringing so much food that Ms. Ella is calling us in every now and then to grub and you know, that's what's up."

"If you give me about five minutes, I will unlock the back gate so you can go shoot on the court. That way you can do your *thang*."

When my parents built this house about 15 years ago, Dad put his foot down about having only three things, two of them a basketball court in the back yard and a media room with state-of-the-art equipment that he could decorate any way he pleased. He said since he had to return to the days of slavery with the big ass house, plantation shutters, and wide porches with ferns hanging off them, he may as well add a ghetto touch with a basketball court. I remember him asking my mom, "What the hell is a keeping room? A place for all the mother fuckers to keep while they wait their turn to be nosey while looking around my damn house. They need to keep they shittinasses at home!" So my dad got himself a half court built of concrete with two baskets cemented into the ground. It also has a set of bleachers and a sound system so he can play his music while he is out on the court. His third demand was a huge barrel charcoal grill beside the bleachers under a small pavilion. So side by side Daddy had the three things he loved the most, besides my mom—a basketball court, a sound system for his music, and a grill. He hung a big sign outside the gate that says, "Gametime—Get your mind right."

"Thanks Ms. Jackie. Make sure you tell Ms. Ella to holler at your boys if she needs us! "Oh, and Ms. Jackie, you sure are looking good. I know I am about 10 years younger, but age aint nothing but a number, and throwing down aint nothing but a thang."

Oh, Lord, not again. This child has been flirting with me for the last four years!

"Scoop, what did Daddy tell you about trying to holler at me! Now get back there before I change my mind about opening up "Gametime." You don't want me to come out there and run a few games with you—you know what happened the last time I came home."

"What happened Ms. Jackie?" asks the player named Junebug.

"Well, I will let Scoop tell you that," I say with a laugh. "I'll see you around back in about five minutes!"

As soon as I walk in the door, I want to go back to the cab. The smell of heavy colognes and perfumes, crying, laughter and the looks of sympathy that come my way are overwhelming. Why in the world my people always feel the need to bathe themselves in perfume before they walk out their door is beyond me. And why do people think that when someone dies a visitation should turn into a party? Black people can always find an excuse for three things. Eating, dancing, and playing cards. I half expect to walk into the kitchen and see four people sitting at the table playing a game of spades or bid whist, and another group in the next room doing the Wobble. I speak to as many people as I can while I make my way to the epicenter of our house, the kitchen. I know that my mother and sister will be in there holding court like the queens they are. The first person I see as I walk through the kitchen door is my mother. Despite going through hell for the last year, she looks like the serene, peaceful beauty that she is. Although I know she is struggling with the death of my dad, I can see a peacefulness surrounding her. The next thing I see is my sister's butt sticking out of the refrigerator. I immediately start laughing because I know that her ass has literally been in the air all day. My sister is a neat freak, and she doesn't like anything out of place. She also has very little tolerance for any foolishness, so to keep herself from talking out of turn she often hides herself in the kitchen under the guise of cleaning up. As she turns around, the first thing I see is her eyes. They look sad. She doesn't have to tell me that she was with my mother when my dad took his last breath. She doesn't have to tell me that although she is exhausted she is going to stay in this kitchen until the last person is fed and everything is tidied up and ready for the next crop of people coming in tomorrow. She doesn't have to tell me that Mom is doing ok. I can read it all in her eyes. When people tell you the eyes are the window to the soul they are right. But at this moment, she is rolling her eyes at the person who walked in behind me. Remember I told you my sister has little tolerance for stupidity. Well, stupid just walked through the door in the form of Keeva's brother Bo. Bo talks nonstop, has no filter, and apparently no intelligence because he is crying, snotting, and yelling, "Aunt Ella, I can't believe Uncle Shorty is gone! I didn't know he was that sick."

Serena immediately sticks her head back in the refrigerator to keep from saying anything, but the baby girl of the family just can't stop herself. I pull myself up to my full 5 feet 11 inches, look down at his short fat butt, and say, "How is it that you don't believe he is gone?" He aint here is he? Are you stuck on stupid? He probably never got a chance to tell you he was that sick because when you called he couldn't get a damn word in edgewise! And would you please stop yelling. You aint outside! We are ok, but if you keep this shit up, we are all going to be in here crying. Now sit your shittinass down so Serena can fix you a plate because you know that's why you came in here!"

Did I say that? Oh Lord, I did just say that! How is it that you can be cussing one moment and then cry for the Lord's help the next minute? You know what happened? My dad left his spirit in my body. I mean, he left here this morning but his spirit stayed right here in my body because I sounded just like him!

And the funny thing is, Bo sat his fat ass right down in the chair and didn't say another word, except to mumble "thank you" to Serena who had fixed him a plate. As he sits there eating, Serena turns her body back to the refrigerator and everyone else in the room looks dumbfounded. I can see Serena's booty shaking, which means she is laughing. My mother turns around to look at me and gives me the sweetest, most beautiful smile I have ever seen—the kind of smile that says, "You go girl!" The kind of smile that says, "My sentiments exactly." The kind of smile that says, "Things are going to be alright." The queens have been holding court, and now the princess has arrived!

None of us really sleep that night. That's why at about 7:30 AM (which is 5:30 AM Seattle time) the next day we all trudge down the steps. Well,

Serena and I trudge down the steps, and mom glides out of her bedroom. Ella promptly announces that we have an appointment with the infamous Prentis Houston of the Houston Funeral Home and Crematory at 12:00 PM that day to make Dad's funeral arrangements. One thing you will find with black folks is that we ALWAYS use the same funeral home for every member of our family. Mostly because one out of every three people that dies doesn't have life insurance and you can usually work with the funeral home to get them buried on the cheap.. Our family used Prentis to bury our grandfather, grandmother, a few aunts, and a cousin a few years back. Prentis also happened to have grown up with my mom and dad.

So at 11:30 AM sharp, all of the Donovan women meet at the door. Now when people say "you were sharp as hell," you will know they are talking about us. Ella walks down the stairs in a black St. John pantsuit with rhinestones on the collar and wearing a pair of three-inch Jimmy Choo pumps. Her hair is combed to perfection and she sports a set of diamond stud earrings. Serena comes down stairs in a black A-line leather dress with a scoop-neck collar, having added a wide red belt and pointed red leather boots with four-inch heels. And I, knowing that I am in the company of Naomi Sims and Beverly Johnson, come down wearing chocolate leather pants with four-inch brown riding boots, a cream Ralph Lauren turtleneck, and a soft brown leather jacket. I put on my diamond hoops and even decide to put a few curls in my hair, which is hanging down my back in a ponytail. Simply being in Ella's presence makes you want to step it up. She always taught us that it didn't matter if you have on Goodwill or Gucci; you need to look your best.

We open the door of the funeral home with Ella in the lead, and we suddenly stop. Standing at the door are all the players from my dad's basketball team dressed in black!

Scoop, the appointed spokesperson, says, "Good morning Donovan ladies. We decided to meet you here so that we can make sure you were protected from all of the people that have been stopping by to find out when Coach D's arrangements are taking place. Until you leave the funeral home we will be standing guard at all the doors to make sure you have what you need."

We look around and notice that there are 10 other men standing around with their mouths open. Prentis, the funeral home director, is at the front of the line. Why is it that funeral homes always have staffs that are 90 percent men and 10 percent women? I need to advise all my single girlfriends that the best places to find men aren't just the gym, church, a home improvement store, or the club, but also a funeral home. I can tell you, the men all paused. I know we are looking good, but it's as if they have never seen three women before. I look over at Scoop, who is grimacing.

"Ms. Jackie, this is one of the reasons why we are here. Before Coach D died he told all of us to make sure we looked after Ms. Ella and his girls."

He then whispers, "Let me know if we need to open up a can of whoop ass on any of these fools. I got yo back…all of it," meanwhile raking his eyes up and down my body.

"I think we are ok from here Scoop, thanks to all of you for being here. You know Coach loved you all like his sons and he is proud that you are here to protect us. Now go on baby, we are good," says Ella.

Scoop gives a quick nod of his head, and the young Donovan Secret Service agents loosen the circle they have formed around us. As we are walking into the office, Scoop looks up at me, leans over, and whispers in my ear, "I got this boo. Go do yo thing for Coach D." I swear, if we hadn't been in the funeral home, which is as close to a church and death as you are going to get, I would have leaned down (did I say Scoop is only 5 foot 6?) and slapped the piss out of him. But since I am a grown-ass woman and he is just 17, I decide I don't want to meet Leo just yet at the Happy House after catching a damn case. It takes everything in me not to laugh at how serious they are. Daddy would be so proud that his young men are for the moment acting like mature adults.

"Prentis, where is the office? My girls and I have a lot to do today and we don't plan to be here more than a few hours," my mother says.

After Prentis picks his big mouth up off the floor, he leads us to his office.

"Ella, it's so good to see you. And you are looking as beautiful as ever. I always told Shorty that he picked the prettiest girl at Pearl High. And I am so pleased that you have selected Houston Funeral and Crematory to handle Shorty's final arrangements. And you girls just keep looking more and more like your momma every year. Such beautiful girls. Jackie, I watched you on TV last summer. That jump shot sure looks good."

"Prentis, that's enough with the kissing up. You know Shorty always thought a lot of you. He always told me that when he died he wanted you to handle his arrangements. Let's get started so we can get this over with."

"Ok, Ella. You sure are looking good, I tell you, that Shorty picked a beauty."

"What makes you think he picked me? I may have picked him," my mother replies while cutting her eyes at Prentis.

Seeing that we are likely to hear Prentis gush over my mother for the next two hours, my sister takes over. She explains to Prentis that we want to have a visitation in two days, followed by the funeral the next day. We have made arrangements at Greater St. James on Missionary Avenue and we want a black coffin. She also tells Prentis that we have brought Daddy's favorite suit, his favorite tie, and the shirt we want him to be buried in, and that she wants the program printed on ivory card stock—she even pulls out a sample. I lean over and say, "Are you writing this down, Prentis?" The fool finally starts writing things on his notepad.

Having lived with a coach our entire life we have gelled into a well-oiled team. You see, my mom is like the Queen of England. She speaks softly but carries a big stick. Serena is like the black Colin Cowie of event planning. Maybe she needs to add funerals to her portfolio. And me, I am the cleanup woman. I sit back, let my sister tell people what they need to do, and then I make sure everything stays on budget. What Prentis and very few people know is that my mother is a closet broker—and a good one at that. She invested sizeable amounts of Daddy's salary and did very, very well before the market crashed. So well that she was able to quit her job and stay at home, and she's the reason they were able to build the Plantation. She also bought substantial life insurance policies for all of us from our State Farm agent—*"Like a good neighbor...State Farm is there."* As a result, Dad left her a sizeable estate. But as I said, Prentis doesn't know that so my job is to see if we can get this elaborate funeral done on the low low! Prentis is writing things on his pad and hitting the keys on his calculator. He finally finishes, looks up, and with a cheesy smile says, "I think I can accommodate all of your wishes. You know at the Houston Funeral and Crematory we do all that we can to make sure that your loved one is laid to rest with dignity."

"How much, Prentis?" I ask with a little bit of the passion I use to guard Tamika Catchings.

"Well, beautiful ladies, it looks like all of that is going to cost about $25,000."

I look over at my sister, smile, and then say, "Everything that Serena said we wanted to include will cost $25,000 even?"

After assuring us that he is giving us a significant discount, I say, "We will pay you $17,500 for all of the items Serena said we wanted. We also will donate $2,500 to the Prentis Houston Scholarship fund, which we know assists young people who want to be embalmers of the future."

"Well, young Donovan lady, because I was such good friends with your daddy, who married the most beautiful lady from Pearl High School, I will do it for that price, especially since you are going to make a generous donation to the Prentis Houston Scholarship Fund and I will throw in a second limo for free!"

"I thought you might say that, since while you were figuring out things on your calculator I was figuring things out in my head, and I came up with $17,500. But I thought we would throw in the charitable contribution since my dad loved the kids and my mom needs a tax write-off. Oh, and Mr. Prentis, my name is Jacqueline, my friends call me Jackie or Jack. Knowing that you knew my father so well, you would also know that he wouldn't take too kindly to you saying for the umpteenth time that he married the prettiest girl from Pearl High. Now are we done here, because I am prepared to write you two checks for the arrangements and the scholarship fund today." With that the Donovan girls walk out the door to meet our teenage body guards so they can escort us back to the car.

Keep your Head to the Sky

Two days later came the funeral. As I look out the window early that January morning, I wonder why the forecast is calling for a beautiful sunny day with a temperature of 60 degrees. Is this God's way of telling us that Coach is smiling down on us? Heck, I would rather it rained. It would match my mood. The funeral starts in five more hours and I wonder if Aunt Lu will make it in time. The last message I got from her was three days ago, when I landed at the airport. Since then, no word from her and she isn't answering her phone. My cousin Keeva commented last night that Aunt Lu must have gotten on the short bus instead of the Greyhound, because only a slow person would settle for turning a 15-hour bus ride into a 72-hour ride.

My dad and Aunt Lu are about 10 years apart, so he was more like her dad than her older brother. She was crazy about my dad, which is probably why she isn't here. Who really wants to go through the pomp and circumstance of burying someone you love so dearly? In fact, Dad always said to throw his ass in a wooden box when he died, and if you had to have a funeral he only wanted singing. He said most pastors were full of shit and talked too much. And make sure someone at my funeral sings a Luther Vandross and a Patty Labelle song. And don't do a bunch of crying. Remember all of the good times we had and just smile. So smile I do, even through the bucket of tears I shed as I sit in my room trying to contact Aunt Lu for the 50th time. Smile I do as I remember Leo saying that, knowing his mom, she would wait until we are about to close Daddy's coffin to show up and throw her body across it.

When Dad stopped talking, I realized how sick he was. Throughout his illness he always talked, giving advice to his players and his family and assuring everyone he would be ok. But about three weeks before he died he stopped talking. He would speak short sentences: "I love you" and "I know" and "Hello" and "Goodbye." He would even wink and smile at people, but when he stopped saying full sentences, cussing and talking smack, I subconsciously knew we didn't have much time left with him. The last full sentences he spoke were to Serena and my mother. When the doctor knew there wasn't anything else she could do for Dad, she gave him a prognosis of two weeks to two months. My dad told us he wanted to go home. I am still not sure if he meant home to the Plantation or to his heavenly home. My guess is both. So we took him home to his man cave with the 64-inch HD screen, a Bose surround system that could belt out songs from Sam Cook to the Commodores. Home to a room that had more movie DVDs than Red Box. Home so he could look out the window and see his beloved basketball court. Back to what he called his comfort zone—the place he felt most at peace and the place he didn't have to worry about how he looked or felt. In those last seven days he told my mom so many times, "I love you." And one day, as my sister sat by his bed watching him while pretending to watch TV, he looked up at her and smiled and said in the clearest voice she had heard in weeks, "You are going to be just fine." Somehow he knew that we would all survive and forget the bad moments of the last year and remember all the good things. That something deep down in our souls would convince us that he was in a better place. That we would find a way to honor him and carry on his legacy. I think he also knew this next year would be a ride that was textbook Shorty Donovan. Fun, exciting, controversial, but oh so gratifying. In later years I would look back and coin it, "The Year of the Shorty!"

We all decided to wear black. Not because black is the color for mourning but because Coach always told us to bet on black. Since my dad was also a lover of all things hats, his girls decided to wear hats. My mom had on a beautiful black fedora with this bad ostrich feather sticking out of it. Serna had on a wide-brimmed Kentucky derby style hat that had a wide black sash around it. And I decided to go gangsta all the way and wear an old school '70s black Kango. Leo even got in on the hat wearing and put on his Neo-like black hat and a pair of my dad's black sunglasses. He had gotten out of the Happy House for the two days it would take for the visitation and the funeral. And even Leo's girl Queesha had the nerve to come into the house wearing a black bandana with rhinestones on it.

I mentioned that my mom comes from a huge family. Her gang was all there, except my Aunt Leslie. Mom had tried calling Leslie a few times on her Cricket, but apparently her minutes had run out so we had no idea where she was...at least until the limo from the funeral home pulled up and Leslie got her trifling ass out. The crazy heifer said she was going to ride over with the funeral home people so she didn't have to drive in the dark. I leaned over to Serena and said, "Remind me to whoop her ass after the funeral for getting in the limo before our mom."

I don't remember much about the funeral. I do know that when we walked into the church there seemed to be thousands of people all over the place. I also remember a lot of songs, one of which was my cousin Babs singing Patti LaBelle's "You Are My Friend." As I listened to the song I thought about the irony of friendships and how impactful they can be. I looked around at all the people my dad had befriended over the years and realized that you really know who your friends are, much like Patty said..."I never knew it till the end." I know why this was one of Dad's favorite songs. He fed into his friends, and at the end those who counted fed into him and our family.

I also remember my mom's boring preacher, Pastor John Ragavan, saying a few words. Why, because my mom took her hand and swept it across her neck as if to say, "Cut it short," right before she elbowed me in the side. He did cut it short and then sat his butt down. And why does it seem that something hilarious happens at every funeral? I think its God's way of showing you that He has a sense of humor. Or maybe it's him telling you that he is happy about getting another angel. Either way I have to thank Harold, one of my dad's closest friends, for this one. When we got to the graveyard for the interment, we sat for a few minutes while Pastor Ragavan said the ashes to ashes, dust to dust stuff. Just as the pastor finished, Harold leans over the coffin to grab a few roses to give to my mom, and he trips and lands on the coffin. Well, that in itself was funny, but then the casket moved about a foot off the brace and Harold almost fell into the dirt along with the casket. Leo yelled out, "Yo, watch it Harold! You trying to get in there with pops?" After about 250 people said a collective "Oh!" my sister and I started laughing. Then Ella started laughing, and then it was just like a dam opened. My dad could not have done it any better. After days of planning his home going, he showed us that even in sorrow it's ok to laugh.

After the graveside service we went back to the church for the repast. I don't know why it's called a repast. Why don't they just call it a meal for people to come and eat for free after a long funeral? This is the part I know I am going to dread because we'll be forced to hear, "Just call me if you need anything. My thoughts and prayers are with you. You know your daddy sure did mean a lot to me. I will call and check on you. Oh, and Jackie, can I have your autograph?" Can you believe a few people had the nerve to ask me for my autograph? Isn't it enough that you got to see my monkey ass for the last four hours? Why didn't you just take a picture? As I sit down to eat once again the obligatory fried chicken, ham, turnip greens, macaroni and cheese made with Velveeta not the fancy gourmet cheese, yams, rolls and hot water cornbread, which is the preferred church meal of black Southerners the whole time I am thinking can I just have a cheeseburger?

One thing that really caught me by surprise came from the principal of the school where my dad taught and coached for the past two decades. I am still a little fuzzy on what Dad taught because he was one of the few people at the school that got to do what he damn well pleased. Some years he taught

26

physical education. Other years health, or science , and some years I think he just hung out in the cafeteria hollering at the kids, "Hey, do right. If I have to come over there I'm going to open up a can of whip ass on you." How did I know he said that? Well, for one because he said that to Serena, Leo, and me until we turned 18, and about 20 of his students shared a story over the last few days and said those words verbatim.

Bud Leevins, the principal of Dad's school, has literally been at the school for 50 years. First as a student, then as a teacher and coach and, lastly as the principal. He walked up to me and said, "Jackie, words cannot express how much I am going to miss your father. Not only was he my colleague but he was one of my closest friends. You know, over the last year we allowed Coach Frazier to stand in since he was your father's assistant. But you know your dad always said that Frazier wasn't wound too tight and I tend to agree with him. I want to continue the winning legacy that your dad built at Seymour High School. He always said that not only could you play the game better than anyone he had seen in a long time, but you also understood the game and what it takes to win. Jackie, I am not trying to put any pressure on you, but I know you have considered retiring from the league. Why don't you consider moving back home and accepting the interim head coach job for the SHS Bulldogs? We could try it for a year to see what happens."

Now you know we just finished putting Daddy and almost Harold in the ground. The last thing I expected Principal Leevins to ask me to do was to replace my dad. First of all, while I have played basketball since I was able to walk, I have never formally coached. I mean, I have been a team captain and leader several times over, but never a coach. Second, did he just ask me to coach a bunch of pre-adolescent, pre-pubescent boys? Do I look like I want to be in a locker room with a bunch of smelly, farting, immature boys? Third, there are only a few cases across the United States where there are women coaching boys, which is crazy because every last one of my coaches was a man. Fourthly (which maybe isn't even a word), does he not realize that I am a superstar in the WNBA? I aint Candace Parker, Lisa Leslie, or Tamika Catchings, but I have held my own over the last six years. After Mr. Leevins tells me to close my mouth, he pats my shoulder and says, "Think about it Jackie. Your dad told me that you were thinking about this being your last year playing before moving to the front office. What a legacy you could continue by taking this position. And you know how proud your dad was. I know he is looking down now just smiling and knowing that you can keep Coach Frazier from messing up his winning record. You know people are saying that we have the SHS curse. Thirteen state championships and none for the past few years. We'll talk before you head home. Ella has all of my contact information. I look to hear from you soon."

OMG, I mean, what the hell! Ok, who says God and hell in the same sentence? And I think I just said it out loud because Ella just turned around gave me the same hand movement across the neck that clearly meant cut it out. I need to go outside and get some air. It's just too much to think about. No wonder so many people look at Principal Leevins in fear. How do you replace the man with the winningest high school record in the state of Tennessee outside of Coach Insell from Shelbyville and Smiddy from Bradley Central High? There is a big difference between being a player and a coach. I have seen many people who excelled as players but sucked as coaches. Am I ready to put my life on hold to coach boys? Can I withstand the pressure of hearing, "Coach D didn't do it that way." As Dad would say, "There's nothing to it but to do it." But he had enough confidence in one hand for about 25 people. Ella would say to pray about it. So as I go outside to catch my breath and to ponder Principal Leevins' proposition, I try to figure out where to go without being bothered. Then I spot Pastor Ragavan's candy apple red Cadillac Deville sitting behind a gate. Yes, pastors in the South still drive Cadillacs. As I'm leaning against one of the illegally tinted windows, I see a large shadow come over me. I look up and low and behold I see an angel! No, I see Adaris Singleton. First Aunt Lu is MIA. Next, Leslie shows up in the funeral home limo, then Harold almost falls into the grave. Then Leevins drops a bomb on me. Now this! The last time I saw him was three days ago at the Nashville Airport.

AJ and I pull up at the church about five minutes before the family walks in. I called Ms. Ella the day before to see if she could reserve a seat for me in a secluded corner at the back of the church. Although AJ would be sitting in a reserved pew with the basketball team, it was important for me to be in a place where I wouldn't call any attention to myself. That is one thing I hate about being back in Tennessee. If I were in New York or L.A., people would treat me like a regular person because everyone in those cities think they are a celebrity. Here in Nashville, if you are a pro athlete or a country music singer you can draw a crowd quickly. Today is Coach D's day and I don't want to do anything to disturb it. To help keep my anonymity I wore a pair of dark black glasses and a dark gray hat to match my suit. I dropped AJ off at the door to meet his team mates and went to park the car. I parked my car, waited for the family to get settled, and then slipped in a side door of the church. There was a seat right by the door with a sign that said, "Reserved for AS." I slipped in right on time.

Then I look up and see Jackie. As Fred Sanford would say, "You got a fine brown frame." I know I'm not supposed to be checking people out during a funeral but it's impossible not to. Jackie has on a black turtleneck, some black palazzo pants, a fitted black jacket, and a black old school Kango. Today her hair is tied up in a low ponytail that hangs halfway down her back. If we weren't at a funeral I would swear she was giving a nod to the Black Panthers. I also knew she was paying homage to her dad, whom many considered a rebel with a cause. In the back of my mind I can hear James Brown singing, "Say it loud, I'm Black and I'm proud." Well, more power to you my sister. I know this is going to be a rough few hours to get through. The last few days have been rough at my own house. It's hard to explain to a 16-year-old that great people die before their time. I know little man is young, but he's old enough to start seeing how valuable life is.

Knowing Coach, this funeral won't be long and thankfully 'cause chairs were not made for a six four, 250-pound man. And how in the hell does anyone see in sunglasses when they are not outside? If I take these off, the four women sitting near me are going to start whispering even louder than they are now. I love my sisters but damn, they have no shame. One just whispered, "Is that that fine ass Dair Singleton sitting in front of me?" Um...I dare him to walk up on this." I guess the sunglasses stay on.

The funeral is finally over. It was really good, especially when the sister sang "You Are My Friend." It looked like Pastor Ragavan was about to get on a roll but then he stopped abruptly. Wonder what happened there? I think I may just hang around the church, lay low, and wait for the repast instead of going to the graveside service.

When the family came back from the gravesite I decided it was time to formally introduce myself to the famous Jackie Donovan. Our first introduction was in the airport and I am pretty sure a do-over is necessary. As I walk through the fellowship hall, stopping from time to time to say hello to a familiar face, I notice Jackie having an intense conversation with AJ's principal. I then see her slip out the side door. I slip off my hat but keep my glasses on, since I am trying to be cool and follow her to where she's leaning on a bright red Cadillac. As I walk

29

toward her I'm wondering what to say, and when she turns around I am speechless. I have been in this world for 32 years, have met a whole lot of beautiful women from every race and age, but for some reason she just takes my breath away. And something about that old school Kango that she's wearing cocked to the side of her head has me going. So I simply say, "Hello Jackie, my name is Adaris Singleton, AJ's father. I think we met briefly the other day at the airport. How are you?"

She sat and looked at me for what seemed like forever and then stuck out her right hand and said, "Hello Adaris, nice to meet you while I'm vertical." Now I know we just buried her father, but I had this sudden vision of getting her horizontal, if you know what I mean.

"What are you doing out here by yourself?"

"Just getting some fresh air. The last few days have been a whirlwind and I just wanted some time to get my thoughts together."

"I'm sure you've heard all kinds of comments over the last few days, but I wanted you to know that I went to see your dad while he was ill and we spent a lot of time talking about you. He told me that you and he had a very special relationship and that you were one of the closest people to him and he knew with you he could share his innermost thoughts. He also told me that if I ever got a chance to meet you that I would be amazed at how much you were like him. He then told me that you were one of the few people that ever beat him in a game of Horse. This was to be my son AJ's first year officially playing for Coach D, and he will be missed."

"Thanks Mr. Singleton. I really appreciate those kind words about my dad. You seem to be a lot more down to earth than I imagined."

"People who get a chance to really know me find out that I'm pretty laid back. I hope I'm not being too presumptuous, but I would love to take you out to have a drink while you are home. Maybe get you out of the house for a while. Can I have your number so I can give you a call?"

Then a funny thing happened. Jackie leaned further back on that Cadillac and put her hand on her face like she was "The Thinker" by Rodin, acting like she really had to contemplate my invitation. I swear, it was like time stopped. Now I aint bragging but the last time I was rejected by a woman was 14 years ago by A.J's mother. After what seemed like at least 10 minutes, Jackie pulled a card out of her purse and said, "You can call me at this number and maybe we can make arrangements to meet." She said it like I was talking about an Underarmour endorsement meeting. I looked down at the card and saw that she was giving me what looked like her business number. You know, the kind that people in our profession use when they don't want to give out their personal numbers.

So I asked her, "Is this your work number?" She looked at me without blinking and said, "I don't give out my personal numbers to people I don't know. I suspect you don't either, do you Mr. Singleton?" Well damn. I just met a woman that beat me at my own game. I am known for pulling out the card for people that I don't want to have access to me personally so they can call my publicist and leave a message, which she forwards to me on my personal cell if she deems it important enough.

"So it's like that? I have to call to schedule an appointment on your voicemail?"

"Mr. Singleton, you don't have to call at all, but if you want even the slightest chance of me calling you back, you can start with that number."

As I stood there tearing up the card she just handed me she gave me the Black Panther, power to the people salute and walked off, just like she did at the airport. Well, until she tripped over the speed bump and stumbled just slightly. She's a clumsy but sexy little wench. As she continued her little strut, I yelled out, "My name is Dair; my father's name was Mr. Singleton." Her response was to flip me the bird. I think she likes me!

Now that the funeral is over I've decided to stay with my mom for a few more days before returning to Seattle. We were sick of all of the heavy food, so we decided to clean out the refrigerator and take the leftover hams, drinks, and other items to the Salvation Army to give to people who would appreciate it. When we got back to the house my mother asked me, "What's on your mind baby girl? I know the last few days have been rough, but when you stop talking I know there is something wrong."

"Mom, did you know that Principal Leevins was going to ask me to come back and coach Daddy's team next season?"

"Yes, baby, I knew. Before your daddy passed away, he came to the house and talked to your dad. Your dad's response was to open his eyes, smile, and wink at him. I know he approved. Have you thought about what you really want to do after you play your last season?"

"I thought I had until two days ago. My plan was to work in the front office helping new players get acclimated to being in the league. I haven't spent much of what I earned and endorsements can keep me for a while. Plus the fact that you quadrupled my money makes me more comfortable. And while I love Seattle, I never got a sense that I would stay there permanently so I didn't buy a home."

"Jackie, what did you plan to do after you finished with the front office?"

"I had thought about going to either law school or culinary school, but first I really wanted to take a year off and do nothing. Maybe hang out with you and Dad. Do a little volunteer work. Go see Serena and Micah and hang out with Jordan. Now I feel kind of lost. Almost like the best laid plans of mice and men have gone astray.

"Jackie, I don't think I ever told you this, but your daddy and I named you after Jacqueline Kennedy Onassis. I thought she was one of the most beautiful, graceful, loving women on this earth, and when President Kennedy was killed she became one of the most courageous. Over the last 28 years I have watched a wild child grow into a courageous young woman. Now, sometimes you can be a little clumsy and you don't like wearing dresses too often, but you have grown into your name. You were the little boy your daddy didn't have. Before we bought this house, you and your daddy would go to an outside court and play basketball for hours, and you went with him to every summer camp. Your daddy was so proud when he took you to practice with him and you beat the crap out of boys that were older than you. The day you got drafted into the WNBA, your daddy cried like a baby. You had realized a dream that he was unable to because of segregation. Even though you were playing clear across the country we watched every one of your games on TV. That's how your daddy knew exactly what you did each game and what you needed to work on to get better. Remember what your daddy used to tell you before each game: "Slim, go out there and play hard and don't stink up the gym. " He inspired you to always do your best, even when you didn't feel your best. So what is bothering you about moving home?"

"When I moved away to go to college I didn't feel any pressure to succeed. I just knew I would. Even when I got picked up by the Stars I didn't feel any pressure because I knew I had a degree to fall back on. But how do you step into the shoes of a legend? A person who was loved and respected by all of his players and knew more about the game than most. A man who couldn't walk two steps when we went down to Kleerview in Murfreesboro for turnip greens without someone stopping him just to get a word of encouragement or to thank him for something wonderful he did. I mean, I am the WNBA star and people pushed me out of the way to get to him! Not that I minded but it's daunting to replace the man they have already named a gymnasium after. How do I live up to that, Ma?"

"You don't, Jack! One thing me and your dad taught all of our kids was to just be you. Don't try to live up to anyone's expectations but the good Lord's and your very own. What most people don't realize about your dad is that he was far from perfect. People were willing to look over his weaknesses because he was so great! And yeah, he loved to win, but the pins, plaques, and points weren't the most important thing to him. He was humble when it came to his success because he knew it could be taken away instantly. We raised you kids to be humble. Yes, also to be confident, but never to think you were better than anyone else.

"If you take this position it will give you a different kind of stress than you have ever known. Kind of like what a parent feels about their child. You have a certain amount of time to teach, train, and mold someone but you don't know how they will turn out. If you take this position, do it on your own terms. Just because you are a Donovan doesn't mean you have to coach just like your daddy. He was old school but these kids need some new school techniques. Yes, people will be watching. You will be one of the first females to coach an all-boys team in this state who just so happen to be one of the most successful teams in the nation. You will jump over coaches who have been waiting in line for years for your daddy to either fail or die. And guess what, Principal Leevins does not give a damn what people think. If he did he wouldn't have hired the young, good looking, cocky son of a gun they called Shorty Donovan so many years ago. Brashness comes with a lot of baggage. Your father caused a lot of trouble over the last 25 years. Remember what those reporters from the Tennessean said about him. I quote:

"Donovan says what he thinks and what he believes, and that sometimes doesn't go over well with others. Make no mistake about it, there are coaches and others in the country who don't like the vocal coach. However he has never changed his style and his toughness has never been tested. Try as they may, fellow coaches and parents haven't been able to break Donovan."

"Baby, your dad always told you kids, your good is most people's best. You do everything with a spirit of excellence. Whether you decide to coach or not, just know I got your back, your front, and your side, just like I did your daddy's. If you decide to take the position you can stay here with me. You stay in the basement—it's like a separate house with two bedrooms, a bath, and a kitchen. It will be like having your own place."

"Let me think about it Mom. I've been away for 10 years now, it'll be hard to come home. It's not that I don't love it here or that I may be getting my groove on..."

"Well baby, I know you and your daddy talked to each other without a filter, but your mom would still like to think that at 28 your groove has not been gotten. But I will say that you'd have a separate entrance in the basement. Now, didn't you promise me a batch of that wonderful lasagna you always make? Get to cooking girl. For the first time in weeks I am hungry!" Mom smiles and gives me a big hug, then pushes me toward the kitchen.

I've been back in town for a week now, trying to spend as much time as possible with AJ and my mother. I'm training four hours a day to get ready for the upcoming season and thinking about the offer from ESPN. But I also have been spending way too much time thinking about that mean ass Jackie Donovan. I'm still laughing about her flipping me off. Who does that shit anymore? Something about that little challenge is going to make me a glutton for punishment. I tore her card up just for show—I have a photographic memory. I am going to call her but I need to decide exactly what to say to get her to respond to me. I thought about sending her some flowers but I don't think that will impress her. Those gestures are too predictable and cliché' d.

I have to admit, I am intrigued. Jackie strikes the balance between being a professional athlete and a very feminine woman—usually you only get one or the other. I want a woman who has a mix of all of that, who doesn't mind going to the gym but also knows how to get fixed up without too much effort. Like Ms. Donovan. Although it seems she's a bit on the clumsy side when she's nervous. I like the fact that I make her nervous.

My parents had a happy marriage, before my pops died. I'd like to find what they had—just because AJ's mom and I didn't make things work doesn't mean I don't believe in a lasting relationship. And I want more children. But with a wife, not a baby mama. At 32 I'm tired of booty calls, blind dates with teammates' sisters or the nice church girl who turns out to be the freakiest ho in the bunch. I want Mrs. Singleton, and I am willing to wait for the right sister.

And yes I want a sister. A thick-hipped, set a tea cup on your booty, big-lipped black woman. She can be black as a berry or light enough to pass, but she needs to be of African descent. Yes, my expectations are high, for my mother set a high standard. I am willing to give my someday queen everything she wants, including my time, my talent, and my treasures—if you get what I am saying. That is why I am meeting my realtor to look at some houses. I'm too old to be living with my mom. It just aint cool to end a date by asking, "Would you like to come by my mother's house for a nightcap?"

AJ has had a rough week, so I decide to take him to school. I want to have a little man-to-man time to see where his head is. One thing I have learned about kids today is they would rather communicate by text message or Twitter. That's why I always try to teach him the importance of communicating and having good oral skills. One day AJ was sitting right next to me in the car and we stopped at Ed's Fish on Buchannan to get a fish sandwich. When we pulled up at the drive through I asked AJ what he wanted. No sooner had I got it out of my mouth when I heard a ding on my phone. Thinking it was a text from one of my boys, I checked it and found it was from AJ "*wnt whtn fsh snwch w/ mstrd, ht sce n pkls n grp drnk.* That's when I decided to take his phone away. Just for a week. After that I made sure we had a father/son pow-wow once a week to tell each other what was really on our mind. With the recent death of Coach D, I expect today's talk to be challenging.

"How are you feeling little man?"

"I'm straight pops."

Since I figure my open-ended questions will only get one- and two-word responses, I try again.

"Tell me what your plans are for camps and practice this summer so granny and I can start coordinating our schedules."

"Well Pops, I haven't thought about it much since Coach died. I planned to help out at this year's camp for disadvantaged kids and then attend the camp for older guys. Coach told me I needed to play some AAU basketball if I want to follow you to an SEC school. Two AAU coaches have been calling Granny to get me to come out, but I'm not sure. I know my defense is off the hizzy and I think that may be my calling card, but Pops, right now I aint really feeling any of it. Coach was, well he was my Coach..."

As I pull up to the school, I can tell AJ has something else on his mind.

"Anything else we need to rap about son?"

He looks at me with sad eyes and says, "This is the first day I'm gonna walk into Seymour High and know that Coach isn't coming back. He won't be walking down the halls yelling for all of us to do right. He won't be in the cafeteria giving lunch money to kids who don't have any. He won't be sitting in his office during sixth period telling us to run drills. It's going to be different, Dad."

"I know son. The saddest thing about life is death, especially when someone you care about so much dies. And it seems so often the good die young. And cancer is no respecter of persons. I am so thankful you don't remember all you had to go through when you were diagnosed with leukemia. You were just five years old and thank God we got you to some of the best doctors at St Jude and the Seattle Cancer Care Alliance. Looking at you now, no one would ever know what you went through. When you walk down those halls today, remember that life is hard but that God will give you the endurance to make it through the rough times. Think about all the great things that Coach D taught you and don't be afraid to be sad. A part of being tough is crying and having sad moments. The key to it all is not staying sad."

"Dad, are you having a moment?"

"I guess I am little man. My role is to help you learn to be a man and a big part of that is teaching you to be sensitive. Now get out of here and have a great day. Later Tater. Your Pops loves you."

"I love you too dad. Later Tater. "

As I drive off, I realize my son is starting to become a man and I'm not sure I'm ready for it. I'm also not sure I'm ready to meet my realtor and start a house search...but, I know I need to start putting down some roots. Mom has hinted that she just might start dating soon. How will it look for her to invite a date over and he see her grown ass ashy son hanging out at her house?

I head to Brentwood to meet my realtor. I'm not really sure I want to live in Brentwood. But, my realtor keeps telling me I need to consider my zip code for resale value. All I really want is for AJ to have a home base that will eventually be his. He told me he wants a house like 50 Cents and Missy Elliott like he saw on MTV cribs, so I decided I would wait to get him involved. I want a nice house but I don't want to go crazy. Mostly I want my home to be my sanctuary.

As I'm driving, I'm thinking I just may break one of my own rules and call Jackie. People say men like the chase. I never had to chase, but this has definitely been an intriguing few weeks. I can't seem to stop thinking about Jackie. She doesn't know I called Ms. Ella the other day to check on her and the family. Ms. Ella and I developed a relationship over the past few years when I would take AJ over to Coach D's house so they could work together one-on-one. I sat at Ms. Ella's kitchen many a day eating some of her homemade potato salad with some of Coach D's ribs. We had a lot of time to talk about life and raising our children. When I called the other day she mentioned that she and Jackie were going out to do some shopping. I wonder if she dropped Jackie's name on purpose...Surely she doesn't know that I saw Jackie in the airport or that I spoke with her at the repast. Or does she?

Three hours and six houses later I still don't think Tiffany knows what I am looking for. Her husband Shelton Presley bka Shelley plays on the Trailblazers with me and she has lived the life of an NFL wife, so I thought she'd have a feel for the kind of home I want.

"Tiffany, do you understand the type of home I'm looking for?"

"Let's see, you want a Mediterranean house with a basement, a wide open plan with no wasted space. You want a large kitchen, big bedrooms and bathrooms and lots of closets. Is that about right?"

"You hit the nail on the head Tiffany—so why aren't we seeing anything I like?"

"The problem is, the only way you can find just what you want is to build it."

"Tiff, how about you find me some land with at least one acre. Try your best to stay in AJ's school zone or as close as you can get. Also, work on finding me an architect and builder. I want the home that I can stay in for the rest of my life and I want to get it right the first time. But keep in mind, I aint no chump. I expect you to help me keep my costs reasonable. The house I want shouldn't be more than $750,000 in Nashville."

"Is that your budget Dair?" Tiffany says with a sly smile.

"That's the most I want to pay. Mrs. Singleton will be living there one day so I want it to be perfect for both of us."

"Speaking of Mrs. Singleton, have you found her yet? You know I've wanted to introduce you to my girl Angel for a while."

"Thanks Tiff, but I got this." As I say that, a long-legged beauty wearing a Kango and flipping me a bird crosses my mind. "You just find me some land and some people to bring my dream home to life."

"I'm on it Dair. I will be in touch in a few days."

Thanks Tiff. I'd like to be in the house by Christmas. Is that doable?"

"Adaris, that only gives us ten months to build a custom house!" Tiffany looks panicked.

"If you can get me in this house by December 31st I'll up your commission to 5%. I know that's chump change to you, but I also know you love a challenge."

"Don't play me close Mr. Singleton. I can definitely get you in a house in 10 months."

"I just bet you can Mrs. Shelley." I jump in the Rover and speed off to my daily workout.

Award Tour

I know what Tribe Called Quest meant when they rapped "Award Tour." I just flew from Nashville to Seattle and back to Nashville in one week. And of all days, I decide to come home on February 14. Since I don't have a man I figured I'd fly from Seattle with a layover in Dallas—that should take up at least half the day. The last Valentine's Day I shared was with that no good Quinton Styles. I thought he was taking me out to a nice restaurant but instead he stopped at Trader Joes and bought me some wilted flowers with the price tag on. Then he had the nerve to walk in the door with the raggedy ass flowers and say, "Hey babe, what you cooking tonight?" That was the last damn straw. So, in my best Pam Greer voice, I said, "Baby thanks so much for the beautiful flowers. I knew you'd be hungry so I called Morton's and placed an order. It's paid for; all you have to do is run in and ask for the order for Styles."

"I sure am glad you paid for it babe cause you know pay day aint till next week and your man is kind of broke."

"You go on down there. It should be ready by the time you get there."

As my stupid boyfriend was walking out the door he became my stupid ex-boyfriend. I never said he was the brightest Crayola in the box. After he left I called Morton's Steakhouse and placed a huge order in his name. I just so happened to have his debit card number…Then I called Verizon and told them to block his number. Can you hear me now you cheap mother? I threw those flowers in the trash, turned on Chuck D's "Fight the Power," and then pretended I was Rosie Perez in "Do the Right Thing." I danced my ass off until I was so tired I had to go to bed.

After a lot of soul searching and prayer, I've decided to forgo a season in the WNBA and come home to coach at Seymour High School. I figure I need to get home a.s.a.p. so I can talk with Principal Leevins about what he expects of me, meet with the parents and start to get to know the players, develop a coaching philosophy and set up a practice schedule, and start a new life—in that order. Wow, I make that sound so simple. I also have to figure out how to fill a corner of my dad's shoes. You know, the corner where your pinkie toe barely slides into the shoe…

As I walk through the airport I think about my conversation with Coach Tricks.

"Hey Coach, you got a few minutes for us to talk?"

"I've got a few minutes but every time one of you girls ask me to sit and talk you are either going to tell me you are pregnant, getting married, or you are sick. I can't tell you how many Tums managing you ladies keeps me going through. Before you share your big story, tell me how you and the family are doing. And don't give me the bullshit answer you give everyone else."

"Coach, we're doing ok. Dad went fast so we didn't have much time to prepare for his death. I couldn't stand watching him waste away over the last few months. The dad I knew was big and strong and full of life. He smiled and laughed all the time. The dad I began to see was weak and frail. He didn't smile as much and his voice became soft. Before he died, he was almost childlike. I would rather him be gone than to see him that way. I'm taking one day at a time…

Speaking of which, I know we talked about me playing one more season before I move to the front office to help manage the rookies. One thing I have always been with myself is honest. The money sucks and the cost of living here is so expensive and I'm halfway across the country from my folks, there aren't many brothers here and I am getting homesick…"

"Why don't you tell me what the hell is going on, Donovan."

"The principal at Dad's school asked me to come home and be the coach for a year, that's what. I told him I wasn't sure I could segue from being a player to a coach and that a whole lot of people would have issues with a female coaching young men. And Coach, how in the heck do I take all that I know about the sport and impart it to young people? How do I convince these kids that a girl can teach them how to play this game? How will I convince them I know as much as my dad?"

"Jack, slow down honey, you need to take one step at a time. No one is putting any pressure on you but you. So what do you really want to do? I know you love playing the sport but you have become a bit of a player/coach. That's why I made you a sixth man over the last three years. I needed you to study the game the first few minutes to help us figure out the best way to win. You have an innate ability to help your teammates figure out how to capitalize on the opponent's weaknesses and how to execute better. You already have been coaching for the last few years. The only difference is I had the pressure of winning, not you."

"Now, do I think accepting the coaching position will be easy? Hell no. It will be one of the most challenging things you've ever done, but you need a challenge Jack. Honestly, life's been a cakewalk for you. You're so talented and smart that you achieved most of your successes without breaking a sweat. You also happen to be a beautiful young lady who dares to be modest about it. You have kept your nose clean over the last six years and have been a good kid—you've been a coach's dream."

"Do I think you should take the job? Hell yeah! Show those racist bastards in the South that a little black girl can coach an all-boys team. I have a spot open for you here if things don't work out in Tennessee. Right now our franchise needs people like you to show the world the value of the WNBA. You being in Tennessee will help elevate our sport, maybe garner more sponsorships and owner loyalty and help raise our salary caps so we can start paying you about 1/10 of what you are worth. I don't know how you can take a nineteen year old male marquee basketball player who is barely getting more than $20 per diem for meals and turn him into a $20 million franchise player overnight. But pay you barely enough to make ends meet. Jack, I need you to be an ambassador for our league. I will miss you, but I think Tennessee needs you more." Then Coach takes out his handkerchief and wipes his eyes.

I lean across coach's desk to look at him closer and say, "Are you crying Coach?"

"No kid, I have something in my eye. You think things over and get back to me in a month. Now get out of here so I can wipe my eyes in peace," he says as he shoots me a wink.

"Well coach, I was about 80% sure of my decision before I walked in. Now I am 100% sure. I'll be going home once I get my affairs in order here."

Coach gives me a wide smile. "Go and make history, Coach Donovan."

Coach Tricks is one of the most important people in my life. He hasn't been easy to play for but he has made me a better player. He knew that making me tougher would help me withstand the taunts from my team mates. I shut them all up after my rookie year. I know he is proud of me and wants the best for me. Having his blessing to go means a lot to me. More now that Dad is gone.

So I informed my team mates and friends that I was leaving, sublet my apartment for a year, and shipped my Beemer to Tennessee. But before I left I had a party of sorts.   It started with me saying, "Goodbye rainy ass suicide capital of the world where the homeless people make more money than the women's basketball players. See ya ole funky Ivar's fish house. Arrivederci Nordstrom, the best customer service experience in the world. Holler at you Starbucks. Adios rich ass Bill Gates. Later, all things North Face and bike riders. Goodbye all things Super Sonics, Mariners, and Seahawks who don't give the Seattle Stars any respect unless they want to date them. I'm out, bikes and hikes and lakes and mountains.

Then I stop and think, boy am I going to miss those wonderful rainy days that help make Seattle one of the most beautiful cities in the world. And I'm gonna miss my buddy Pat the homeless man who I see on the corner every day on the way to practice. What am I going to do without the cod and haddock from Ivar's while settling for Captain D's BKA as the "great little seafood place?" What the hell am I going to do without the shoe department at Nordstrom's, where everybody knows my name? Boy, will I miss the free tickets to Quest Stadium and the pride of being around great athletes.

Seattle has been very, very good to me, and I will miss the organic city. Suddenly I'm wondering, what self-respecting professional athlete would quit her job and move clear across the country to coach a bunch of hormonal teenage boys? Apparently me. I wonder if I am making the worst mistake of my life...as I walk yet again through the Nashville airport I wonder what the future is going to bring. Will the rolling hills of Tennessee be kind to me? Will a friendly drawl hide the racism I am sure to encounter here in the South? Will I find that special Mr. Right here, or only Mr. Right Now in Nashville? Based on the last message I received from Adaris Singleton, things could get interesting. I listen to it again as I walk through the airport— officially the place where we first met.

"Jackie, uh hello, this is Adaris Singleton. We met at the airport in January and then at the repast. I know it's been a while but when you gave me your work number it kind of pissed me off. Anyway, I thought I would call just to check on you and see how you are doing. I mean, I know you are fine, but how are you? If you ever want to talk, please give me a call on my personal cell number not my work number. I have it on me 24/7. My number is 615-895-5555. I look forward to speaking with you very soon."

Now how do I interpret that message? He gives me a backhanded compliment about being fine knowing the last thing I did was flip him a bird. I haven't flipped a bird since the day Leo showed me how and told me it meant I love you. I was about six at the time. I went into the kitchen where mom was cooking breakfast and flipped her my middle finger while wearing a big smile. The next thing I knew I was getting choked and my mother was asking if I had lost my damn mind. I couldn't say anything because she was squeezing my windpipe, but when she finally let go of me I said, "I was telling you I loved you Mommy." She then explained to me in no uncertain terms that if I flipped a bird at any one else she would choke the life out of me. I never flipped a bird at anyone until 22 years later.

Oh Lord, was I subliminally telling Dair I loved him! I mean, I love looking at his long strong legs, his wide shoulders, his flat stomach and that rippling chest, but those come a dime a dozen on professional athletes. I may call him back, but only after a few days—I gotta make him sweat a little. Let me get out of Nashville BNA and go meet my cousin Keeva who is picking me up.

I step out of the airport into a balmy February day, and the first thing I see is my cousin Keeva's bright red Mercedes coupe, top down, zooming through the short-term parking lot. Well, I actually hear her before I see her. It sounds like she is bumping the song, "Baddest Bitch" by Trina. Now I know that song is a few years old, but this is the song that represents her best. Keeva may be small but she sure carries a big stick. She's not only beautiful but unabashedly single and always looking. Not to mention, she is the owner and CEO of her own marketing firm. She has accounts all over the world and can mix business with pleasure better than anyone I know. Keeva was working for a Fortune 50 company in Chicago making them more money in one day than she made in five years. One day she got sick of the grind, walked in her boss's office and put in her two weeks' notice. Shortly thereafter she started KeMarketing. She makes her own rules and offers no apologies.

"Hey girl, looks like I got here just in time! Let me pop the trunk so we can put your bag in," says Keeva.

"Ke, do you mind putting the top back up? It's cold as hell out here."

"Girl, you need to seize the day! I have the heat on at 80 degrees. Get yo long-tailed self in here and let's be out."

Favorite cousin that she is, Keeva puts the top up, as we pull away from what I hope is the last time I see the Nashville Airport for a long time, Keeva turns to me and says, "So what's going on cousin? We haven't had a chance to really talk since Uncle Shorty's funeral. You left Nashville so fast and then I had to fly out to Paris so what's up?"

"It's a long story girl. I never got a chance to tell you that I met Adaris Singleton."

"That fine ass Adaris Singleton that plays for the Tennessee Trailblazers? You know, I thought I saw someone that looked like him at Uncle D's funeral but he looked like Michael Jackson in the Smooth Criminal video. Was that him?"

"Yes, girl that was him. I guess he was wearing it to throw people like your fast tail off his scent. The thing is, I really met him at the airport the day Daddy died. I was walking down the concourse and tripped over this fat chick's suitcase. I looked up and there he was blinking at me with those pretty brown eyes and that slow smile. I was so embarrassed I ran off as fast as I could. I forgot that his son was going to play on Dad's varsity team this year. He formally introduced himself at the repast and I was so shook up that I gave him my card with my business number. You know, the one I give to the scrubs I don't want to be bothered with. He was a little pissed and tore up my card. And then I flipped him a bird. Hell, that day I couldn't figure out if I should scratch my nose or dig in my ass, girl!"

"Let me get this straight. You met one of the finest, smartest, wealthiest, single men in Nashville and you ruined it...twice? I thought I taught you better than that, Jacks! That would have been the perfect time for you to get your groove back. Oh, I forgot. You never had one to lose. Is he as fine in person as he is on TV?"

"Yes Ke, he is as fine and his voice is Barry White deep. Apparently he didn't lose the number because he called me yesterday and left a message."

"What did he say, Jacks?"

"He said he was just checking on me and wanted to give me his number that could be used 24/7."

"Do you plan on using the number or are you going to make the brother wait to hear from you?"

"That brings me to the reason I am home. I didn't get a chance to tell you before that Principal Leevins asked me to coach the boys' varsity team for a season."

"And what did you tell him?"

"I called him a few days ago and accepted the position. It only pays a $1,500 monthly stipend, no benefits, and I have to help the booster club raise money for equipment. I also have to sign a one-year contract. Oh, and get this! Principal Leevins hasn't broken the news to the parents yet. You and Mom are the only people who know I accepted the position—I haven't even had a chance to tell Serena yet. I don't think I should call Adaris back. If I'm coaching his son it might get awkward."

"Jacks, you know more than anyone else that the team is business. Don't you think the two of you can separate business and pleasure?"

"Ke, all we have going are two chance meetings, one phone message, and a finger flip. I felt a spark when we met but I'm not too sure about going on a date with a professional athlete."

"Aren't you also a pro? And you're beautiful and smart and you have a lot going on. You can hold your own with anyone out there."

"Yeah, I know Ke, but Adaris Singleton makes more in one day than I make in an entire year and he's a household name here in Tennessee. That doesn't intimidate me but it does make me hesitate to date him. I want to live like a normal person—well, as normal as I can considering I am about to step into one of the most publicized coaching positions in Tennessee. And I'm just not sure I can compete with the memory of one of the few people I know who could walk their talk."

"Uncle Shorty didn't walk he pimped, but I digress. You don't have to, Jacks. What did Uncle D always tell us? To be our authentic selves. You couldn't be him if you wanted to. The funny thing is, you're the closest damn thing to Uncle D as you can get. You walk like him, talk like him, have his smile and his temperament. And you know the game of basketball because he taught you. What makes you different is you have tits and a vjay jay. Seriously, being a woman gives you an edge that Uncle D never had. Just a sway of that apple bottom alone will have those boys walking like toy soldiers!"

"Keeva, leave it to your nasty ass to insinuate that I would try to sway them with my feminine wiles. I am not trying to catch a case for assault with a deadly booty! But I may just swing my apple bottom at AJ's dad…!"

"How do you do it Ke? How do you date without worrying about if you are one of many? Without thinking about if he's on the down low or has a sexually transmitted disease? How do you keep up with all the guys you see around the world?"

"Well cuz, the operative word is date. Dating means you are spending time getting to know someone. It means you are having dinner, going to the movies or whatever grown-ups decide to do. Dating does not mean you are in a relationship. I decided a few years ago after my divorce from Damon that I would date like a man. If I see you and something about you interests me then I might allow you to spend time with me. We can hang out and get to know each other. It doesn't necessarily mean we are going to be intimate. It just means we have made a commitment to see where things go. If we decide together that we want to take things to another level then we do. Most times if things start getting too heavy it's my cue to move on. I am not ready for a commitment. I did that with Damon for six years. He didn't hold up his end of the deal in our marriage. I told myself if I became single again I would take my time and date until I found the person who was the best fit for me. So far I have met some great men. Some have been well off; some have been poor as hell. Some were beautiful and some were ugly. Some had great careers and some were jobless. Hey, I am an equal opportunity woman. If there is one thing about him that intrigues me I will give myself an opportunity to get to know him. Until I find that one person that as Stevie would say "knocks me off my feet" I am going to be an equal opportunist. Now you might get fired, might get laid off or you might get a raise. Those that get raises get called when I am in their city. I make my own rules. I suggest you do the same thing little cuz. Life is short. Carpe Diem. Call Adaris back. A phone call doesn't mean you are committing to a wedding, 2.5 children and a house in the burbs. Call the brother back and see if his rap is as tight as his ass..ets. "Oh snap, my girl is back in town! I have a feeling this is going to be a very interesting year," Keeva says as she turns up the volume on "Baddest Bitch" and we head to the heart of the city.

Who's who?

I meet with Principal Leevins and we decide to meet with the parents and the team in the near future. In preparation I go to Dad's old office to grab the current roster and some videos from previous seasons. Everything is just as he left it. I can even get a whiff of the Aramis Cologne Dad used to wear. I'm not ready to go through his desk yet so I get the items I need and head back to the Plantation. As I look through the roster I can't figure out who is who. All of these boys have nicknames—Scoop, Li'l Daddy, Popper, Junebug, and Peaches. I don't think Dad ever called them by their real names. There also are three sophomores joining the team, including AJ. Dad didn't get a chance to nickname them so I guess it will be up to me. The only person who can help me sort out these names is mom.

"Mom, I'm glad you're home. I can't figure out who any of these young men are by their legal names. Can you help me decode?"

Ella looks at me with a huge grin and replies, "Sure I can baby. Once you get to know those boys you will be able to see why your daddy gave them their nicknames. Scoop likes his so much he asked your daddy if he could legally change his name, like those Ochocinco and Metta World Peace characters! Scoop's real name is Josh Stevens. He was really nosy and could always tell your daddy who was doing what, so Daddy started calling him Scoop because he always "knew the scoop." Let's see, Little Daddy's real name is Jordan McCullough. Your daddy named him Li'l Daddy because he played football with Jordan's granddad in high school. There's Lance Nixson, the football player who is a defensive back. Since he uses his body to hit people your dad started calling him Popper. Leslie Grimes, better known as Peaches, is the pretty boy who always comes to practice smelling like some peach cologne. Your daddy said no boy should go around with a name like Leslie at his age and since Leslie always smelled so good he would call him Peaches, Pe for short. And then there's Chauncey Smith. Your daddy started calling him Junebug just because he was born in the month of June." Let's see there's Robin Leeks or Bird and Samuel Hall or Shaky because he gets a little nervous. And then there's Baby Baby who is actually Junebug's younger brother who is really the 6"6 Bass Smith. Oh, and Shelby Brown who your dad calls Slim since he is so darn skinny to be so tall. And last but not least is Hector Sanchez or Homeslice. Homeslice got the name because he so stupidly walked up to your dad and said what's up Homes. After your daddy got through cleaning his clock he gave him that nickname. Mom fills me on the rest of the roster and says "I swear those boys wear those names like a badge of honor. In fact, they won't answer to their birth names. Even the game announcer calls them by their nicknames. So it looks like you will have to find names for the newbies. I know you want to create your own culture, but this is one habit that would be hard to break. Kind of like you being nicknamed Jack."

"So on top of me trying to figure out everything else I also have to name three new babies." I shake my head.

"Yes, but that's the fun part. Take the good things with the bad and make the most of it."

"Thanks for your help Mom. I hope you know that you will be my unofficial assistant coach and I am gonna rely on you more than you might want."

"Since I am your unofficial coach, let me leave you with this advice."

"Ok Mom, lay it on me."

"Don't take anyone's advice. You have a clean slate. Make your own rules. Keep the things that make sense. You will figure it all out, little grasshopper."

Dang, Mom drops her bomb and walks away, and I feel like Daniel did in *The Karate Kid* when Mr. Miaygi said, "Wax on, and wax off."

After getting a pep talk from both Keeva and Serena, I decide to call Adaris. I've waited a few weeks and I don't know what he'll say now that I'm finally calling him back. Keeva told me to call him and act like he just left the message a few days ago and not to mention that I waited so long to call. She also said not to talk too long, just to feel him out...but then I remember Ella told me not to take any advice. Finally I decide to just wing it.

Doesn't it seem like when you call someone new, half of you prays they won't answer and the other half hopes they do so you can get it over with. I sit there as the phone rings once, then twice, and just when I thought I was home free, this deep voice says, "Hello."

"Uh, hi, is Adaris available?"

"This is Adaris speaking."

"Hi, this Jackie Donovan returning your call."

"So you finally decided to return my call after two weeks Ms. Donovan. To what do I owe the pleasure of this return call?" he sounded out of breath.

"What are you doing Adaris? You sound kind of winded. Did I catch you at a bad time?"

"Actually you caught me at the perfect time. I just finished a five-mile run and am cooling down now."

"How often do you run Adaris?"

"During the off season I run every day. Since I am getting a little older, it's harder for me to stay in shape. Are you back in Nashville?"

"Well, I've actually decided to move home for a while to help my mom get Dad's estate settled, and take some time to decide what to do in my retirement. And how did you know I left town?"

"You retired?" Adaris sounded surprised. "I knew you left town because I called Ms. Ella a few weeks ago, and she told me that you and your sister had returned home and your brother had gone on vacation. How many years did you play?"

"Vacation, now that's funny! I actually played six years. If I decide to go back I have a job in the front office, but I really need to think about what I want to do with the rest of my life." I let out a deep sigh.

"Sounds like you're at a crossroads. I know last year wasn't very kind to you. You probably need some time to unwind and relax. I've been in the league 12 years now and this is definitely going to be my last. Don't tell anyone this, but the older I get the more fearful I get about concussions and other injuries. It's been a great ride but my priorities are shifting some.

"So tell me Ms. Donovan, why did it take you so long to return my call? I sure didn't think it would take more than two weeks." Adaris laughs.

"When you called I was just moving back to Tennessee and needed time to catch my breath. I'm calling you from my personal number, so if you want to lock it in your phone you'll have it."

"Does this mean I have been upgraded from associate to acquaintance?"

"Don't press your luck, Adaris. We have had a good two minutes, but you might blow it if you keep teasing me." He can't see it, but I said this with one of my first genuine smiles in a long time. "Oh, and my mom is Ms. Donovan, you can call me Jackie or Jack. That's what my friends call me."

"Another promotion to friend status–I will be pleased to call you Jackie if you don't mind. Since we have had a…let's check my watch…a very nice three-minute conversation, could you please tell me when we can have an actual face-to-face somewhere other than an airport or the fender of a Cadillac? It would be nice to catch up with my new friend." I can feel him smiling now too.

"How about if we try working out together? I've been a little lazy since I moved home and need to get back on track."

"Well, Jackie, I was hoping for something else—but ok, let's make it a workout. How about tomorrow at the Nashville Athletic Club on Harding Place Road?"

"You got it. I'm glad you know a good workout facility. So much has changed since I left town, and I've been so busy helping my mom that I haven't had much time to scope things out. It'll be nice to get reacquainted with my hometown."

"I hope you'll let me be your guide as you get to know our fair city again. I can take you to a lot of the old spots and show you some terrific new places."

"Let's see what happens at the athletic club first Adaris. Let's take one step at a time. What time should we meet tomorrow?" I ask with a chuckle.

"The early bird catches the worm. I drop AJ off at 8:00. Let's make it 8:30."

"How about we make it 10:30, which is 8:30 Seattle time. I'm not used to the time change yet, and I don't want your third impression of me to be grumpy black woman."

"The first two times were eventful," he said chuckling. "It's a date then."

"Have a good day Mr. Singleton."

"I see we're back to last names again. See you tomorrow Jackie."

I didn't get much sleep last night. Guess I'm nervous about seeing him this morning. Might as well figure out what I'll wear today. Isn't it funny how the thought of seeing the opposite sex makes you think about what to wear? My wardrobe consists mostly of hundreds of shoes and purses. Guess you can say I have a fetish. Nordstrom in Seattle has the best shoes in the United States. I collected so many shoes I made a pact with myself that for every new pair I got I'd give a pair away. I also sent my mom and sister shoes from time to time as my way of letting them know I'm thinking about them. Then one day my dad calls me and says, "Jack, what day is Christmas this month? Your mamma has been so excited trying to figure out when her new shoes are coming." Since it seemed like Daddy wanted in on the excitement, I started sending him shoes too from time to time. And then I got a call from Leo about shoes.

"This is a collect call from the Matthew Thomas Correctional Facility. I have a call from Inmate Leo Donovan. If you accept this call there will be a one-time $5.00 charge with a $.50 charge per minute. Press one to accept and two to decline." I accept the call.

"Hey Sis, what's up in rainy ass Seattle?"

"Not much, just balling, what's up in confining ass jail Leo with the three hots and a cot?" Leo and I always keep it real. It couldn't get more real with him already in federal prison.

"Pops told me you was sending kicks to the peeps in the fam. When you going to hook ya boy up? I know you can get all the shoes you want and what not."

"I don't get men's shoes Leo, and you know I don't need to send you brand new shoes to jail. You can't even keep the laces in the ones you have."

"Sis, I don't want them to wear. I want to use them as trade for cigarettes and food and shit. You know they know my sis is the bomb ass Jackie Donovan. They want me to get them some free loot since you ballin and all."

"Leo, I am your sister, not theirs. I am balling literally, not figuratively. And I told you to take all of your pictures of me off the damn wall in your cell! If the front office gets one more letter from the Matthew Thomas correctional facility addressed to me I am going to come and put my foot in your ass. Stop bragging to your fellow convicts about me and tell Pookie to stop trying to be my Facebook friend."

"OK, Sis, damn! I will tell Pookie to stop. How 'bout you send your big brother $50 to put on my account?"

And so it goes. But since I'm no longer playing for the Stars I've also retired from being the shoe Santa. But back to what to wear to the gym this morning. Why do I feel like I'm getting ready for the prom!?! I can't make up my mind so I call Keeva. She is my Dr. Ruth, Oprah, and Wendy Williams all rolled into one.

"This is Keeva with KeMarketing how can I help—"

"Ke, it's me Jack." I interrupt her in the middle of her spiel.

"Hey girl. I am so used to getting business calls early in the morning so I didn't look at my caller I.D. What are you doing up so early?"

"I have a predicament and I need your help. I took your advice and called Adaris yesterday. We had a very nice conversation and he invited me to work out with him this morning."

"So you decided for your first date for him to see you at your absolute worst. That's my cuz. No sexy red dress and four-inch stilettos but some raggedy ass gym shorts and a sports bra that makes you look like you have a uniboob, all so you can sweat like a pig and smell like hell. Who knows, you just might pull it off Jackie."

"Ugh, sure glad I called you. When he suggested we meet at the gym I thought it was a great idea, but now you're making me feel like it's a very bad one."

"Well, actually it's pretty genius. After this date you won't have anywhere to go but up. If he likes you all sweaty and funky he is going to love what he sees when you fix up. Now what was it you needed to ask me?"

"I need some advice on what to wear. I don't want to look too casual but I don't want to look like I'm trying too hard either."

"Jackie, you have more workout clothes than Richard Simmons and Billy Blanks put together. Dress according to how you feel. In the words of Digital Underground, 'Doowutchyalike…' I don't think there are any rules in gym dating because you are the only two nuts I know of who have your first date at the gym!"

"Thanks for being such a big help cuz. I'll let you know how it turns out. Have a good day."

"Make sure you call and give me the 411 as soon as you leave the gym. Gotta go make that paper, girl! Love you, bye."

I jump in the shower and get out with 20 minutes to spare, and walk into my closet. I decide to wear all black. I haven't worked out in about a week and I figure it'll hide any bulges that have appeared. I pull on tights, black gym shorts, a black sports bra, and a black sleeveless shirt. I decide to add a black hat, black socks, and black shoes. Now I'm in black Nike from head to toe. I put my hair in a ponytail and finish my Shaft look off with some small diamond studs, my g-shock watch, and some light pink lip gloss. Gotta break the black up just a bit with some pink! The last thing I do is pop a piece of strawberry peach gum in my mouth. I am a gum fanatic. Since I'm feeling a little peachy I decide to go with that flavor.

I check myself out in the full-length bathroom mirror and I am pretty impressed with what I see. I grab a jacket—black, of course—and a pair of my Tiffany sunglasses and jump in the car with 32 minutes to get to the gym. As I walk out the door, my mom looks up from the paper and says the words I have heard every time I leave the house since I learned to drive, "Have a great day baby, and please be careful."

I say, "I'll be back in a few hours Mom. I'm headed to the gym for a workout."

I walk out to the garage and jump into my baby, which just arrived by a carrier from Seattle. She has been my most expensive indulgence. Keeva convinced me to buy it. I planned to do my car shopping during her visit so I'd have someone to test drive with me. I was looking for something reasonable like an SUV or a truck. Ke always encourages me to walk on the wild side. By the time she was finished with me, I was driving off the lot with a brand new white BMW 650 convertible. It was one of the best decisions I ever made. This car reminds me that life is short and that I should treat myself from time to time. So I jump into "Ivory"—I myself am Ebony—and zoom off down I-24. I start thinking, what the hell I have gotten myself into. I am either about to do one of the best things I have done in a long time or set myself up for epic failure.

I get to the gym a little early so I can meet Jackie as she walks in. I'm a little antsy about the workout today. I would not qualify this as a date but I can't recall ever working out with a female. All the women I've been involved with in the past did things like Pilates and yoga and other bougie activities. Jackie said yes to a workout and didn't make one comment about her hair which immediately gives her more brownie points. I check with the facility manager to make sure he has everything set up for me. Jackie doesn't know this but I have a private workout room set up with a few treadmills, elliptical machines, bikes, mats, exercise balls, and some free weights. I tried to think of every piece of equipment she may want to use.

I'm standing at the front desk talking to Matt the manager when out of the corner of my eye I see Jackie walk through the door. I swear she gets more beautiful every time I see her. And today she is in her most natural state. She walks with an elegance that belies her athleticism. Almost like she took charm school classes and walked with a book balanced on her head. She exudes a confidence unlike anyone I have ever seen. How a woman can look so sexy in all black athletic gear is beyond me. She's also wearing this black hat with her hair swinging out the back. She smiles hello as she walks by people like she never meets a stranger. She has on some sunglasses so I can't really tell if she is looking my way. I almost hope not because I can feel a little bit of slobber in the left corner of my mouth.

"Adaris man, get yourself together," I whisper to myself.

Matt, who is standing right beside me, shakes his head. "How can you get yourself together man? She is a sight for sore eyes."

By that time, Jackie has sauntered through the lobby and she walks up to me with a smile on her face.

"Good morning Jackie," I say, doing my best not to drool.

"Good morning to you."

"Are you ready to work out?"

"I haven't been in the gym for at least a week so I hope you'll go easy on me."

"We can work at your pace. I reserved a workout room so we can have some privacy. I hope you don't mind?"

"Uh, well, that was nice of you. Are you sure you didn't go out of your way?"

"It was my pleasure. Follow me so we can get started."

I follow Adaris down the hallway and start to get a little nervous. I distract myself by watching him walk. The man is effortlessly fine. He has on gym shorts that hug his butt and a Trailblazers t-shirt, and a hat turned backwards on his head. He's shaped like an inverted triangle—wide shoulders, huge chest and back, a washboard stomach, and a small waist. As my eyes travel downward I come to a tight butt and some of the most beautiful legs I've ever seen. This man is a chocolate dream. I'm staring so hard that I fail to notice he's come to a stop at the door and I bump into him. Hard. I bounce off said huge back like I'm bouncing off a brick wall. Adaris turns around with the agility of a running back and catches me like a football. Now I don't know if it's the collision or excitement of being in close contact with him but I'm suddenly a little lightheaded. As he sets me upright with those tree trunk arms, I look into his eyes and smile. As he was holding me about six inches off the floor he smiles that killer slow smile with those braces wrapped around his teeth and says, "If I'd known we'd be tackling today I would have put my pads on baby." Still a little unsteady, I put my hands on his chest and before I know it I'm rubbing my hands up and down his pecs. He smiles even wider.

I feel my face get hot. "You can put me down now Adaris. Sorry I ran into you. I wasn't watching where I was going." He sets me down and grabs my hands, which are still rubbing his chest, then leans over and says in a whisper, "That's one of the best sneak attacks I've had in years, Jackie. I need to decide if I'm gonna give you a penalty. What say you?"

"Uh, well, uh, I say you should take a time out and think about it." I snatch my hands out of his grasp and ask, "Is this our room?"

"Yes it is." He smiles slyly and opens the door.

I walk through the door and my jaw drops. The first thing I notice is the soft music playing on hidden speakers. There's every kind of workout machine known to man and some I have never seen before. I look at him in awe and ask, "Did you do all this for me?"

"I wasn't sure what you wanted to do today so I made sure we'd have everything we need. Your wish is my command little lady."

"Wow...I figured we'd be in a room with 100 other people! Adaris, thanks for being so thoughtful. Oh damn, here come the tears. I am so sorry but I am still very emotional."

"Dang, if I can impress you by arranging a private workout room, it must not take much to make you happy," he says, moving a little closer. He reaches down and gently wipes the tears from my eyes. Then it's back to business. "I only get this room for a few hours so I suggest we get started. What's your pleasure, ma'am?"

"My pleasure is to start on the treadmill," I say, giving Adaris a small smile.

"Then you get started. I'm going to lift some weights." Adaris turns his back to me and says in a serious voice, "Let me warn you right now, Jackie, that when I work out I am serious, so don't be looking at my butt or anything."

I respond by giving him my first real laugh of the day. "I feel the same way, Mr. Singleton, so you take your own advice and keep your eyes off my booty."

"Don't worry Jackie. I memorized the way that onion looks when I saw your clumsy ass fall in the airport. Now get to work."

Suddenly I'm not nervous anymore. He has diffused my anxiety, and I feel a sense of peace come over me that I haven't felt since before my father passed away. I was around someone that would allow me to be myself. I was one moment glamour girl, the next minute clumsy ox, and finally workout diva. I jump on the treadmill, turn the speed up, and start running for my life. I toss off my hat and my shirt and just let myself go. Before I know it I've run for an hour. I haven't felt this good in a long time. I feel great!

Lord help me! How am I going to get through this workout? As I stop at the door to the workout room I can sense Jackie behind me and then all of a sudden I feel some 36 Ds crash into my back. And what a feeling it is! I turn around to catch her and the next thing I know I have picked her up off the floor and she is looking me right square in the eyes. I just about lose my mind. From what I can tell she is around 5 foot 11, without heels, but to me she is the perfect size. Then she starts palming my chest like a basketball. Is she trying to give me a heart attack? I know the rubbing is innocent, but what will I do if she ever rubs me the right way! I put her down and grab her hands. They are big for a woman, but they're feminine. A perfect fit for holding onto a big man like me.

After that I don't really know what's happening. I feel like someone has slipped me a mickey. I vaguely hear her saying she wants to get on the treadmill, then off she goes. I mean, she runs for an hour straight and she has the nerve to take off that hat, almost in slow motion, and then she rips her t-shirt off over her head. I almost drop a damn weight on my foot when she does that, even though a sports bra covers up all her delightfuls. The funny thing is, she is so deep in the zone that she doesn't even know I'm there. About the time she finishes her run I'm beginning to get my bearings. She starts her cool down and my phone rings. My surprise is timed just right.

"This is Adaris speaking," I say into the phone.

"Mr. Singleton, your appointment is in the lobby waiting on you," I hear the receptionist say.

I reply "Thanks Jessica," and hang up. When I dare look at Jackie I say in my most sincere voice, "Jackie, I need to take care of something up front. I'll be back in a few minutes."

She smiles and says, "No problem."

As I walk out the door, I say a prayer of thanks to God for getting me out of that room. What the heck was I thinking? There is no way I can work out with her in private. I almost did myself in dropping that weight on my foot. Jackie Donovan could cause me a career ending injury. How would that look, telling my coach I injured myself while gawking at a woman. And what is that scent? She smells like peaches and strawberries.

I've had the feeling Jackie hasn't been pampered much in the last few months and I wanted to do something special to help her relax. She doesn't know it yet, but I arranged for a masseuse to give her a massage in our private room. Before we arrived at the gym today the masseuse brought over her other supplies, including an outfit for Jackie to change into after her massage and shower. I pass Griffin the masseuse on the way out, giving her a smile as I head over to the stadium where I can get a good workout without any distractions. I should know how my surprise went over sometime this evening.

As I'm cooling down from my exhilarating run I wonder what Adaris rushed off to do, but at this point I don't really care. For some reason I feel like I can run forever today. With the pace of retiring, moving home and trying to decide my future, I haven't had much time to think and reflect on the last year. Now I know that it was the most stressful time of my life. Somehow Adaris knew I needed some private time to unwind. I even forgot he was in the room. Hey, what's with the funky Zen music that just came on? You know, the kind of music you hear when you're having a massage. I stop to take a sip of water when a woman walks into the room with a portable massage table. I say, "Hello, you must have the wrong room. This room was reserved for a workout."

"Hello, my name is Griffin and you must be Ms. Donovan. Mr. Singleton sent me here to give you a full body massage. Would you like stone, Swedish, deep tissue, sports, or reflexology?" she asks while gently shaking my hand.

I stand there with my mouth wide open and tears in my eyes for the second time that day. She looks at me with a gentle smile. "Mr. Singleton told me to make sure you didn't get up from the table until you are completely relaxed, so let's do a deep tissue massage today. Here's your robe, you can change in the bathroom. While you do that I will get set up."

I take the robe and like a robot step into the little bathroom that I haven't noticed before. On the sink is a handwritten note. I plop myself down on the toilet seat to read it:

Jackie,

I know the last few months have been overwhelming for you and your family. Please take this time to rejuvenate and relax. Griffin is the best masseuse in town, so you should be feeling great in no time.

Your <u>Friend</u> Adaris

P.S. In the bag behind the door are toiletries and clothes for you to change into after your massage. I hope I got the size right. I guessed that you are a size 10.

Now I'm really bawling. But for the first time in a long time they are tears of happiness. No flowers, no jewelry, no flowery words. Just a one hour run, a massage, and a new outfit. What am I thinking, *just!* Adaris just spent more time and money not to mention the thoughtfulness on me than all the men I ever dated put together and we haven't even been out on a date yet…have we? This is one of the best gifts anyone has ever given me. As I sit reading the note again, I hear a soft tap on the door and Griffin says, "Ms. Donovan, I'm ready for you now."

I open the door and see that the workout room has been transformed into a massage parlor. The big equipment is gone, the lights are dimmed, and a burning candle is emitting the sweetest scent. Now that funky music I noticed a few minutes ago is like music to my ears. I lie down on the table to start another relaxing hour. Courtesy of Mr. Adaris Singleton.

After an amazing massage, I drag myself into the bathroom to take a shower. As I unzip the garment bag and start to pull out the items Adaris bought me, I am thinking, "Is this man not amazing!" He—or maybe some woman he knows—has thought of everything. First I pull out Chanel No. 5 soap, lotion, and perfume. Also a shower cap to protect my 'do,' a comb and brush, deodorant, and even toothpaste and a brush. Next I find a matching bra and panties—in the right size. And then I pull out a beautiful yellow Juicy Couture jogging suit that has the word "juicy on the butt. And a matching shirt and tennis shoes. I shower and dress and put my dirty clothes in my garment bag. I leave the gym with a huge smile on my face. Guess I won't wait for two weeks to call Adaris back this time!

"Hello"

"Hello Adaris. This is Jackie. I want to thank you so much for everything today. It just felt so good to exercise without any stress. And Griffin was awesome! She truly has magic hands. And did you pick out that outfit by yourself?"

"Hey Jackie. I am so glad you enjoyed your day. I really wanted you to relax. I wanted to stay around to see you after the massage, but I didn't want to risk taking you out of chill mode. Griffin is awesome isn't she? I've referred her to so many people she doesn't have to advertise anymore, and yes I picked out the outfit."

"Everything you did was so thoughtful. I'm trying to figure out what I can do to repay you. I was so relaxed when I left the gym that I came back home and took a long nap."

"Great! Griffin does tend to rock you to sleep with her magic hands. How about if you repay me by letting me see you somewhere outside of a gym? I have to fly out to Bristol tomorrow for a few days but would love to see you when I get back."

"Why are you going to Bristol, to see a car race?"

"Not Bristol, Tennessee. Bristol, Connecticut. I've been talking with the execs at ESPN about doing some commentating after I retire and we're close to reaching an agreement."

"I got it. I want to hear more about that when you return. I actually thought about taking you for a ride."

"Now I like the sound of that Jackie, First you tackle me, now you want to ride me."

"Not so fast, Tonto. I'm talking about a bike ride. Living in Seattle I became somewhat of a cyclist, and I've been doing some research on bike trails here in Nashville. I want to check them out before I take anyone on them. Do you ride?"

"You better watch how you word things baby. I guess the G-rated answer would be that yes, I rode a bike as a kid. From time to time I ride an exercise bike at the gym, but I haven't actually ridden a real bike in a long time. They say you never forget how to ride though, don't they?"

"It should come back to you. I have my own bike, but if you're game I'll be happy to rent a bike for you. How about we schedule it for later this week? Does that work for you?"

"No need to rent a bike for me. If you plan to take me for a ride I'll invest in one. It may be one of the best investments I ever make."

I swear, this man can make something so innocent sound so sexy. "If you plan to ride a lot buying one may be a good idea. Do you have any idea what to look for?"

"Oh, you can be sure I plan to ride as often as I can...with you. How about this? Why don't you pick out a bike for me, and I'll go pick it up before we head out to the trail. Once you decide on the trail and the time, give me a call so I can put in on my schedule. I'm good any time after Wednesday evening to ride you. I mean ride with you."

"I am going to pretend that you didn't just make that comment and I am going to replace the word ride with cycle. What's your budget for a bike? You can really go crazy. Also, should I pick out some biking gear for you?"

"Pick out whatever you think I need and then call me with the total so I can take care of it. And let's try to go riding, I mean cycling, sooner rather than later this week."

"Adarissss...you are killing me softly. I'll give you a call in a few days to update you on everything. Have a safe trip, and please be careful." I think to myself, oh Lord, I'm starting to sound like Ella.

Adaris says in a whisper just before he hangs up the phone, "I look forward to seeing you soon."

It's Just an Ordinary Day

The next day I drive over to a bike shop in Nashville and pick out a Schwinn Hybrid bike for Adaris. My bike is a little dated so I splurge on a hybrid for myself. I pick up a helmet and some gear, then call Adaris to give him his tally.

"Hello."

"Hi Adaris. Hope I'm not interrupting anything, but I'm at the bike shop and I have the total for your bike and gear."

"You're not interrupting me beautiful. How much did you get me for?"

"I got you a bike, helmet, an extra-large seat, and some gloves–it adds up to $700. Plus tax. I hope it's not too much."

"Seven hundred G's Ms. Donovan. You are a cheap date. I figured you'd get me for more than that. Ask the clerk if they take AmEx."

"Yes, they do take American Express. Ummm, do you have one of those infamous black cards?"

"I do, Miss Lady. I have to run to another meeting, so write this number down and call me later with a time and place to meet. I know you modern ladies don't like to be picked up."

He gives me the number, then whispers, "I can't wait for our ride. I will talk with you later."

I hand the phone to the salesperson so Adaris can verify his identity, and I wonder why he's looking at me with a huge grin. I ask him, "Do you mind telling me why you look like the cat just swallowed the canary?"

So Pete, which is the name on his name tag grins at me and says, "I can't believe I just talked to Dair Singleton. He even promised to stop by the shop sometime to autograph one of our bikes. He told me to put the entire purchase on his tab. Including yours."

Well I'll be damned. He just turned my date into his treat. I am not going to get used to this. It's too good to be true...

I find a nice bike route that will take us across a couple of college campuses, and I figure we can take breaks along the way. Once I'm sure everything is in order I send Adaris a text. I am feeling too vulnerable to have a conversation with him, I need time to get my mind right:

Hllo. Need u to pck up 2 bkes and gear from Estside Cycle on 11th strt on Thrsdy mrng and meet me at TSU at Shrader COGIC's prkg lot at 10:00am. B rdy to roll. Wll tke bout 4 hrs to fnsh our rte. C u Thrsdy and I have a bne to pck w/u re: the pymnt of my bike @gear. Thnk u ☺

Within two minutes I hear my phone ding with a return message:

Got ur msg. Fraid to cll huh...LMAO. Will c u at 10 in 48 hrs. Cnt w8t to ride...I mn cycl. No thnx nesecry. Lst I cld do 4 ur trble. TTYL.

I'm sitting with a few of the ESPN sports analysts, who have just ganged up on me. It reminds me of the college recruiting trips I took in high school. They set me up with the best players on the team to convince me to join ESPN instead of Fox or Sports South. As they're telling me how great it is to be a sports analyst, my phone rings. It's Jackie. I've been waiting for her to call all day. I feel like a kid waiting on Santa Claus. After the first ring I excuse myself and say I need to take this call. I can't help but smile when I hear her voice. She explains something about finding me a bike and I remember that I told her to get me whatever I need. So I pull out my wallet and give her my black American Express credit card number. Then I'm on the phone with someone named Paul or Paco or Pete and I promise to come sign a bike for his shop. All that really matters to me is hearing her smile. Then I think I told her to hang on to the card number just in case...Have I lost my damn mind! Who gives a woman he has seen three times, two of which were five minutes or less the capacity to have an unlimited amount of credit? My dumb, nose wide open ass, that's who. So I get off the phone with this corny smile on my face and turn around and see the two analysts looking at me and laughing. One of them says to me, "No wonder we can't get you to commit to ESPN. Some chick has you signing your life away. I saw you pull out your Centurion card, my friend."

And then it hits me. Am I really hedging on this deal because I see a chance of something developing with Jackie? The main reason I have reservations is that next year AJ will be a junior and I don't want to miss any of his games. But am I also hesitating because I'm not sure I want someone else once again to be in charge of where I go and when? In football you have very little say about your schedule. I respond to John with a wink and a smile, but I'm thinking, "It's none of your damn business, dude who I am talking to and if I just emptied my bank account. But I'm on the first thing smoking tomorrow and I can't wait to see my family—and to see Jackie on Thursday.

Now that I have all the bike gear in place and have scoped our route, I need to call in Special Forces agent Keeva McGhee-Hudson. I almost hate to 'cause I'm not really ready to talk much about Adaris, since I have no idea where things are going. Keeva is going to be nosy as hell, but I need her help. It's time to put "Operation around the Hood" in play so I punch the number to Keeva's Nashville office.

"KeMarketing, this is Keeva!"

"Ke, it's me Jackie"

"What's shakin' bacon," she yells into the phone.

"You are so corny. What's shakin' is, I need you to help me put "Operation around the Hood" in motion."

"What the hell is "Operation around the Hood"? It's not a tour of homes in the JC Napier projects is it? Are you asking me to devise a marketing plan for that?"

"Hold up swole up. "Operation around the Hood" is our code name for my next outing with Adaris."

"Well, you never even told me about the gym and now there's already a round two? And are we calling these outings now?"

"Yes, outings. I will give you the details about the gym later, but I tell you, I have never been so relaxed in my life…"

"Did you screw him Jack? I knew you would give up the goods."

"Keeva, you are so crass! I did not screw him. Not even close. But he did put me to sleep for a while...Now will you shut up for two seconds so I can tell you about my plan?"

"I will table the gym outing but I want to hear about it," Keeva replies, sucking her teeth.

"You know how much I like to cycle, right? Well, I decided to take Adaris on a bike ride around the city that starts at TSU, and moves on to Fisk and Meharry. Ride around to Vanderbilt and then ends up at Hadley Park. I want to have a spread laid out at the park so we can eat a late lunch and I need your help. Can you take the food and set things up, and then hang out till we get there so no one steals our food?"

"Shut the front door! Did you just say you are going to do some cooking tomorrow? You actually plan to cook for the man? You must really be feeling him to pull out the pots and pans. I can't remember the last time you let a man see you throw down in the kitchen."

"I don't know what else to do. He has been so wonderful to me and I want to show him how much I appreciate him."

"So you cook for him. Are you crazy! You know when you cook for men you can never get rid of their asses. And the way you cook, you must want to be his wifey. Why don't you just let me run over to Swett's or Ed's Fish and pick up a few plates for you?"

"No Keeva, I want him to eat some home-cooked food. I was thinking I'd open up Dad's grill and throw on some chicken and ribs. We haven't used the grill since last summer. I'm hoping to convince mom to make some potato salad and I'll make some of my baked beans, with fruit tea and cupcakes for dessert. What do you think?"

"I think you are going through a whole lot of trouble for a man you just met. But if it means your cousin is going to get a slamming meal out of it, then I am down. I expect to be paid in swine and bird!"

"Ok, I got you. I'll drop everything off at your office on Thursday morning before I meet him at Schrader Lane. I need you to hook up a decoration for the table. Don't go crazy, just something simple. Remember we're going to be in Hadley Park not Centennial Park."

"I take it back. You obviously don't want to impress him if you're going to Hadley. I hope you are licensed to carry a concealed weapon 'cause you may need it," Keeva says with a peal of laughter. "Now I see why you are calling this little escapade "Operation Around the Hood". By the time you get the poor man to bike all over the damn city he's going to be so tired he won't be able to go past Hadley Park."

"Hush up girl. We'll be fine in the middle of the day. I feel more comfortable in Hadley then I do in most places. I have blocked out four hours for the ride. It probably won't take that long so I need you to be ready to roll around 1:30? I'll call you when we get close to Vanderbilt so you can put everything in motion."

"I'm your girl. When will you start cooking?"

"When I get home from the gym tomorrow afternoon, why?"

"Because I will be over with my Tupperware around six. That should give you enough time to get the ribs and chicken off the grill, right?"

It's Thursday morning and my stomach is doing flip flops. I don't remember the last time I put this much effort into trying to impress a man. Something in me wants Adaris to feel as pampered as I felt at the gym. I haven't spoken with him since we talked at the bike shop other than a few texts , which is ok, 'cause I feel like a blithering idiot around him most of the time. Add clumsy to that. Yesterday I picked up the ingredients for my lunch. Before I left I asked mom if she'd mind fixing me a small bowl of potato salad. Now, everyone in our family can throw down, but I have seen people almost come to blows over my mom's potato salad. If you want to find out how she makes it you better sit your butt down at the kitchen table and watch. If you ask her how many potatoes or eggs to use, she'll just tell you, "I figure it out based on how much I need." When my dad died my Aunt Leslie even had the nerve to ask mom if she planned to make a batch of potato salad since we were expecting so much company. You should have seen the people scatter from the kitchen after that stupid comment was made. I don't know what my mom said to Leslie but all I know is that Leslie is now on potato salad punishment. She gets none! Anyhow, my mom is no dummy, so I have anticipated that she'll be asking me what I need it for. I start the countdown. By the time I get to seven she says, "Who are we making this small batch for baby? I want to make sure we don't need a big batch before I start boiling potatoes and eggs."

"A small batch will be plenty mom. I'm putting some things on the grill and I thought it would be good to add some baked beans and potato salad." I'm pulling a Serena with my butt hanging out of the refrigerator, and I turn and sneak a glance at Ella.

"Baby, you know I'm happy to make your small batch even if you won't answer my question. I hope this young fellow is worth the hassle. When do you need this done?"

You can't put anything past Ella. She may not ask me anything else but the wheels will be churning. Ella says to me as she goes into the pantry to get the potatoes, "That smile on your face sure does look familiar. I had that same smile over 30 years ago..."

"Well, greedy Ke is coming by tonight with her Tupperware, so if you can have it done by five that would be great. And Ma, I don't know yet if he is worth it, which is why I am not telling you who he is." I give her a smile.

The ribs and chicken come out perfectly. The potato salad is tasty as ever and my baked beans are awesome. I also throw together some vanilla cupcakes with chocolate icing and a pitcher of fruit tea. I drop everything off at Keeva's office and head over to Schrader Lane to meet Adaris. I get there about ten minutes early so I can settle my nerves. I pop a piece of spearmint gum in my mouth—might as well have minty breath.

I'm just starting to get a good minty chew going when I see Adaris pull into the parking lot in a Range Rover. He sees me and flashes a huge grin. Boy is he a sight for sore eyes. It's only been about a week, but I am so excited to see him. I remind myself to keep all of my cool points, but I don't even know if I should stay in the car or get out? Get out fool! I wait for him to pull up beside me and then get out. I'm still wondering if I should give him a handshake, a pound, or a hug, when all of a sudden I'm enveloped in a hug so tight it takes my breath away. This is no half hug that your mom teaches you to give men so they don't feel your boobs. It's the I can feel every muscle and bone in your body" kind of hug. The kind where you can smell whatever kind of cologne he is wearing for the rest of the day or your life. The kind of hug that feels like home. I feel him smell my hair—thank God I put some Carol's Daughter Tui in it before I braided it up this morning. Then he pulls my braid back gently so he can look me in the eye and stares with this huge smile on his face. "It's so good to see you Jackie," he murmurs.

"So where are you taking me, baby?" Adaris asks with that Barry White voice.

Meanwhile, I'm still wrapped up in his hug with my face about three inches from his. Thank God I decided on spearmint and not bubble gum!

"I found a bike route that will take us across most of the colleges around town. We'll end up in Hadley Park and have lunch."

Now it seems he has pulled me even closer to him. I can feel every inch of his chest, his stomach, his thighs...everything is so big, so tight, so compact.

"Uh, Adaris, we are in the parking lot of a church and people are riding by. Do you want to let go of me now and get the bikes out of your car?"

"Well...I don't want to let you go, but I guess we should get going. Let me get the bikes out of the car." He moves his arms down my back for one final squeeze and then lets me go. I swear I almost fall to the concrete. Thank God I was really cool with it. By the time he turns around with my new bike in his hands, I manage to look like I'm just chilling but I am really checking him out in his biker shorts.

I look at his tight buns and whisper, "What a rump roast."

"What did you say?"

"Oh, I said that's the bike I liked the most. What do you think of the bike I picked out for you?"

"It's very nice. I notice you got me a wider seat. Are you trying to tell me something Jackie?"

I grimace and say, "Let's face it, bike seats are not made for black people. Just be glad someone had the presence of mind to make bigger seats."

I figure I better take charge so I don't make any more rump shaker remarks, so I say, "Our route should take a few hours. Let me know if you want to stop for a beverage break. Any questions?"

"Yes, one. Am I the first man you ever rode with?"

"Actually you are. Does that matter?"

"I wouldn't want your first ride to be with anyone else," he says looking intensely into my eyes. "I'm glad to be your first."

Without further comment, I get my big ass on the oversize seat that still isn't quite big enough and take off down the trail. All of a sudden I hear laughter.

"Aren't you going to show me how to use the bike?!" he yells.

I think about flipping him another bird, but since that means I love you, I quickly decide not to. Instead I ride on as fast as I can. He's a pro football player. He can keep up!

We cycle up Ed Temple Parkway past the Ted Rhodes golf course, then turn onto Clarksville Highway and pass Ed's Fish. When we reach the corner that separates Fisk University and Meharry Medical College, I decide we need to stop for a pulse check. I brake at the corner and turn as Adaris pulls up beside me.

"How's it going back there?"

"It's great. You see a whole lot more when you're on a bike. Where now?"

"I thought we'd ride across the Fisk campus. I haven't been here in a while and I think it's pretty fascinating that Nashville has three historically black colleges within a few blocks of each other. Are you ok with that before we move on toward downtown?

"It's your ride. You lead the way."

After we leave Fisk, we loop around Music City Row and past the famous Musica statue, commonly known as the "naked people" statue. Then we hit the Vanderbilt campus and stop for another break in front of Vanderbilt Hospital.

"This is our last break before lunch. How are you doing?"

"Great! I'd love to do this more often. I forgot how much history there is in Nashville. You know, Vanderbilt offered me a full ride, but I didn't think it could give me the exposure I would need to play pro ball."

"I don't love being around Vanderbilt. My dad was in and out of this hospital for over a year. He had great care, but if I never have to come to this hospital again it will be fine with me."

"I have similar memories. When AJ was five he was diagnosed with leukemia. We started his journey at the Vandy children's hospital, but we had to transfer him to the Seattle Cancer Care Alliance."

"I had no idea you spent time in Seattle. How long were you there?"

"Well, we had to stay six months, since he had a bone marrow transplant. My mom and I were with him all the time, and his mother flew out when she could, but she wasn't very helpful. I take that back. His half-brother Noah, the child she had with her husband, was a match for AJ and helped save his life. After AJ went into remission we went back to Seattle for check-ups for five years, but I haven't been back except to play football. Since then AJ has been very healthy, and thankfully he doesn't remember much about that time of his life.

"What a story—I had no idea AJ had leukemia."

"We don't talk about it much, but we do participate in the leukemia Relay for Life every year and I help the Red Cross recruit people of color for the bone marrow registry. Our race is grossly underserved. Are you on the registry Jackie?"

"No, I'm not. What does it take to join?"

"Just be healthy and under age 44, then go to the local blood bank where they'll swab your mouth. If you're a potential match you'll take more tests, and if you clear the tests, you donate bone marrow or stem cells. It's a small commitment, considering you can save a life."

"I'll think about joining. Maybe I can get some of my family and friends to commit too. Thanks for telling me about it. Since daddy had cancer I've become more aware of cancer prevention. And Hospice." I feel myself welling up so I cough and say, "Well, enough on that. Are you ready for the last leg back to Hadley Park? I have a surprise for you. Just let me step in here and use the restroom. I'll be right back!"

As I head to the restroom, I pull out my phone and call Keeva.

"Thank you for calling KeMarketing this is—"

"Keeva, it's Agent Jack in the Box. I'm calling to confirm that the goods are en route. Copy?"

"Jackie, is that you girl? Why in hell are you talking in code? Are you ready for me to set things up at the park?"

"Our ETA is thirteen hundred hours. Copy."

"Girl, I don't know military time. What the heck is thirteen hundred hours? Is that 1:00?"

"Yes Ke, its 1:00. Central Standard Time. Are you down?"

"Like two flat tires girl. Oh, sorry, that is Ebonics. I mean the ribs are slamming and the beans are the fye. Over and out."

As I end the call I wonder what Keeva has up her sleeve. I walk back outside, and Adaris is leaning against the bike stand watching me with a smile. I have never seen anyone with braces that has such a beautiful smile.

"Are you ready to head to our final destination?"

"I am hungry girl. You've had me out three hours and you haven't fed me. Don't you know I'm a growing boy?"

"Why didn't you tell me? I have some granola bars in my fanny pack. Would you like one?"

"I don't want any bird food woman. Get me some meat!"

"Meat you will have, cave man. Follow me."

"To the ends of the earth girl, to the ends of the earth."

As we head toward the park my stomach starts to turn. I start rethinking everything I have done over the last few days. We could have easily stopped at Swett's, got some good soul food and kept it moving. But noooo, I wanted to show him that my culinary skills can rival Marcus Samuelson or G. Garvin. What if he doesn't like my food? What if he doesn't eat meat? Oh wait, he just told me he wants meat. What if he has food allergies? Wait, only white people have food allergies. Correction; white people actually go to the doctor to find out they have food allergies. As I see Hadley Park come into view I start to slow down. I can hear Adaris coming up close behind. He yells out, "You aren't getting tired on me are you Jackie?"

"No, I just want to make sure we're going to the right area."

As we enter the park I start looking around to see where Keeva has set up our spread. I'm hoping one of the Pavilions is vacant so we can use a table, but I see people sitting at all the tables. As I look around for Keeva, Adaris rides up beside me. All of a sudden I see something that makes me dread ever putting "Operation around the Hood" in play.

Under a tree in a secluded section of the park she's laid a thick blanket out on the ground. Spread out on the blanket are two wine glasses, a bottle of sparkling cider, and a beautiful picnic basket filled with what I presume is the food I cooked. There's also real silverware—not plastic—rolled up in cloth napkins. I'm so amazed that I almost miss Keeva walking back to her car. She turns and gives me a little wave, then keeps on walking. As I pull closer I see she's also left an IPOD with a note under it, and another blanket. I hop off my bike and grab the letter:

"I know you just asked me to set up the food, but it's too beautiful a day not to enjoy it with someone you like. You should have everything you need. Choose the Operation Hood Playlist on the IPOD. Toodles, Keeva."

I don't know if I want to strangle her or hug her. Adaris pulls up next to me and puts his bike down. I turn around with a huge grin on my face and say, "Lunch is served!" I wish I had a camera to capture the look on his face. I know exactly how he feels. What I don't know is what the hell Keeva has put in that basket.

I motion for Adaris to sit on the stadium seat that Keeva has left leaning against the tree, wondering if she forgot the other one or is trying to set me up. As he sits down I say, "Let me get everything out so I can serve you." With shaking hands, I pop open the cooler. Inside I find some wet wipes (good thinking Keeva), a bowl of mixed berries, and some cheese cut up in wedges. I assume the heifer intends this to be the appetizer. Under the fruit I see the potato salad, the tea, and some water. I hand Adaris the wet wipes, and as he washes his hands I hesitantly open the picnic basket. Inside are the ribs, chicken, baked beans, some plates, more napkins, and the cupcakes. I grab a few of the plates with a huge sigh of relief. I was praying she didn't have a fondue and some oysters in there. I lay out the food, then reach over to turn on the IPOD. Surprisingly "I don't see nothing wrong with a little bump and grind" didn't start playing. I'm surprised when Norman Brown starts playing. I finally get the nerve to look at Adaris. He is sitting on that stadium chair like a king on his throne. I instantly thought of the movie "Coming to America" and started to say "whatever you like," but I had a feeling he would say "bark like a dog!"

"I hope you're hungry because we have a ton of food."

"Are you sure I can't help you with anything?"

"No, just sit tight and let me get organized so I can fix our plates."

"Did you cook all of this food Jackie?"

"I cooked the chicken, ribs, beans, and cupcakes. My mom fixed the potato salad for me," I say while scooping food onto his plate. I brought chicken in case you don't eat pork."

"Oh, I eat pork from the rooter to the tooter!"

"What part of the chicken do you like?"

"I'm a leg man, but I'll take whatever you give me. I thought I recognized Ms. Ella's potato salad. When I dropped AJ off at your parent's house one day your mom invited me to eat. I almost killed myself eating her potato salad."

"It is wonderful. My sister and I have watched her make it so often that we don't eat it much. Come to think about it, mom doesn't eat much of it either. Is this enough to get you started?" I nod at his heaping plate.

"It's perfect. I'll open the wine while you fix your plate, then I'd like to say a blessing, if you don't mind."

I finish fixing my plate and sit down on the blanket facing him. Adaris reaches over grabs both of my hands and says one of the sweetest prayers I have ever heard. He finishes with a squeeze of my hands, then takes a huge bite out of a rib and lets out a moan that almost makes me drop my chicken leg.

"Ohhhhhh Jackie. This rib is the bomb, girl. And you say you grilled this?"

Smiling around my full mouth, I say, "Grilling is one of my specialties. Daddy taught me how to grill when I was little. Low and slow is what he always told me. That, and always use charcoal."

"You will have to forgive me for sucking and smacking, but this is so damn good. All of it."

We eat in silence for a few minutes, and then Adaris looks at me with a dreamy expression and says, "Will you marry me Jackie? If I weren't so full I would get down on one knee." I laugh so hard that I can't catch my breath. We sit there eating for about 20 minutes, looking around the park and asking between bites, "Can you pass me this? Do you want more of that?"

"Now what's for dessert, wifey?" he says with a teasing voice.

"Looks like homemade cupcakes and fruit. Which would you like?"

"Some of both. Why don't you put a few cupcakes and some fruit on one plate and come and sit between my legs so we can talk a while. I know sitting without back support has got to be killing you." Adaris moves the seat so he can lean back against the tree.

I look at him for about 30 seconds trying to decide if I should get that close. He senses my hesitation and pulls out the extra blanket that Keeva left us up against his chest to make a barrier. I fix the dessert plate, take a deep breath, then turn around and scoot my back up against him. He folds his arms around me and takes the plate.

"Feed me, wife," he says with a gruff voice.

"You're taking this wife thing a little too far. Next thing you'll be wanting me to cook your dinner and feed you every day," I say, teasing back at him.

As he gathers me closer in his arms he says softly, "You know, I am just teasing you, but thank you for the bike ride and the delicious meal, but most of all for the dessert. And I'm not talking about the cupcakes. Holding you even with a blanket between us is the icing on the cake."

Should I tell him he had me at "Hello?" Naah, I need to keep him on his toes because he has definitely knocked me off my feet! I pick up the fork, stab the cupcake, and put a big bite into his mouth. I never knew watching his lips grab food off a fork could be so sexy. I feed him bite after bite until one cupcake is gone. He closes his eyes and groans in ecstasy after every bite. I am hypnotized. Then he grabs the fork and starts to feed me the second cupcake. After a few bites, I shake my head so he can finish it off. A girl has got to watch her hips. He opens a bottle of water and holds it to my lips so I can take a sip, then he takes a gulp and sets it down. Suddenly I realize we have been eating from the same fork and drinking from the same bottle! Me, who is germ phobic. I have just swapped slobber with Adaris and he hasn't even kissed me yet.

The thought of it sends a shiver down my spine. Apparently he thinks I'm cold, because he pulls the blanket out from between us, holds me against his chest, and wraps it around us, and leans his head against mine. "That was one of the best meals I have had in a long time. I am honored that you took the time to do that for me. The only woman who has cooked for me like that is my mother. I hope to sit down at your table again soon because you got bill making skills."

"It was my pleasure. I love to cook but when you live by yourself it's easier to fix a sandwich or order out. In Seattle I had a rule to try a new recipe once a week. My team mates loved it because I either had them come by to eat with me or brought leftovers to the gym. It got so bad that they started leaving Tupperware by my locker so that I could put their food in it," I say with a laugh. "I am going to miss some of those girls. Wait, I take that back. They are going to miss me."

"Was it easy for you to retire Jackie? Did you decide over time or just wake up one day and say, I'm done?"

"I was pretty sure that this would be my last season even before my dad got sick. After six years in the league the game was no longer exciting to me, and I always told myself that I wouldn't hang on just because I thought I needed to play. I actually had planned to move up to the front office and help the rookies adjust to the league. When Daddy died I decided to come home for a while. What about you? How long do you plan to play?"

"This is my last year. I've been in the league for twelve years and played for three great teams, but my body is tired. The boys coming up behind me are bigger and quicker. I knew when I was more concerned about escaping a concussion than I was with the game that it was time to go. I don't want to get hurt because I'm playing too tentatively. AJ will be a junior next year and I don't want to miss any of his games—guess I just want something else for my life now. I have already missed enough of his life as it is. I still don't know what I want to do, that's why I'm checking out the opportunity with ESPN."

When Adaris mentions AJ's games I tense up a little. Apparently he notices because he starts rubbing my shoulders. "Are you trying to put Griffin out of business Adaris?" I ask with a nervous chuckle.

"I am so in tune to you that I felt you tense up a few seconds ago. I don't make you nervous, do I?"

"Truthfully, you make me very nervous. I feel like I need to be on guard when I am around you."

"I really hope I can make you drop your guard, Jackie, because I really want to get to know you better. I will be pretty free in the next few months and I'd like us to spend some time together, working on being friends."

"Friends...do you mean friends, or friends with benefits, Adaris?"

"I won't lie, Jackie. I think you're really beautiful and I think we may have a lot in common. Right now I'll settle for being your friend. Let's just take one day at a time and see where things go. How does that sound?"

"I like the idea of having a new friend. But I know how it is when you're preparing for a season. Not to mention, you have a teenage son who needs your attention. I'm ok with being third or fourth or even tenth on your list–I just don't want you to lose focus, especially since this is your last season. How about we shake on seeing where this friendship will take us?"

Adaris sits there for a moment, tilts his head, and looks me in the eyes. "How about we seal the deal with a kiss?" He pulls me closer, reaches around and turns my face to his, and gives me the sweetest kiss he can—on the corner of my mouth, then on my cheek, and then on my closed eyelids. Then he scoops me up as he gets to his feet and gently puts me on the ground. He makes me feel as light as a feather. He whispers in my ear, "I will let you set the pace, my friend. If I feel like you are stalling on me then I will take over the ride. You feel me?"

Oh, I definitely feel you Mr. Singleton, every single inch of you. I am not sure what happens after that. Somehow we gather up our items and walk back to our cars. After we get everything loaded up, Adaris asks the age old question: "When can I see you again?" My heart is pounding and I want to blurt out, "Right now or tomorrow or every damn day," but common sense prevails and I say instead, "My sister and a close friend are flying in tomorrow and we're having a girls' weekend. How about we touch base next week?"

Adaris smiles that killer smile, leans over and says, "Have a good weekend. Now let me walk you to your car." He opens the door and I climb in, he closes it, winks at me, and walks off chuckling.

The Hen's come home to Roost

Jackie and I just finished biking a few hours ago. She seems to find ways to spend time with me that don't require much communication, like running and biking. At first that was cool, but now I want time to get to know her better. I can't believe I am actually saying that. I typically meet women, go out a few times and lose interest. The last time I actually craved time with a woman was over 16 years ago when I was with AJ's mother, which was before I grew hair on my chest. Back then I didn't know what love was, I just knew I wanted to get with AJ's mom as much as possible. I mistook that for love. When she got pregnant I panicked. Don't get me wrong, I love my son more than anyone in the world. The mistake I made was not loving his mother enough. We tried to stick it out, but broke up our senior year in high school. After we graduated, she broke the news to me that she wanted to relinquish shared custody of AJ and move to California. I wasn't surprised, since AJ was with my mom and me most of the time. My mother took care of AJ so I could go to Auburn, and I came home to see him as often as I could. AJ and I have a great relationship despite my playing football away from home.

When I got the chance to move home to play with the Trailblazers I was ecstatic. I made sure the organization knew that this is the place I want to end my career. It's important for me to be here while AJ goes through puberty. My mom has done an excellent job, but boys need their fathers. My dad passed away when I was 13, and I know I missed out on things only a man can impart to a boy.

Jackie is an enigma to me. She handled my checkbook the way I would. I have had women insist on cars, diamonds, and one even asked for a boob job on my dime. They assumed because I had it they did. I have never given any woman my credit card number. I just sensed she would be a good steward with not just my money but with anyone's money. And then there was our picnic in the park—that lunch just took me over the edge. That girl can throw down. Every bite was amazing. Cooking for women, even southern women is a lost art these days. Most women I know can't boil water and they expect me to wine and dine them.

The best part of the day was just sitting under that tree with Jackie in my arms, listening to music and talking. Sex did not cross my mind, I just wanted to hold her and comfort her. The physical part of a relationship is still important to me, but I really long for a mental and spiritual connection with a woman. I know Jackie is vulnerable, having just lost her dad, and I know I need to give her space and let our friendship develop naturally. I just pray that God gives me the patience to let that happen and not screw it up.

I am so excited! My sister Serena and I decided to surprise our mother by bringing in my Aunt Dorthea, her oldest sister, for a long weekend. My mom has a ton of siblings, but she and Dorthea have a special connection, maybe because Aunt Dorthea is old enough to be her mother. Aunt D as we call her is 85 years old and she is still the sassiest, smartest woman I know. She always tell us how she used to pull in men. She has outlived two husbands, a few boyfriends, and is still pulling in admirers. The funny thing is, she isn't interested in old men—she says "old men give you worms." When she comes to visit she holds court, and we all gather at her feet as she tells us what the real law of attraction is all about. My dad often refers to these meetings as Hen parties. Aunt D says that when we really want something from a male, we should sizzle up to him, shimmy down beside him and bat our eyelashes, put a hand on his leg and rub, pat, and slide. She is convinced that the best way to get what you want is to rub, pat and slide. She even dared us to try it! Mom has confirmed that it does really work—that is how she convinced daddy to build the plantation!

My closest friend, Maxine Hilton, is also on her way in from the Virgin Islands. Max and I met as college freshmen when I was wandering around campus introducing myself. She describes me as a country ass tall skinny girl from Tennessee who had an accent so bad that she thought I was speaking a foreign language. When I walked up to her and introduced myself, she looked at me with a huge grin and then opened her mouth. Her Crucian accent was absolutely beautiful, like a song. Ten years later we are still the best of friends.

I swear I hang out with overachievers. Serena is a master event planner, Keeva is a marketing guru, and Max can tell you to go to hell in such legal-ease that you think she is complimenting you. Max flew in for dad's funeral, but decided to come back for a few days so we can really hang out. Keeva decided to cancel a trip so she could join us. It's like the perfect storm. The hens have come home to roost!

Serena and Aunt D's flight arrive within 30 minutes of Max's, so I can pick everyone up together. I pull up to the parking garage and jump out. We've decided to meet in the baggage claim. Even though Max is thirty minutes behind, she will easily catch up with the others. Serena and Aunt D will stop twice to pee, and once to rest, with Aunt D dropping antidotes the whole way and she often repeats stories but Ella reminded us that at her age she can repeat what she damn well pleases. As I walk in the door I see two of the three divas waiting for their bags near the carousel. They are easy to spot because Aunt D is the only person I know who can put a Tam to shame. She has one in every color. As I get closer I hear Aunt D shout out, "Look at that shape, if I had hips like that I would still be in business." My Aunt D can make you feel like a million bucks.

As I hug Aunt D, I wink at my sister and say, "Aunt D, why don't you let me walk you over to the seat over here so Serena and I can get your luggage and go find Max."

"Baby, you know Aunt D packed light. When you get my age all you need is a few muumuus and a toothbrush," she says with a chuckle.

"What about your panties?" I ask Aunt D.

"Panties, what panties?" she says with a huge grin. The running joke in our family is that Aunt D has the first penny she ever made and is tighter than Dick's hatband. If you ever buy her a gift, watch out—you might get it back in a year or two. Aunt D made regifting popular before Oprah stepped on the scene, even though she has enough money to buy and sell pretty much anything she wants. She is like the Godfather of cash, the one you call when you're a little short on money.

I sit Aunt D down and walk back to the baggage area to meet Max. She is also easy to spot, as she is the most colorful person I know, in more ways than one. She rocks the sorbet colors all year long because in the Virgin Islands it's always summer and she believes people need to get in tune with her fashion sense. I head over to the baggage claim area and see her instantly. She has the biggest tatas I have ever seen and wears them like a badge of honor. She jokes that she has put plenty of men to sleep with her boobs! She is wearing a beautiful white blouse with a long orange skirt and banging brown riding boots. Living in a tropical area, she is always cold when she comes to Tennessee. I walk up to her yelling, "Celieeeee!" and she yells back, "Nettieeee!" Then we hug each other and start singing, "*Me and you must never part, maki da-da,*" while we clap our hands. We notice that the white people look at us aghast, but the black people start laughing because they understand our chant from one of our favorite movies, *The Color Purple.*

We scoop up Aunt D, who is busy telling Serena about the first time she flew on a plane, back when integration first started. Suddenly my aunt, who has no filter, looks up at Max and says, "Girl, your breasts are so big that I bet you have men wagging around behind you saying 'Got milk?' If I had breasts like that I would put a cow out of business." This comment brings tears of laughter. What a way to start the weekend! The last year has been so heavy that it feels great to be basking in the light.

We get to the house and pull into the garage. Serena and Max go in first so they can get their greetings out of the way, while Aunt D and I bring up the rear. As we come around the corner, my mom stops mid-sentence, looks at Aunt D, and bursts into tears. As mom runs to hug her sister and they coo at each other, Serena, Keeva, Max, and I look at each other and smile. Then Max says, in her Crucian lilt, "Come now ye old broads. I have libations. Let's get our holiday started."

We decide to go down to Shorty's Shack and have a slumber party. For the first time in a long while we came into his room and feel a sense of peace. It's almost as if he is saying, "Come in and do what you do." So we do. Once we've all had our first round of food and wine, I bring out the big reveal. I go to the hall closet and pull out five brightly wrapped packages. Now my mother and sister are   professional gift wrappers; they even took a course to learn how to do it up right. Since they love all things holiday, especially Christmas they decided a few years back to take a gift wrapping class at one of the department stores. They even wrap their own gifts every Christmas. I just tape up the box really good, ask them to wrap it for me and then put the gift tag on when they are done. This time I had asked Mom to wrap up the shoes I had bought everybody before I left Seattle. I look at Serena and say, "I know this looks like an Ella wrap job, but these are actually from me. Since I'm a poor retired basketball player now, this will be the last of them."

I have never seen five women jump up and down with such excitement over shoes. Each of these women could buy and sell me at a discount, but they are elated. I decide that we need to have an impromptu shoe fashion show, so I put on Lisa Lisa's "Let the Beat Hit Em," and we strut down the runway like we're Beverly Johnson or Tyra.

We all sleep in the next morning and have a delicious brunch prepared by my mother and Aunt D. Aunt D calls this "big breakfast." You know, the breakfast that includes bacon, potatoes with onions, grits, homemade biscuits with sausage gravy, white rice with butter and sugar, and scrambled eggs. The kind of breakfast that makes you want to go back to bed. After we eat, the younger girls head to Greenhill's Mall to do a little shopping, and we decide to head out to BB King's tonight to celebrate Max's 29th birthday, which has just passed.

We hang out at the mall a while and then head to the spa to get a "mani-pedi." Then we stop by Keeva's house to rest for a while before heading out to BB King's before we head out. Max pulls out the libations. I'm always amazed that she had the guts to sneak into the states with not one but five bottles of liquor.

"How does an attorney have the nerve to sneak all this booze into the United States?"

She looks at me with a grin and says, "Don't you know that attorneys make the best criminals? I would have told security that I was bringing these to you for medicinal purposes."

"So what did you bring to heal us with tonight, Dr. Hilton?"

"Let's see, I have two bottles of Kahlua, some Crucian white and dark rum, Vodka, and a little homemade Blackberry wine for boogie ass Serena."

"Well, since you got the Kahlua I got the cream, let's get it on." The Kahlua is a throwback to our college days, when we would sit around and drink in our dorm rooms. We would spring for a bottle and get a few pints of milk from the cafeteria. We actually thought we were having a sophisticated drink. Now we drink it just for old time's sake.

At the mall we all purchased outfits to match our new shoes. Maxine bought a beautiful white V-neck blouse with maximum cleavage and a pair of white riding pants to go with the four-inch silver boots I bought her. She is the only person I know who dares to wear white in the winter. Not winter white or cream, but copy paper white.

Serena, who is Ms. Manners commented, "Only you would dare to wear all white in the winter time and in a club where idiots could spill a drink on you at any moment."

"I always thought the don't wear white before Easter or after Labor Day was stupid and I dare a bitch to spill something on me," said Max.

The biggest risk-taker of the group, Keeva has picked out a chocolate dress that's about five inches above her knees to go with a pair of brown suede booties with five-inch heels.

Serena, the only one of us who is married, is wearing a pair of dark skinny jeans with black boots that come up over her knees, and a suede turtleneck. Only Serena can make such a casual outfit look so sharp.

And I, feeling once again like the underachiever among these fashion plates, wear a black sweater dress that is fitted at the top, cinched at the waist, and flared around my hips. I pair it with black stilettos and tights. Keeva has set my hair and it is hanging past my shoulders in beautiful curls. Serena makes up my eyes with dramatic gray shadow and thick mascara, topping off the look with dark red lipstick. I must admit, we are looking sharper than a two dollar pistol, as my dad used to say. After a few drinks we are feeling easy like Sunday morning. Keeva, anticipating that we would be three sheets to the wind, has ordered a limo to take us to BB King's. The driver is patiently waiting on us in front of Keeva's house. We have a running joke that when we go out we will use make believe names like Sasha Fierce.

"Who are you going to be tonight, Max?" I ask her with a grin.

"Tonight I am going to be Angel, since I am dressed in white."

"What about you, Serena?"

"I am going to be my damn self. The only reason I am going is to be your chaperone. How about you Keeva?"

"I am going to be Trina because, after all, I am—"

"We know, the baddest bitch!" we all yell.

"What about you little sis? Who are you tonight?"

"I am going to be—"

"She is going to be Nene," says Keeva. I mean Trina.

"How did you come up with that one?" I ask her.

"'Cause you, heifer now hovering at 6'2" with those Louboutins on look like that amazon Nene Leakes from the Atlanta housewives. Now, let's be out!"

Chris Map, one of my old teammates and closest friends, is in town to hang out for the weekend. Somewhere along the way he picked up the nickname World. When I asked him about, it he said that one of his college professors called him World instead of Map, and the name stuck. World recently went through a nasty divorce and wants to get away for a few days.

World is one of those men who draw women like magnets. Now, I am no judge of men, but apparently he is pleasing to the eye. Although he has no problem getting women, after the messy divorce he is taking a much needed sabbatical from women. My boy Shelley is also joining us. His wife Tiffany, who also happens to be my realtor, told him that

World and I are the only two men Shelley can hang out with that she trusts to bring her baby back home in one piece. World has reserved a two-bedroom suite at the Hutton Hotel downtown, so he and I are hanging out there for the weekend.

World wants to hang out at BB King's on Saturday night, so Shelley picks us up at the hotel and we head to the club. We decide to go early so we can grab dinner before the band comes on stage. We have reserved one of the small dining rooms so we can have some privacy and talk without having to yell. The three of us have a lot to catch up on and we don't want to deal with people asking for autographs and photos.

We arrive at the club around 8:00 PM and order some food. After lingering over a few beers, we decide to go out and mingle with the crowd, as it sounds like the crowd is jumping and the music is bumping. Even though I'm not much of a dancer, my idea of a good time is great music, great friends, and a good drink.

The chauffer has decided to take the scenic route around Nashville so we can see how beautiful the city is at night, so my girls and I arrive at BB's at about 10:30. Most of our buzz has worn off by now. As we climb out of the limo, I laugh at what people must think when they see us. We look like something out of an episode of *Girlfriends*, four uniquely beautiful women getting out of a stretch Mercedes. They will never know who we are, but we are surely important women in our own minds. As we scoot past the guard into the club, I hear the music pumping. There's a band on stage playing some great jazz. We settle in at our reserved table and order some appetizers and a bottle of wine.

It's damn near impossible to have a conversation over the music, so we settle in to listen, and just take in the atmosphere. The later it gets, the looser the crowd is getting–heavy liquor consumption has clearly lowered inhibitions. We meet some new people and dance a few jigs. I tell the guys my name is Nene, which is hilarious because several of them say they swear I look like that girl named Jackie Donovan who played for the WNBA.

We all get sassy when we assume our alter egos. Keeva plays a dingbat, while Max becomes a sexy vamp who flaunts her tatas with a "look but don't touch" expression. Serena...well, she is just Serena. Several admirers stop at our table to offer us drinks or ask for a dance. One guy, clearly hypnotized by her breasts, asks Max if she will marry him. When the band starts playing some R&B hits, things get really interesting.

My boys and I leave the dining room about 11:30 and walk around the club to take in the scene, when I spot a site that takes my breath away. Out on the dance floor I see a woman in a black sweater dress that outlines every curve of her body. I continue down her legs and see she's wearing heels that must be at least four inches. As my eyes travel back upward, I slow down at her flat stomach and considerable cleavage, and then I finally come to her face. She looks like a super model, with deep red lipstick and hair that frames her face with giant curls. Her gracefulness is stunning—I can imagine she was just as graceful on the basketball court. I continue watching her dance, and notice that the dude she's dancing with is getting a little too close. She smoothly evades him, then whispers something in his ear with a wicked smile on her face. He steps back immediately—a good thing, as I could feel myself about to head in their direction. I notice that Shelley and World are now beside me, also watching Jackie.

Shelley says, "That looks like Jackie Donovan out there Dair. Is she the one that has you standing looking like you are about to sprang on that dude?"

"Yeah D, what's up? You got something you want to tell Shelley and me?"

"I'll fill you in later. World, do me a favor. Get them to move our table downstairs."

About that time, Jackie walks off the floor to a table where three other women are sitting, each of them beautiful in their own right. Judging by the number of drinks on the table, the men are coming to them like moths to a flame. As Jackie sits down, I hear World give a low whistle.

"Dair, please tell me you know those women and that they are single. I haven't seen dime pieces like that in a long time."

"I only know one of them, and I have a feeling I don't know her well enough. World, get us a table where we can see them but they can't see us. I want to watch the show before I make my appearance."

World gets us a table and I watch Jackie for about an hour. She's friendly to men, but not overly so. She dances a few times, but mostly just sits talking with her girls. I watch in awe as men approach their table, most leaving a little shorter than when they came. By now our table is also getting some attention, as the groupies are out in full force. There was a time when all three of us would have been very interested, but not anymore. We keep watching Jackie's table. One of the guys they just rejected heads my way, so I decide to stop him to find out why.

"Hey man, you got a minute?"

He looks up at me and says, "Dair Singleton! You are one of my favorite Trailblazers. Of course I have a minute what's up bru?"

"Well, I noticed that you just approached the babe in the black dress at the table where those four beautiful women are sitting. What's up?"

"Man, you must be talking about that girl NeNe. I thought I would offer her a drink and see if she would give me the digits but she turned me down cold. She is beautiful but she is lethal. She might give up the digits for you since you got paper. I guess her and her girls are having a *Waiting to Exhale* moment. I started to say, Bitch breathe," he says with a drunken chuckle.

I start seeing red when I hear the word bitch. I lean over and get as close to him as I can, "What's your name, man, I didn't catch it?"

"My name is Frank my man."

"Frank, let me give you some advice."

"What's that Dair," he says, putting his hand on my shoulder and leaning in close.

"First, my name is Adaris. Only my friends call me Dair. Second, if I ever hear you call NeNe a bitch or see you near her again I will whip your ass. Don't ever assume that buying a woman a watered down well drink is going to get you her number. Those women over there deserve top shelf. Now get your hand off me and get the hell out of here. Are we clear, Frank?"

"Uh yes, Dair, I mean Adaris. I got you loud and clear. Can I get your autograph before I leave? You know what, don't worry about it. Peace!" he calls over his shoulder as he hastily leaves the club.

World says with a chuckle, "Damn Dair, you just scared the shit out of that man. That girl must have you wide open. What's up man?"

"I'm not sure, but in a few minutes we need to head that way. I want her to know I'm here."

"I was hoping you would say that man. I want to meet that chocolate sister with all the white on. She is banging!"

I wave the waitress over and say, "Nikki, can you ask Chef Elester if he can do me a huge favor? Tell him I will give him two tickets in the box at our first home game."

"I'm sure he will help you with anything you need, Adaris. What's up?

"Ask him to prepare four vanilla cupcakes with chocolate icing. I want you to deliver them to those beautiful women sitting at that table," I say, pointing to Jackie's table. "But come back first and pick up a note for the girl in the black dress." I slip her a C note and she heads toward the kitchen.

I scrawl a quick note to Jackie: *Thinking about our time in the park the other day. I missed you so much that I conjured you up in my mind. I hope you are having fun with your girls this weekend. Have a bite of something sweet. Yours, Dair.*

It takes about 30 minutes for the cupcakes to be delivered. With my note...

My girls and I are having a ball! The music is awesome and the drinks keep coming. If the guys would just stop coming it would be perfect. Don't get me wrong, the attention is flattering, but they all have the same tired old lines.

I've had this feeling all evening that someone is watching me. Not like a rapist lurking in the trees but like a warm caress. Suddenly a waitress stops at our table to deliver four beautiful cupcakes with chocolate icing. Serena says, "You must have the wrong table. It's not anyone's birthday. "

"My birthday was just a few days ago!" Max yells.

The waitress just smiles at Serena, puts the cupcakes on the table, and hands me a note. I read it with shaking hands, and then I look up at my girls with a huge grin. "Let's have something sweet, ladies." As soon as I pick up my fork, I feel a tickle in my ear and a warm body against my back.

"Hello NeNe."

I whip around, and there is Adaris. He's wearing brown silk pants that cling to his body and a cream-color sweater that accents his magnificent chest. He's wearing chocolate brown ECCOs. This girl knows her shoes.

"You haven't tasted your cupcake baby; let me feed you a bite." He takes my fork, scoops up a bite of cupcake, and tenderly feeds it to me. Then he has the nerve to lick the chocolate off my fork and say, "Delicious."

Keeva mumbles "Damnnnn." I'm not sure if she's reacting to Dair's moves, or because she's looking at his friend, who I believe is Chris Map, a New York Giant. Chris is staring at Maxine so hard it seems he'll burn a hole right through her. Serena, with her Ms. Manners butt, formerly introduces herself and everyone at the table—using our make believe names, of course. I thank Adaris for the cupcakes and ask, "Have you been here for a while?"

"You are welcome and yes, we met Shelley here a few hours ago. Shelley went home to his wife, but we decided to hang out and listen to some music. You, pretty lady, are quite the dancer."

The music is really loud, so Adaris is leaning over me so we can hear each other. All of a sudden he spins me around to face him, plants his big body between my legs, put his arms on the table behind me, and says, "Every time I see you, you look totally different. You are a chameleon."

I don't know how he does it, but he keeps me so off kilter that I don't know what to do with myself. "Uh, what did you say?" I ask.

"I was saying that you are a great dancer."

"Thanks, I love to dance. What about you?"

"I am not much of a dancer. I can move around on the floor but that's about it. Then he spins me back around and starts talking to the group.

I notice that Chris has worked his way around the table and is talking with Max. He is smiling like a Cheshire cat, but she is frowning like she caught a whiff of chitterlings. I'm about to lean over and ask if she is ok, when one of my favorite songs starts playing. Some man walks up and asks me to dance, but before I can answer, Adaris grabs my hand and storms onto the dance floor. He molds me to his body and breathes in my ear, "I can't stand watching you dancing with anyone else." Even though we're almost at eye level, thanks to my heels, I feel like a china doll in his arms. As one dance merges into the next, Adaris pulls me closer, moves his hand to the curve of my butt, and kisses me softly on my ear. At the end of the song, he bends down, puts his hand in my curls, stares into my eyes, and with those juicy lips gives me the softest sweetest kiss I ever had…a gentle caress that makes me want to beg him for more. Then he lifts his head and says, "Sweetness, I hope you have a nice morning with your girls." I swear I almost swallowed the spearmint gum I sneaked into my mouth. Adaris escorts me back to the table, lifts me back into my seat, then says to Chris, "Let's be out man. It was nice meeting each of you ladies. Do I need to make arrangements to get you home?"

Keeva, who has been watching the scene unfold between Chris and Max and me and Adaris leans over and says, "I have a feeling some of us will be floating home on cloud nine. The rest of us have a limo waiting outside."

Adaris and Chris smile, nod their heads, and walk out of the club, looking like two big black statues as the crowd opens up to let them pass. For a moment we all are speechless, and then Serena says, "Let's go Nettie and Celie. You got some splainin' to do."

We pile into the limo, and Keeva yells, "What the hell just happened in there? We were sitting enjoying drinks and suddenly all hell breaks loose. Let's start with you Max. Why do you have that mean look on your face?"

"You can use your inside voice now," Max says, rubbing her ear. "I was blindsided by this 6 foot 1 mountain with the most beautiful caramel skin and a killer smile who just walked up to me and said hello. He took me by surprise!"

"OK, what about that surprised you?" asks Serena.

"He did not look at my chest. Most men I meet only look at my chest. He didn't look south one time and he seemed to be genuinely interested in me."

"Why wouldn't he be interested, Max, you are beautiful. What person with your Hershey brown complexion also has bewitching green eyes?"

"My mom, duh... but he was just too fine and too nice. Who is he anyway? He said his name was Chris and he is a friend of Adaris, but who is he?"

"Well Sherlock," I say, "he happens to be Chris Map, bka World of the New York Giants. He has been in the league ten years as a running back. Started with the Cowboys, which must be how he knows Adaris. He just went through a nasty divorce and let's see...no kids. He—"

"That's enough Jackie, it doesn't matter. He asked if he could call me sometime, but I told him no, that I'm only in the States a few more days. Besides, he has no idea who I really am."

Serena leans back in her seat and says, "Let me get this straight. You meet a single, fine as hell good-looking man who doesn't disrespect you by looking at your breasts. The entire time you talk to him you are frowning. Then he asks for your phone number, even though your evil ass has frowned the entire time, and you tell him no?"

"That sounds about right, except he told me I had the most beautiful eyes he has ever seen," Max says with a sly smile.

Serena erupts. "Don't interrupt me counselor. Don't you complain to me all the time about the black women to black men ratio on the island being something like 20 to 1? Didn't you say you haven't been on a decent date in two years? Don't you want to settle down one day and have children?"

"Yes to all the above, Serena. But what is your point?"

"You remember the story about the man being stuck out at sea and asking God to save him? The guy has three chances to be saved, but he is so busy watching for God that he doesn't notice God is sending people to help him. Well, my dear friend, you don't get too many chances with men like Chris Map, and I'm afraid you are about to miss your boat. You can rectify your wrong by letting Ms. Cupcake here call Adaris to get a number for Mr. Map. Speaking of Cupcake, what was that all about?" Serena asks me.

"It all started on Thursday, when Adaris and I went for a bike ride. Keeva helped me set up the picnic lunch at Hadley Park. I made cupcakes for dessert. We had a wonderful time, and he asked if he could see me again. I keep getting cold feet, so I told him you guys were coming into town. I'm really afraid of the baggage that goes with dating a professional athlete who also has a teenage son. Oh, and said son will be playing on my basketball team this year. I have no idea what will happen when I tell him that I will be coaching his son."

"Stay on track, Jackie. What happened tonight?" That's my Max.

"We still aren't done cracking your case, Counselor, but I will finish my story. Apparently Adaris and his buddies had dinner in one of the private dining rooms, and then he spotted us. I don't know where he got the cupcakes 'cuz they weren't on the menu, but he sent them over with the sweetest note."

"What did the note say?" the three women ask in unison.

"He said seeing me reminded him of our time at the park, nosey."

"Then he comes over, feeds you like you're at your wedding reception, drags you out to dance to the two most romantic songs ever sung, kisses you sweetly on the mouth, then puts your big ass back up in your chair and leaves. Does that sound about right?" asks Keeva.

"Dang, Keeva, are you Inspector Clouseau? Yes, you got it right. That was our second kiss."

"Ok ladies, listen up, 'cause I am about to take you to school," says big sister Serena. "Since I am the only married broad in this group and the oldest, let me drop a little knowledge on you all. You need to learn how to let a man court you—it doesn't mean you plan to walk down the aisle! Max, why in the world would you not want to see Chris again? Oh wait, let me tell you. You live two different lifestyles, you in the Virgin Islands and he in New York. He is recently divorced and you are unhappily single. He is a professional athlete and you are a teacher. He is fine and you are one of the few women on the Islands who don't have a man. Does that sound about like what you are thinking?"

"That sounds about right except I am a professor," says Max, rolling her eyes at Serena.

"Let me put your worries to rest, boo. Chris is a multi-millionaire. What makes you think he can't fly anywhere he wants when he damn well pleases? A long-distance romance is irrelevant when you have money. And you, my darling, aren't doing too badly with a law degree and a doctorate in English. And you are beautiful, more beautiful than hundreds of women on that island. You are writing the man off before you have conversation number two. What's wrong with you girl?"

Then she swings around and starts on me. "And you Ms. NeNe. When have you ever seen such a man, one who gives you cupcakes and abides with bike riding and picnics when he is used to panties dropping? He is a man who is willing to wait to get what he wants. Don't you two get it?" she says in exasperation.

"No!" We cry in unison.

"Max, you expect to lose something you don't even have yet. Jack, you are afraid to meet someone like daddy. Handsome, strong willed, unique, smart...someone who won't let you run over him. These men want you two. Now the question is, what are you going to do about it?"

"I don't know Oprah, but I am sure you and Gale over there will come up with something. We will let you sleep on it and get back to us in a few hours," I say around a huge yawn.

World and I don't say a word during the cab ride back to the hotel. Or in the elevator. As soon as we enter his suite, he walks to the bar and pours us each a shot of scotch. Then he slumps down on the couch and asks me, "What the hell just happened, man?"

"I can't answer for you, but I can tell you that I met Jackie over a month ago at her father's funeral. We've been out twice, but I can't really qualify it as a date. I have given the girl my black Am Ex number, gone clothes shopping for her, bought two bicycles, and about killed myself by almost dropping a 50 pound weight on my foot. And we hadn't even kissed yet at that point. And those have been the best two dates of my life. I have had a month—what happened to you in those 60 minutes?"

"I don't know. One minute we're watching your girl, the next minute I'm looking into the green eyes of a woman named Angel who is dressed all in white, and I feel like I've been hit with a 2x4. I told her she was beautiful and asked for her number, but she frowned and told me no. Now I know I'm out of practice, but she was looking at me like I'm small or something. What am I missing?"

I bust out laughing and say, "I doubt very seriously her real name is Angel man. Jackie was going by the name NeNe—my guess is they all were using made up names for some reason."

He shoots up off the couch and shouts, "You mean to tell me the first woman who has interested me since Mia gave me the wrong damn name!"

"Pump your brakes, World. I think I have a solution."

"I'm idling man, what's up!"

"Just for you, I will call Jackie in the morning to see if the four of us can get together. That way I can kill two birds—get the chance to talk to her and also find out who her friend is. Sound ok?"

"How many hours until you make that call, man?" World asks me with a gleam in his eye.

"It's 2 in the morning. Let's give them at least 8 hours before we pounce."

"Looks like I will be changing my flight back to New York. See you in seven hours and 59 minutes."

Call a Spade a Spade

We don't get back to Keeva's house until about 2:00 AM, after making a pit stop at Krystal's to grab a sackful of the little burgers I missed while living in Seattle. Keeva and Serena have early plans, but Max and I decide to sleep in and then go out for a late breakfast. The excitement of the night plus a few too many drinks put me in a pretty deep sleep. I vaguely hear a chirp from my cell phone, so I drag myself out of bed, fish around in my purse, and pull out my phone. I've received a text from Adaris that says, *"Mrng NeNe. Chris and I wntd 2 c if we cld meet u n Angl for brkfst to get betr acqantd u pck the time n the plce."*

I sit there for a minute grinning. Then I walk over to Max's bedroom and knock. She hollers "What!" Max is not a morning person.

"It's me, Jack. Can I come in?"

"Only if you have coffee or a scrambled egg," Max mumbles behind a huge yawn.

"I have something better than that, girl," I say as I jump on her bed.

"I said you can only come in if you have food" she says laughing.

I pull out my phone and say," I just got an invitation from Adaris and Chris to join them for breakfast. He told me to pick the time and place. Are you up for starting over today, Max?"

I see about five emotions cross Max's face...excitement, worry, fear, anxiety, and then, finally, a small smile.

"If you promise not to leave me alone with him during breakfast so he won't steal my panties, I will go."

"I have an even better idea. Keeva has a massive kitchen that she hardly uses. Why don't I ask her if it's ok for us to have guests? If she is cool, we can invite them over here for brunch."

"You know Keeva won't care and that's fine with me, as long as you don't make me be your damn sous chef. These nails aren't made for cooking," she says, holding up her hands.

"How about I text him back and tell them to come at 1:00 pm ? That will give us about four hours to pick up groceries and throw something together."

"Sounds good. That'll give me three hours to get some beauty sleep and an hour to get dressed," she says, ducking to evade the pillow I throw at her.

I stop in Keeva's room to make sure she's ok with our plan. She says its fine, as long as I put some biscuits and casserole in her freezer.

As I walk down the hall I send Adaris a text: *c ya at 1 for brunch at 2395 Beacon Court. Brng a bttle of champagne pls.*

I figure if he gets the champagne that will save me one stop, so I can focus on the groceries and cooking. As I head to the shower I prepare a menu in my mind that includes a : breakfast casserole, fried chicken, bacon, home fries with onions, scrambled eggs, waffles, fresh fruit, mimosas and coffee. I figure that will give us plenty to eat and enough for leftovers if anyone wants to take something home.

I shower, throw on jeans and a sweatshirt, and head to the store. When I get back to the house, Max is sitting on the couch, typing on her computer. "What are you doing?" I ask.

"I am Googling Chris Map to see if I can find out anything interesting about him. When I finish, do you want me to Google Adaris?"

"No girl, I want to learn about him organically without the blogs and gossipers tainting my opinion. I don't care how many friends he has on Facebook or if he is Linked In. I like the good old fashioned way of going on dates, walking in the park, and holding hands. All of that social networking moves things along too fast—hell, I don't even like to Google myself!"

"Well, I personally don't have time for all that old fashioned crap. Since we live half way around the world from each other, I need to find out as much as I can, and quick. With a nasty divorce, I'm sure Chris has lots of baggage," Max says with a sigh.

"Well, don't put him on trial before he is charged with a crime, Attorney Hilton. I'm going to start cooking. If you get bored with your research, come in and help me."

I walk into the kitchen with several bags of groceries and get to work. I apparently lose track of the time, because I'm just turning around from grabbing eggs out of the fridge when I bump into Adaris. I almost spill the eggs all over him, but he grabs the bowl and puts it on the counter. Then he reaches for my hands.

"Good afternoon, sweetness. I didn't mean to scare you, but I said your name several times when I walked into the kitchen."

I stand there for a few minutes and just take him all in. How does someone so big walk so quietly? Adaris is wearing jogging pants, a Trailblazer sweatshirt, and white tennis shoes. A girl loves a guy wearing a fresh pair of kicks. He's wearing his glasses and smells like he just stepped out of the shower, which is way better than even the best colognes.

He gives me that slow smile and says, "What can I do to help? I had no idea that you were doing all the cooking by yourself. We would have been happy to take you out for brunch."

"I'm almost finished. You can take the food that is done out to Max." I hand him jelly, butter, syrup, ketchup, and hot sauce."

"Her name is Max, huh? I told Chris that I doubted Angel is your girl's real name."

"I'll tell you about that later. Let me get the eggs and waffles done so we can eat while everything is hot." I finish scrambling the eggs, make a batch of waffles, and help Adaris carry it all out to the dining room.

I look at the display of food on the table and grin. Chef Jackie has done it again, I must admit. Then I notice that it's really quiet and that Max and Chris are standing close to each other with strange looks on their faces. I look at Adaris who is behind me with the bowl of eggs, and say, "Would you like to bless the food before we eat?" because I figure we needed it at this point.

We hold hands, bless the food, and the men start fixing their plates. I had prepared so much food that the guys fix two plates each. I've forgotten to prepare the Mimosas, so I ask Adaris to come help me. As soon as we're in the kitchen, I ask him in a whisper, "What the heck is going on with those two?"

"I'm not really sure. One minute they're smiling at each other, then Chris asks your girl why she used a fake name at BB's and says only groupies have fake ass names, and then I got the hell out of dodge. It looks like maybe they made up. Now, show me how to fix these Mimosas so we can get back in there before the next smack down," he says, giving me a wet kiss on the cheek.

We finally begin eating and the conversation is flowing. By the time we finish, everyone has loosened up and we're having a good time. Max shares some stories about her students, and the men talked about some of their funnier moments when playing football together. Chris and Max offer to put all the food away so I can rest. Adaris grabs my hand and says, "You are a wonderful cook, Jackie. "

I tell him, "Everyone in my family loves to cook except Keeva. I've been cooking since I was about five, and I actually thought about going to culinary school. It's nice to see people enjoy my food. That's what a foodie loves best, seeing smiles on her diner's faces."

"You can make me smile anytime. If you ever need someone to test your skills on, I am your man," he says, wearing a Cheshire cat grin.

"Well, I will keep that in mind Adaris. Do you think we need to go help them in the kitchen?" I say, trying to change the subject.

"I think World and Max have it covered. Now when do you plan to stop putting me off? When are we really going to spend time together? My training camp starts soon and then football season and I want to spend as much time as I can before then getting to know you better." He says this as he strokes the back of my hand with his thumb.

"Well I..."

Just then Max and World came into the room, arguing again. Something about looking on the Internet and how did anyone know who tells the truth. And then, did you think that most of that crap is true? Since you are a big time attorney you of all people should know about slander and libel. And speaking of truth, who in the hell gives out a fake name at your age? Then I heard a lot of words I couldn't understand with some cussing peppered in. Max has started speaking Crucian and it is not pretty.

Adaris stands up and says, "Alright Tyson and Holyfield, you can go to your corners now."

This helps break the tension for all of us. Then Adaris leans over to me and says, "Our conversation is far from over, sweetness. You can use this little time out to get your thoughts together." Then he turns and asks, "How about we play a few games of spades? We're all feeling a little heated, so this might be a good way to let off some steam. What do you guys say?"

Max and I look at each other and grin. These two fools have no idea that we used to take people's money playing spades in college. When we were broke we'd walk through the dorms to hustle up a few games of spades, then beat the hell out of people.

Max says, "I'm not sure. I haven't played Spades in a long time. But I'm up for a challenge." She looks at Chris and says, "How about we put a little wager on the table?"

Chris narrows his eyes, crosses his arms, and replies, "We play to 500, no one can go less than board, if you renege you lose 100 points, and if you run a Boston you get 100 extra points. Jokers are wild. Is that enough of a challenge for you, Counselor?"

"Hell no," Max says. Now she crosses her arms and walks closer to Chris. "The best two out of three games win. We set the wager now and the loser has to pay up within 24 hours. Come into the kitchen, Jackie. We need to decide what we are going to make these chumps do after we beat the brakes off of them."

"While you're in the kitchen, maybe you can grab another one of those girly Mimosas so you can cool off. And grab me a beer," Chris yells after Max.

"You must think I am one of your brainless groupies. Get your own damn beer!"

"Well, I am just calling a spade a spade," World says, with a burst of laughter.

About five minutes later, the guys barge into the kitchen. We have the table ready for our game.

"Can we come in now?" Adaris asks sheepishly.

"Sure," I say. "We have come up with our wager."

"What is it ladies? Something tells me this is going to be a doozy," says Adaris.

"Nothing like that. We've decided that since we won't be done until about dinnertime, the two of you can cook us dinner, including dessert. You can't hire someone to cook it, you can't order it from a restaurant, and you can't grill it. And, the dinner must be served with a great bottle of wine, and the dining room table must be set to perfection. We don't want to lift a finger, which means you also will clean up the mess you make in the kitchen," says Max.

"That's easy, isn't it Dair? Heck, I can maneuver around the kitchen almost as well as I can around the football field." World adds with a smile, "And my boy Adaris is a great sommelier. You want to add anything to that?"

I pipe in. "Yes. We want you to serve dinner wearing suits. And we don't mean your birthday suits."

"Thanks for the clarification smarty pants," smiles Adaris. "Now, are you ready to hear how you'll be paying up, once we beat your beautiful well-endowed rump shakers?"

"Bring it," says Max, glaring over at Chris. "You aren't staring at my rump shaker, are you?"

"Damn right. I am staring at your rump shaker, your mammary glands, your eyes, and your soup cooler! Hell, if I could see your feet I would be in hog heaven," he says with a huge grin.

"Stay on task man. There is plenty of time to channel your foot fetish. If we win, you two have to go out to the golf course with us tomorrow and be our caddies. You don't have to carry our bags, but you do have to wipe our brows, spot our balls, and make sure we have plenty to drink, and when we're done we want you to cook us lunch."

"And we want you to do it barefoot," World says with a chuckle.

"You little freak!" Max yells. "It could be 45 degrees tomorrow. Why can't we play a round with you? Are you afraid we might beat you? And you should be able to watch your own damn balls! And you must be some pervert asking us to cook you dinner barefoot. You better be glad I live in the Islands and my feet are always on point. Come on Jackie; let's beat these chumps so we can get ready for our dinner later on."

"You haven't seen anything yet, Angel. As for golfing in the cold weather, don't worry—if your feet get cold I'll rub them for you."

"My name is Max you assho-"

"Round two is over!" I holler. "Put your bet where your mouth is. Let's play!"

Three hours later the game is tied one to one. All I can say is that Max is a crafty mother. As we're about to lose the last hand, she suddenly takes off her shoes and socks. Her feet are so darn pretty that World almost loses his mind. He loses his focus, reneges on the last hand, and we beat them by two books. We had so much fun that we decide we'll let the guys cook us dinner, but we'll also go with them to the golf course when it warms up.

"Well gentlemen. That was the best ass whipping I have given in a long time. Let's see, it's about 5:00 now. How about Jackie and I take a load off while you two head to the store and shop for our dinner?" Max looks at the men with a smug smile.

"We will be back here around 6:30 to get cooking, and we'll have dinner on the table by 8:00. See you both later," Adaris says, as he and Chris walk out to their car.

As soon as they walk out the door, I say to Max, "Counselor, you should be ashamed of yourself. We could have beat them in round two if you didn't let Chris win those two books. What in the heck were you thinking?"

"Girl, you've got to let a man think he's doing something right. It would have been awful to sweep them so I let a few books slide to make things more interesting. Now what are we wearing tonight?"

"Yo man, what happened in there? Why did you throw that last hand?" I ask Chris as we pull out into traffic.

"I aint gonna lie man, Max's feet got me for a minute, and then I decided it would be fun to cook for them tonight. I want to show that girl that I have other skills than playing football. I know you can't cook worth a damn, so why don't we divide and conquer. You can drop me at my rental car and I'll find a store around here. You take care of the wine and dessert. We can meet back at Keeva's."

"I'll need to know what's on the menu so I can pick a suitable wine."

"Ahhh, grilled salmon, rice pilaf, fresh asparagus, and a spinach salad."

"I'll get a few bottles of white and some Moscato. I also need to check in with AJ to make sure he is good at Scoop's house, and then I'll run over to Mom's and pick up some of her famous fruit tea and a chess pie."

"I have another idea. Knowing Max, she'll convince Jackie that they should stay in those jeans they're wearing just to mess with us. Let's mix things up a bit."

"What you thinking, homey?" World asks me, narrowing his eyes just a tad.

"Hold tight. Let me make a call."

"Hello, this is Griffin."

"Griff, this is Dair Singleton, you got a minute?"

"Sure Dair, what's up?"

"Aren't you good friends with Chloe Mains, that stylist?"

"Yeah, she is my home girl—we just so happen to be hanging out right now. You want to talk with her?"

"Bet!"

"Hold on a minute," she says, and then she puts Chloe on the phone.

"This is Chloe, how may I help you?"

"Chloe, my name is Adaris Singleton. I am sorry to ask you this at the 11th hour, but I need you to style two ladies for me this evening."

"That shouldn't be a problem. Tell me what you have in mind and give me the sizes."

"I would like you to take some outfits in a size 8 and 10 over to 2395 Beacon Court within the next two hours. I'd like you to take size 9 shoes and—hold on a minute. Hey foot freak, what size is Max?"

"My guess is an 8, smart ass," Chris says, grinning.

I give her further details about the ladies—their height, build, and complexion—and ask her to send an invoice to my assistant. When I hang up the phone, I give World a pound and we silently contemplate the evening ahead.

We have a few hours before the guys come back, so we decide to sit and chat over a glass of wine. Just as I'm getting to the heart of why Max was tripping, the doorbell rings. I open the door to this chick, an odd little thing wearing a weird combination of clothes that somehow looks great.

"Hi, I'm Chloe Mains. Mr. Singleton and Mr. Map asked me to come over here to style you and your friend for the evening." She whips out a business card, which I take from her warily.

Max yells from the couch, "Who is it Jackie?"

"It's Chloe, our stylist," I shout back.

"Our what? Get the f—"

"Come on in Chloe," I say, and close the door behind her.

An hour later Chloe heads out the door with a half-empty clothes rack. Somehow she picked out styles and colors that suited us to perfection. Instead of the jeans I had on I'm now wearing a halter-style pea green dress that stops about two inches above the knee, paired with pointed nude stilettos. Max chose a yellow V-neck sweater and a black pleated skirt, which she paired with strappy black sandals that have a five- inch heel. For

110

once in her life, Max is speechless. While Chloe picked out clothes for her to try on, Max stood there like a toy soldier. I decide we should wait to change after the guys arrive so we can do the big reveal.

They come back around 6:30 carrying several grocery bags and a few garment bags—it appears they've decided to change later too. I show them to one of Keeva's guest rooms, then go back to check on Max.

"Max, what the heck is wrong with you? You haven't said a word for over an hour. Talk to me, chica."

"Jack, for the first time in my life I am speechless. I don't know what to say. No complaints and no critiques. You know how after a while you get used to the status quo. You have the occasional date with a loser who has a jacked up car, won't open your door, doesn't ask you anything about yourself, has no conversation and then asks you to go Dutch at the end of the meal. But you are so damn happy to be out that you convince yourself that this date was good enough."

"Yeah girl, I know exactly what you mean, it's called Quinton Styles."

"Exactly! The last two days have shown me that I shouldn't settle for 'good enough.' This man hasn't known me 24 hours and he already has made me smile more than I have in a year, had a conversation that has kept me interested, and did not let me run over him rough shod. He didn't stare at my boobs but looked at my feet like they were gods, and then he makes me feel like a queen by dressing me for the evening. He even let me beat him in spades, even though I know from my Google search that he's highly competitive and was a math major."

"And...what is wrong with that?"

"What's wrong is that when I fly back home on Tuesday I will know that good enough isn't good enough anymore. This man makes me feel he wants to spend time with me! And I get the sense that he isn't settling for good enough either," she says, wiping tears from her eyes. "I realize this might be it after tonight…"

I take Max's face in my hands and look into her eyes. "Max, a few days ago I felt the same way but I couldn't verbalize it. In fact, these last two days seem like a cliché. Two best male friends meet two best female friends in a club. They hang out, fall in love, and that's where the story begins. But we don't know what's next, if there will be a happy ever after. There are so many things that can get in the way. Tomorrow morning things are going to get complicated, as four people make decisions about what happens next. But for the next three or four hours, let's just take it for what it is. Two handsome as hell black men who are catering to two beautiful babes, who are us! Now, stop obsessing and go wash the stink off, then put on that new outfit Chris bought you, lotion up those pretty suckable feet and have a great time." I give her a big hug, and as she sashays off to the bathroom, I sit down on her bed and give myself a pep talk.

At 8:00 PM on the dot, Adaris and Chris knock on Max's door and out we walk. Apparently we've made a good choice of outfits, because Adaris gives me a huge grin and Chris gives Max a once over so hot it almost melts her. He almost has a heart attack when he looks at her feet. The men aren't looking so bad either. Adaris is wearing a black Armani suit with a pale green tie, while Chris sports a charcoal gray Gucci suit with a yellow and black tie. I feel like we're going to the prom!

Dinner is delicious. The salmon is grilled to perfection and topped with Cajun seasoning and remoulade. The rice pilaf and asparagus are fork tender. For dessert Adaris pulls out a homemade chess pie that puts mine to shame. After grilling him about how he made it, he finally admits the pie is from his mother. After the guys clean up the kitchen, we sit and talk for hours about politics, race relations, steroids, professional athletes, and even family. At about 2:00 AM, Chris looks at his watch and says, "Its the bewitching hour, and time for us to get a move on so these beautiful ladies can get some rest. Max, may I see you in the kitchen for a moment?"

About 15 minutes later Chris comes strutting out of the kitchen and tells Adaris he will wait for him in the car. I'm thankful he came out because our conversation was getting pretty heated. After the guys leave, Max and I are too exhausted to talk, so we just go to bed. The next morning I knock on Max's door.

"Max, you up?"

"Yeah, I am, come on in."

"What happened last night Max? When the guys left I sensed you didn't want to talk."

"Things were going well until Chris and I stepped into the kitchen."

"What happened when you went into the kitchen?"

Max looks at me with a dreamy expression and says, "As soon as we got in the kitchen, Chris picked me up, put me on the island, settled between my big juicy thighs, and kissed me."

"OMG, Max. How was it?"

"Girl, that man wrapped me in those big arms and it was, as you say, on and blowing."

"Ewww, it's on and popping! Then what happened, Maxine Hilton?"

"He took a step back, looked at me, took a deep breath, and then he kissed me again." Max now has a dazed expression. "I swear I felt like I had been sucker punched."

"So, that's good, right?" I ask her.

"It was more than good, Jack. But I knew we needed to talk so I pushed him back a little bit and told him we can't keep doing this."

"You can't keep doing what, Max?" I ask.

"I was thinking that he couldn't keep kissing me. It made me want too much. Then he asked me what would happen when we go back home."

"What did you tell him Maxine?"

"I told him that we could keep in touch from time to time."

"What do you mean, from time to time? Are you going to be his Facebook friend or follow him on Twitter?" Now I'm getting sarcastic.

"Then he grabbed the base of my head and started massaging my scalp, and all I can really remember is him saying something about not wanting to be pen pals. I was so mesmerized by then, it's all a daze."

"Sooo…?"

"Girl, he started whispering sweet nothings in my ear. He told me that he wanted me, Jackie. Me girl! He said he has a few weeks before training camp and that I need to make time to see him, even if he had to come to the island. Then his voice dropped several octaves and he asked me if I understood."

"Please don't tell me you got offended by him asking if you understood?"

Max laughs and shakes her head. "Well, after the shivers wore off I got just a little offended, but before I could say anything he walked out of the kitchen."

"Now what girl?"

"I don't know…" she trails off in a whine. "Let's talk about you. What happened with you and Adaris?"

"My story is not as juicy as yours. As soon as you and Chris walked into the kitchen, Adaris walked over to where I was sitting, picked me up, and sat down on the couch with me on his lap."

"Jackie, you know they do that crap to throw us off," says Max.

"He's very touchy feely but not in an 'I want to get in your panties' kind of way."

"Does that make you uncomfortable, Jacks?"

"No and yes."

"Then what happened?"

"He kissed me on my eyes, then on my cheek, and then softly on my lips. When he knew he had me, he asked me if we could spend more time together."

"And you said…?" Max is pushing like she has me on trial.

"I told him that he has a lot going on, with his son and football. Then he told me his son is busy, football is a few weeks away, he is building a house, and about three other things. Then he said I was at the top of his 'to do' list."

"He said he wants to do you. That was fresh!" Max says with a laugh.

"He is full of innuendoes, but I'm always too scared to ask him what he means."

"Then what, girl?"

"He pulled me closer, put my head on his shoulder and kissed me again. He said, 'I know you and your girl probably need some time to hang out on Monday. How about you let me pick you up on Tuesday afternoon and you go with me to look at some land I might be building a house on?"

"Are you kidding me? Sounds deep, girl. What man is gonna take a woman to look at property unless he is serious?"

"Max, you know how much I love looking at floor plans. This will be a great diversion to keep me from thinking about the upcoming basketball season."

"Speaking of which, when are you going to tell Adaris, Jackie?"

"When the time is right. I want to get to know him better first. I only have you here for one more day. How about I take you to Off Broadway and Nordstrom to do some shoe shopping so we can stop thinking about Frick and Frack?"

"I just hope this little coaching opportunity doesn't blow up in your face, 'cause you have such a pretty one. Remember that keeping secrets is not a good way to start a relationship. But speaking of shoe shopping, I did bring an extra bag with me, so let's get started."

I knock on Chris's door at the Hutton Hotel and he opens it after a few minutes.

"Hey man, glad to see you're up. Last night was something else, wasn't it? How did things turn out with you and Max?" I ask him.

"Man that was one of the best evenings I have had in...it's so long I can't remember. At least until I asked Max to go into the kitchen with me so we could have a few minutes alone."

"What jumped off in the kitchen, World?"

"I couldn't help myself man. Remember before brunch when Max and I were standing close to each other? I was about to kiss her, then but you two walked in on us. After that I was determined to get a few minutes alone with her, and once we got in the kitchen I picked her up, placed her on the island, put my chest against her 42 Double Ds and kissed her."

"Damn, World, you didn't waste any time!"

"Hell no, I didn't waste any time. I felt like I was running out of time. I'm heading back to New York today!"

"You didn't stop at just one kiss, did you?" I ask World.

"Man, I wanted to suck her damn face off." Chris smiles at the memory.

"Well, so what happened?"

"She pushed me back a little and said in a tiny voice, 'We can't keep doing this, Chris."

"Can't keep doing what?" I ask World.

"I wasn't really sure what she meant, so I attacked the big ass elephant in the room and asked her point blank what was gonna happen after I go home and she goes back to the Virgin Islands."

"So what did she say, man, and hurry the hell up!" Now I'm getting impatient.

"She told me that the last two days had been wonderful and she was glad we met, and maybe we can keep in touch from time to time. Can you believe that shit, Dair?"

"What does 'time to time' mean bro? How did you react to that?"

"I put my hand in her hair, tilted her head back so she could look in my eyes, and asked her what she meant. Did she mean like we'd be pen pals or something?"

"Sooo...," I coax him on.

"I kissed her again so she would just shut up. She talks too damn much! Then I whispered in her ear, 'I am too damn old to be anyone's pen pal. When I find what I want I don't stop until I get it. It's been a long time since I have seen anything I want, and I want you Maxine Hilton, and I don't care if you live in Timbuktu. I have a few weeks before training camp and I want you to make yourself available to spend time with me. If it means I need to fly to St. Croix, then I will. So, I suggest you get used to me being around so we can see where this thing is going. Are we clear?" I said this in my deepest voice."

"Did she get your drift?" I ask World.

"I don't know. I was so nervous I just turned and walked out of that kitchen and told you I would meet you in the car," World says with a laugh.

"Now what man?"

"I fly back to New York today, but my plan is to be in St. Croix before the end of next week. Now, what happened with you and Miss Tall Drink of Water, Dair?"

"I was glad you guys left. I was starting to feel like we were on a high school double date. After you guys went into the kitchen, I picked her up and put her on my lap. We had a conversation earlier we needed to finish."

"Sounds like you needed to take control man," Chris says while pounding his chest.

"Man, I can't keep my hands off her. I feel a need to touch her as much as I need to breath."

"Does that bother her dude?"

"I think she likes it, and I asked if I can see more of her now that she's moved home. But to be honest, it can be hard to read her."

"So what's the deal, man?" asks Chris.

"She reminded me I have AJ and football. I told her yes, I do have a teenage son, but he's more concerned with his friends than his father. I laid it all out on the table, including the fact that I plan to build a house and am contemplating a career with ESPN, but I stressed that she is at the top of my to do list."

"Man that was brave of you. How did she react? If I had said that shit to Max she would have slapped me. I mean, I want to do her but she aint ready to hear that shit yet." Chris gives me a grin.

"She knew what I meant. I have made no bones about where I want things to go between us."

"So what did you say next, Shakespeare?"

"I pissed on her to mark my territory," I say, grinning back at Chris.

"It's better to be pissed on than pissed off," World laughs. "But what really happened?"

"I kissed her again with some authority and told her I would pick her up on Tuesday so we can go pick out the land where we will build our house. That's not what I really said, but I sure wanted to, man. I did ask her to go with me to look at land."

"Whoa man. Are you crazy? You haven't even advanced to the 'this is my boo status' on Facebook yet and you are already taking her house hunting? You can take the L off of Lover 'cause it's over!"

"I don't have a Facebook page, jack ass. And she is my boo, she just doesn't know it yet. Land hunting will be a good way to spend some more time with her and get a woman's opinion on the floor plan. And I would deny it if your big mouth went back and told some of the boys, but it is over."

"When are you going to tell her how you feel, man?" Chris is serious now.

"I want her to get used to me being around a lot first, and then see where things go."

"Enough talk about our future baby's mamas. Let's hit the gym before I catch my flight," says World.

I laugh and tell Chris, "I'm two steps ahead of you. I reserved us a private room at the club. Meet you back here in ten minutes so we can get going."

Men are Like Houses

Max and I head out to shop on Monday morning. Six hours and sixteen pairs of shoes later, we're back at the plantation to have dinner with Mom. Max has gotten two texts from Chris, including one to let her know he has cleared his schedule so he can head down south in two weeks. I have never seen so much blushing. Hell, I grabbed the phone to make sure they weren't sexting.

As we sit down for a dinner of smothered chicken, mashed potatoes—with gravy of course—collard greens, and Ella's famous hot water cornbread, Max says to my mother, "Ms. Ella, how are you doing?"

"If you had asked me about a month ago I would have told you not too good. You won't understand until you have been married to the man you love for like one hundred years," she says, smiling. "I thought up until the last two weeks of Shorty's life that he would be ok. I knew we would have to make some major adjustments but the girl's daddy had the biggest will to live, and we had the biggest will to help him. He always said he did not want to suffer. Now that I look back I know there were days when he was in so much pain. He also hated being confined. How do you take a man from running up and down the floor with his kids teaching them to use their bodies to play a game to not being able to move his body unless someone or a walker assists him? That really took a toll on him, mentally and physically. When he realized the cancer had spread all over his body I sat and watched him decide to let the good Lord take him home. Even when I knew he only had a few days left, I still felt a sense of peace. I knew that God had different plans for him than any of us did. That's the thing about life. You don't know how much time you have here. One thing Shorty did better than most people I know is that he lived every minute of his life to the fullest. He loved waking up every morning. He loved teaching and coaching. He loved his hens, you know that's what he called Serena, Jack and I. And he loved Leo. And Jordan was the light of his life.

But how am I today? Today I am good. I fall down sometimes and cry, but I get back up. I miss Shorty, but he wouldn't come back down here with us for anything. I am resting in my faith in God and know that I will see him again. I am so thankful to God for the years we had together and for our three beautiful kids. A lot of people can't say that.

"And how are you girls? I know you hung out at Keeva's for the last two days and I sense some big things might have happened?"

Max turns around looks at me and takes a deep breath, then she asks, "Ms. Ella, how did you know that you were in love with Mr. Shorty? How did you know that you would be with him and have his kids, that you would be his haven when he needed a rest from his own self?"

"Maxine, I think finding a man is similar to finding a house. Some will look great on the outside but the inside is raggedy, or it's built on sinking sand. But when you walk into your home, you just know it. The amount of rooms are just right. The closets are perfect, and the kitchen is built to suit. That doesn't mean you don't have to maintain the home. Sometimes you may need to paint to keep things fresh or get new furniture. It just means it's the right one for you." In fact maintenance adds appreciable value."

"I guess what I am saying is that I think it's the same when you meet the right person. You just know it. You feel settled in your soul. Shorty was something else when we first met, and I can tell you it was not love at first sight. In fact, he irritated the hell out of me. He always said he wooed me, but I picked him. You ladies need to make sure you pick your man. And you don't want a foreclosure or a short sell or a prefab model! Now things move at warp speed. You can find out about someone with a keystroke but remember, men like a mystery. Yes, I picked Shorty and I made him work to get me. I knew that I was signing up for controversy, haters as you young people say and a lifetime of having to share their father. But I knew I was his resting place. I was the person he could be the most vulnerable with. I knew ALL of his weaknesses. I understood the things that made him sad and fearful. When you are not afraid to make yourself vulnerable with someone than you know you love them. About a year ago I heard him tell one of his friends that he was away coaching and teaching a lot but when he came home we were always so glad to see him. He was so thankful that we didn't mind sharing him."

"Shorty and I married for love. That's all we had back then. Jackie, you remember what your daddy told you and Serena? He said, 'Me and your momma married for love, but you two better marry for love and money! I don't necessarily think you should be looking for someone that just has money, but do make sure you are evenly yoked. You two are beautiful, intelligent, savvy girls. Don't settle; life is too short."

And after that soliloquy there is nothing left to be said!

The next morning I take Max to the airport to catch her flight back to St. Croix. I hate to see her leave. The time always goes by too fast when we're together. Right before Max gets out of the car, she looks at me and says, "Just because I am leaving doesn't mean I can't come back for your first meeting with the team and parents. I can fly back up here as quick as a whip."

"I know you can Max, but I can't depend on you to fight my battles. This is one I am going to have to work through myself. Just promise me that as soon as we finish the last game I can get my ass on the next plane heading to the Henry E. Rohlsen airport. I will be ready to lie on the beach, eat mangos, and drink rum, not necessarily in that order," I say, reaching over to give her a big hug.

As I squeeze her as tight as her giant tatas will allow, I whisper in her ear, "Give Chris a chance to court you Max. Let him show you that you are worth traveling the 1631 miles from New York to the island."

She whispers back, "Girl, you Googled it too, huh?"

"Yeah, I Googled it. Now go on before you miss your flight."

"Oh yeah, I forgot you've got a date with Adaris this afternoon. Take some of your own advice girl and remember what Ms. Ella told us last night." She quickly hops out of the car so she can have the last word.

Adaris and I decided to meet back at the sports club. Well, actually I decided it would be a good place to meet. I just wasn't comfortable yet with him coming over to my mom's. Not that I'm keeping a secret from my mom, but things are just too new for me to tell her about Adaris–even though she suspects something is going on. Ella aint no fool. She knows that if I have her whipping up potato salad I must be interested in someone.

I've decided to stay in the house as Mom suggested, since she's in the Plantation by herself. I want to be there with her to help her get through all the firsts without dad--his birthday, their anniversary…who am I fooling? I want her to be there for me as well. I also don't know if I will be staying in Nashville, so I feel like this is where I need to be right now.

I pull up at the gym to meet Adaris. It's already March and the temperature is about 50 degrees. I dressed warmly so I'd be prepared to walk around. I have on skinny jeans, a cream turtleneck, a brown leather bomber jacket, and my new brown Timberlands. I'm also wearing the brown tam Aunt D recently gave me. Funny thing is, Serena gave her that tam just two Christmases ago! You should have seen the look on Serena's face when I pulled out the tam on Christmas morning!

As I get out of my car, Adaris is walking out of the gym. I haven't seen him since Sunday morning, and it's like seeing him for the first time. He's wearing jeans, boots, and a black cashmere sweater. He walks up and gives me a back-cracking hug, grabs my hand, and starts walking to his car.

"You ready to find a house today?" by way of greeting.

Running to keep up with him, I ask, "Do you want a house or a home?"

He stops, swings around and grabs my other hand, then pulls me close so we're standing chest to chest. He looks deep into my eyes and says hoarsely, "When I hold you in my arms I feel like I am at home."

Did he talk to Ella last night? Did he read my mind? Did he just say...

He leans down and works my lips as if they are a piece of candy. He starts on one side of my mouth and nibbles his way over to the other side. Once he gets to the other end he bites my bottom lip, then he sucks where he bit and says, "Umm, you taste like strawberries."

Before I could let out a moan and beg him to bite me again, he swings me around, puts his arm around my shoulder, and lifts me up into the seat. Then he fastens my seatbelt and gently closes the door. Next thing I know, we're pulling off the highway and heading to the first stop to meet his realtor. I start to get a little pissed off. How in the hell can you kiss someone like that and then just stop!

"Where are we going first Adaris?" I ask him, while still trying to recover.

"We're heading out to look at some land where I might build my house. I built a house for my mother a few years ago, but I want something for me and my future family."

"Your future family? Do you have plans to have one in the near future?"

"Actually I do. When I retire from football I want to plant my roots here in Nashville. AJ is getting older and will be gone to college soon and I want a family that includes a wife, more children, and maybe a few dogs. What about you Jackie? What are your plans for the future?"

"I've always thought someday I will get married, but I never felt the pressure to settle down just because I felt like men were scarce. I know that when God is ready for me to find my mate, I will. I never have worried much about my biological clock either. I just think timing is everything. But let's get back to the subject at hand. What are you looking for in a house?"

"I want southern comfort, smooth but with a lot of flavor. It doesn't have to be huge, but I want to have all the comforts—wide open spaces, big rooms, and big closets. I also want a space for me and my boys to play and relax. I want to be able to watch TV and movies, work out, hit golf balls, and I want plenty of space to keep all of my man toys."

"Man toys—"

"Yeah, my footballs, golf clubs, basketballs, tools, and yard items. I want a place to put my stuff where my wife won't bother it."

"Kind of like us women feel about our closets. We want plenty of space to keep our shoes and purses. Has your realtor found any existing houses that might be what you're looking for?"

"Nope. I am not sure if there is anything out there that comes close to what I want, which is why I'm thinking about building. We will be looking at two houses in Brentwood to see if I like them, but the realtor has also arranged for me to meet with an architect today. Johnny Fulton of Fulton & Associates."

"That name sounds familiar."

"I heard they have been around for a long time."

We pull up at a mini-mansion in Brentwood and get out of the car. As we walk up the stairs to the house, the door opens and a beautiful woman steps out to greet us.

"Good morning Adaris and hello, my name is Tiffany Shelley, and you are..."

"Tif, this is a good friend of mine, Jackie Donovan. I brought her with me to help me out today."

"Nice to meet you Jackie. Let me introduce both of you to one of the architects I want Adaris to talk with. She's in the dining room making a phone call."

"She? I thought you told me the architect's name is Johnny?" Adaris says with a puzzled look.

"It's Johnnie with an ie. Apparently her dad wanted a boy but had three girls. Johnnie is the youngest, hence the name."

I enter the house a few steps in front of Adaris. As Tiffany leads us to the dining room, I hear a husky voice talking on the phone. As we round the corner, I see Johnnie. A sense of dread sends shivers down my spine and my hackles immediately go up. Not because she is beautiful—she reminds me of Halle Berry and she is flawless, right down to the false eyelashes and slamming steel gray stilettos—but because of the look Johnnie gives Adaris when we walk into the room. The look that says, I know you are gorgeous, young, single, and unattached and I am gorgeous, young, single, and unattached. You know, the look women give men that says, I have done all the research. The look that says, we can excuse ourselves right now and get down to the business in the next room. The look that says, I don't give a damn if you just walked into the room with another female because I am gunning for you.

I immediately think to myself, I wish Keeva were with me, she would make some comment to let that girl know that she isn't running anything up in here. But my technique is a little different. My sister and I were taught by our father "not to take any wooden nickels." He also taught me that "game recognizes game," and since I think of myself as a master player, especially after the last spades beat down I figure I will just sit back and let Johnnie with an "ie" self-destruct.

No, Adaris is not my man. Not yet. But she doesn't know that and I can sense her lack of respect for me. I stop abruptly, cross my arms, and narrow my eyes at her. I can feel Adaris stop right behind me and put his hands on my shoulders. I don't know if he senses that a battle of wills is about to take place, but I am glad his manners take over, and just in time.

The heifer walks up to Adaris, holds out her hand as if I am not even in the room, and says in her best bedroom voice, "Hello Adaris, my name is Johnnie L. Fulton of Fulton & Associates. I have been a huge fan of yours since you were first drafted to the Cowboys. I'm looking forward to working with you."

As I stand there watching Johnnie make her move on my man-to-be, I wonder if he is naive enough to go for it or if he is as sprung as most men probably are when they're in her presence.

"Nice to meet you Johnnie. Let me introduce you to a special friend of mine, Jackie Donovan. Jackie, meet Johnnie."

Johnnie shakes my hand with a sly smile. What she doesn't realize is that I'm hip to the game, and I plan to play it with my mind rather than my body. Yes, I know she is smart, and yes, she is beautiful—if you like her painted on, plastic look. Something tells me Adaris has been around that mulberry bush a time or two and that the fruit has soured. I decide to bench myself and get my game plan together...if I even need one. I know I am pretty easy on the eyes, but I never considered myself a pretty girl or a LSLH. Yes, a light skinned, long hair girl. Pretty girls are those girls that have or had long hair at one time. They are typically light skinned, and have teeth that never needed braces or they have invested in veneers. Their parents told them so many times how pretty they are that "pretty" becomes who they are. They get so caught up in it that they ostracize everyone around them including their five year old friends. That "pretty" young ego becomes a pretty teenage ego and it goes on and on. Pretty girls are so busy with themselves that they don't have any friends. Well, they have one, but she is ugly. "Ugly" is the only person who will deal with "Pretty" cause she will feed pretty's ego and pretty will make "Ugly" feel wanted. Eventually they create a cloud around them no one can penetrate, and after a while nobody wants to. Oh sure, pretty can reel the men in. But pretty can't keep them. 'Cause pretty is as pretty does.

So I decide to let pretty, I mean Johnnie, hang her own damn self. I know Adaris won't be able to help but notice her, but slow and steady wins the race every time. I don't have to say a word. I sit down in the chair farthest away from the meeting so I can get a full view of what is about to go down. I mentally give Johnnie the nickname PYT. It will be a great code name when I talk with Keeva and Max later.

PYT leads Adaris by his big strong strapping arm to the dining room table so she can show him a few of the houses she has designed in the past. As she leads him away he turns and gives me a look that says, "Why are you all the way down there when you should be up here with me?" I looked at him and smile, and give him a wink that says, "Handle your business." Then I put my elbow on the table, put my big head in my hand, and start watching the movie. Damn, I wish I had some popcorn!

For the next 15 minutes I watch PYT stand behind Adaris and graze her silicone breasts across his back as she shows him her design plans. She touches his arm as often as possible. Too bad PYT didn't know about Aunt D's rub, pat, and slide move. Every now and then Adaris looks up from the drawings and gives me a smile. I rub my tongue across my lips and smile back at him. After that he doesn't have a clue what PYT is saying, he is too busy looking at me.

Adaris clears his throat and says, "Johnnie, excuse me for interrupting, but I would like to take a look at this house first before we go through any more plans." With that he gets up from the table, slithers past PYT, who is standing way too close, and walks over and grabs my hand to pull me up out of the chair.

"Ladies, give us 15 minutes to walk around a bit and then we'll meet you back here to discuss some more options. Jackie, let's start in your favorite room."

I looked at him and innocently ask, "The master bedroom or the kitchen?"

"You lead the way," he says with a huge smile.

Since the kitchen is adjacent to the dining room, we stop there first. I can see PYT's eyes narrow, and the look on her face says, "I guess I need to try another tactic." When we step into the kitchen, Adaris spins me around and says, "You better watch what you say to me sweetness. Anytime you even hint about getting me alone I will jump. And I swear if you lick your lips like that one more time, I am going to pounce."

"What are you talking about Adaris?" I ask. Then I lick my lips again.

Before I know it Adaris has me backed up against the cabinets. He takes my face in his hands and whispers, "This is your payback for leaving me down there with Johnnie." He smashes his lips against mine, licks my bottom lip, and then whispers, "Open."

And open I do. He plunges his sweet tongue into every corner of my mouth as he flattens his body against mine. This is the first time he has touched me this intimately. He grabs my butt, settles me closer to his groin, and then says, "It's a shame we have company or I just might be tempted to eat you for lunch."

Right then PYT yells out, "Do I need to show you any of the amenities in the kitchen, Adaris?"

"No thanks. I found them all and they feel, I mean they look great," he calls back, and then he kisses me on my neck, right below my ear. "Ok," he whispers, "Playtime is over. I have a feeling we may have company pretty soon. Let's do a tour and then I want to hear what you think." Meanwhile he is rubbing his hand back and forth across my butt cheek.

"If you don't stop doing that I won't be able to tell you," I say, pushing him away. "Let's go and look at this mini-mansion."

"What did you and Jackie think about the house Adaris?" Tiffany asks.

"The house is beautiful and has a lot of great features..."

"I sense a but. Tell me what you like about it?"

"I like the layout. I like knowing that all of the living space is on one floor and the play space is below. I can't really put my finger on what I don't like."

"We can certainly use this layout to design something for you. Just tell me what you want," Pretty said with a suggestive smile.

Adaris looks at me and says, "I can't really describe what I think is missing or what I would change. Help me, Jackie."

Ahhh, it's finally time to show Johnnie what's up.

"Ladies, the rooms Adaris felt most comfortable in were the kitchen, the master quarters and the basement. This entire house is really too formal. Adaris wants a nice home, but one where people can fall asleep on the couch or be at ease in any chair. He's a big man who wants to be able to wander freely without feeling confined. Johnnie, please make a note that all of the doors should be 10 feet and the sinks taller than the standard size. He also wants his basement to be a play area where people feel instantly relaxed."

"Well, I will be damned. What she said! Jackie, you just helped me design my house. Tiffany and Johnnie did you take notes?"

"Of course not! I thought I would be discussing your vision with you, not with your friend," says Johnnie in a huff.

"Johnnie, one thing you need to learn about me is that I don't waste time. I brought Jackie because I wanted her opinion, and I expect you and Tiffany to listen."

Tiffany says eagerly, "I took notes, Adaris, and I can share them with Johnnie. What other items need to be added?"

Adaris gives them a long list of must haves—a full chef's kitchen, a master bathroom with a sauna and huge whirlpool tub, a state of the art media room, a full gym, and so on. Then he asks, "Ok ladies, are we clear on the direction we need be headed?"

"Uh, I think we are Adaris," says Johnnie. "It looks like we will need to redo your plans from scratch, but I can't wait to work with you to get it perfect. How about we get together on Wednesday and review the first draft over dinner?"

"There's no need for us to meet yet Johnnie. I think we need to find the land first before we can proceed with the plans. Tiffany, Jackie, and I can handle it from here. We will get you linked in once we find the property."

"Well, I will need your contact information so we can speak freely while we are going through the process," Johnnie says, now sounding just a little desperate.

"You can get my contact information from Tiffany, but I'll be traveling for the next few weeks so you won't be able to reach me. You can send me the specs over email."

"Well, here is my information. You can call me anytime," says Johnnie as she hands Adaris her card.

"I doubt I'll have a reason to call you at home Johnnie, but thanks. Hold on to this for me please, babe," Adaris says as he hands me Johnnie's card. "Tiffany, why don't you jump in the car with us so we can take a look at this property. If I see something I like today, I want to put the offer in so we can get going a.s.a.p."

"But Adaris, don't you think I should go along? I will have the best idea about the elevation and grade of the land." Yup, she is desperate.

"Johnnie. I understand elevation. Tiffany can call you once we settle on some land. In the meantime, please get started on the floor plan. Come on ladies let's go," Adaris says while grabbing my hand.

Now I just have to look back at Johnnie and give her a little smile. Not the kind of smile that says, "He is mine, mine, mine." Just the kind that says, "Round 1 goes to Jackie Donovan."

So off we go to look at the land. All of the lots are great, but one in particular catches Adaris' eye. It is three acres located between Murfreesboro and Franklin in a place called Arrington, about six miles from the interstate. Far enough from Nashville but close enough to the stadium. After we walk around the property for about 15 minutes, Adaris looks at Tiffany, gathers me in his arms, and says, "This is it ladies. This is where I will build my home."

"Let me call Johnnie and get her to do some research on the land to make sure the house you want to build will work. If it checks out I will tender an offer. I suspect that you will be signing closing papers by sometime next week."

"That sounds great. And Tiff, please make sure Johnnie remembers this is a business transaction. If she can't do that, then we can go to another person in the firm or find another company."

"Adaris, you of all people know how football players attract people," Tiffany says with a smirk. "Johnnie's opinion is that you are available."

"I need you to tell her that I am off the market," Adaris says while he looks at me, intensely.

"I will handle it Adaris. If you want to be in a house by the end of the year we need to get the floor plan finalized, and pronto."

"Tiffany, I will be out of town for almost two weeks, so please have Johnnie email me her first stab in the next few days, and I will forward it to Jackie. I will need both of you to help me. Are you ok with being my second set of eyes, Jackie?"

"Uh sure Adaris. Why would you want my opinion about how your house should look?"

"You have great style but you don't go overboard. I loved the way you handled the bike which means you are a good steward of money. And, you figured out in 30 minutes what I wanted and didn't want. If it's too much for you to take on, just tell me."

"It's not too much. I just don't want to overstep my boundaries with Tiffany and Johnnie."

Tiffany steps in to reassure me. "If you can help us move this along quicker we can get the build out done sooner."

"Then it's settled. Jackie will work with you and Johnnie's firm to bring the house to life."

We drop Tiffany off at her car with her promise to touch base about the land in the next few days. Then Adaris leans over and says, "Sweetness, thanks for helping me out with the house. I have to fly back to Bristol for a few days and then to New York to meet with my agent. When I get back I want to take you out on a real date. Just me and you. No parks, gyms, friends, or realtors. I want some time with just Jackie. Can you make time for that?"

"You make it very difficult to say no, Adaris. Especially when you kiss me..."

He leans over to kiss my cheek, then my ear. He removes my hat and runs his fingers through my hair, then he nuzzles the nape of my neck and whispers, "Say yes, please..."

"Fall back dude. We are both too big to try anything in this car. Yes I will go out with you when you get back. Ouch! You just bit my neck!"

"Damn right. I have to leave my mark so you don't forget about me while I'm gone, and what is that smell?

"It's my gum."

Adaris leans back over, buries his nose in my hair, gives me a slow kiss with a hint of tongue, then leans back and says, "I am entranced by a piece of gum? Give me a few pieces of what you have in your purse so I can keep them in my pocket while I am gone."

"Seriously?"

"Unless you plan on taking off your panties or your bra for a more intimate scent, he said with a huge burst of laughter."

"Here are a few pieces of gum," I said while digging in my purse. "You will have to make it to home base before you get any of those other items."

"At least you are talking as if it can happen so I will settle for the gum for now."

"Good compromise. Now take me to my car so you can go home and get ready for your trip."

Two Peas in a Bucket

It's been a week since Adaris left town. I really miss him, although I would never admit it. But, it's given me time to get my game plan together and get closure on a few things. Dad has been gone for over two months but his presence is still very much in our home and on our minds. There's a picture of him in every room of the house, and we can't go to the grocery store without running into someone who knew him. And, we get calls almost every day from someone wanting to give their condolences as people around the country who knew him hear of his death.

A few local TV and radio stations caught wind of my retirement and I've done some interviews. ESPN did a 15-second blurb on my retirement, from which they segued into a 30-second blurb on my dad's passing. That gave me a huge chuckle. Dad is still besting me, even on ESPN. I have come to accept that he will be present in our lives for at least another generation— that's just how many people he touched.

We were also trying to figure out how to get rid of our "peace lily greenhouse" as Serena had coined it. Whatever freak of a florist coined the peace lily the plant to give to the bereaved was, well a freak! At one time we had so many plants and flowers that we could have easily started a floral business. Serena and I laughed because every time someone came over to the "Plantation" to visit my mom would send them home with a plant. If she really liked you or if she knew that my dad did, she would let you pick your own plant! She would tell them to keep it alive in remembrance of Shorty. We were down to about 25 plants and Ella had put me on water duty. I had gotten so good at watering the plants that I had decided to name each of them.

I decided that I really needed to put myself on a schedule. My entire life had been regimented so order was very important to me. Since I've been home I've gotten kind of lazy, and I'll need to get back into a routine to get ready for coaching. I decide to make mornings my time to exercise—I already joined the gym Adaris took me to. It's off the beaten path so not many people have recognized me. After my workout I'll make lunch for mom and me. Ella and I like to lunch like queens. Sometimes she even sets the dining room table with her finest china and dresses up a little. I'll spend the early afternoon watching game tapes and laying out plays. I've pretty much taken over Shorty's Shack. Somehow I feel more connected to Dad there, almost like he is still whispering hints in my ear, as he always did.

I know I need to set aside time for Mom, so I decide that late afternoon will be my time to help her take care of the house and settle my dad's estate. This reminds me of one of the items I really need to resolve: I still don't know who my assistant will be. Principal Leevins wants to give Coach Frazier the first right of refusal, but this bothers me a little. I know that Frazier can be a loose cannon. Dad was able to rein him in, but I'm not sure if I will be able to do that.

Another thing that's been on my mind is where the hell my Aunt Lucy has gone to. We have not heard one word from her since the day daddy died. I've called her dozens of times but only get her voicemail--you know, the message that indicates that the phone is off. So I call Leo to see if he has heard from her. I have been avoiding Leo for the last few weeks. I love my brother, but he can be a pain in the ass and he is needy like a female dog. I need this, I need that, can you hook your brother up with that. It's like he and my sister and I reversed roles, as we are tough as nails. All I can figure is maybe once Daddy saw how Leo was, he changed the way he raised Serena and me. I had decided to practice some tough love with him or to borrow a quote from Shorty, "get lost on him". I take a deep breath before I dial his number, as I know I'll have to give something up if I want to get some answers.

"Happy House, may I help you?"

I learned from my last call to put on my most professional voice. "Yes, may I speak with Bill please?"

"Uh yeah, hold on a minute."

"This is Bill, how may I help you?"

"Hi Bill, this is Jackie Donovan, Leo's sister. How are you doing?"

"Doing just fine Jackie. I am assuming you need to speak with Leo?"

"Yes please."

"Hold on just a second, let me get him."

"What's up sis? You been avoiding your boy, haven't you? I spoke to Ma a few times last week and she told me you were out. What you been doing since you've been home?"

"Hey bro. I have been a little busy working out and figuring out what I want to do. Did mom tell you I decided to retire?"

"Yeah, she told me. What's up for you now, Jack?"

"Well, I decided to take dad's place coaching his basketball team at SHS."

"No shit? How did you manage to take that job from that dumb ass Frazier?"

"Principal Leevins asked me to be the interim coach for a year and see what happens. I decided to take him up on it."

"Maybe I need to hurry up and get done here so I can be your assistant coach. It would be just like old times sis. Remember when we used to beat the breaks off the boys at the YMCA!"

"Oh yeah, I remember. Do you also remember the whipping we got from Mom when the director at the Y kicked us out for betting and taking all their money?"

"Pops laughed about that shit for days. He told me he used to do the same thing with Lu when they were little."

"Yeah, Aunt Lu used to have some game too. Speaking of Aunt Lu...have you talked to her Leo?"

"Yeah, I talked to her trifling ass a few days ago. I had to get Queesha to ask one of my boys in New York to go 'round her way to see if she was still alive. Peep this, he knocked on the door and she answered like it wasn't nothing. He told her we were worried about her and gave her the number here, and she called me a few days ago. All she said is 'I'm ok.' Not, how are you, my only son? How was the funeral? She didn't say shit. It's like she threw Pops away like she did me when I was a baby. Sis, I swear Ma Ella and Grandma Peggy have been more of a mother than my own. That's why I call her Lu. I aint got enough respect to call her anything else."

"I am glad she is ok, but pissed that she went MIA on everyone. I have left so many messages for her. I didn't tell you I wired her some money to come home a few days before daddy died."

"One thing I learned from selling is not to give an addict money. Why didn't you just buy her a bus ticket?"

"I don't know! That last week was a blur. We brought daddy home to die and I didn't think about what I was doing. Serena put me in charge of Lu so she wouldn't have to deal with it. I must have had a brain fart."

"More like a brain shit!"

"You should have been a comedian instead of a drug pusher. I just don't understand Aunt Lu. She came home for six months to help Mom take care of Daddy. She was wonderful, aside from the constant cussing and her average five beers a day."

"That's better than five snorts of crack per day. If she was using she would have stolen everything out from under Ma and Pops."

"Yeah, you're right, just being her beer pusher got pretty expensive. But it was well worth it, knowing she was helping mom when none of us could be there."

"I have a lot of regrets, sis. You can't get a furlough from a federal pen, even if your dad is dying from cancer. I didn't want Ma bringing Pops to the pen, so I didn't see him the entire time he was sick..."

"You called enough. Daddy said you could really get down when you called. He made me put a chart together to see how much it cost per minute. It was like I was back in school completing an assignment. By the time I got to fifteen minutes he started cussing. He told momma not to let you two talk more than ten minutes. Then he told her to check into investing in federal prisons cause those mfs were taking all his damn money!"

"Yeah, but after a while he would talk for about a minute and then say, 'Here's your Ma.' I guess he was trying to save money."

"No bro, he just didn't have the energy to talk, that's why he put Mom on the phone. He did the same thing with me and Serena."

"Damn, I thought it was me because I let them down."

I don't' know what to say to that, so I change the subject. "Leo, I have decided to write Lu a letter and let her know how I feel."

"You know she can't read. She claims to have dyslexia."

"She can read, believe me. I would catch her butt reading the paper all the time when I was home. She would grin at me and say she was just

136

looking at the pictures. I need to write the letter to give me some closure. I really thought we had gotten pretty tight over the last year. She is crazy as hell but crazy smart!"

"Yeah, the only person Lu couldn't outsmart was Pops. He knew her like a book. He always said the only difference between him and Lu was he got out and she couldn't. Now I really understand how two people with the same parents can turn out so differently yet be so much alike. That may be why Lu didn't come home, maybe Pop's passing was just too much for her to handle."

"Leo, if she had said that I would have understood, but how do you say you are on your way to Nashville and then never show up. Telling the truth would have been so much better."

"Write that letter sis. It may make you feel better but let me give you some Shorty Donovan advice."

"What advice would that be, little brother?"

"I may be shorter than you but I am still older. My advice is, 'two peas in a bucket...fuck it.' That's what Pops always said when he knew he couldn't change a situation. I suggest you do the same and if I can say that about my own mother for once in your life you should listen to your big bother. I love you Coach Donovan. Before I get off the phone, tell me one thing: when are you going to hook a brother up? I need some new threads and some kicks."

"I love you too Leo. I'll try to bring you a box of stuff next week. It will give Mom a good reason to go to the mall."

I feel a lot better after talking to Leo. Talking to him is like a coin toss. You either end up pissed off and frustrated, or you feel like you just talked to the best shrink in the world. Leo's advice gave me some food for thought. Would writing Lu a letter really make me feel any better? Would she even read it? Maybe I should just fly up to New York and give her an old fashioned beat down. That's what Max would tell me to do. I decide to write the letter—if nothing else, it may help me release some of my hurt and confusion and finally give me some closure.

So I sit down and write to Aunt Lucy.

You want this

I thought I would be gone one week tops, but once I got to Bristol I ended up meeting with the ESPN executives for over a week. I even flew my agent in to help. Now we are at a standstill. I told them I am not willing to fly all over the United States for a story, and their last offer was to report on games south of the Mason Dixon line. That would keep me close to home and allow me to attend most of AJ's games—I am not going to break my promise to him. I told my agent I'm willing to walk away if ESPN can't agree to a schedule that worked for both parties.

I didn't realize how attached I had gotten to Jackie. I miss her too much. We've texted back and forth and talked a few times, but I sensed she was preoccupied with family stuff. She told me we can talk about it when I get home. The good thing is, she did speak of seeing me in the future. That makes me feel pretty good. Damn good!

Since I've been away, Tiffany finalized the land deal. I am now the proud owner of a piece of Tennessee. Now we have to get the floor plan finished. Johnnie emailed me her first draft the other day. I sent Jackie a copy so we can look at it together when I get home. I want her to love this house. I don't want to jump too quickly, but I can actually imagine a future with her. I expect to be home in the next 48 hours, so I tell my agent I need to step out and do a little shopping. I've noticed that Jackie has an affinity for shoes and purses and I want to get her a little something from the Yves Saint Laurent store to show her I've been thinking about her.

Adaris has texted me several times a day to say hello and even called me a few times, but I'm not much for talking on the phone since it proved to be more frustrating. I miss him and am ready for him to come home. I have gotten myself into a really good routine and am back on track with my workouts. I even tried a little Pilates. I've just gotten home to make lunch when the doorbell rings. Mom is out, and didn't say she was expecting anyone so I'm a little leery about answering the door. I peek outside and see a Fed Ex Truck and a delivery man.

I open the door just as he's leaving a box on the front porch. I turn the box around to inspect it and then run to get the scissors. I cut the box open and see two smaller boxes. One is a shoe box and I'm not sure about the other.

Of course I go for the shoe box first, which has a YSL label. I slowly open it and pull out a pair of beautiful black suede booties with a four-inch heel and a platform toe, with gold piping around the platform. I notice a note sitting on top of the shoes, but I am too curious about what's in the other box to stop to read it. I open it and find a black suede YSL clutch that matches the boots. By now I am grinning so hard my teeth hurt. The only YSL I know of is in New York City, which is where Mr. Singleton is currently located. I open the note and read:

"Hey sweetness. I was out and just so happened to see this little store called YSL. These boots and the clutch were calling your name. I thought these shoes would look beautiful on those gorgeous legs when we go out on our date. Meet me at Sambucas at 7:00 on Wednesday evening. I miss you. Until then...Dair"

OMG, I only have 48 hours to get myself together! I call my hair stylist and make an appointment for Wednesday, and ask her to set up a mani-pedi too. Now what to wear? I decide to keep it simple to show off the shoes, and thank God for mom and Serena, who over the years have bought me some beautiful little black dresses.

I arrive at Sambucas about 7:15. I planned to be a little late so I can make an entrance—and make Adaris sweat just a little. We haven't spoken since I got the shoes and purse. I think both of us wanted to save all of our conversation for tonight. When I had my hair done I decided to go with the Snookie look, so it is slicked back on the sides and puffed at the top, the rest hanging down my back. I'm rocking a suede Grecian dress that has one arm completely exposed and the other covered. My only jewelry is a pair of diamond studs. My booties are outrageous—they make me look over six feet tall and my legs seem to go on forever. My new clutch holds a tube of lipstick, some spearmint gum, my driver's license, and a twenty dollar bill. I always keep a bill in my purse when I go on a date...I guess old habits die hard.

As soon as I walk through the door, the hostess looks at my shoes and says, "Ms. Donovan, let me see you to your table," and she leads me to a private table way in the back. I am vaguely aware of red curtains, black marble floors, and low lights, and then I see him. He is also dressed all in black. He is so striking that I let out a gasp. As I walk toward him I see the look on his face and find myself humming Janet Jackson's "You Want This." The bar that said "What's my name boy..."

I arrive at the restaurant at about 6:45. I want to make sure that everything is in place for our date. I ask the manager to put us at a table that will give us some privacy, and I also make sure I'll be able to see Jackie walk into the restaurant. I have been imagining her legs in those boots for the last two days and praying she wouldn't wear pants. Hell, I have been imagining her legs, her arms, her mouth, her eyes...everything Jackie. Nine days was too damn long to be gone. Now I understand what my boys who are married mean when they say they are ready to get back to their wives. Jackie energizes me and I miss her vibe. As I sit there enjoying the music, I see her walking behind the hostess. My jaw drops as I start admiring her at the bottom and work my way up. Those boots make her legs look like she is ten feet tall. And that dress! She looks like a vamp and I am completely captivated. I jump out of my chair to meet her before she gets to the table.

"Good evening Adaris!"

"Hey baby. You look...you look, oh hell!"

"I look what?"

"You don't want to know what I am thinking. I am so glad to see you." He gathers me close for a hug and a light kiss on the mouth. "I better stop or we won't eat."

"Did I say I need to eat?"

He gathers me closer and gives me another gentle kiss.

"Spearmint tonight?"

"Yeah spearmint."

"Let me have some."

"Ok, let me get it out of my purse."

"Damn the purse, give me a taste of what you have in your mouth." After that there's no conversation for a few minutes. Adaris gathers me even closer, moves his hand to the curve of my behind, put his other hand behind my neck into my hair and kisses me like he needed to get to know my mouth and lips again. He leans back over and runs his nose from the top of my head to the nape of my neck.

"I have missed your smell, your lips, and your hair. But most of all I have missed you here," he says, moving my hand to his chest so I can feel his heart. "Do you know what you do to me? I am breathing harder than when I go out for a pass."

"I missed you too. And thank you for my shoes and my purse. You have exquisite taste."

"I imagined how your legs would look in those booties and knew you had to have them. You have beautiful brown legs," he says while he picks up my leg and brushes my calf up and down his thigh"

"Adaris, please put my leg down. People are staring at us."

"I don't give a damn about people looking. I can't keep my hands off you. But maybe we should sit down." Adaris lets go of my leg but keeps his hand wrapped around my thigh. It's your fault for wearing this dress. You knew this outfit would drive me out of my mind."

"Yes I did. I'm pleased to see that my hard work is paying off."

"You could have come here in a sack with your hair jacked up and you still would look beautiful. Remember, I have seen you sweaty and funky. You looked just as beautiful then as you do now."

"If that's the case, next time I will just stay all jacked up to be damned. And I was not funky," I say with a grin.

I unwrap my arms from Adaris' neck, and he gives me a hard kiss before seating me at the table.

"I hope you're hungry. This place is known for having great food, and I want to get you full so you'll be more accommodating with my after dinner plans."

"If you feed me good food you can get me to do almost anything."

"Good! Let's order, then I want you to tell me how you have been doing. I could sense that you didn't want to do a lot of talking while I was out of town."

"I knew you had a lot of business to handle and I didn't want you to be worrying about me here at home."

"I don't worry about you but I am concerned. Actually, I wanted to ask you to join me for a few days in New York but didn't want you to think I was moving too fast."

"And who was going to keep Johnnie company if I came to New York? You needed me more here."

"I think what I want and need is too much for you right now. Now tell me what's been going on with you."

"I don't want to talk about me. It will take too long, make me sad, and probably piss you off. Let's talk about your meetings."

"Thank you sweetness," Adaris says, reaching for my hand.

"Thank you for what?"

"For giving a damn about me. I haven't dated a woman in a long time who didn't think my world should revolve around her. And for dealing with Johnnie and the house. Thank you for being here with me."

"That's enough thank yous, cornball. And are we dating? I thought we were getting to know each other—"

"Dating, talking, gathering, booed up, conversing, hanging out. You can call it what you want, but I am interested in you Jackie. Not Johnnie, Missy, Lori, Jill, or, Kim."

"I know who Johnnie is. But who in the hell are Missy and them, Adaris?"

"That doesn't matter..."

"Well, you keep saying you want to get to know me better, so let me ask you some questions and you can ask me some too."

"I can ask anything I want?"

"Yep. I'll start. What's your favorite color?"

"I guess blue or black. What's yours?"

"I have two, yellow and green. What's your favorite food?"

"Jackie's ribs, and lately I've been digging Frosted Flakes. What's your favorite food?"

"Mine is something Italian or Japanese. What is your favorite pastime?"

"Looking at your smile..."

"Adaris, be truthful. That is the only way this will work."

"That is true. But I also like to relax—watch TV or go for a long drive, maybe hit some golf balls or work in my mom's yard. What about you?"

"I love to cook and read when I have the time."

"You certainly have an affinity for cooking. When I get my house built will you christen my kitchen?"

"It depends on what you mean by christen."

"We can start with cooking.......but speaking of christening, what's your favorite Bible verse?"

"That's easy, Philippians 4:13. 'I can do all things through Christ who gives me strength.' What is yours?"

"James 1:2, 'Count it all joy even when you go through various trials because you know the testing of your faith develops perseverance.' Jackie, what's the hardest thing you ever had to do?"

"Watch my father die. It was so sad, but beautiful at the same time. I have never seen something so peaceful. What about you?"

"Leave my mom and son to go to Auburn. I knew it would be the best thing for our future, but AJ was so young and mom had just barely finished raising me. It was a huge sacrifice on her part. That's why it's so important for me to have a good relationship with my son. Now, something less serious...what's your favorite car, Ms. Donovan?"

"I happen to love my own car, but if I could have any kind I wanted it would be an Aston Martin. And yours?"

"I like the Aston too. So much that I bought one last year."

"No kidding, what color?"

"Black."

"The one I saw was also black...wait a minute, I bet it was your car I saw at the airport!"

"Indeed it was. I don't drive it much, but my Rover was in the shop and it was too late to call a car service. I am terrified that AJ is going to pull a Ferris Bueller and take my car for a spin one day."

"Or me! Where does your mom live?"

"You can drive it any time, just say the word. And my mom lives in North Nashville."

I think for a minute, then ask Adaris, "What do you hope for?"

"Getting deep on me now, aren't you Jackie. I hope you can learn to trust me and see where our friendship will go. What do you hope for?"

"I hope I can learn to trust you. I hope that my heart will stop hurting from the death of my father. I hope for peace for my family."

"Wow, you are something. Let's go back to something lighter. What's your favorite sleeping position?"

"I like to sleep on my side. I'm almost afraid to ask what yours is..."

"I prefer sleeping naked...and I have a feeling I'd like spooning you, but for now I sleep on my back."

"TMI Adaris. But for future reference, do you snore?"

"I do not snore, at least not that I know of. What is your deepest fear, Jackie?"

"Hmm, back to heavy. My deepest fear is that I will get in my own way. One of my favorite poems is by Maureen Williams that talks about our fears. What is yours?"

"My deepest fear is that my son will make a decision he can't recover from."

"And what makes your heart go pitter patter, Adaris?"

"You in my arms. Smelling your hair and your scent. Watching you walk into a room," Adaris says slowly, looking at me intensely. "What makes your heart beat?"

"You watching me walk into a room."

"If you could travel anywhere in the world, where would you go?"

"I always wanted to go to Africa, to visit our Motherland before I leave this earth. And you?"

"I want to go to Aruba, but right now I need to run to the restroom. This wine is running through me. I'll be right back."

Adaris excuses himself and disappears around a corner, which gives me a chance to breathe. I didn't realize the conversation would get this deep. Adaris is not your average athlete, and being an athlete myself, I can't believe I am thinking that!

"I am back sweetness. Now where were we?"

"I have one last question. Who were those five women you named earlier?"

"I knew you wouldn't let that one go. You obviously know I have been around. I once was dating five women at the same time. I dated one because she was really smart, one liked to throw down in the sheets, and one was a football fanatic so she could relate to what was happening on the gridiron. One other chick was a great cook, and the last one really helped me connect with my spiritual side. Then one day I realized this was a pattern for me, dating several women without committing to any of them. As I thought about this, it hit me that those five women collectively had the things I wanted in one woman. So, I decided I was going to wait on the Lord to send me that seven."

"Wait a minute, I thought you said five?"

"I did, but I want the perfect mate for me. I want a woman who can do those five things, but also love and accept AJ and deal with my profession and all the baggage that comes with it."

145

Adaris leans across the table, takes my hand, and looks into my eyes. "I think the Lord has brought my seven to me. She isn't quite ready yet, but she is sitting here. For the first time in a long time I am ready and willing to wait."

"So does that mean you have gotten rid of the other five? Because I am competitive in sports but not in competing for a man. I need to know what you want so I can make a decision about what I want to do."

"I am a free agent. I have female friends but those friendships are platonic. In fact, most of them are now married and trying to hook me up."

"Ok Mr. Free agent, I will take your word for it. But if anything changes I expect full disclosure."

"The only thing I expect to change is the subject. Right now. I want to know what you think of Johnnie's floor plan."

"Are you sure? I don't want you to think I am throwing salt."

"Throw whatever you want, I value your opinion. Once I finalize the plans it's a go and...what the hell is that noise?"

"It sounds like you brought me to this beautiful place on country-western night—right now they're playing "All my exes live in Texas."

"Does that mean you do country line dancing?"

"I have done some line dancing, but I'm more into the electric slide, the cubic shuffle, and the wobble."

"Well, I suggest we dance on out of here to a much quieter place."

"Are we going to your mammy's house or mine?"

"Neither. I have a hotel room at the Hutton. And don't worry, I'm not going to let you seduce me tonight. I have an early meeting with coach in the morning so I decided to stay downtown. Ride with me over to the hotel and let's look at the floor plan. I'll bring you back later."

"On two conditions. One, I get to drive the Aston, and two, you promise you'll bring me back."

And with that I get up and do my "you want this" walk right out of the restaurant.

The Aston Martin is awesome. It's good that we're just going a few blocks away or I would put it in the wind. I feel a little nervous, as this kind of car is very intimate. It seems like Adaris' scent is wrapping itself around me, and it doesn't help that he has been staring at me the entire ride.

I pull up in front of the hotel and the valet meets us to open the car doors. I find myself wondering what he must be thinking. Judging by the way he greets Adaris they have met before, and I wonder if I am one of many who have made the walk of fame to Adaris' hotel room. One thing I know for sure is that I will not be making the walk of shame out of the hotel later. I am determined to take my time getting to know Adaris. We will go upstairs to look at his floor plan and then I am going back to the Plantation. We get on the elevator, and as soon as the door closes, Adaris turns and traps me against the wall.

"Why are you trembling, Jackie? Am I making you nervous?"

"Uh, hell yes, you are making me nervous. I feel like little brown riding hood about to be eaten by big bad Adaris."

"Oh, I plan to eat you, but not tonight," Adaris whispers in my ear, then he softly kisses my ear lobe. "Relax Jackie. I really do need your help with the house plans and I know you are not ready for anything too heavy. Trust me, sweetness, I will handle you like a china doll."

"Then back up about 12 inches, please," I say, pushing on his rock hard chest.

Thank goodness the elevator opens and we walk to his room. Adaris goes to the closet and pulls out a set of plans. "Come over here to the desk so I can spread everything out," he says, and we look over the floor plan for about five minutes.

"What is it? You haven't said a word, Jackie."

"It's nice—"

"But, what Jackie? Tell me."

"Johnnie didn't listen to anything you said. It's like she printed off one of those stock floor plans on a big sheet of drafting paper. The rooms are too small, there aren't enough bathrooms, and there are no bookshelves in your study. The basement is also all wrong and she is wasting her time and your money...wait a minute! I know what Johnnie is up to," I say with a sly laugh.

"What do you mean?"

"You men can be a little slow sometimes. She is obviously a brilliant architect and I know she heard every word you said, since she seemed to be dissecting you with her eyes. She is playing games with you, Adaris. She jacked up the floor plan so you will have to make contact with her."

"You're kidding. I made it clear I don't have much time—it's already the end of March. I also thought I made it clear I'm not available. I guess I'll have to fire her and get Tiffany to find another firm."

"No need to do that. You want the best and Johnnie's firm is the best in Nashville. We can beat her at her own game. I want you to call Johnnie tonight and tell her you want to meet her first thing in the morning to review the plans. Now, she is going to want to meet you tonight, but stay firm that you'll meet her at 10:00 tomorrow morning."

"I can't meet with her tomorrow at 10:00, sweetness; I have my physical to get cleared for camp."

"You aren't meeting her. I am."

"Oh snap. You are scaring me now. What are you planning?"

"I plan to step in there and tell her the gig is up. Then I will show her our changes and make sure she understands that I don't appreciate her wasting your money or time. I also will put her on notice that she has one more chance to mess up. If you are ok with that, let's mark up these plans and make this house your home."

"You just gave me a mental hard on. I love it when you get in Mama Bear mode and protect me. You are the only woman other than my mother who has ever done that. Hell, you seem to care more than my agent and my accountant—maybe I need to fire them and let you manage my career and my money."

"Let's get through tomorrow before you start firing people. But I will need to negotiate my payment for handling Ms. PYT."

"I will give you anything, but who is PYT?"

148

"PYT is Johnnie—the day we met her I named her Pretty Young Thing. And I want my payment to be taking Beauty out on the highway."

"Who the hell is Beauty?"

"Beauty is your Aston Martin, which the valet took for a spin while we have been looking at this floor plan. I figure if you can let a stranger drive Beauty you can let me take her out for a drive."

Adaris bellows, "The valet is driving my car?"

"Calm down beast! As long as you get it back without any dents you should be fine. And here's a tip—check your odometer before you leave your car and make sure the valet knows you do it."

"I think I need to be comforted. I have just fired my agent and my accountant. I just found out the architect is running a game, the valet is playing with my toys, and you are dropping knowledge on me that is making my head spin. I need a hug and a kiss and I need to touch your booty."

"You were doing really well until you got to the booty part," I say with a grin. "Sounds like you have been around the groupies too long. Come here big baby and get your hug. Then we have a lot to do to fix this floor plan."

"How about you lean over the floor plan with that red pen, and I will wrap my arms around you. That way I can hug you and touch your booty all at the same time," Adaris says as he moves behind me and wraps me in his arms. Then he lays his hands on my stomach.

"Adaris..."

"What sweetness," Adaris says while kissing my bare shoulder and rubbing against my back.

"If you don't stop moving your pelvis against my behind you are going to have a hard time sleeping."

"I haven't slept soundly since the day I saw your ass lying on the floor in the airport," he says, now kissing my neck. "And I got your hard time right here." Now he's grinding himself against my body.

"Ok, that's enough Adaris," I say shakily. "Go to the bar and get me some water, and grab yourself a beer. Then sit down so I can fix this jacked up floor plan. When the valet gets back from Chattanooga with your car you are going to take me right back to Sambucas to get my car."

"One last kiss, please baby," Adaris says as he sucks on my neck like he's sipping a milkshake. "Now make sure you show Johnnie that at your meeting tomorrow." He laughs and walks away.

"Did you just put a hickey on my neck?" I scream.

"You bet your fine ass I did. Serves you right for trying to seduce me with that dress and those legs and those shoes and that brain and those pheromones and that attitude…."

Now we both are laughing. "I am going to get you," I say with a huge grin.

"I can't wait! Now, get to work with that red pen."

"What if you don't like the changes I make?"

"If I don't like the changes I will go over them with my green pen. Now, I'm gonna sit over here and drink my beer and study your onion while I wait on Beauty to arrive from Chattanooga."

It's a Small World

The next morning I go for a run around 8:00 AM, then come back to take a shower before I head over to Johnnie's office. I've already gotten a good morning text from Adaris saying, *"Make sure you call me the minute you come out of Johnnie's office, Iron Mike Tyson."* I had to remind him that he is the biter, not me.

I arrive at Johnnie's office at 9:50 wearing a jogging suit and tennis shoes just in case I have to make a run for it. Trust me, I am a lover not a fighter. After the steamy night with Adaris and my morning run, my adrenaline is pumping, but I'm ready for a battle of wills, not a physical altercation.

I'm tempted to call Keeva for moral support, but I don't have time to fill her in, so I take a deep breath and I walk into the building. I am instantly stopped by the receptionist. Have you noticed that the receptionist is always either a beauty queen or a barracuda? This one is a barracuda and she looks like a center of a football team. I decide to try to throw her off, so I smile and say, "Good morning, my name is Jackie Donovan. Adaris Singleton and I have an appointment with Johnnie Fulton at 10:00."

The barracuda looks at me and frowns. "I don't see your name in the appointment book."

"Adaris must not have told Johnnie that I will be joining them. If you would, please just call Johnnie and let her know I am here and that Adaris is on his way."

"Humph...we will see," she says while dialing Johnnie's extension.

"Ms. Fulton, this is Mary. There is a Jackie Donovan who says she is scheduled to meet with you and Mr. Singleton at 10:00." There's a lot of head nodding and some um-hms, then she hangs up the phone and looks at me like I'm small. "Ms. Fulton will see you now. I will send Mr. Singleton up when he arrives. Go down the hall, make a left at the next hallway—her office is the second on the left."

I smile and say thanks, then take off down the hall. I knock on PYT's door and hear someone say, "Come in." I open the door and see another receptionist, and this one is a beauty. She also seems to be much nicer. "Ms. Fulton will be available in a few minutes. Can I get you something to drink?"

"No thanks, I'm fine."

After about five minutes, she says, "Ms. Fulton will see you now."

I feel like I'm walking the "Green Mile." My dad would tell me not to punk out, so I keep whispering words of affirmation to myself, like the maid in *The Help:* "You is kind, you is smart, you is important." I walk into Johnnie's office, where she's sitting behind her desk hanging up the phone. She looks up and says, "Good morning Jackie. Is Adaris on his way?"

"Actually, he had a physical this morning and it ran a little long." There, I've told about half the truth. He did have a physical this morning...I just didn't say where.

"Oh, ok. Well, are you here to drop off his changes to the plans?"

"Actually, I am here to go over the changes with you. Adaris wants you to make them and get them over to his assisant's office by 5:00 this afternoon."

"There is no way those changes can be done in seven hours. I have other clients and appointments today."

"Well, then I suggest you move some things around so you can get this done. If the plans had been done according to Adaris' wishes, I wouldn't be here."

"I don't have to talk with you about this. What time is Adaris going to be here?"

"Adaris isn't coming. He sent me. I have all the modifications he wants made, and he instructed me to make sure you understand his wishes."

"Let's get this straight. I don't take orders from anyone, especially if you aren't my client. I don't have to do a damn thing until I see Adaris." By now PYT is seriously frowning.

"Here's the deal John…"

"It's Ms. Fulton to you."

"Ms. Fulton then. Regardless of what I call you, you need to understand that Adaris has put me in charge of making sure you get these floor plans done correctly. If you can't get them done by 5:00, he will terminate your agreement. If you want to lose an influential client, it's your choice. I'll be calling him after this meeting to let him know what you've decided."

"You little bitch! You think you have him wrapped around your finger. This is my company and I will do what I damn well please, so don't threaten me!"

"Listen up Joh…Ms. Fulton. Adaris knows what you are up to. I suggest that you not ruin your business relationship because you want him to be your flavor of the month. If you do this right it could bring you a lot of business. Now, can we get to work? You now have only 6 hours and 50 minutes to get it done."

"You won't last. Adaris needs a real woman on his arm and not an ex-basketball player who can't walk and chew gum at the same time. I will make the changes, but you make sure to let Adaris know I don't appreciate him sending a messenger."

After that I spend the longest hour I can remember suffering through in a very long time. When the edits are complete, I have to admit to a grudging respect for Johnnie. The girl knows her stuff. As we're wrapping up, the door opens abruptly and a big hunk of a man with cocoa colored skin walks in. He appears to be in his early sixties and is very distinguished looking. He looks at me and says, "I'm sorry Johnnie honey, I didn't know you had a client. Wait, are you Jackie Donovan?"

"Yes sir I am. You must be Mr. Fulton. Nice to meet you."

"Young lady, I was so sorry to hear about my dear friend Shorty's passing. Your father and I were childhood friends, we grew up in the same neighborhood in North Nashville. I was in Africa when he passed away. Some buddies of mine and I were designing irrigation systems so the people there have safe water and couldn't get back in time for the funeral. I have spoken with your mom several times since then. How are you and your sister doing?" By now he's holding both of my hands.

"Daddy, you never mentioned you know the Donovans," Johnnie says.

"I had no reason to honey. Shorty and I didn't speak every day, but we saw each other every year at our class reunion and we spoke from time to time. That's how we are at Pearl. We have a love for each other that can't be explained. We may not see each other for a year but we pick up just like we saw each other the day before. In fact, I helped Shorty and Ella design their house. I drew up the plans and he paid me with tickets to some NCAA playoff games. I really miss your daddy. Johnnie's mom passed away about seven years ago, and Shorty really helped me deal with her loss."

"It is a pleasure to meet you, I'll make sure to let mom know I saw you. Your daughter and I were reviewing some plans that she has promised to have done later today. I'm really impressed by her knowledge. She must take after you, Mr. Fulton."

I can feel Johnnie staring daggers at my head. If looks could kill I would be graveyard dead.

"Are the plans for your house, Jackie?"

"No sir, they are for a friend of mine, Adaris Singleton."

"Dair Singleton is one of my favorite new school football players. I am delighted he chose our firm to develop his house plans. I know Johnnie will do her best for your friend, won't you honey? Now young ladies, please excuse me, I have a meeting. Jackie, tell Ella that Skip says hello!"

"*You* are Skip Fulton? My dad had some hilarious stories about the two of you growing up—he used to call you Skip to my Lu! Now I can put a face to the name. Oh, and thank you for the delicious Edible Arrangement. Mom really loved it."

"Your dad and I got into quite a bit of trouble in our young days," he said with a chuckle. "And sending that fruit was the least I could do. I have got to run. Johnnie, make sure you cut 20% off Dair's bill. If he is a friend of Jackie's, he is family. Have a good day, ladies." He bows to us slightly and walks out the door.

"Jackie, tell Adaris I will have the plans to him by 5:00. Since you are family, you can also tell him to delete my personal number from his phone," Johnnie says, now wearing a sincere grin.

"I will give him both messages. Thanks for working with me Johnnie.

"After seeing the message he sent me, what else is a girl to do?"

"When did he send you a message?"

"Oh, I got it the moment you walked in with that big ass hickey on your neck. Message received."

I leave Johnnie's office and head to the grocery store. I have a sudden urge to do some baking, which I usually only do for two reasons: Christmas and stress. Since Christmas was over months ago, I guess I'm feeling stressed.

My mom is out again when I get home, so I get busy in the kitchen and grab a snack for lunch. After a few hours I have a huge pile of chocolate chip cookies, a sour cream pound cake, brownies, and some pralines. I decide to take a break and call Serena to see what she is up to.

"Hello!"

"Hey sis, it's Jackie. What are you doing?"

"Hey sis, I'm cooking sausage links, fried rice, and fried okra. And keeping one eye on your nephew. He is supposed to be studying his Algebra."

"That's an interesting fusion of food. Creole and Asian?

"Yeah girl, I call it Creasian. You should try it sometime."

"I'll take your word for it."

"What are you doing? I hear some pans banging around."

"Baking. I just took a pound cake out of the oven and am about to put in some banana bread."

"Is the team having a bake sale already? Daddy used to hate trying to raise money. You remember that year he decided to do a fish fry and a bake sale at the same time. He and his friend "Captain" fried the fish and, and he made you do all the baking while Mom and I wrapped it all in pretty packages. That was the best fundraiser ever!"

"Yeah I remember. I didn't want to bake for a long time after that. But I'm not worried yet about fundraising, I'm too worried about my first meeting with the kids. It's three weeks away and I have no idea what I'm going to say."

"That's why you are doing all that baking. You must be on edge. What are you gonna do with it all?"

"I am going to take some of it to the Fellowship of Christian Athlete and the Habitat for Humanity offices. I'm also going to save some for Adaris."

"So how's that going little sister? Are you two going steady yet?"

"Well, he did ask me to spend more time with him. I really like him more and more every time I see him. He is sweet, sexy, and smart. But I'm nervous what he'll think when he finds out about me coaching."

"Ahh, the three S's. A man with the three S's is hard to come by," Serena says.

"Oh, and I didn't tell you that he's building a new home in Nashville and has somehow convinced me to work with his architect to help him design it. Do you remember daddy telling us stories about his friend Skip Fulton? He owns the architectural firm Adaris is using."

"So you met the infamous Skip, huh? I kinda thought he was a figment of daddy's imagination. But seriously, now that you two are playing house, don't you think it's time to tell your 'husband' about your new occupation? You are running out of time..."

"Honestly, I just don't know what to do at this point. By the way, what I do know is that our mother has been acting awfully strange lately. She goes out at about the same time on Monday, Wednesday, and Friday."

"Didn't you ask her where she's going? Maybe out to the gravesite to check on daddy's headstone?"

"Who would go to the gravesite three times a week. I'm not really sure why people go at all. Daddy aint there! He is heaven with God."

"I bet Mom would tell you where's she's going if you ask her. How do you think she really is doing Jackie? I talk to her every day but I can't see her face. She seems to be dealing with daddy's death pretty well. I just never thought he would die of cancer and it still hurts like hell. I can't imagine how Mom must feel."

"You don't think she's doing anything crazy do you?"

"Ella! Of course not. Mom has more sense even at her worst than most people have at their best. Ask her Jackie, but remember, she is your mother, not your child. I gotta run. My Creasian is almost done and I think

Jordan is texting under the table. I'll call you later. I want to hear what's going on with Max and Keeva."

"I plan to call Max when we get off the phone. As for Keeva, she told me the other day that she is thinking about becoming a nun 'cuz she hasn't had none in so long."

"Now that is some Bruce, Bruce funny shit right there. What did you say when she told you that nonsense?"

"I told her she is too old and tarnished to even think about being a nun. Can you believe that heifer had the nerve to get offended and hang up on me!"

"Tell the nun hello for me and give Mom a big hug when she comes in from her outing. I love you sis."

"I love you back."

I get off the phone, mix up a batch of fudge, and dial Max's number. She has been awful quiet lately, which tells me she has been up to something she isn't ready to talk about. I can't wait to probe and make her uncomfortable. Let the cussing begin!

"Hallo."

"Hey Max. It's Jackie. I haven't talked to you since you got back from Tennessee. What's going on?"

"Hey bitch. I could sense that you were going to call today. Why is it that you always call at the strangest time? Don't you Negro Americans sing some hymn about not coming but coming on time?"

"You my dear are also an American and of Negro heritage. And the phrase is, 'He may not come when you want him but he's right on time.' Are you comparing me to God?"

"Lord I hope not, because after what I did, you may just strike me down. I am still trying to recover from it all—"

"Wait a minute, stop the presses. What are you saying Max?"

"I am saying that Chris came here last week and turned St. Croix upside down. He had my mom, my sister, and everyone else on this island eating out of his hand. And he rocked my world. Now I know why they call him World."

"Are you going to give me the Cliff notes or the whole story?"

"Your virginal ears can't take the whole story. Just know that I have got his nose wide open and he had some other things of mine wide open and I really like him but I didn't tell him because he already has a big head...literally."

"Uh, I can't tell if that was supposed to be nice or nasty. You obviously aren't ready to discuss this, are you?"

"Ok, I like him a lot and I'm flying up to Orlando to meet him in two weeks. He has never been to Disney so we'll spend time there together. I aint too excited about seeing that damn mouse but the snake will be great."

"What? I don't really understand a word you are saying. Just tell me you're ok and are happy and I will get off the phone."

"I am still limping but I am just fine."

"Alright, call me after you finish riding the teacups Minnie. I love you."

"I love you too. And remember, Small World!"

I get off the phone and start on a batch of vanilla cupcakes with chocolate icing. Between the Creasian and the Disney characters, I am just as confused as I was before I started. And where in the heck is Ella!

I get a text message from Jackie saying that everything worked out ok with Johnnie and that the revised floor plan will be delivered to my assistant's office before 5:00. I text her a quick thank you before I go in to finish my tests. I hate this part of my work. They test you for everything, including drugs and steroids. Over the last few years signs of arthritis in some of my joints has become more pronounced, but what should I expect after playing football since age eight. Sometimes I am amazed I can even walk. That's one reason I'm so glad AJ has decided to play basketball, it's just not as hard on your body.

I finally finish around 4:00 that afternoon, and I see I have a text from Jackie asking if I can meet her later on. I want to have dinner with AJ and my mom and hang out with them for a little while, so I tell her to meet me at my hotel room around 9:00. I'm happy Jackie is actually asking to spend time with me. Lord knows I have been trying to take it slow, but when I see her my future flashes before my eyes. I still don't think she is aware she's designing her own dream house. I see marriage and babies and am excited about introducing Jackie to my mom and AJ really soon. But I want her to get used to me being around first. I'm thinking that over dinner tonight I might test the waters of talking about her with my family.

I pull up in front of my mom's house and notice an unfamiliar car. I figure my mom must have company and don't think much about it. Now that AJ is old enough to look out for himself, I have been encouraging Mom to spend more time with her friends and to think about dating. I can't believe I said that, but I really wanted her to be happy and she is still very young. She had me when she was only 19.

I walk into the house and hear a voice I haven't heard up close in about 10 years. I stop to make sure I am not hallucinating. The voice I hear is that of my baby's momma. My first love. The one who broke my heart for the first time. The woman who has been a constant disappointment to her son and to me. It is none other than my ex-girlfriend Lisa. I'm reminded how irritating her voice is, several octaves too high, like she never hit puberty. Nails on a chalk board irritating. As I'm wondering how I can back pedal out of the room without anyone noticing I was there, I hear AJ call out, "Pops, is that you?" I am actually a little pissed that neither he nor my mom had called to tell me that she is back.

I still have a lot of anger toward Lisa. She has missed out on most of AJ's life, swooping in only when he began his cancer treatments or when he begged her to come to one of his sporting events. AJ became so uncomfortable going to her house in California that he begged me not to make him go anymore. I had primary custody and knew she wouldn't have a leg to stand on if she took me back to court, so I decided it was time to let AJ decide what he wanted to do during the summer. As long as I didn't ask Lisa for the child support the judge had ordered her to pay, she kept her mouth shut.

Over the last few years, AJ has seen his mother and half-brother Noah sporadically. Somehow he and Noah have managed to build a great relationship. Noah actually spends time with AJ in Tennessee during the summer and holidays. Despite my feelings about his mother, I love

159

Noah and treat him like he is my own child, and my mom treats him like a grandson.

Lisa and I get along by communicating through our son, and I can't figure out why a woman I haven't seen in ten years is sitting in my mother's kitchen, eating my collard greens and fried chicken. AJ gives me a cross between a stunned and a scared look when he meets me in the kitchen. Something tells me the shit is about to hit the fan and that my life is about to be altered in a big way.

I walk over to the breakfast nook, and there sits Lisa and my mom talking as if they do it every day...except that my mom has this look on her face like she is about to throw up, and Lisa is looking as pleased as punch.

"Hello Lisa, what brings you to Tennessee?"

"I guess no hugs from you, huh Dair? I came over so I could see my son and Ms. Katherine."

"You haven't been back to Tennessee in years. What's going on and where is Noah?"

"Noah is at my parent's house. I didn't want to bring him over until I finished talking with you and Ms. Katherine and seeing AJ. I swear he looks more like you every year, Dair. If I didn't carry him for nine months I would think you spit him out yourself."

"So why are you at my mother's house? We could have brought AJ over to your folks' place."

"Dad, wait until you hear what Mom is doing," AJ says with a huge grin on his face.

"Spit it out Lisa. I came home to hang out with my family and relax."

"I see you want to skip the pleasantries Dair. Well, I decided to move back home for a while. California is not the best place to raise Noah and I miss my AJ. I want to spend more time with him before he goes off to college."

"Isn't that cool, Pops! Mom will be here in Tennessee so she can come to all of my games and I can spend more time with Noah. She even said she'll try to get Noah into my school next year!"

"That is cool son. I am excited that you and Noah can spend more time together. Do me a favor. Take my bag up to my room and then call Noah to see what he's up to. I need to talk to Granny and your Mom for a few minutes."

"OK dad," AJ says while running up the stairs two at a time.

"I think I'll go watch some TV," my mom says. "It was, well it was good...I am glad you made it home safely, Lisa."

"I am so glad to see you too Ms. Katherine. I plan to spend as much time as I can with AJ so you will probably see me quite a bit."

"Well, next time you be sure to call before you come over. I know you have been gone a long time, but you need to be mindful of your manners," Katherine says with a huff, then she walks out of the kitchen.

My mom is quiet but lethal. In that one sentence she told me she had no idea Lisa was coming and she also gave Lisa a tongue lashing.

I fold my arms across my chest and say, "The audience is gone now, Lisa. Why don't you tell me what you're really doing home?"

"I have decided to move back to Tennessee. My parents are starting to get older, Noah is at an age where he needs to be in a more stable environment, and I want to see AJ as much as possible. I really want to just start over."

"AJ is 16. Do you think that moving home now will improve your relationship? You have been absent from his life for, let me see...oh yeah, like his entire life."

"I would think you'd be glad to have me share in some of the responsibility of raising AJ. A boy needs his mother."

"That boy *needed* his mother. He's a teenager now and he needs his father to teach him how to be a man and the support of good friends. He has both here. So cut the bullshit Lisa and tell me what you want."

"I want to undo all the mistakes I made. I want to have a great relationship with AJ. I want him and his brother to see each other more than twice a year. I want to restart my career. But most of all I want you and me to become friends again," Lisa says while walking closer to me and putting her hand on my shoulder.

"Don't touch me Lisa. The time for you to worry about our friendship was 14 years ago when you walked away from your child and me without a backward glance. If AJ hadn't gotten sick you would never have given a damn about him. So I'm asking you again, what do you want?"

"I want our family back! I want you to give me a chance to show you that I have changed. That I can be what you needed me to be 14 years ago. I realize that I made a huge mistake and prayed that if I could ever make things right with you I would."

"You are crazy! You are trying to make things work with the wrong man. I didn't know what I wanted at 16, but at 32 I damn well know I don't want you!"

Lisa is moving her hands down my chest. "Don't you miss me Dair?"

"Get your hands off me! And no, I don't miss you. You don't miss what you never had. Focus on loving our son. He's the only man you need to take care of in this house."

I turn and bellow up the stairs, "AJ, your mom is getting ready to go. Come down and say goodbye." Then I turn back to Lisa and say, "Remember what Mom said. Call before you come the next time." Then I walk out of the room.

I go upstairs to take a shower and cool off from my confrontation with Lisa. I'm still a little shocked. Lisa's timing is unbelievable and I still can't process the idea that I have fallen in serious like with my son's deceased coach's daughter and now my baby's mammy has returned home like the prodigal daughter. She is still beautiful, and she still expects everyone to bow down to her. I can't help but compare her to

Jackie. There is no way Jackie would abandon her child and then come back after 14 years as if she never left. It feels like the same ole crap with Lisa has come back to haunt me. But, we will be in each other's lives for a long time to come, so we need to learn how to co-exist. But, as usual, her timing sucks.

After I get out of the shower I hear some pots banging in the kitchen and I figure it must be AJ eating again. This seems to be a good time to talk to him and see how he is taking the news of his mother's abrupt return. I slowly walk down the stairs to gather my thoughts. Sixteen year olds are peculiar. I figure I will play it cool to see what direction the conversation heads.

"What's up son?"

"Hey Pops, want me to fix you a plate?"

"Bet. What pieces are left?"

"I left you some thighs and some wings. That's a trip about Ma coming home, aint it?"

"Isn't it? For so long I wanted her here to help Granny and me raise you. But now that you're 16, I just don't know."

"It's pretty dope that Mom is back. But you, me, and Granny kind of got our own routine going Pops. But at least Noah and I can really hang out now."

"It is definitely cool that Noah is here. It's cool you have a brother. That is something I really miss. I guess that's why Shelley and World are so important to me."

"I just don't want you to be mad at Moms. I know you don't really like the way she does things at times, but I don't have any beef with her. I had you and Granny. Noah needed her more than me. Now that she is here, I can throw a little love her way and watch out for my little brother."

"Son, you are wise beyond your years. I guess in a way Noah did need your mom a little more than you did growing up. I want you to carve out how your relationship with your Mom will change. I have been resentful of your mom in the past, but the thing I hoped for the most has come to fruition. She is home to spend more time with you."

"So what did she say to you Pops? It sounds like it got a little heated down here."

"Not much, son. I wanted your mom to understand that I am glad she is home for your sake, but that our conversations from here on out would only involve you, and Noah if she needs any help with him."

"So there is no chance of the two of you hooking up again, Pops?"

"Son, I will always love your mom because she gave me you. But any chances of us getting back together are gone. I want you to understand that you can spend time with her whenever you want, but just know that those grades better stay at a B or higher and that you better do what your new coach asks you to do. This is a very important year for you and your team. A lot of people will be watching to see what happens to the Tennessee Dream Team now that Coach D is gone. And you'll have more college teams watching than ever before, which can be a blessing or a curse. Don't block your blessings, my boy."

"I feel you, Dad, you aint got to worry about your boy's grades falling or me not listening to the new coach. I want to get a scholarship in two years, and no chicken heads are going to mess that up."

"Son, I hope to God that when you go out in public you don't talk like that. I understand you throwing slang but make sure it's with me or your friends and not your teachers or coaches! Part of being scouted by schools is your ability to communicate. And don't get too comfortable with me either boy, you feel me?"

"I feel, I mean, I got it Pops. After I clean up the kitchen I'm gonna call Noah again. We need to get our game plan together for this weekend. If we are in the same school next year I'll have to make sure no one messes with my little brother because he will be fresh meat!"

"You are growing up. See you later son. I'm going to run out for a while."

"Hmm...another reason why you are kicking Moms to the curb, right dad?" AJ says with a big chuckle.

164

"Mind yours son, and I will mind mine," I say, laughing over my shoulder as I head out to meet Jackie.

After talking with Serena I start making some chess pie squares, which are her favorite. I'll pack them up tonight and ship them to her tomorrow. My mom has a lot of baskets left over from the flowers she received when Dad died, so I gather up four, cut up all the sweets, and divide them among the baskets. In the smallest one I put a sample of each item for my mom. I'll deliver the others tomorrow.

One basket is for Adaris. I know today was rough for him. I tuck in a few cupcakes, some pralines, about a dozen cookies, a few pieces of banana bread, and some chess squares, along with a note that reads, *"Sweets for one of the sweetest persons I have ever met. Thanks for being so sweet to me."*

By the time I finish packing everything, Mom comes downstairs. She has been home for a while but went to her room to take a nap.

"Wow, baby girl, you really showed out with the baking today."

"I know. Once I got started I just couldn't stop. I know you don't eat a lot of sweets, but I have samples of everything for you over there."

"Thanks baby. I think I might fix myself a cup of coffee and taste a few. You want to join me?"

"No, I'm going to run out to meet a friend."

"I was wondering who the extra baskets full of goodies are for, but I guess you aren't ready to tell me yet, are you?"

"It's complicated mom. But you will be one of the first to know. I just hope this one doesn't bite me in the ass."

"Well, have a good time and please be careful. After I drink this coffee and eat these chess squares I'll probably be up all night bouncing off the walls."

"See you later mom. I love you!"

As I head over to the Hutton to meet Jackie, I decide to check in with World. I haven't talked to him since he left town. I hoped to see him in

New York, but when I got there he was in St. Croix. I need to bounce a few things off him, so I connect my cell to the Blue Tooth in my Rover and dial his number.

"What's up Dair? I was going to holla at you this week."

"I just finished my physical today and I am so glad it's over. What's up with you man?"

"I just got back in town a few days ago from hollering at Max."

"How was it man?"

"You know I hate to be sensitive and shit since everything went down with the ex, but I am really feeling Max, man. I got a chance to meet her folks and just chill with her a few days. She is mad cool, man, crazy smart, and sexy as hell. And her feet! I didn't want to leave her."

"How are you going to manage a long distance relationship?"

"We plan to meet in Orlando in a few weeks. I always wanted to go to Disney World and I figure my first time should be with her. I also plan to fly her up here as much as her schedule will allow. She's really independent so we had to have a long discussion about me paying for her to travel. I know she does well teaching and practicing law but, well, you know..."

"Yeah I know. It's nice that you were able to discuss it. Most women would make the assumption that you are going to bankroll all of your outings."

"What's going on with you Dair?"

"Man, you won't believe who just moved back to town?"

"Who man?"

"My baby's momma. I haven't seen her in almost ten years and have barely talked to her over the phone. Then she just shows up at my mom's house sitting at the kitchen table like she used to do when we were teenagers."

"Was she fat as hell with thin hair and sagging titties? At least tell me she was busted."

166

"She was just as beautiful tonight as she was years ago. She is a little curvier, but the years have been good to her. Can you believe she told me she wanted to give us another chance?"

"Hell yeah, I can believe it man. Why do you think she came home? She knows that anytime she wants to see her child, you will make it happen. She sees the dollar signs man. Her ex must either be broke or not paying his child support. Not that you are ugly or anything..."

"Thanks World. I think. I told her we need to keep our relationship focused on our child. But I know how Lisa is. She has a trick up her sleeve."

"She can't do what you don't allow. Besides, she doesn't have a chance with Jackie around. Jackie is still around, isn't she?"

"That is moving slow but it's moving. I have her so busy helping me build our future house that she doesn't have a clue I'm sneaking in on her."

"Like a thief in the night! That's my boy. Look, I gotta run. I am doing two a days to get back on track from my trip. I exercised but I didn't work out, if you get my drift. Holla at me next week. We need to hook up before we start the pre-season."

"Alright man. Take care."

I pull up at the Hutton, check the mileage on the Rover, look at the valet and say, "It looks like about 67,250 miles my man. Take good care of her."

His face gets real red as he mumbles, "Yes sir, I will pull her right around the corner."

"You do that, my man," I say, and hand him a generous tip.

I walk up to the room, put a stopper at the bottom of the door, and lay on the couch with the lights down low. I just wanted to relax until Jackie gets there and try to tune out football, the house, and Lisa.

I'm not sure how long I've been lying there when I hear a light tap at the door.

167

"It's open!"

I can smell Jackie as soon as she walks into the room. I keep my eyes closed just so I can remember her unique scent on those days when I can't see her.

"Adaris, why are you sitting in the dark?"

"If you need the light, turn it on. If not, come join me on the couch."

"I am good without it, ouch! I think I just tripped over your shoes."

"Turn the light on sweetness. I forgot you were clumsy."

"Scoot over and let me sit down. Why don't you put your head in my lap and let me see if I can relax you."

"Oh baby, thanks. It's been a day from hell. What is that smell? I smell something sweet."

"Dang Ray Wonder. You got the smell sense working like a mother. I brought you some sweets I baked this afternoon."

"Don't tell me what they are. Grab a few and feed them to me. There is nothing sexier than eating something sweet in the dark."

"Is this the negro remake of *Nine and a Half Weeks?*"

"I am going to try to keep this G rated tonight. I don't have the energy to do the nasty."

"Wow, you really had a bad day. Pick up your big head so I can sit down."

Adaris moves down on the couch so I can sit at the end. I put his head on a pillow in my lap and lay the basket on his chest.

"Now tell me what is going on," I say, removing Adaris' glasses and massaging his temples.

"Can I have just one kiss first? It will warm my lips up for the surprise you brought for me."

"Don't move."

I lean over Adaris, grab both sides of his head, and kiss his forehead. Then I move down to kiss each eye, then his nose, and I end with a gentle, lingering kiss on his lips. I slip my tongue slowly into his mouth and licked from side to side.

"Umm, what flavor do we have today?" Adaris whispers against my lips as he grabs my ponytail.

"Today's flavor is green apple golden pineapple."

"I like it, but I have a feeling I am going to like what is sitting on my chest even better."

"Why don't you tell me what happened to you today while I feed you."

"I need a few bites before I start talking." Adaris settles himself more comfortably against my lap, turns his head, and nuzzles his lips against my stomach. Thank God for pushups! He inhales deeply and says, "Mmm, you smell so good."

"Thanks. Now turn around so I can start feeding you. Open your mouth."

Adaris obeys like a baby bird and I slip a morsel into his mouth. He bites down before I can move my fingers away and gently sucks on them.

"Damn, I don't know what tastes better, that cookie or your finger. Give me another bite."

"Adaris...you said you weren't going to seduce me, so stop sucking on my fingers. Now tell me!"

"Ok, that was something with a chocolate chip, peanut butter, some vanilla, and a pecan. Yum, that was good. More."

"Another bite only after you tell me what happened today," I say.

"AJ's mom moved back to Tennessee today. And ouch!"

"Oh sorry. I didn't mean to squeeze your head. Did you just tell me your son's mother just moved to Tennessee?"

"Yes. Now give me another bite, please, I need it after that admission."

"As long as it's not an admission of guilt, here you go," I say as I slip him a piece of a chess square.

"My God! What was that? I want another bite, please!"

"Oh no, not until you tell me more."

Adaris moves his head back to my stomach and gives it another wet kiss.

"I walked into the house after a full day of doctors pushing, prodding, poking, and picking on me. I was looking forward to spending some time with my mom and son and then seeing you. I heard her voice before I saw her. I swear, it was like fingernails on a chalkboard. I have talked to her briefly over the years about our son, but I hadn't seen her in almost ten years. Now can I have another bite please?"

"Here you go. What do you think this is?"

"I taste bananas. Is that banana bread? Hit me with another shot of potassium please? So, she is sitting at my mom's table like they are long lost buddies. Except my mom looked like something stank and AJ looked confused. Another bite please."

"So what did you do?" I say as I offer him a sip of milk.

"That milk is so good. Please don't tell me you got it from a cow in your back yard. I swear, you are a keeper. Anyhow, I sent AJ upstairs to call his brother Noah and I asked her what she was really up to."

"Please tell me you don't have another son," I say, spilling milk on Adaris' chin.

"Sweetness, don't drown me with the milk. Noah is Lisa's son. He donated his bone marrow for AJ's bone marrow transplant. I only have one son that I know of—ouch, did you just squeeze my temple again? You are supposed to be relaxing and nourishing me, baby, not pinching on me."

"Sorry, but either you are moving too fast or all this baking is making me slow. Open up for another bite." I put a piece of the Praline in his mouth.

"Ummm, now that's what I call a Praline. Lean down and give me some more sugar," Adaris says, grabbing my head for a quick sugary kiss.

"That Praline does taste good. I rarely eat my sweets. By the time I finish I can't stand to look at them. So then what happened?"

"I will eat your sweets any time, baby. I asked Lisa why she really moved home. She said something about wanting Noah to be close to his grandparents and brother, needing help with him, and me—"

"Wait a minute." After that comment I lean over and set the milk on the table. "Did you say 'me'? I thought she was married."

"Damn, you just smushed my head again. Yes, I said me. She has been divorced for a few years now and she wants us to be friends again. Can you believe that shit? She hasn't said more than five sentences to me in almost ten years and tonight she says she wants to be a family again."

"What did you say?"

"I aint saying nothing else until I get another bite and you promise not to keep abusing me."

I put the vanilla cupcake up to his mouth and he takes a bite.

"You changed the recipe! I fell in love with the cupcakes from the picnic and you changed the recipe. That is the bomb!"

"What did you say Adaris?"

"I told her that the only communication we would have is about our child. Then I told her to call the next time before she came over. I swear, I need to get my house built as soon as possible. I can't tell Mom who to let in her house, but I sure as hell can keep her off my own property. Milk please."

As I give Adaris more milk, I wonder what the future will bring. I have heard nightmares about baby's mommas. With AJ's mom moving back to Tennessee, not only would Adaris see her more but so would I, and very soon. I suddenly feel like my world is tilting in the other direction. Then Adaris nestles his head further into the pillow on my lap, puts his arms around me, and kisses my stomach again.

"Thanks for my treats, sweetness. What did you put in these things? I should be bouncing off the wall after all that sugar but I feel like you gave me a sleeping pill. Will you stay for a while just like this?"

"I'll stay until you go to sleep. Just relax. We both had a rough day."

"I want to hear about your day, baby. And I want to talk about the house plan..."

"Adaris?" Damn, I just put him to sleep. I am running out of time to reveal my little secret. I sit there for another half hour, rubbing Adaris' head. As his breathing gets heavier my apprehension rises. When I was sure Adaris was in a deep sleep, I slowly move out from under him. I find a blanket and another pillow in the closet, so I ease the pillow under his head, cover him with the blanket, give him a gentle kiss on the lips, and head back to the Plantation. Lisa's move back to Tennessee has thrown another wrinkle into our already complicated and fragile friendship. I have a lot to think about...

The next morning I wake up about 7:00. As I lie there getting my bearings, I realize that I have fallen asleep on the couch in my hotel room. The last thing I remember is my head in Jackie's lap and her feeding me the most delicious desserts. I look around and see that I am lying on two pillows with a blanket over me. On the table beside me I see a basket with desserts in it. And a card. I read the note and smile. Jackie thinks I am sweet. I think she is amazing. Even after her rough day she took the time to listen to me vent about Lisa. She baked for me. And she put my ass right to sleep like a baby. I haven't slept this well in months. I slowly get up, stretch, and then grab my phone to send her a text.

"Thanks for rocking me to sleep with your sweet treats and your sweet kisses. I hope you have a wonderful day. It's my turn to listen to your story. Make time for me on Friday evening...Dair.

Before I know it, March is gone and it's the end of April. Things with Adaris have been going great. I have been impressed by his willingness to move slowly—I can imagine that most of his relationships went from 0 to 100 in a matter of hours. Still, in the back of my mind I wonder if he is spending his time with one of the five, since we have decided to wait to become intimate. It is not easy. In fact, it is becoming harder to resist him every time I see him. Adaris is charming, loving, giving, and modest. We talk very little about work, and a lot about our hopes and dreams for a future.

I also find myself sharing my feelings about the loss of my father and the pressure I feel to be the protector for my mom and my brother.

The construction on Adaris' house has started and the coaching job is looming like a dark cloud over my head. Before I know it I have just a few days before my meeting with the parents and the team. Principal Leevins and I have discussed our game plan. I still haven't found the time to talk with Adaris about it. I take that back, I still haven't found the nerve to talk to Adaris. For the life of me I can't figure out why talking to him makes me feel so nervous. I don't think he will judge me or be mad, but I am a little fearful of what will happen to our relationship once he finds out.

The meeting

Principal Leevins and I meet with the team and their parents to discuss my position today. I'm at the school walking to the meeting when I run into Scoop's mom, Ms. Stevens.

"Hey Jackie. How are you doing child? I haven't seen you since, well, you know..."

"Since my dad's funeral."

"Yeah baby, since then. I have been waiting for this meeting for a while. Ever since Coach Donovan got sick, things have not been right with this team. Coach Frazier did ok, but there is something about him that just aint right. That man aint wrapped too tight," Ms. Stevens says with a frown.

I don't comment on her remark, but I agree wholeheartedly. I start thinking back to when Dad started declining, and Serena and I happened to be home at the same time. We made a pact that one of us would be with Mom as much as possible to help her with dad's care. Coach Frazier came to visit Dad throughout the last season. They would review game tape and Coach Frazier would solicit Dad's advice. It was a great way to keep Dad involved with his players. After Coach Frazier left, daddy would rub his head; roll his eyes and say, "it's got to be because that boy is from Chattanooga. You know those Brainerd and Howard High boys aren't wrapped too tight." As Daddy started to get weaker, Mom starting limiting his visits with Frazier because she could see they took too much of Dad's energy.

One day Serena was with Dad in the Shack. He was so weak by then that he only spoke when absolutely necessary. He spent most of his time sleeping. He would wake up from time to time and we would get him to drink his favorite drink which was pineapple orange juice that week, and eat if he was hungry. I know beyond a shadow of a doubt that he heard every word that was said even right before he died. Coach Frazier came to see Dad without calling first, and Serena let him in. I was up in the kitchen cooking dinner when I noticed that Frazier was down in the Shack. I felt a sudden chill— not the chill of the death angel but the pissed off chill.

I greeted Coach Frazier and plopped down on the couch. My sister was sitting in my dad's chair. You know the chair that every man in the house has that is his chair only. This chair happened to be a deluxe, leather, remote controlled massage chair. As soon as my butt hit the couch, my cell phone dinged that I had a text message. I saw that it was from Serena. Now mind you I am sitting so close to Serena that I can smell the Lemonheads that she is currently smacking on in her mouth. I looked up at her and realized why it was so cold in the room. Her message said, "*I m redy for his ass 2 leave!*" Now, I assumed that his ass was Coach Frazier, but I was a little confused so I texted her back and asked, "*who?*" Meanwhile, Coach Frazier was talking about his kids. From time to time my sister says, "um hum" or really. Instead of answering me back with a text message Serena decides to go the sign language route and looks over at Coach Frazier and cuts her eyes at him. Since I am not too good at sign language I decide to go back to texting and I say, "*wht hppnd?*" She texted back, "*the MF is askg bout dad's cncr n f we had stpd dng trtmnts n if Hspc was cmng. I tld the MF he can hear u.*" Now I was pissed off too. When we brought dad home from the hospital, we posted a note on the basement door that said, "Please enter Shorty's Shack with a positive attitude and a prayerful spirit." Apparently Frazier failed to read it. But who comes into a room where the patient is and talks about cancer and hospice? When the doctor told us that there were no other treatment options my dad made the decision to come home for the rest of the time God gave him on earth. We decided that if he had 2 days or 2 years left we would make that time as positive and as peaceful as we could in his comfort zone. Although Hospice had been called in we decided not to speak of Hospice to each other or to him. The connotation of Hospice is often death and as long as he was alive we were going to speak life. Now this ding bat came in and singlehandedly blew peace right out the door. Daddy always said Frazier was stuck on stupid.

Coach sat there for a few more minutes and then finally said, "Well, I guess I better go now." Serena replied to Frazier, "I think that would be a great idea. The next time you want to visit, Coach, you should call first. instead of dropping in, and did you happen to see the sign on the door before you knocked?"

"What sign? "He said with a dumbfounded look on his face. As he gets up to leave, he leans over my dad in his hospital bed and says, "Coach, I appreciate everything you have done for me. You have taught me a lot about the game of basketball and life. I will never forget all you have done for me. I love you."

At this point, I am literally begging Serena with my eyes not to get up and choke the life out of him. I had even sent a text saying *"don't choke him"* with a sad face for good measure. If that isn't a farewell speech I don't know what is. Serena jumped up, herded him to the door, and literally hit him in the back with it as he was leaving.

A funny thing happened that night well after Frazier had left and Mom and I went to bed. One of us always slept in the room with dad during those last few days. In the back of our minds we knew that each moment he decided to say something or even do something would be precious. Serena decided since she was leaving the next day to head back to Chicago for a few days she would sleep downstairs with my dad. As she was sitting there watching TV, she just happened to look over at my dad. He looked at her with eyes as clear as could be and said to her with the sweetest smile, "You are going to be just fine." Then he closed his eyes and went back to sleep. I guess that was his way of telling her I know Coach Frazier is ignorant but no matter what comes your way when I am gone, you are going to be ok.

"Jackie, Jackie, baby, are you ok. You look like you are in another world," says Ms. Stevens, waving a hand in front of my face.

"Sorry Ms. Stevens, I was thinking about something just then. Now what were you saying?"

"I was saying that I am glad you are here. I bet you are just as anxious as we are to hear who will be replacing your father. Coach Leevins has been so tight lipped about it. I heard that Leevins received over 125 resumes from all over the country and that Coach Frazier and the JV coach don't even know who has been chosen for the job. Your family must be so proud of your dad's wonderful legacy. I would love someone to step into his shoes that can really help these boys advance to the next level. If we have another season with Coach Frazier at the helm, I am afraid recruiters are going to stop looking."

"Ms. Stevens, I am sure that whomever Principal Leevins chooses will be well qualified for the job. But you shouldn't expect them to immediately make the same impact as my dad. He had more than 25 years to turn water into wine." I'm feeling a bit sneaky by this point.

"Scoop doesn't have time for no fermentation. He is a senior and I need this coach to be able to pop his cork without getting any stuck in the bottle, if you know what I mean," she says with a chuckle.

"I gotta run Ms. Stevens. I need to use the ladies' room before the meeting starts." I suddenly feel I might be sick...

I walk into the gym and see that most of the boys and their parents are talking quietly. Well, the boys actually are in a corner laughing and punching each other the way boys do. I say a quick hello to everyone then

176

sit down next to my mother. Funny, but no one seems to think it's odd that my mother and I are here. I guess they assume we're curious about who will be replacing my father. Just then, Adaris and AJ walk in, and I feel as if someone has just sucked the air out of the room. My goodness, he is a specimen The women are openly gawking. AJ joins the guys in the corner and Adaris walks right over to me and Ella.

"Hello Mrs. Donovan," he says, giving mom a big hug. "I didn't know I would see you here tonight. It's great to see you."

"Hello Adaris. I am just as excited about the news as anyone else here. When are you coming by the house to have dinner with me again?"

"When you ask me to come Ms. Ella. I can't wait to eat some more of your potato salad."

Then Adaris turns to me and says, "Hello Jackie. It's great to see you again as well."

"Again? When have you two seen each other since daddy's funeral?" Ella looks at us with a puzzled look.

"Uh, we've run into each other a few times since then Mom. It's good to see you too, Adaris."

"I better take a seat back here. The last time we had a meeting, Scoop's mom cornered me in the hallway and talked to me about him for 30 minutes," Adaris says with a laugh and then walks away.

"Jackie...Jacqueline Coretta Donovan, will you stop looking at him like he is a pork chop."

"What Mom? What did you say?"

"What I said is now I know why you have been doing all that baking. The look was written all over your faces," Ella whispers in my ear. "Please tell me you told him about your interim appointment?"

"I didn't tell him Mom! This man has been wining and dining me for over two months and I have been baking and caking him and I just couldn't find the time to tell him."

"Well, my child, there is no time like the present. While you are over there explaining what you plan to do this season, I am going to be over here praying...I must say, that Adaris is a keeper."

"Momma, I need you to do more than pray. I may need you to be my bodyguard after this announcement."

"Here come the principal and Coach Frazier. Take some deep breaths and get yourself together baby."

Principal Leevins calls to the crowd, "Can I have your attention everyone? I promise I won't keep you too long. I called this meeting to announce our interim coach for this next season. I can't tell you how much it pains me to have to make this announcement, as I miss my dear friend Coach Donovan every day. I didn't think I would have to make this announcement for at least another ten years—"

Scoop yells from the back of the room, "Spit it out, Principal Leevins, so we can stop guessing."

"Young man, you obviously forgot your manners over the last few months. You boys sit down and pipe down!"

Pipe down. I haven't heard that term in a long time, I think with a chuckle. I need to add it to my repertoire. Just then I look up and catch Adaris staring at me intensely. All of a sudden he gives me a quick wink and my phone dings to tell me I have a text message. Before I can check my phone, Principal Leevins says, "As I was saying before I was so rudely interrupted, Coach Donovan is deeply missed around our school. He wasn't just a coach but also a friend, mentor, teacher, and father figure to a lot of kids over the years, and I know he would want us to carry on the winning tradition he established over 20 years ago. The person who will replace Coach Donovan for the next year has been playing basketball all her life— high school, college, and professional ball, and she was trained by Coach Donovan."

People have caught the "her" and "she," and are whispering and looking around. The look on Coach Frazier's face shows that he knows he's out and is not happy about it.

Principal Leevins signals to the crowd to settle down and then he says, "It is with much excitement and anticipation that I present to you our new interim coach...Ms. Jacqueline Donovan!"

Well, you could hear a pin drop for about two seconds, and then the proverbial shit hits the fan. It can only be described as about two minutes of pure unadulterated chaos. Coach Frazier puts his head down and I can swear he is wiping away tears. Scoop's mom says, "What the hell! Aint no way Scoop is going to get a college scholarship with this shit." Hector's mom yells out, "Dios mio!'" which I think means "Oh my God!" As Peaches yells, "Does that mean we got a girl coach now?" another player is saying, "That fine ass Jackie is going to be our coach!" I need to make sure I remember that voice because his ass is grass once I get them into practice. Finally Principal Leevins steps in and says again, "Pipe down!" this time addressing the adults as well. "Jackie and I will be happy to address your concerns in an orderly fashion. Jackie, please come up and introduce yourself, and then we can take questions."

I slowly walk to the front of the room and stand beside Principal Leevins. I actually stood about one step behind him just in case I needed to duck behind him if a flying object came my way. I suddenly think about President Bush and the infamous shoe throwing. I give a nervous chuckle and then I clear my throat and say, "My name is Jackie Donovan (and I am an alcoholic). At least that is what I would become as soon as I got out of this room. I have met many of you over the last few years. As Mr. Leevins said, I have loved the game of basketball my entire life. You probably think I didn't have a choice, but I did. Dad never pressured me to play, but I guess it was just in my DNA." I sneak a look at Adaris, who has a blank look on his face. I can't begin to guess what he is thinking, but his eyes have narrowed and those tree trunk arms are crossed over his chest. Focus Jackie, focus!

"At first I wasn't sure I was the right person to coach these young men, but I have watched the tapes and spoken with some of them, and I can see they have the talent and drive to be winners. I want all of the you parents to know that it will be an honor to coach and train your children and that I will not take this opportunity for granted. And I want all of you young men to know I'm looking forward to leading the Bulldogs. I will do my best to honor my father's legacy, but I hope you'll understand that our style of coaching is a little different, so you'll get a little old school but a lot of new school too. Now, I can imagine you have a lot of questions for me."

"Jac, I mean Coach Donovan, I have a question," shouts an older man from the back. "You have never coached before, especially not boys. How are you going to get these young boys to listen to you? And you have no track record—so why should my boy listen to you?"

"I am sorry, sir, I didn't catch your name."

"My name is Mr. Smith. I am Junebug and Big Baby's father."

"Nice to meet you Mr. Smith. It's true I have never coached before, but I have played this sport since I was three years old. My father and my coaches taught me how to pace the game and how to outsmart your opponents and yes, how to win. I believe I can get the boys to listen to me the same way I can get anyone else to—including you parents—by building relationships and earning respect."

"My name is Jordan McCullough and Little Daddy is my boy. I knew your dad for a long time, Jackie, and I have nothing against women coaching, but how in the hell are you going to cope with all the people who will say you can't coach boys?"

"Mr. McCullough, what people say doesn't really bother me. All I can say is that I promise to do my best to teach these young men to be better athletes and better people."

Ms. Stephens stands up next. "Jackie baby, you know who I am."

"Yes Ms. Stephens I do. What is your question?"

"I want to know how you plan to get my baby and some of the rest of these seniors a scholarship to college?"

"Ms. Stephens, it's going to be up to Scoop and the rest of the boys to earn their scholarships. I will guide them and teach them everything I can and we can expose them to college scouts, but they will have to do the rest. This team will have to decide that they want to be winners. Once they do that, I will help them reach their goal."

"Hey Jackie, I got a question for ya," yells Scoop.

"It's Coach Jackie or Coach Donovan, Scoop. Now, what is your question?"

After the snickers quiet down, Scoop says, "Uh, Coach Jackie, when do we get this party started? I mean, when do we get to start practicing with you?"

"We can't start until school is out. I have camps scheduled at the Universities of Tennessee, Kentucky and Vanderbilt. Until they start, you will run the court during sixth period as often as you can and work to stay in shape. Next week you can weigh in and we'll set up your training and eating plans. Official practices will start November 1."

Principal Leevins steps in and says, "OK folks, before we adjourn we will take one more question. If you want to talk with Jackie after tonight, she will be in her office every day from 3:00 to 5:00. You can schedule a meeting with her directly."

"Thanks so much to the parents for being here. I know this is a bit of an awkward time but I think we are going to have a great season. I do want to talk with all of you in the next few weeks about raising money for the booster club so we can send our team to all of the camps I mentioned as well as make sure they have all of the equipment and uniforms that they need. I have someone that has already committed $5,000 to help support the program. You know that will barely put a dent in all that we need. I want to discuss some fundraisers and some potential sponsors."

"I also want to ask for your patience. My dad had this team for more than twenty five years. For those that knew him you also know that it took him a while to build a winning team. I only have a year. And because I only have a year, and because of that our practices will be closed to the public-"

"What the hell do you mean the public? We aint the public we the parents," yelled Ms. Stephens.

I can see that she is going to be a problem. Now I know where Scoop got his mouth from.

"Ms. Stephens, I am aware that you are the parents. I am closing the practices to the parents, the students, the public and the media. I don't want any unnecessary distractions.

As people start filing out of the room, I can't help but look at Adaris again. He has not said one word and looks as cool as a cucumber. Some people stop to congratulate me, others walk past as if I'm not there. A few ask me questions, and Hector's mother comes up to me, makes the sign of the cross, and walks away mumbling "dios mio" again. I can see I won't have to worry about the boys, but the parents are another thing. They are off the chain. Adaris still hasn't budged from his seat, and I fear he will wait for hell to freeze over before he talks to me again.

181

As Scoop takes his exit he leans over and whispers, "I guess whatever I planned to start with you is over now isn't it boo?" After that comment he moves so quick that I'm unable to put him in a choke hold. His mom wouldn't need to worry about him being recruited to college ball. He wouldn't make it that far.

Mom walks up to me looking worried. "Jackie baby, it looks like Adaris is waiting to ask you some questions in private. Since you got yourself into this mess, I am going to let you dig your way out. If all else fails, remember what Aunt D says—rub, pat, and sliiiide... I love you and I am so proud of you. And remember, nothing is too hard for God." Mom beams up at Adaris and scoots out of the room. I am relieved to see that he beamed right back at her. I swear my mom can make any man drool.

I finally get rid of Ms. Stephens—she asked me damn near everything including my shoe size! I don't know how daddy put up with that crap. And she was a breeze compared to the 6-foot-4 arctic chill still sitting at the back of the room. I can feel his eyes raking me up and down, and it's not in an "I think you are sexy look." I suddenly think this might be a good time to seduce him. I mean, balls to the walls stripper pole seduction. But then I remember we are in a high school gym surrounded by the scent of sweaty armpits and feet that smell like Fritos. I can see Adaris isn't budging, so I walk over and gingerly sit down in the seat in front of him.

"I know what you are going to say Adaris!"

He leans forward with narrowed eyes and says, "What am I going to say, Jackie?"

"You are going to say, why didn't you tell me you were going to be coaching my son?"

"No, actually what I was going to say is, why didn't you tell me that you were going to be coaching, period. You told me you moved home to figure out what you are going to do, and the whole time you had already decided to coach."

"I actually didn't decide until a month ago. I just had to deal with so many emotions. Not wanting to disappoint my family. Not wanting to take too big a step too quickly. Still mourning my dad. And then I met you and I knew your son would be on the varsity team. Things were going so well and I just wanted a piece of happiness in my life for the first time in a long time."

"What made you think we couldn't be happy Jackie? All you had to do is talk to me about what was going on, tell me you were thinking of taking this job. Give me a minute to absorb the fact that a piece of my child's future was going to be in the hands of the woman that I have come to care about. What hurts me is that you have been hurling in my face the fact that you don't want me to hurt you, and I have been brutally honest with you about my relationships and my fears and my child...and all the while you have been deceitful. Don't you think I have a right to be upset?"

"Yes. Yes you do. But I didn't tell you because I was afraid that I couldn't handle being your girlfriend and your child's coach. Think about it—I will be spending more time with your child than you do most days, and he doesn't even know that we are seeing each other! Hell, my mom didn't know until she saw the stupid look on my face when you came in the room. So I'm afraid of what we talk about during our time together now, like, why isn't AJ playing as much as he should?"

"I know that Jackie. That is why I am pissed. I had planned to let you meet my mother and AJ in the next few weeks. I really wanted you to get to know the two most important people in my life. I think I can handle balancing things, but I don't know if he can. Now you haven't left me any time to figure it out–get him in another school, give him time to get used to us being together. None of that."

"So what do we do now?"

"I don't know Jackie. I have to adjust to you being a huge influence in my kid's life. AJ will be coming home and talking about you– you praised him and said it was a great practice or you raked him over the coals. Maybe this is a good time to take a break. Let's sleep on it and talk in the next few days. I need to get out of here now and check on AJ. He either is excited because he has the finest coach in the state of Tennessee or is wishing he had gone to Whites Creek."

"That's why I had such a hard time telling you. I knew your answer would be like this." Now I can hear myself whining. "I was just so afraid that you would put us on hold or give up what we have– "

"Yeah, so you can focus on doing your best, and so my son can play without people thinking he has an in because his daddy is sleeping with the coach. Jackie, these people are unforgiving and they will be watching you like a hawk. They will say things that will hurt your feelings, and I would probably try to kick someone's ass for talking about you, AJ included. So maybe I need to keep my distance..."

"But we aren't sleeping together."

With that, Adaris leans over, grabs my hands, and pulls me between his legs. Then he looks up at me and whispers, "We aren't sleeping together *yet*. But in my mind I have slept with you hundreds of times. And we both know it is just a matter of time, sweetness. But this is going to be a pivotal year for both of us, and I want us to be at 100%. I would not want anyone but you to coach my son, because I know you will protect him. Just give me some time to think this out, Jackie." And with that he stands up and gives me a kiss– the kind that says we may not do this again for a while...a goodbye kiss. Then he walks out the door.

I lean over and put my hands on my knees in the universal "I am exhausted" stance. What in the world have I gotten myself into? Have I taken one of the greatest opportunities of my life but pissed away my future with the man I am falling in love with? I pick up a basketball and dribble out to take a shot. As I shoot I remember something my dad used to say to me: "Slim, whatever you do, don't stink up the gym." As I dribble around and take a few more shots, I pray not that I won't stink up the gym but that I won't stink up my life.

After shooting for about an hour I suddenly remember that I don't have a ride home. I dig my phone out of my purse and remember that Adaris sent me a text message right before the big reveal. I check my phone...

"Spearmint gum tonight. I can't wait to taste it."

Damn, damn, damn! I will have to hang on to that text to get me through the lonely nights that are coming up. I call Keeva.

"Hello!"

"Hey girl. I hope I didn't wake you up. Can you come and get me?"

"I was awake. What are you a car rider now? Where is the Beemer and where are you, Jackie?"

"At the SHS gym. We had our meeting tonight to announce me coaching the team. Mom left me here to talk with Adaris, he broke up with me, I shot the lights out, and now I am stuck like Chuck."

"On my way little cuz!"

Just when things seem to be getting better they take a turn for the worse. Jackie and I have been getting along so well. We've broken ground on my house, Lisa has stayed away, AJ and Noah were getting along great...and now I have to deal with this shit. I'm not ready to go home yet, so I decide to ride out to Arrington to check on the house. AJ is out with the guys on his team, so I decide to call World.

"Hello."

"What's up man? It's Dair."

"I know who this is. What's going on man? I can hear it in your voice."

"I just left a meeting at AJ's school where they announced his new coach. Remember me telling you that the last coach was Jackie's father."

"Yeah man, I remember that. Is this new dude going to be alright or what?"

"The new chick is going to be great at coaching the team, but not at being my future wife...at least not right now."

"The chick? What the hell are you saying, man?"

"What I am saying short bus is that the new interim coach is Jackie."

"Get the fu...sorry man. Max said I need to stop cussing so much. You are bullsh..., man, are you serious?"

"As a heart attack. She has known for more than a month that she was going to be AJ's coach and she hasn't said a thing."

"What was she supposed to do, man, say 'by the way, I am going to be your kid's coach while you were out on one of your corny ass bike rides?"

"Yeah, she was supposed to say that. Man, I have been planning our future and she has been sneaking around behind my back figuring out how to play a 2/3 defense."

"Let's see, you didn't find her in bed with another man, or another woman. She didn't take any of your money. You didn't catch her going through your cell phone. She isn't boiling chicken in your kitchen because your baby's momma is in your back yard. Man, it could be a lot worse. So she coaches your kid through the season—just keep your relationship on the down low until the season is over. It will be better for both of you that way. She is going to have enough stress coaching."

"I don't want to keep it on the down low. I'm building a house that I want her to love. I planned to introduce her to my mom and AJ in the next few weeks. I was about to tell this girl that I am falling in love with her! You know I go balls to the walls man. I can't just repress my feelings."

"No one told you to repress a damn, I mean a darn thing man. But do you think this is a good time to tell your son that your future baby's momma, who is his new coach, is going to be his step mammie?"

"World, I have always both appreciated and despised your candidness! I don't know what to do at this point. The spotlight has been on me for most of AJ's life. I really wanted these last few years to be about him. This is not the time to tell him that I am sniffing behind his coach."

"That's some deep shi...I mean stuff, man. It's the end of April. Can you make it through a basketball and a football season without being around this chick? I mean, I have seen you two together. She has your nose wide open man."

"For once I have to put how I feel on the back burner and think about what is best for my son. Looks like I am going to have to shut my nostrils for a while."

"Tell me how that goes, dude, 'cause you got a big nose. My guess is that crap won't last too long. If Jackie is anything like Max, she is going to have you more than sprung, man. I can't stop thinking about Max."

"Do I hear wedding bells in your future, World?"

"If it were up to me, I would have brought her ass back to New York, but I am going to have to move slow with Max. Obviously some punk has hurt her in the past and she doesn't trust what I say. I will give her a little time to get used to your boy and then I am going to put that voodoo on her!"

"I knew you would cheer me up. I just pulled up at the house. Let's get together before I meet you on the gridiron and whoop yo ass!"

"Whatever man. Holla at yo boy when you need some more advice."

My whole world has been thrown for a loop in the last few weeks, and talking to World always makes me feel better. For the first time in my life I allow myself to think about bringing in some permanency, and now I get this news from Jackie. At first I was just mad as hell, but as I think about it, I am mostly disappointed. I am happy for Jackie and I know she will be an amazing coach. But I know she is going to face a lot of criticism and I hate that I can't be there to help shield her. I also hate that I can't shout out to the world how I feel about her. But now is not the time. It's time to focus on my son, reshape my career, and build my future home, in that order. Jackie and I, well, that will have to be put on the back burner. If we are meant to be...

While I wait for Keeva, I walk around the gym to pick up some loose balls and then lock my office door. As usual, I hear Keeva before I see her. She gives her horn a short toot and I walked out to the car.

"Can you please ask me to pick you up sometime when you have something positive to say? Ever since you came home there has been nothing but drama," Keeva says as soon as I opened the car door.

"It's great to see you too, Keeva."

"What's up with all the sweating? And where is your car?"

"Let's see, where do I start. I broke the news to the team and parents that I'll be the new coach and got cussed out in three languages: Spanish, Ebonics and dead silence. Then Adaris broke up with me. Need I say more?"

"Honestly, Jackie, what did you expect him to do? You wait to tell him about a major decision that affects you, him, and his son in front of everyone like he doesn't matter and you expect him to be happy about it?"

"Wow, I almost forgot how subtle you are. Right now I need someone to tell me I did the right thing. Tell me I am not screwing up my professional and my personal life!"

"I can't do that little cousin. Only time will tell if you made the right decision. Just take one day at a time and focus on what is best for Jackie. If it's meant to be with you and Adaris, it will happen. He may need to take a few steps back to get his mind right, but he is obviously really into you. Believe me, he wouldn't do half as much as he has if you didn't mean something to him. Men like him don't have too. Don't get me wrong, you don't need to dumb yourself down Jackie. That is part of what intrigues him. For now put your energy into the boys. All the other stuff will work itself out in the end."

The next few weeks go by in a blur. I'm spending more time at the gym watching the boys run through drills and shoot around. Most of the time I keep my distance, watching them from the top of the gymnasium and taking notes here and there. All communication with Adaris has stopped. We both realized that it should either be all or nothing at this point, and I am experiencing a restlessness I haven't known since before my father died.

One day before practice I am sitting at the kitchen table reviewing the player's profiles. I can see that in two years this group will be amazing, but I have only one year to prove my coaching chops. There is no time to make many mistakes. As I sit contemplating how to structure the team workouts, Mom walks in.

"Hey baby, what are you working on?"

"Hey Mom, where have you been?"

"I had an appointment. You didn't answer my question."

"I am sitting here trying to figure out how I am going to get a group of boys, including a new batch of underclassmen, to gel as a team in one season. Mom, how did dad figure out what to do?"

"The question is, how do you figure out what you need to do when you are going through something?"

"Mom, why do you always answer a question with a question?"

"Because neither I or anyone else can give you the answers. God and you have to answer those questions. Most people didn't think your daddy was very religious. And he wasn't in the traditional sense. But he did believe in God's power to help him find the answers. A lot of answers are in your heart and soul. Hold on a minute, let me grab something for you."

Ella goes down to Shorty's Shack and comes back with a disc.

"I want you to listen to this CD. I put this together for your daddy a few years ago when he was really struggling with one of his teams. He was frustrated, aggravated, and so off center that it was affecting everything around him. You are a lot like your daddy, Jackie, and you can't afford to be off kilter. Your dad had skin in the game and a reputation that could afford him to make a few mistakes. You don't. Take this and really listen to it, and let it minister to your heart and soul. The words will help you decide your path."

Ella leans down, kisses me on the forehead, and walks out of the room.

"There is no time like the present," I say, and head down to the Shack to listen to the CD. At first I just lie in my dad's recliner and listen. I've heard these songs countless times, but I never really listened to the words. As I sit there I start to pray. I pray for the Lord to bless my family and to keep us all healthy. I pray for the Lord to help me lead my team. I pray for God to reveal to me what to do about Adaris. And as I pray I hear a voice whisper to me to write it down, and I remember what the Bible says about writing the vision and making it plain. I play the CD again and start writing out my first practice schematic. The words continue to wash over me. I listened to songs by Bishop Paul Morton and Donald Lawrence about encouragement. I reflected on my blessings while listening to Fred Hammonds. Kirk Franklin reminded me to smile. Patti Labelle reminded me once again about the value of my friends and family. Fanny J. Crosby reminded me to keep Jesus "Near the Cross." Marvin Sapp helped heal the wounds over the last few years with "My Testimony," and Donald Lawrence proclaimed that the "Best Was Yet to Come."

By the time the CD finishes, I feel a sense of peace about the upcoming season and about my relationship with Adaris. God has shown me through his music that He is in control, and if I relinquish my life to becoming his best, that will be enough.

I walk back upstairs and join my mom in the kitchen. "Mom, I think it's time to bring the team over so we can run some games again. This is where the boys need to be to get ready for camp."

"I think that's a great idea honey. Let me get started on my potato salad," Mom says with a big grin.

I send out a text to all my players and their parents:

"Meet Coach Jackie at Gametime Saturday morning at 10:00am. We will be running 5 on 5 and 3 on 3 games most of the day, grilling out and having movie night in the evening. Parents are welcome to come and go as they see fit. We will have food, fun, and fellowship. Bring clothes and toiletries to shower, shave and shine! Any who want to spend the night can stay in Shorty's Shack."

Within seven minutes I receive 16 texts in return. Most are from the boys, but some of the parents also responded. I don't receive a response from Adaris.

I'm walking out of the gym about to head back to the Hotel when I hear my phone ding. I look down and see a text from Jackie, and my heart does a flip flop. God, I miss her so much. I look down and see that it's a group text. I read it and smile, as I see an opportunity to kill three birds with one stone. I can take AJ to the Donovan home, eat some of Ms. Ella's potato salad, and lay my eyes on Jackie. I realize how much I'm looking forward to seeing her.

They're playing Basketball, We love that Basketball

The court has been cleaned and is ready to go, the racks of basketballs are pumped up, and the music is blasting. The burgers and hotdogs are in the refrigerator ready to go on the grill and the drinks are chilling in the cooler. I look around "Game Time" and all I can do is smile. Dad would be so pleased with everything. He taught many a person to love the game of round ball on this hard court. We still have an hour before the boys start arriving, so I grab a shower and change into basketball shorts and a T-shirt. As I head to the kitchen I hear what sounds like my nephew's voice. I round the corner and stop in my tracks. Jordan looks so much like my dad, the same dark chocolate skin, long wiry build, and a smile that lights up a room. I fell in love with this little person the day he was born, hook, line, and sinker. The minute Serena went in labor we caught the first flight smoking to Chicago. As Serena's contractions got stronger she kicked all of us out except her husband Micah. As soon as we walked out the nervousness began. My dad who was the coolest of the cool, and the calmest of the calm was pacing and rubbing his stomach. "Slim, my stomach is paining," he said. "I can't seem to get rid of this stomach ache. I have taken Tums, and everything."

"Come on dad. Let's run out to the store and pick up a few things and get you a coke to help calm your stomach."

"Ok, babe. You know how I hate hospitals anyway. Go tell your mama to call us if anything happens with Rena while we are gone."

We went out to Wal-Mart, bought a lot of crap that we didn't need, stopped and got dad a Coke and about an hour later headed back to the hospital. Ella was not leaving. Although she had been banished from the labor room she was sitting quietly in the waiting room and from time to time walking to the door to see what was going on. By the time we got back Rena was starting to push. We sat there for another hour, the entire time my dad burping, farting and complaining about how much his stomach was hurting. All of a sudden he looked over at my mom and me smiled and said, "Oh wee, my stomach feels so much better now. As soon as Rena has this baby I want to go downstairs and get something to eat." No sooner than the words spilled from his lips, Micah came around the corner with a smile and said, "Jordan has arrived!" My mom rushed back with Micah so she could check on Serena and baby Jordan and I looked at my dad and shook my head.

"You are the first dad I have ever heard of that can have sympathy pains for their child."

"You can call it what you want Slim. All I know is I feel so much better now. Maybe I was taking some of the pain from Rena."

Ten minutes later we got to see what would be the love of all of our lives. Jordan was a beautiful and delightful child. And now he is twelve years old and standing in my mom's kitchen smiling at me.

"Hey Auntie. Surprise! Mom, Granny, and I wanted to surprise you. I flew in this morning and Granny picked me up at the airport. I flew all by myself. When Granny told Ma you were opening up Game Time I wanted to be here to help you."

"Oh Jordan! This is the best surprise I have had in a long time. I am so glad you came in to help me. You wanna run some games today?" I ask, giving him a big bear hug.

"Oh yeah! These chumps may be a few years older than your boy but I can hang!"

"You are Shorty Donovan's baby boy and I know you can hang. How about you play on Auntie's team?"

"Are we going to bet any money like you and Uncle Leo used to do and take all they ends?"

"You have been talking to Uncle Leo too much nephew. I know we could take all of their money but today we are going to play for bragging rights. Stop eating all the snacks and get ready to play some ball!"

About 30 minutes later the doorbell starts ringing and Jordan is the self-appointed doorman. Most of the parents drop off their kids with a promise to come back later in the day when we start playing 5 on 5. Principal Leevins drops in under the guise of checking on my mom, but he really wants to see how the boys are adjusting. I think he also wants to be around the people that were closest to his dear friend.

As usual, my parents' house is open to anyone. We send the boys out to the court to shoot around and get loose before we start playing. Mom tells me she needs more cups and drinks, so I run to get them from the pantry. I have just bent over to lift some drinks off the floor when I smell him. His scent almost tips me right over. I still get so damn clumsy when Adaris is in the room.

I have some reservations about taking AJ and Noah over to the Donovan house. My mom could easily have done it, especially since she and Ms. Ella get along really well. But I am so excited about seeing Jackie that I had a hard time sleeping last night. I get up early and go for a very long run just to settle myself down some. When I get in from my run, AJ is sitting at the kitchen table stuffing his face with Fruit Loops.

"Yo pops! You taking Noah and I over to Coach Jackie's house this morning?"

"AJ, I swear you would never know that your Grandma and I taught you not to talk with your mouth full of food. Yes, I am going to take you over to Jac, I mean Coach Jackie's house this morning."

"Sorry Pops. Are you going to stay and hang out for a while? Maybe you can run some games with us while you are there. Show my boys you got skills other than on the turf?"

"I hadn't thought about that. I may bring some Jordan's just in case you guys don't have enough. I hadn't planned to stay too long after I dropped you off...although I did promise Ms. Ella that I would stop by the next time she was making potato salad."

"I get it pops. You aint taking me and No to check out our skills on the court. You just want some of Ms. Ella's potato salad!"

I start to say the hell with the potato salad, I want some of your coach's sweet potato pie! But I figure AJ isn't ready to hear that I am pining for either his coach or her pie. So I say instead, "You got it sporty. All I want to do is eat." I am telling the truth—I want to eat Jackie's face off! I miss kissing her so much. But I know I need to practice some restraint.

We pull up to the Donovan compound and AJ and Noah jump out before I can put the Rover in park. Hell, I am just as excited as they are but I am too cool to let on. I get out of the truck and amble slowly up to the house. Every time I pull up at this house I feel so at peace. It's like a throwback to the early 1900s, when the houses were large, the porches were broad, and the homes were wide open to friends, family, and even strangers. I am so desperate to see Jackie that I literally stop, take a few deep breaths, and say a quick prayer for the good Lord to keep me from having a heart attack.

Ms. Ella meets me at the door and gives me a big hug. "Adaris, I am so glad you decided to come. Are you going to take in some of my potato salad and the trimmings while you're here?"

"Hey Ms. Ella. You look beautiful as usual. I didn't get a chance to visit with you at the meeting last month. How are you doing?"

"There was a lot going on at the meeting. Maybe we can get a few minutes to catch up while you are here," she says with a sly grin. "Do you mind helping me get some drinks out of the pantry to take outside?"

"You know I don't mind Ms. Ella. Just point me to the place and I will grab whatever you need."

"It's right through the kitchen, the door on the right. You can't miss it," Ella says with a smile, then rushes outside to check on the boys.

I open the door to the pantry and the first thing I see is Jackie's rump shaker and legs. The second thing I notice is her scent. Today she has on something fruity that clings to her skin. I stop to soak it in. All of a sudden she starts to fall over, so I grab her around the waist before she hits the ground. I lean over and whisper in her ear, "I am starting to think I bring out the worst in you." And then I plant a quick kiss on her lovely neck.

"Adaris, what are you doing in my mom's pantry?"

He leans over again and kisses my neck and then my ear and then my cheek. "Your mom asked me to come in here to grab some drinks. She didn't mention that there was a long, tall drink of water in here." As he says that, he inches his arms up to my stomach and starts slowly kneading my six pack. "Are you afraid to turn around?"

"Yes, and if you don't stop doing that, there is going to be more than water in here."

"Stop doing what, this?" he murmurs as he slowly grinds his pelvis against my butt. "I can't seem to stop. Absence makes the hard, I mean the heart grow fonder. Just be still and let me hold you and smell you before we get caught."

"Ok, but if you are going to stay—oh baby, do that again!"

"Do this?" he says, sliding his tongue from my ear to my neck. "I feel like a damn dog in heat. You smell good, you feel good, you taste good. What are you wearing?"

"Ralph Lauren," I say while trying my aunt's rub, pat, and slide move again.

"If you rub your hand against my leg again, I won't be responsible for what I do. Now turn around and kiss me like you missed me."

I turn around slowly, move my arms up his thighs, graze the sides of his groin, then smooth my fingers over his nipples, then I throw my arms around his neck, grab his head and give him a passionate kiss. "How is that for showing you I've missed you?"

He grabs my ass, lifts my legs around his waist, and backs me against the wall, then says, "Show me again!"

As we stand in the pantry kissing like two teenagers in heat, time stands still. All of a sudden we hear footsteps in the kitchen and Ms. Ella yells, "Adaris, did you find the drinks?"

"Yes ma'am, I found them. I'll be out in just a minute."

Adaris puts his forehead against mine, looks into my eyes and smiles.

He gives me another heated kiss and slowly puts my legs down, then whispers in my ear, "Go upstairs and get yourself together. I need to stand here for a few minutes so I won't scare the shit out of your mom with this hard on you gave me. Maybe we can finish later."

As I turn to walk out the door Adaris says, "I missed you too," as he blew a huge bubble. "And don't lose any more weight. I love you just the way you are."

Before I could recover from the 'I love you comment' I noticed that my gum was missing. "Hey, are you chewing my bubble gum?"

"I figured your spit was the closest I could get to you so I took it. Tastes like Bazooka."

"Damn, I didn't even notice you took the gum out of my mouth..."

Lord, what have I gotten myself into? I think as I run up the stairs to redo the ponytail Adaris has just taken down.

As Jackie was rushing up the stairs, I stood in the pantry taking deep breaths like I had run for a pass, pasted a big grin on my face and said, "Thanks Ms. Ella, I owe you one!"

Ms. Ella stood between the kitchen and the dining room, patted herself on the back and said, "I haven't lost my touch."

I went upstairs to redo my ponytail, air out my panties, and get another piece of gum. As I get myself together, I wonder how I'm going to make it through the day with Adaris lurking around. I do want him here, as I have missed him so much, but I also sort of want him gone so I can concentrate on the boys. I walk past the kitchen and hear Mom, Principal Leevins, and Adaris talking. I decide to steer clear of that conversation, so I walk outside and find myself in the midst of another interesting conversation.

"Yeah, this court is the bomb, aint it? I still can't figure out how in the hell coach could afford this shit. This is the kind of stuff you see in LeBron's or Shaq's house," says Junebug.

"You think coach was doing something besides teaching and coaching, like slinging or something?" asks Peaches.

"Coach was so damn cool that he could do whatever he wanted. He was cooler than a fan. Hell, I am just glad that Jackie with her fine ass finally got us back out here. It's been so long since we got to run out here that I almost forgot what it was like," says Little Daddy.

"My pops is building a house. Maybe I can get him to do something like this. This is the joint!" AJ yells from across the court.

"Your rich ass daddy could build two of these if he wanted to. Why don't you work on getting your boys some tickets to the game, newbie? And I don't want none of that regular shit seating either, I want a seat in the box with the owners," Scoop hollers back at him.

With that the boys give each other high fives and pounds, while AJ stands to the side with a funny look on his face.

Oh, the dynamics of a team. The new ones have something to prove, the old ones have something to protect. On top of that, these boys have a new coach who happens to be a girl. I decide not to interrupt yet. This conversation is bound to get better.

"Speaking of fine ass Jackie, what's up with Principal Leevins making her our head coach? That shit is foul," says Junebug.

"Yo man, she said not to call her Jackie. She is Coach Jackie or Donovan to us," says Homer.

"Shut up Slice. You just got your damn green card five minutes ago. You are barely on the team your damn self. And the only reason you got on the team is because Leevins needed to do the affirmative action shit," yells Popper.

"I got your affirmative action shit right here." Hector grabs his crotch. "I got skills homes. Just wait until I get your coola out on the court."

"Home slice is one of the best Mexicans I ever seen that can get down on the court," yells Bird.

"I aint from Mexico! I am from Puerto Rico fool," Hector hollers. "And it looks like for once in your life you are in the minority too, White boy!"

"Mexico, Puerto Rico, Spain, it's all the same shit," taunts Scoop.

Then Jordan suddenly says in a voice as clear as the sky outside, "All you fools need to put up or shut up. We playing basketball and if one of you makes another smart ass remark about my Auntie I am going to whip all of your asses today. She is fine, but she is your coach and you better respect that shit."

Wow, Jordan can really cuss! I know I shouldn't be admiring that, but he did get it honest. My dad was the director of Cussiolgy for the state of Tennessee so naturally the tradition would carry on right? I can see it's time for me to step in. I really appreciate Jordan taking up for his Auntie, but I don't want anyone to kick his 12-year-old butt. I come around the corner and yell, "Ok guys, thanks for coming out. Let's get the day started, shall we? We need to get a good workout in, then we can have some fun and eat some good food. Now, today we are going to run some 3 on 3 and 5 on 5. We will play to 10 by 1s and if you lose you cruise. I am going to mix it up a little bit so you can play with different people. Any questions?"

"Yeah Coach. What's the prize for the winning team?" Scoop asks.

"Well Scoop, the prize is that you get to play on the court of a man and woman who earned every penny to pay for it with hard work, sacrifices, and by investing their money well. The prize is that one of the best female basketball players you have ever seen is now your Coach, and that you are not in Spain or Mexico but in Tennessee. The prize, young men, is that you'll be doing the things you love most: playing basketball, eating great food, and being in the presence of some great people. Any other questions?"

"No!"

"Nada!"

"I think that covered it."

As I walk off the court I hear someone mumble, "Do you think she heard us talking out here?"

I walk back into the kitchen and find Mom, Principal Leevins, Adaris, and Mr. Leeks having a heated conversation about the upcoming election. I stick my head in and say, "We are about to get started. Come out at your own risk." As I turn away I hear Adaris chuckle and blow another bubble...

The rest of the day is awesome. We play 3 on 3 until lunchtime, and I notice that we have quite an audience. Most of the parents and a few of my dad's friends who caught wind of the play date have stopped by, and Keeva is here too. As I play a few games with the boys I can sense that Adaris is lurking nearby, but he is keeping his distance from me by design. At one point I'm staring at him so hard as I a run down the court that I almost miss a pass from Noah. He yells out, "Coach Jackie!" I somehow manage to catch the ball and lay it up.

Principal Leevins, Adaris, my dad's friends Captain, Bubba and Calvin are putting the hotdogs and hamburgers on the grill. It was just like old times except my dad wasn't there laughing, cooking on the grill and dancing around. We break for lunch, eat way too much, and decide to rest for an hour so everyone's stomach can settle. Adaris walks up to me and says, "How about a game of Horse, coach? You up to it?"

"You know I love a challenge, Adaris."

"How about we have a friendly wager?"

"The last time I bet on a game, my opponent had to eat humble pie—I mean chess pie. What do you have in mind?" I look around and see that we have an attentive audience.

"How about we write our wager down on a sheet of paper, give it to the lady of the house to hold onto, and then read it after the game."

"You got it."

"Hey Pops, can we make a wager too? 'Cause my money is on you, Coach."

"Mine is on Mr. Singleton. He's got some ups!" says Shaky.

"Let's get this over with Adaris, so the boys can get back on the court. Shoot for who gets the first shot."

As we walk toward the court I look at Adaris and ask him, "Are you playing me for my heart?"

"I hope I already have it. Today is for bragging rights," he says with a huge smile.

Adaris and I exchange shot after shot which included shooting with the opposite hand, and a dunk by Adaris which moved the young crowd. A granny shot by yours truly moves the old school crowd. The game goes on for about 30 minutes, and when we get deadlocked I decide to take some three-pointers. Adaris is athletic but he's a football player, and it only takes about five minutes for him to get the S and E. The applause is mixed with lots of boos and yeas, but the game has set a playful stage for the rest of the afternoon. As soon as we walk off the court, Adaris gets a text and says, "I have to run. One of our rookies just had an accident and I need to go check on him. Ms. Ella, may I have Jackie's wager."

"Sure Adaris. Here it is."

He looks at AJ and Noah. "I'll come get you two in the morning. Stay focused." He tucks the paper in his pocket, looks at me, and says, "Thanks for playing with me, Coach."

After Adaris leaves I breathe a huge sigh of relief. Thank God he didn't read my wager in front of the crowd. I hope my payoff will make him smile and give me some time with him. After all, he made the decision to pull back, not me.

I walk to the car thinking at least I got to see, smell, and smooch Jackie. I feel like a thirsty man who just had a long drink of water. Hopefully the time we spent will hold me for a while. I jump in the Rover, turn the air on full blast, dig in my pocket, and pull out her note.

"After I win Horse, which I will, I would like you to find some time in the next two weeks to let me take Beauty for a drive to Murfreesboro to get a Buster burger! Oh, and you can come too!"

I throw my head back and laugh harder than I have in months. "I got your ride and a burger, Coach Donovan," I say to myself. I would have given her anything in the world and she wants a damn burger and a ride. You can't beat that!

The day is a hit. The boys play a few more games of 5 on 5 and then we break again to eat. At the end of the day, when the boys are downstairs relaxing, Mom hands me Adaris' wager.

I walk up to my room, sit on my bed, and unfold the note. It has been such a long time since I had any communication with Adaris that my hand is shaking. I turn the slip of paper around a few times, smell it to see if I can get a whiff of his Cool Water scent, and then I read it, quickly at first and then again slowly, taking time to absorb his words.

"I don't just want your heart; I want your mind, body, and soul. But until the time is right I will settle for a stolen moment with you, and not in the pantry. You choose the time and place."

I sit there smiling and know I will get to see Mr. Singleton again soon. Until then I will anticipate our reunion as a child would Christmas.

Down Goes Frazier

The time has come for me to meet with Joseph Frazier. Something in me just can't call him Coach. For the sake of the kids I know that it will be important to forge a relationship with Frazier, because he has been the one constant the team has had since Dad got sick. I want to introduce some new techniques. I hope and pray Frazier and I can come to a consensus and merge our coaching styles. If we can't, I know how to assert my authority— my dad made sure of that. It's not my natural style, but my dad always said, be respectful but don't take any wooden nickels, from a man or a woman.

Before I walk into the gym I bow my head and close my eyes really tight, because that's the best way to get a prayer through according to Sister Hattie Lou and say a quick prayer.

"Lord, please help this meeting to go well today with Coach Frazier. Please let us figure out a way to compromise and do what is best for these young men. Please let the words of my mouth be acceptable to you and if I have to cuss his monkey ass out please forgive me for I know not what I do. Amen."

As soon as I open my eyes after saying that jacked-up prayer, I see my new bestie walk into the gym. I decide to start the conversation off on a good note, so I paste on a smile and say, "Good afternoon Coach. How are you doing today?"

Now I didn't mention this before, but Coach Frazier is short, about 5-foot-6 on a good day. He has a bit of a paunch—some would even say he has a big gut. He has big bug eyes and a receding hairline, which he covers up with a purple SHS hat that is older than my nephew Jordan. He also wears glasses that are as thick as a Coke bottle. Suffice it to say, Coach Frazier doesn't look like he played basketball a day in his life, but to hear him tell it, he was a high school basketball playing fool! The best thing Coach has going for him is that he was under my father's tutelage for the last ten years and he has the same name as the famous boxer. So, I figure that with his coaching experience and my playing experience we can put together a dynamic team if we can keep our egos in check.

Coach Frazier looks up at me with those coke bottle glasses and says, frowning, "I am as well as can be expected considering what just took place in the last few months little lady. I have been looking forward to this meeting. I want to talk to you about my vision for this team and the things I have been doing for the last year."

"I would be very interested to hear your thoughts Coach Frazier. I think with your vision and some of my thoughts we can come up with a great game plan for the season."

"Little lady, I know you don't have any coaching experience so I am willing to take the lead with these young men. I have been here for over ten years and have been a huge part of the winning tradition."

"First, Coach Frazier, I would appreciate you calling me Jackie, Coach Jackie, or Coach Donovan, and not 'little lady.' Second, I think we need to talk further about our respective roles. I have been appointed the head coach and you are my assistant. I want us to be able to work together, but the final decisions on how we execute will be mine. If you have a problem with that, this is the time to tell me. We need to present a united front. If the boys see anything different, they will walk all over us."

"You are more like your dad than I thought. I figured we would have this conversation sooner than later. Since we are getting it out on the table, let me tell you what I really think."

"I think you should Coach Frazier."

"What I really think is I am pissed that you got the damn job that I have been waiting on for the last five years. I knew your dad was slowing down and he was preparing me to take this job. I thought your dad would retire in the next few years and tell Leevins to give me the job, but it looks like his slick ass was greasing the wheel for you to take his place. He always was a crafty motherfucker and once again he got the best of me. I am the most qualified person in this state to take the job, but because of affirmative action and the fact that Leevins thinks you can bring some publicity and funding to this school by being one of the first bitches to coach a bunch of boys, he appoints you."

"Are you done, Mr. Frazier?"

"Not really. On top of that shit, you don't even know how to coach boys. The pace of the game is different. I am going to have to show you how to coach. I'll be doing all the work but you'll get paid for it! People are already talking about the fact that I have to play second fiddle to a Donovan once again."

"Is that all you got to say?"

"That's all I have for right now."

My parents taught me to take the high road until someone had my back against the wall. While Frazier is ripping me a new one he is he walking steadily toward me. He gets so close I can smell his funky breath and he is literally spewing his rage all over me. I have finally had enough and am trying to decide if I should shove him away, but then I remember Martin Luther King, Jr and I decide to take a more peaceful approach.

"Coach Frazier, I need you to back up about two feet so I can look you in the eye without looking down. I want to address all of your issues so we can move on to doing the job you are paid to do or you can you leave my gym. My dad may have been getting a little older but his mind was as sharp as a knife until the day he took his final breath. He taught you the game of basketball just like he taught me. The biggest difference is you didn't play beyond the high school level and I did. It was Principal Leevins idea to hire me as the interim coach. Whether he made a good decision or a bad decision is up in the air at this point. I am pretty sure Affirmative Action did not play a part in his decision but I know it played a part in the decision to hire you ten years ago at the height of the movement. And if you use the word 'bitch' again to refer to me or any other woman, I will file a complaint against you. I want to teach our boys the proper way to refer to all people. After all, it is our job to teach them life skills, not just basketball."

"As for the money, do you think $1500 a month is going to help me for a 5-6 month season? Just so you know, and this doesn't need to go any further than this gym, I am giving $1000 a month back to the program. With dad passing away some of our major sponsors have backed out no thanks to your sorry efforts."

"This is my team and I don't give a rat's ass what people say about me. Let them talk. Hopefully that will generate more publicity for our school. A wise man once said, you can show people better than you can tell them, and I plan to do some showing this season. And if people are talking that much, that means I am relevant. I asked Principal Leevins to allow you to stay. It was my decision point blank period. Now, I am going to the office to get started on our game plan and I will give you five minutes to decide if you are in or out. If you are going to be in, you will need to stop running your damn mouth and accept that I am running this show. So, get yourself together and join me if you wish."

About 4 minutes and 47 seconds later, Coach Frazier walks into my office. I guess he wanted to make me sweat by waiting till the last second, but little does he know that I already have a short list of potential assistants, all of them female. We meet for the next two hours, working out a plan to build the team's strength and stamina. Although we disagree on a lot, we do agree it's best to see how the three camps shape up before we start making any concrete decisions. Just when our conversation was at its most lively, there's a tap on the door.

"Come in," I yell with some aggravation.

"It sounds like the good ole days in here," says Principal Leevins. "This scene looks familiar and I must say I have missed it. Can you two take a pause from your cause? I have some great news to share with you."

"Sure thing, we were just trying to figure out how to get these kids to the three camps this summer. I think I can get them to cut some of the costs, but it looks like we'll still need about $10,000. There's only about $3,000 left in our account."

"Then you'll really like my news. We just received a $25,000 check from a group called Game Changers. The letter was addressed to me, but it specifically said that all of the money should be used for Jackie Donovan's new basketball program in honor of her dad, Coach Donovan. Since Shorty's death we have already received about $7,000 for the program as well. If you two are ok with it, we can use that first chunk of cash to make some improvements in the gym, including renaming it the Theodore 'Shorty' Donovan Gymnasium. The latest gift will be used for camps, equipment, and uniforms. Jackie, I can't release any money without receiving a voucher, so you'll need to get one to me at least two weeks before the camp so we can get you guys moving"

"Principal Leevins, I don't think we will need all the money. Can you find out if we can allot any extra funds to the girls' basketball team? I have a heart for girl's athletics and I know it's grossly underfunded."

"That's the Jackie I know and love. I will be happy to check on that. Now I'll leave you two to figure out how to get the Tennessee State Champion trophy back in our house."

"Well I'll be damned," says Coach Frazier, rubbing his head. "I haven't seen Leevins that excited in a long time, Jackie. It's almost like Shorty has come back to life except with a vagi..."

"I get it Coach Frazier, I get it," I interrupt him again, but this time with a laugh. Down goes Frazier!

It's been over a week since the game of Horse and I am chomping at the bit, pun intended, to spend time with Jackie. Her basketball team is due to go away for a week to a basketball camp, and I feel a little trepidation knowing AJ will be going away for the first time by himself. It helps to know that Jackie and Coach Frazier will be watching over him. My son is growing up and I need to turn him loose.

I'm wondering if Jackie wants me to pay off my debt before the team leaves. I miss her like crazy, and I want to try to soothe some of the nerves she must be feeling about her coaching debut. I am sure the pipeline is full of gossip about her coaching. I even heard some of my teammates talking in the locker room. Of course, they mostly talk about how fine Jackie is and say she could coach them any day–typical locker room conversation.

After listening to the guys talk about Jackie's butt, hair, and even her teeth, I step in and try to shut it down. "Can't you fools find something else to talk about? You need to be focusing on getting ready for camp."

"What are you so uptight about? You act like you boning her or something!" yells one of the defensive linemen.

"He may not be boning her but I sure wish I was. She is fine as hell! And those hips are just perfect for pushing out some of my babies," says Amos, one of the centers.

As I sit there fuming, Shelley puts his hands on my shoulder and whispers, "Chill man before you give yourself away and we start a locker room fight. I got this."

Shelley turns and yells, "All of you shut the hell up! Jackie Donovan don't want any of your ugly asses. I want complete silence in here for a few minutes! The captains need to meet, and if you piss any of us off we can make camp a very unpleasant experience for you."

You could hear a pin drop. When one of the captains raises their voices the team knows he means business. Except for this captain obviously! As I walk out of the locker room with the other captains, Shelley looks at me with a sly smile and mumbles, "The look on your face is just like mine was when I met Tiffany."

After the captains meeting, I send Jackie a text to ask if I can come get her on Sunday after church to go for our ride and a burger. As I wait on her to respond, I start to get nervous. I have never in my life had to wait on anyone to respond to me about going out on a date. After about two hours she texts me back and says that any time after 2:00 will work for her, and she says to dress very casual. I text back that I will see her at her mother's house at 3:00. For once I'm glad that she doesn't have her own place, as being alone with her is dangerous. It'll be hard enough to ride around in the Aston Martin since it's known for speed, not space. It's going to be pure torture.

It seems like I've been waiting forever to hear from Adaris. I can't very well call him and ask why it's taking so long to pay up. Luckily I have been distracted by getting ready for camp, my first as head coach, and I am pretty nervous. There aren't many females working with any of the teams, but they found a section in one of the dorms where they can put me so I'll have some privacy. I hated being away from the team, but my new best friend Coach Frazier will be nearby.

I have noticed that Mom is doing a lot of humming and mumbling around the house lately, and I can tell she's in prayer warrior mode. She used to do this when dad was starting a new season or something stressful was going on. Because of her faith she was able to stay calm and peaceful most of the time. I know it's me she is covering with prayers and that the angels are watching me.

Adaris finally texts to ask if he can pay up on Sunday after church. I think about skipping church, but I need the Lord to help me get through the camp—and the time alone with Adaris—so skipping church is not an option. We make arrangements for him to pick me up and I go upstairs to pack for camp. It's a relief there's no longer a need to sneak around.

For the first time in a long time I'm really concerned about how I look. Not in a vain way but in the "I want people to talk about how I coach not what I wear" way. Men never have to give it a thought, but a woman doesn't want to look too masculine or people will say she is butch. She can't look too girly or people will say she is trying to use her looks to her advantage or to get attention. I want to avoid wearing anything that will draw too much attention, especially to my well-endowed bootay. I decide on dark color jogging suits for most of the week, and I will keep my hair in a ponytail, and makeup to a minimum. I want people to remember me as a solid rookie coach and not a hoochie mama.

I decide to poll my girls to see what they think. I may be a glutton for punishment, but I wouldn't trade my girls for anything. I call Keeva first and say, "Hold up for a minute Keeva, I need to get Serena on the phone." I get Serena and then hit flash so we can all be on at the same time. Max is teaching so she'll miss this one.

"Make it quick baby sis. I am in the middle of getting my Sunday dinner ready."

"And I'm getting ready for a date. Before you ask, he's a young tenderoni I'm just wasting a little time with," says Keeva, a little defensively.

"I hate to interrupt both of you from cooking and serving it up especially the one cooking her Sunday dinner on Saturday but I need some help. I'm leaving tomorrow for camp at the University of Kentucky and I need some advice."

"Run the 1-3-1 defense. You guys are really quick and that defense will shut them down," says Serena.

"I have no idea what a 131 defense is but what she said. Now speed it up, I still need to put my makeup on before I pick tenderoni up at the bus station."

"What? Keeva, are you really going to meet him at a bus stop? How is that going to look, you pulling up in a Benz to pick up a scrub? Is he too young to have a driver's license?" hollers Serena.

"I just wanted to see if you two were listening. He's not jail bait but he is young. And I am meeting him at the bus stop so I am assuming he is riding the bus. What's up Jackie?"

"Thanks for the advice on the defense Rena, but I need to know what to wear during the camp."

"You wear clothes girl, what do you mean?" asks Serena.

"I don't want to look too sexy, too butchy, or too contrived."

"I can never figure out why we as women always have to think twice about what we wear. This is the twenty first century. The women's movement gave us the right to wear what we want. Why do you think you need to worry about what you wear?" says Serena.

"For once I agree with Serena. Those horn dogs are going to talk no matter what you wear, so you might as well do what you want. You have great taste Jackie, don't dumb yourself down," says Keeva.

"And remember you're setting a precedent for future women coaches. Wear what looks best on you but is also comfortable and breathable. It's hot as hell!"

"And most of the people at the camp have Googled you, checked out your Facebook, LinkedIn, Instagramed and had small tribal meetings about you. They already know what you look like. If you make any changes in your appearance do it for your damn self. Now I gotta go put these Spanx on so I can meet my new boy toy. Speaking of which, fuck the Spanx. I am going to let it all hang out tonight. Call me during the week and give me an update!"

"I gotta run too sis. Do what you do! I am proud of you. Call and give me an update as well."

I get off the phone and take everything out of my suitcase that I've packed so far. I replace it with bright-colored sweat suits and shorts, all with matching hats and shoes. Max would be proud!

Mom and I decide to go to the early church service so we can have breakfast together. Mom holds my hand extra tight at church and prays longer than usual. She must be sending up some extra prayers for me in preparation for the upcoming week.

The doorbell rings at about 2:55. My stomach does a flip flop right before I open the door. Adaris stands on the porch wearing gym shorts and a T-shirt. He looks casual and comfortable. Mom has decided to take her Sunday nap so we don't need to linger.

Adaris reaches in his pocket and pulls out a set of keys. "You looking for these sweetness?" he says with an indulgent smile.

"You know this man! I can't wait to get Beauty out on the interstate so I can see how fast she'll go. Let's do it!"

"No hug, no kiss, no nothing?"

"I'm scared."

Adaris raises his eyebrow, crosses his arms over his chest, and asks, "Scared of what?"

"That I won't be able to stop. Now give me the keys and let's hit the road," I say, reaching out my hands.

"Damn, you are a sight for sore eyes. I don't know if I like seeing you more from the front or the back."

"If that was an offhand compliment, thanks. Oh, and thanks for finally paying up on your bet Adaris. I couldn't wait to drive this car," I say, putting an extra sway in my step.

"Wait to drive the car or wait to see me?"

"Both," I say with a huge grin. "How have you been for the last few weeks?"

"I've been doing well. I'm in the gym as much as possible, trying to get used to the heat before camp starts. I also have a young man at home who is excited about going to his first high school basketball camp tomorrow. He thought he should get a couple pair of new Jordan's to celebrate."

"Well, did he get them?"

"He got one pair. He already has a closet full of shoes in every color."

"How is the house coming?"

"Great—it's completely framed out now. The builder is going to start putting the Tyvex up next week. Once they get the roof on we should be done in about 90 days. I can't thank you enough for helping me create the floor plan. I want you to come by when you get back from camp and tell me what you think."

"But I thought you wanted us to chill for a while."

209

"I'm not sure if that is what I want Jackie. But I also don't know how AJ would feel about me seeing his coach. Hell, I don't even know how I would feel. Some of the guys had a conversation about you in the locker room the other day and I damn near lost my mind."

"I would have loved to be a fly on the wall! I remember some of my locker room conversations about men and they could get pretty X-rated."

"Your reputation is intact, thanks to Shelley. He had to keep me from whipping a 350-pound center's ass. Or I should say, he kept me from getting my ass kicked and Amos is my friend!"

Adaris leans over the center console and gives me a light kiss on the neck, then nuzzles his nose back and forth. He moves his hand down my neck, across my shoulder, and down my arm. "I know I shouldn't be doing that but I just want to touch you."

"How about you stop that and stop staring a hole in me."

"Will it make you slow down? You're driving 105 miles an hour, sweetness."

"Oh shoot! I had no idea I was going that fast. This car is amazing. It's sure not meant for the foothills of Tennessee."

"Talk to me Jackie. If you won't let me touch you, at least tell me what has been going on with you."

"I'm a little nervous about heading up to Kentucky tomorrow. I feel like I am going to be on display the entire week. The boys have been working hard to stay in shape but this will be the first time I coach them officially."

"You will be on display baby, much to my chagrin. There will be hundreds of men and boys checking you out at every turn. Another reason why I probably need to put a mark on you before you leave."

"You are too funny," I say, laughing.

"I have other ways to mark my territory, but I know I don't need to be possessive. I can't ask you to wait and not date anyone while we are going through this...whatever this shit is."

"I guess that means you plan on dating?"

"Hell, I don't know what I plan on doing. At this point I plan to take a picture of you on the sly and look at it all the time," Adaris says, then he lifts up his cell phone and clicks the camera.

"Hey, you got my bad side. Wait until we get to my hole in the wall. We'll probably be the only black people in the joint and we can get one of the waitresses to take a picture."

"I have a feeling I would follow your ass to the ends of the earth."

"There is power in the booty," I say under my breath.

"What did you say?" Adaris says, leaning closer to me.

"Nothing!"

Adaris leans over the console and whispers, "Obviously there is enough power for you to drive my car. You can take me for a ride anytime, baby."

We pull up at the hamburger joint in less than 30 minutes, find a booth and put in an order for burgers and fries.

"Yumm! This burger is the bomb, Jackie. How did you find this place?"

"This was one of my mom and dad's favorite places. Back when they had just started integrating M.T.S.U., seeing four black boys come into a restaurant with five white boys didn't sit too well with the locals. One employee here recognized that they were the basketball team and welcomed them with open arms. After a while my dad was a weekly fixture here."

"It's amazing how often sports are the great equalizer. People may say they hate black people but once they find out you are a great athlete, actress, musician you become the exception to the rule. People don't notice color when you are Oprah, Jordan, Tiger…or Dair," I say with a sly smile.

"Yeah, but the good ole boy network is still very much alive. Remember I played in Texas and now here in Tennessee. I have been in situations where people didn't see anything but a big black man walking into their establishment. I have seen white women grab their purses and look at me like I'm a monster. I do think that sports helps break down some barriers and often transcends race. But I also know that once I step off the gridiron for good, things will change for me. Most people aren't prepared for it, but I look forward to it. I want to be in a public place without someone recognizing me, to live a regular life."

"Alas, the difference between an NFL player and a WNBA player. All I can say is, thank God for Title 9. At least it gives girls and women a chance to play sports and get some recognition for being great athletes. Oh oh, here they come, Adaris!"

"Who is coming?"

"A few of your fans."

After Adaris gives out autographs to some of his most loyal fans and gets them to take a picture of us with our cell phones, he lets them take a picture of him to hang on their wall of fame. We get back in the car with me still at the wheel and head to Arrington to check out the construction progress. I pull onto the property and immediately start smiling. The house is about 500 feet off the road so we can't see it at first. After driving for a few minutes we arrive at the house. As we walk around it's hard to envision how things will turn out, but the rooms are starting to take shape.

"It looks like Johnnie cooperated and went with most of your ideas for the floor plan."

"Thanks to you, things are moving along smoothly. We made a few more moderations, like adding floor to ceiling windows across the rear of the house. I won't have any close neighbors so I don't have to worry about privacy. We also oriented the house so the morning sun comes through in the front and the evening sun in the back."

Looking at the house is almost overwhelming. I know Adaris is building his dream home based on some of my ideas, but I am afraid to admit it. On the way back to the Plantation, we talk about mundane topics, avoiding anything too personal. I pull into the driveway and say to Adaris, "Thanks for letting me drive Beauty today. The drive was great, and your house is going to be gorgeous Adaris."

"Just seeing the way your eyes twinkle when you talk makes it all worth it. I am so glad we got to spend time together Jackie. This is going to be a pivotal week for you. I know you and the team are going to do great.

Camp is the best time to take some risks and try some new things, so don't put too much pressure on yourself or the team. You have a blank slate baby, draw your own picture. Now lean over here and let me draw from those lips before you get out of the car."

Adaris leans over and puts the palm of his hand on my face. Staring at me intensely, he lays two fingers over my mouth and whispers "Open for me."

I silently obey and Adaris slips a finger in my mouth. I gently suck on his finger, then he pulls it out and replaces it with his mouth, and gathers me as close as he can in the cramped car. After a few minutes of necking like two teenagers, I push him away and say, "I need to go Adaris. Staying in here is just making things worse for me. It makes me want to drive back to your hotel and take all your clothes off!"

Adaris gently massages the back of my head while planting little kisses across my neck and says, "That sounds like a great idea, baby, but it is the wrong time. Give me one more kiss and then go get ready for your week."

"I wonder if it's always going to be the wrong time."

"The older I get, or I guess the more mature I become I realize that with intimacy comes a commitment. At least with you and me. Once we sleep together I want it to continue. Now is not the time. You would become addicted to me."

"Me addicted to you?"

"Actually I would become addicted to you. I am already addicted to the smell and taste of you. I want you all of the time." With that he plants one more kiss on my neck, then jumps out of the car, runs around to the driver's side, and grabs me out of the car. He gives me a bone crushing hug, then walks me to the door.

"I feel like we are two teenagers who have been kissing in the car. You kept me out too late and now you are sneaking me back to the house so I can slip in before my mom and dad catch me."

"There are a few changes we need to make in your little movie."

"What's that John Singleton?"

"We are grown ass people, and it's a little too late to be trying to sneak past Ms. Ella. And thank God I have more self-control now than I had sixteen years ago. If not, you would have got gotten in the front seat of Beauty and I would have kept your panties to show my boys. Now go in. Be safe this week and text me when you can to tell me how you are doing." He plants one more kiss on my forehead and walks back to Beauty.

I unlock the door, walk into the house, and close the door behind me. I go to the window and watch Adaris drive away. I finally know what people mean when they say, "Absence makes the heart grow fonder."

This is a Man's World

This camp has been a blessing and a curse. It's a blessing that I get to spend time with these 13 stinky, cocky boys, but a curse that I found out I will be coaching 13 stinky, cocky boys. I had forgotten what boys do when they get together—mostly eat, fart, and burp. Thank God we were able to rent a small bus so I can sit in the front and keep a little distance from their antics—and their odors!

I also had the presence of mind to recruit—actually I begged—a young lady to join our team as the statistician/manager. She would be the first of many firsts, as I was determined to get girls involved with the team. Of course doing so would bring its own set of problems. Take Sophia, for example— she happens to be drop-dead gorgeous so while I'm trying to train her for the job I also have to keep an eye on the boys, especially Peaches, who was practically drooling over her and strutting his stuff. He thinks he not only smells good but he also thinks he looks good. And, of course, she is also a PYT. I had to swear on a Bible; yes and promise my first born that she would be taken care of in front of Mr. Leevins and her father Mr. Graham. I know I need to mentor Sophia, but it's really hard when she's getting on my nerves. At this moment the little heifer was working on my right temple. Can you believe that she came with terms? She told me, "Ms. Jackie, I will join your little team as long as I don't have to go in the locker room. I am not interested in seeing any of those boys without any clothes on or picking up their funky clothes!"

After I got over the initial shock of a sixteen year old saying my team was little and dictating to me what she was and wasn't going to do I agreed that she didn't need to come into the locker room. And I tend to agree with little Miss PYT. There is nothing more disappointing than seeing small things if you get my drift.

Sophia thankfully has done her research on how to keep the stat book properly. I had her practice a few times while the guys were messing around on the courts at school. She is pretty good, I must admit. I also need as much girl power as I can get, so for now Sophia will have to do.

The first few games go off without a hitch. Coach Frazier and I are getting along as smooth as butter, and we decide to switch out acting as head coach for the games, which will give me the chance to both observe and coach the guys in live games. Of course I have to remember Joe is a stupid MF and make sure he understands that this is for camp only.

Scoop has assumed the role of team captain. The other players can't seem to figure out that they are better leaders than Scoop, so I decide to let him reign. He'll figure out soon enough that a leader isn't the one who talks the most but the one who models leadership. I've played on several teams and I know that the team leader is not always the smartest, loudest, or smoothest but the one you want to follow when the going gets tough.

As I was saying, the first two games flowed fairly well. The boys are moving the ball, taking some good shots, and playing good defense. But I realize suddenly that something has shifted, and that things will get out of hand pretty quickly if I don't reign them in. This is one of those defining moments, and I remember something my college coach told me: "Talent is cheap but dedication is costly." And then I realize that dedication had just left the gym. Let me explain. It's the seventh game. We played two games early in the day, and the boys were instructed to eat lunch and then go back to their rooms and rest. The bad thing about not having a male manager is that I don't have anyone to keep an eye on the boys in their dorm. Frazier is usually too busy campaigning for his next job so I can't count on him.

When the boys get back out on the court, I notice that they look fatigued. They are getting beat on defense and are missing a lot of easy lay-ups. When the score hits 16 to 6, I lean over to Frazier and say, "Coach, we are getting beat up and down the floor. I think we need to make some adjustments pretty quick."

"Jackie, we're just five minutes into the game. Let's see if they can recover and get into a groove."

About that time, the other team runs a fast break that results in an alley oop and slam dunk, which advances the score to 18 to 6. Now I'm really getting anxious, so I say to Joe, "If nothing else you need to call a timeout and regroup. The boys look tired. We have a great bench. Let's substitute and get some fresh legs out there."

Coach Frazier turns to me, puts his hands on his hips, and says, "Little lady, don't make me repeat myself. I got this. Just sit over there and be quiet."

When he put his hands on his hips I almost lost it. And did he just call me little lady again and tell me to be quiet? That just about takes me over the edge, so I think about what my dad would do in this situation. First off, there is no way in hell he would let his assistant coach take the lead in something that was obviously over his head. In fact, he probably would have told him to sit down and shut the hell up. Because people were being

216

pretty nosey about the new female coach I didn't really want to show my ass, but enough was a damn nuff, because by the time I finish fuming over that snide remark the score is 22 to 8.

I stare down my nose at Frazier as Scoop dribbles slowly down the court like he is my Aunt D. As soon as he gets close to our bench, I yell as loud as I can, "time out!" I make the sign so the ref will give me 60 seconds. Apparently I scare the hell out of Scoop and everyone else that was within five feet of me, including the referee.

I get the team to huddle up real close cause that's what you do when you need to get some cussing in. Right before Frazier opens his mouth to say something stupid, I yell "Scoop, what the hell is going on out there? The score is 22 to 8 and this team is running over you. You are stinking up the gym!"

"Well coach—"

I really don't give a rat's ass about his answer, so I yell some more. "I don't want to hear it. Scoop, Little Daddy, and Peaches, it's a damn shame that Popper is beating all three of you up the court. They are running rough shod over your defense and breaking the full court press. You three take a seat. Bird, Baby Baby, and AJ, check in. I want you to pull back in a 1-3-1 defense with Bird at the top and AJ in the back. You have got to shut this running and gunning crap down or the next three quarters are going to be painful. Pass the ball and take your shots. Use Baby and Popper to get the rebounds and bust the boards. Put it in and let's execute!" I knew I should have asked Rena to be my assistant. She knew the 1-3-1 would work before we got to this damn camp!

The team joins hands in the huddle and yells out "Execute!" As they walk back onto the court, Frazier looks over to me and says, "I don't appreciate you making the decision to substitute without talking to me first!"

I get as close to him as I can, smiling so the public won't suspect I'm about to go gangsta, and say through clenched teeth, "I changed my mind about switching up our roles. We can discuss this later in private. Let's do what we can to turn this game around before they run us out of the gym."

We end up losing the game by four points, but it's a far shade better than the 14 points we were down in the first quarter. The underclassman really played well, but the other team simply outplayed us. After the game I ask Sophia to tell the boys to meet me outside by the bus.

"Coach Jackie wants your little asses to meet her by the bus, you losers," Sophia says as she sashays away with her nose in the air.

I have to keep my back turned so no one will see the smile on my face. It is good to know that Sophia is a competitive and has my back, but I know I will have to keep an eye on her. As she runs to catch up with the boys, I call out, "No cussing, and remember that whatever a man thinketh, so is he."

"Sorry coach—what does that mean?"

"It means, if you keep telling yourself or anyone else something it can become a self-fulfilling prophesy."

"Uh... I don't get it."

"Take the word 'loser' out of your vocabulary, Sophia."

"Got it, Coach!"

Actually, what I have just told her not to do is what I want to do—cuss and call them losers! As the little losers gather around me I start asking questions.

"What happened out there guys?"

Everyone is either looking at the sky or at their Jordans, and you could hear a pin drop. Mind you, a few days ago I couldn't get them to shut up.

I try a different tactic. "You guys were getting beat up and down the floor from the jump. What changed from this morning to this afternoon?"

Silence.

"I guess since no one has anything to say, we can head back to campus and start doing some running. You appear to be more out of shape than I thought, so you can just run until the next game which is two hours away."

After that I get a few people to look at me, but most of them look over at Scoop as if he is the Godfather and has to give his blessing for them to speak. Just then Scoop decides to make a comment.

"Coach, we were just a little tired. And then you took almost all of the starters out of the game and—"

"Scoop, who appointed you the spokesperson for the team?"

"Well I did, but everyone else feels uncomfortable talking to you because you are a woman."

"What does me being a woman have to do with you getting beat up and down the court? Were you trying to prove a point?" I say with a frown.

Shaky, who never really says much, speaks up. "Coach, it's embarrassing to be at this camp with all of these great teams with a girl coach. The guys from the other team have been making fun of us since we got here yesterday. And all of the coaches, even the white ones, are checking you out. Before we came over here we almost got into a fight with this team from Ohio because they were saying things about you."

"Yeah coach," says Slim. "They think because you are coaching us that we are weak and a bunch of pus-, I mean sissies."

"Good save, Slim. Any other comments?" I say, rubbing my head.

Bird jumps in, "No one even asked us how we felt or what we wanted after Coach Donovan died. It's like Principal Leevins just put you here and now we have to deal with it."

"I still can't see what me being a female has to do with how badly you played. Are you telling me it's because a team from Ohio punked you out? It's time you remember you are here to play ball, not get into it with another team because you have me coaching you. Basketball is not just a physical game, it's also mental. Are you going to let a team you didn't even play get you beat just because they think you shouldn't be coached by a woman?"

The boys shuffle nervously and I turn to Sophia.

"Sophia, how many turnovers did we have in the first quarter?"

"We had eight, Coach."

"How many did we have in the other three quarters?"

"We ended up with 15 turnovers, so that makes seven in the last three quarters."

"So we had more turnovers in the first quarter than in the last three combined?"

"Yes Coach!"

"You cannot win games with that many mistakes. You lack focus and you are out of shape! Stop allowing people to get in your head about me being a girl. At this point we have no starters, so everyone should be prepared to play at any time. We also don't have a captain until Coach Frazier and I appoint one. Finally, it was not up to you who would replace Coach Donovan, so get over it. You are here to play basketball, anything else is secondary. Now, we have two hours before our next game. I suggest that you all sit down somewhere and get your minds right. If you guys want to be contenders in the state of Tennessee, you will have to toughen up and learn to be more aggressive, and to execute."

"Now, this conversation is over. I suggest you get on the bus, keep your mouths shut, and think about what you can do to win the next game. Coach Frazier, can you hang back? We need to discuss a few things."

As the guys start walking towards the bus. I turned to Coach Frazier and ask, "What happened out there coach?"

"I wanted to see if they could pull it out and get themselves together."

"Really! And when were you going to decide we needed a change—we were almost 20 points down?"

"This is camp Jackie, not a game."

"I know what this is, Coach, but you are letting the boys think that being mediocre is ok, and it isn't."

"Sometimes it's good to teach them a lesson, little lady," he says with a glint in his eye, while patting me on the shoulder.

"Don't get too comfortable with me, Coach Frazier. And you need to chill with the little lady comment—I have spoken to you about that before. Furthermore, the time to teach lessons is during practice, not in a game. Were you perhaps trying to teach me something?"

I tell Frazier that from now on I will be the only head coach. As I'm walking to the bus, I hear Frazier say, "There are a lot of people up here talking, Jackie. They don't think you can do it."

I turn around so fast that Frazier jumps back about two feet. "Are you sure they aren't making fun of the 10-year assistant coach because he didn't get the position left behind by the great Coach Donovan?" I say with a nasty laugh.

"More like your dad left a bunch of money to the school so Leevins would appoint you."

"And you honestly believe that bullshit? When did you start caring what other people say about you? You are a grown ass man. Are you going to let some young immature coaches allow you to cause dissension among our team? That is pathetic!"

"Imagine how I must feel. I acted as head coach all last season and was left in the dark for months." Frazier says whining.

"My dad was dying, you asshole! You should have been honored to coach last year. But instead you took a prime opportunity to shine and you pissed it away with a 12-18 season. You are lucky I kept you on after that crap! If you don't want to be on my team, walk away now. All your friends in there will cheer you on for not staying with a woman, and pretty soon they will talk about you and laugh when you can't find a coaching job. But if you decide to stay, we do it my way!"

I turn around again and don't stop until I get on the bus, where everyone is sitting down, blessedly quiet. Coach Frazier can kiss my ass until his bitch ass lips catch on fire!

After that epic failure I take over all the coaching, which I should have done from the jump. My dad always told me I was too nice and that people will take your kindness for weakness. We end up having a fairly good week, and I can sense the boys' resistance easing up just a little. I still have a long way to go, but I feel they at least realize that I know what I'm doing. It is interesting to watch their personalities on the court. AJ is a constant reminder of his dad. They not only look alike, he also has his dad's laid back demeanor. And the young man is quite the ballplayer, playing with the maturity of an upperclassman though he's only a sophomore. It will be exciting to see how things turn out for him in the next three years. I am also

221

very pleased with Junebug and Popper, and Shaky is proving to be an excellent six man.

The rest of the week is pretty uneventful, except for a botched panty raid. On Wednesday about 300 cheerleaders converge on the campus, which improves the mood drastically. It doesn't matter if you are 16 or 60—when men and women get around each other the birds start chirping and the bees start stinging. Sophia and I get back to our dorm to find about 200 girls screaming and shrieking. It was fairly quiet the first two days, but not anymore. When I inquire about our new roommates, I am told that the dorm they were supposed to stay in had bedbugs so they moved to our quarters at the last minute. All of my peace and calm are out the door. Even Sophia is a little miffed, as she has gone from being the only pretty girl on campus to being one of 301! The look on her face is priceless when we walk into the hall full of perfect teeth, 32DDs, and luxurious long weave!

After we get over the initial shock of the invasion and having to stand in line to take a shower, we are finally able to settle down. Suddenly I hear a blood-curdling scream that scared the pants off me. Then I hear several more screams. My natural instinct is to check it out, so I run out into the hallway and smack into Sophia. As I bounce off her I see that the hallway is sheer chaos. But it's organized chaos, not the kind that makes you fearful that something was serious but yells that said there was excitement in the air. When I finally get my bearings, I notice that boys are spilling out of several rooms, and some of them look very familiar. It finally dawns on me that this is an authentic old-style panty raid.

At first I see red, but then I snap back into the land of the living and realize that what I have here is a dormful of the dumbest boys in captivity. They have to know that Sophia and I are staying in the girl's dorm, but they don't seem to notice me. Then I feel someone pinch my butt! I look down and realize I have on only a pair of boy shorts and a tank top, so I quickly go and put on my robe, then I step out into the hall and blow my whistle for a good 30 seconds.

You know when dj's really have the dance floor going and they have the crowd doing what they want and then they yell out, "freeze!" Well, the whistle is the universal sign to freeze, which is what about 50 girls and half that many boys do. And then things start to move in slow motion. I yell out, "Hey, everyone shut up! Now I want all of the girls to get back in your rooms! And lock your windows so no one else can get in." They stand and look at me in shock and awe. Apparently the panty raiders didn't know a coach was staying in the dorm. The bunch of idiots! I say, "Girls, in your rooms right now! I will deal with you in just a minute. Boys, you stay put. I want to get a good look at you!"

I start marching down the hall toward the boys with as much force as I can muster up in my bathrobe and house shoes, hoping to keep the fear of God—and me—in their little hearts. I get to the end of the hall where the little heathens could have just walked in instead of coming through the window, I holler, "You get outside now and you better march like little soldiers!"

The boys walk outside and I motion for them to gather around so I can take a good look at them. Such stupid kids, they didn't even have the presence of mind to wear disguises! I run my eyes across the group and see Scoop, Peaches, Little Daddy, Homeslice, and, surprisingly, AJ and Peter. The first four were no surprise but I assumed since AJ and Peter were the youngest they had succumbed to peer pressure or a dare. And then I remembered that AJ was his father's child and started wondering if he had a young harem of five women as well. I move in close to them and ask, "What the hell were you thinking?"

One of the boys I didn't recognize says, "We were just trying to have a little fun, Coach."

"Your little fun could have turned into something disastrous. You broke into a dorm and you are out past your curfew. How on earth did you get over here?"

Scoop pipes in and says, "Well Coach we actually just walked right in."

"That is not what I asked you and I suggest you put it on pause, Scoop. Someone else better answer my question or I am going to start making calls back over to the boys' dorm."

Suddenly they start singing like canaries.

"We paid one of the bus drivers 20 bucks to give us a ride over."

"It was the girls' fault, they told us to come."

"They told us which rooms would be unlocked."

"This shit is just like Adam and Eve. The men always get jacked up!"

"I am the only person old enough to cuss up in this piece!" I yell.

"We were just coming to hang out for a while."

"So you thought..."

"Please don't call our coaches on us, they will kill us."

"No they won't. They will probably give you a high five!"

The comments go on and on until I blow my whistle again.

"Pipe down! AJ, go find Sophia and get me a pen and piece of paper."

As he runs to find Sophia, I start circling the group. "I am very disappointed in every one of you. Not only are you out past your curfew, but someone could have been injured tonight. Each of you is here to focus on basketball, not to fraternize with cheerleaders. I want each of you to write down your name and the team you play on. Who are the seniors in this group?"

About half the guys raise their hands. I look at one of them and say, "What is your name, young man?"

"It's Lawrence Brown!"

"Lawrence, here is my phone number. You and the rest of the seniors are responsible for making sure that everyone on this list gets back to the dorm, except the six who play for me. Call me when you get back. I am going to keep the list with your names on it, and if I see any of you get out of line the rest of the week, I will report you to your coach. Are we clear?"

"Yes ma'am, I am clear."

"Now start writing and make it quick! And if I find out that any of you hoodlums writes the wrong name or team, I will take all of you down. Capiche?"

"What coach?" one of the players says.

I take a deep breath and switch into thug language. "Do you feel me?"

Obviously they do, because boys write down their names and team names. When they are finished, I say, "Be safe getting back across the campus and tell any others who are on their way over that the gig is up."

As they start walking back toward the north side of the campus, I hear,

"Thank God she isn't going to tell coach on us."

"She is a cold-hearted bitch, but I am glad she is letting us go."

"Shut up fool. What she did was cool. We are already in enough trouble. I just got a text from Moe and coach knows we missed curfew."

I turn around look at my team, shaking my head in disappointment. I sit and stare at them, hoping to make them squirm while I figure out how I should handle the situation. I am disappointed in them for doing something so stupid, but I have to chuckle just thinking about how stupidly brave they were to come invade the dorm where their coach is staying.

"I am very disappointed in all of you. Not only would you be featured on the dumbest thief show by having a panty raid in the dorm where your coach was staying, but you also could have just got the code from one of the girls and walked into the dorm quietly so you wouldn't get caught. You are out past your curfew so you have disobeyed one of my rules. Since you all seem to have so much energy, I think we need to do a few things before you go back to the dorm. Sophia, do you have your stop watch on you?"

"Yeah Coach, I figured you might ask for that."

"Smart girl! I want each of you to give me 20 laps around this building. I figure that should be about a five-mile run. You need to do it in less than 40 minutes, and if one of you doesn't make it you all start over. When you're done, I'll give you 10 minutes to get back to your rooms--and not on the bus. Scoop, since you want to be the leader, I'll expect to get a call from you by... it's now 12:30, so by 1:20. If you don't make it by then, we'll do the same thing in the morning, which is now about 6 and half hours off. Any questions?"

Hector takes a deep breath and says, "Coach, are you going to tell the rest of the amigos that we got in trouble?"

"They already know, Hector. Check your Facebook and Twitter accounts. Time is running—any more questions?"

225

With that Scoop takes off running and the chain gang follow. It's like watching the blind lead the blind.

"Come on Sophia. We can watch them from the comfort of our rooms," I say with a huge grin.

The next morning we have a 9:00 AM game. Half the team is pretty tired, and so is the coach. Rumors are running rampant and the boys are feeling pretty ashamed. I decide to have my little criminals sit out the morning games to make sure they understand that there are consequences for their actions. That leaves me with my second-stringers to play the entire first two games. They play pretty well but are kind of timid, which shows me that we need to be more than six deep. At the end of the first quarter I give them my "be aggressive" speech.

"Guys, you're shooting the ball pretty well but you have got to be more aggressive with the full court press. Jump on them as soon as the ball is thrown in and make them turn over the ball. I want you to be more physical—the referee will tell you if you need to back off." Then I look at each of them and bark, "Be tough, be tough!"

They apparently take my little pep talk to heart because the next thing you know they are running and fouling and being way too aggressive. Guess I'll have to be careful what I say to these boys–seems they thought I meant to foul. While I'm proud they were listening to me I have to get them to chill out with some of the aggression. Just as I'm about to call a time out, Shaky hits a three pointer and the team moves in for the full court press. Before I can blink, the other team throws the ball in and my boys run to trap. Well, as luck would have it, the trap is right beside where I'm standing and all of a sudden Popper, also a defensive end who is aggression at its best, forgot he was playing basketball and shoved a kid on the other team. He loses his footing and slams into me. It happened so fast, that next thing I know I'm on the floor seeing stars. And then I suddenly see Adaris reaching over to help me up—but wait a minute, it's not Adaris but AJ. At least he has the decency to help me get up—the rest of his criminal cohorts are sitting on the bench chuckling. For a split second I want to go straight ham, but then I realize how funny it is. The referees take pity on me and call a timeout so I can catch my breath before the other team takes their technical shot. After a few seconds I grab AJ's hand, adjust my jogging suit, plop my hat back on my head, and yell to my team, "I want you all to get back out there and keep playing hard!" Coach Frazier of course takes perverse pleasure in asking if I am ok. Hell yeah I'm ok because my boys are finally playing basketball! I looked around the gym and realized that this camp would go down in history with me being the single woman coach who cussed out the assistant coach, broke up an infamous panty raid, and got ran over during the game. Basketball...it's fantastic!

After Lexington we go to two more camps. By the time we're done, school has started and so has the NFL football season. Adaris and I have kept in touch sparingly over the last month, and I missed him more than I can express. I think he misses me too, but our priorities have shifted. Love, if it is to be, will have to wait.

I do have an opportunity to meet AJ's mother, Lisa. After our final camp, we decide to cap the summer off with a cookout at the Plantation. When the boys start to leave, a car I don't recognize pulls up in the driveway and a woman who can best be described as a West Coast beauty gets out of the car. She is about 5-foot-7 and skinny, but with perfect boobs and about a dime's worth of ass. Her highlighted blond hair is about shoulder length in a perfect blunt cut. Her makeup is flawless and she is wearing a fuchsia maxi dress that clings to her curves. As she walks up the driveway I keep chanting to myself, "I don't feel envy, I don't feel envy!" I paste a huge smile on my face and say, "Hello, you must be AJ and Noah's mother. My name is Jackie Donovan. It's nice to meet you."

"My name is Lisa Patrick. And you must be this wonderful coach I have been hearing about. I can't wait to watch the games this season. I haven't been able to see AJ play in a while."

"He has been doing a great job at the camps. Even though he's only an underclassman he should see quite a bit of playing time this season."

"I am looking forward to it. Let's head out son. I'm taking you to meet your dad in a few minutes."

"Ok mom. Thanks for inviting us over for the cookout, Coach!"

"Nice meeting you again Coach Donovan," Lisa says before walking back to her car.

Not only is she pretty, she is also nice. I wonder if she would have been as nice if she knew I had kissed her baby's daddy. And I realize with a pang that she's driving off right now with their son to go see said baby's daddy. My first impulse is to call or text Adaris, but I am not going to stoop to being like most of the women he is used to. She is just taking AJ to meet his dad, right? They aren't going to spend family time together... so why is she dressed up like she is going on a date? Maybe she always dresses like that on a Saturday afternoon. Adaris and I have already agreed that we can see other people... Now I am getting paranoid and I need to talk to someone who will be a voice of reason for me so I call Max.

"Hallo!"

"Hey Max, it's me—"

"I know who this is. Who just pissed on your party, girl? I can hear it in your voice."

"It's rain on my parade, girl. You remember I told you that Adaris and I have decided to put things indefinitely on pause since I am coaching his son?"

"Yeah, I remember that stupid decision. Now what's going on?"

"We saw each other again at the end of July. We played a friendly game of Horse and made a wager that I won. He ended up paying up right before we left for camp and we had a wonderful time just hanging out. We didn't do anything special, just took a ride, ate a burger, and went to look at his new house."

"Ok, so the decision you made was undone, right? So you are seeing each other again?"

"No, at the end of the evening he kissed me like he was going off to war, and I haven't seen him since. He has sent a few texts to check on me and we have talked a few times, but that's it."

"Jackie, you had to know that when you decided to coach that—"

"Wait, let me finish. Coaching his son is a constant reminder of Adaris. The kid looks just like him. And then today, just when I was aching for a hit of Adaris, AJ's mom pulls up in Mom's driveway looking like black California Barbie."

"You knew it was just a matter of time before you saw her, Jackie. She is the mother of one of your players."

"Yeah I know, but I was hoping she would be ugly as hell with a big 'I swear I am going to lose this baby weight, stomach, nappy hair, and jacked up teeth. She is beautiful Max!"

"And I am sure she looked at you and thought the same thing, Jack. She probably thought you would be some butch coach who weighs 250 pounds."

"But she has no clue about Adaris and I, Max, and I know she wants to get back with Adaris!"

"Shut the front door! Come again Jackie? What the hell do you mean she wants him back? I thought she was married!"

"She was married, but now she's divorced. When she moved back a few months ago she made it clear to Adaris that she wants her family back, including him. At the time I wasn't too intimidated because Adaris was sniffing under my skirt, but things have changed since then and I don't know where his head is at."

"His head definitely isn't in her v jay jay! You don't need to worry about baby's momma. He has been there and done that. You only need to worry about all the new coochie that is lurking around waiting to give out coochie coupons." I hear Max heave a big sigh, then she asks, "So what are you going to do, girl?"

"Just because I can't have him doesn't mean I need to try to block him, so I guess I do nothing. So tell me, what is going on with you and Chris?"

"Well, we said the L word."

"Oh my gosh, you said you love each other?!" I scream.

"Hell no, we told each other we like each other. Love is a little too strong at this point. Although I love what he says to me and I love how he treats me and I love some of his, well, all of his body parts, love is too much of a commitment for me right now."

"And you don't trust him...I suspect your coochie comment is more about you and Chris than me and Adaris."

"I trust him but I verify. And we're thousands of miles apart so I can't really forbid him to accept any coochie coupons."

"Why not Max? If you are intimate, why can't you talk about not being intimate with anyone else? I might be a little jaded, but I still believe there are some men who can have a monogamous relationship, and that includes jocks."

"Even though he makes me feel like I am the only woman in the world when we're together, I am assuming he is like most men."

"Why can't you give the brother the benefit of the doubt, best friend? Trust and have faith."

"Well aint you the pot calling the kettle black. Maybe you should trust that things are not over with you and Adaris. He seems to be an all-in kind of guy, and my guess is he has cut communication with you to keep from going crazy. Hell, the way he looks at you makes me swoon. He looks like he can sop you up with a pork chop."

"You mean a biscuit. In any case, this pork chop needs some sopping but I am afraid it aint going to happen with football and basketball season coming up."

"Well, hold your sheep. You know that Chris and Adaris play each other in the first regular season game in Nashville in a few weeks, right?"

"Honestly Max, I have been so caught up with these boys and my pity party that I haven't even looked at the football schedule. And its hold your horses, not your sheep."

"We aint got no damn horses on the island, only sheep. Chris said just the other day that he wants to fly me in a few days before the game so I can hang out with you, so when he comes to town I will be all his. He's gonna ask Adaris to get us a pass for the team's box."

"Adaris hasn't mentioned anything yet, but I would love to have you come and hang out, girl. I am overdue for some shoe shopping and some girl time. Maybe I can see if Keeva is going to be in town."

"What about Rena? Can she fly in?"

"I think she has weddings scheduled for the entire month. What's the date of the game?"

"I believe its Sunday, and it's a day game. I'll ask Chris tonight if he's mentioned it to Adaris. He wanted me to talk to you first before he books my plane ticket. If you're good that weekend I will fly in on Thursday."

"That weekend is fine with me. If I don't hear from Adaris, I'm sure Chris can get you a ticket to the game."

"He won't need to, Adaris will come through. Let's talk in a few days."

"You have more faith than I do, girl. I love you. Talk with you soon."

"Hello."

"Hey, it's World. What's up dude? You ready to get your ass handed to you in two weeks?"

"Seeing that you are coming to my house, I think you should ask yourself the same question. Can you stay on after the game and hang out, or are you heading back to New York right away?"

"That's why I called. I want to fly Max up to Nashville so she can hang out with Jackie and spend a little time with me. Can you get them tickets to the team's skybox? I want them to sit in the AC, it's hot as hell in Tennessee."

"Man, you know how to pick a game for a family reunion don't you? You know I can get them into the box—along with the other ten people who have put in requests."

"Just say the word if it's a problem. I can make arrangements for Max to sit in the sorry ass, I mean the seats you leave for guests out in the hot sun."

"No man, it's a done deal. I will give Jackie tickets for her and two guests in case she and Max want to bring another person. I guess this will give me an excuse to see Jackie again."

"Damn, I thought you were cool. What's up? You sound like you lost your best friend."

"I feel like I have, man. I haven't seen Jackie in more than a month and I miss her so much I can't stand it. I have women coming out of the damn woodwork and I can't even pretend to be interested. I am getting pathetic—I took a picture of her the last time we were together and I look at it about a hundred times a day."

"So the game is as good a time as any to see her. I know you want to keep your distance for right now, but don't look a gift horse in the mouth. You can justify it if you need to because this was my idea, so take advantage of it.'

"What's up with all the clichés man? Max must be making you soft."

"Fuck you Dair! Just set my baby and her friends up in the box so she can watch you get your ass handed to you on your home turf," World yells before hanging up the phone.

"Now that's the Chris Map I know and love," I chuckle.

Exactly one week before the game I receive a text from Adaris inviting me and two of my friends to be his guests in the Tennessee box at the first regular season home game. It's been over a week since I talked to Max and I've been on pins and needles hoping for a call from Adaris. Max had assured me that he would come through, but I wonder if he came through to please Chris or because he wanted me to be there.

I wait a week before I send Jackie a text inviting her to the game. I was hesitant for several reasons, but I finally decide that everyone involved is a grownup and can conduct themselves accordingly. Just knowing she'll be watching me play makes me nervous, so I decide to see how the game goes before I decide whether or not to see Jackie. I receive a text from her the next day thanking me for the invite and wishing me well for the game.

Max flies in on Thursday evening so we can spend some time together. Keeva is in California but she'll be flying in on Saturday evening and will join us for the game on Sunday. Max and I decide to hang out with my mom on Friday, and then we spend the entire day at the spa on Saturday. Max is hoping to spend an hour or two with Chris before his curfew on Saturday night, so she wants to be at her best. I must admit, I am so happy to see my girl. Max has a glow and a serenity that I haven't seen before. Life is good for her and I need to make sure she knows it. As we sit down for our pedicure at the Essence Day Spa. I look over at her and say, "I have never noticed you coaching the pedicurist before—I guess you want to make sure she gets all the dead skin off your feet." And then I started counting, 10, 9, 8, 7...

"If you must know, bitch, I want to make sure my feet are on point because Chris thinks they are beautiful."

"Yeah, I vaguely remember him talking about how much he loves your feet. What is tripping me out is that you are actually doing something you think will please him. That is some growth, girl. I am proud of you."

"I know I can be hard, but was I really that bad, Jackie?"

"Yes, you were really that bad, Max. I think you have conditioned yourself over the years to be able to handle rejection so well that it became a part of your persona. But I love this softer side of you, Max, it becomes you. You've got the 'I like him glow' and it looks good on you."

"I do, don't I girl? And I more than like him Jackie. I really, really like him!"

"Really, I couldn't tell. Hell, girl, I don't remember the last time you let someone fly you off island, let alone to see a football game, and you didn't complain even once."

"Don't push it, Jackie. Remember, game recognizes game. Speaking of which, what are you playing, some kind of Monopoly? You have not said a word about Adaris since I flew in, but I know you can't wait to see his sexy ass cushioned in all those pads tomorrow."

"Right now I am sitting in jail and can't get past Go. We'll see what happens tomorrow. In the meantime I will keep looking at this picture we took in July and remember the time we had together."

"OK, but tomorrow I am going to pay $200 to get you out of jail. Make sure your feet are nice and smooth too—you never know what might happen," Max says with a big smile.

Who's Zooming Who?

Today is my twelfth season's first game, and I am more nervous than I was in my rookie year. I kept telling myself it's because this was my last first game but most of the butterflies are because of who is sitting in the box about 300 feet above my head. There is a cast of characters gathering there, and I just hope that things down here and up there go well today. I say a final prayer, gather around the coach for his final battle cry, and run out onto the field with my team. There is nothing like the yells from exuberant fans that greet us as we enter the stadium. It's a sound I love, and I will miss it.

Since the game starts so early, we decide to go out for breakfast before heading over to the stadium. Keeva has hooked us up with another limo so we won't have to find a place to park. The temperature is still in the upper nineties and the divas are wearing some bad stilettos, so walking any distance is not in the plan. I'm nervous about seeing Adaris play football. I'm hoping I will have a chance to see him after the game. If I latch on to Max and Chris, maybe that will increase my chances. As usual, I had a hard time figuring out what to wear. It is still hot as hell outside but the box will no doubt be air conditioned. I opt for a pair of jeans and a bright yellow top. I decide to wear my hair so it frames my face in curls and hangs down to my shoulders. I keep my makeup pretty light—just mascara and bright coral lipstick. I strap on orange Michael Kors sandals that make me look about 6-foot-1. Max says my hair and outfit make me look like a lioness. Grrr...

Keeva is wearing a beautiful black maxi dress and black mules. Dressed all in black, she looks absolutely gorgeous but lethal. Max has on a navy top that gives a hint of side boob, which in Max's case is a lot of boob, with white pants and red sandals. She is not so secretly paying homage to her baby, as his team's colors are red, white, and blue. I must admit, we all are looking fierce.

On the ride to the stadium, Keeva convinces us to have a glass of Pinot Grigio to help calm our nerves. For once in my life I am thankful that Keeva encourages me to drink, and it will likely be the first of several I'll need to get me through the game. We get to the team box and I immediately walk up to the window to see if I can catch a glimpse of Adaris. I spot him immediately. His number 14 stands out from the crowd, not because he is so big but because he has a confidence and swagger that most of the players do not. After staring at him for about ten minutes, Keeva gives me a nudge.

"Cuz…"

"Yeah Keeva," I say, still distracted by Adaris in his uniform.

"I know you want to keep your eyes on Adaris, but I need you to look around the room."

"Why? I don't really care who is here, I came to watch the game."

"And so did a few others. Max just so happens to be getting acquainted with Adaris' baby's momma as you ogle her baby daddy. You better wipe the drool off the window before you turn around."

I slowly turn around and search for Max and Lisa. I have to be cool because you can't let people know you are trying to look at them. As I'm scanning the room, I notice Johnnie in a corner talking to Tiffany, Adaris' realtor. I wonder if she has moved up the totem pole in the last two months. The heifer has the nerve to give me a saucy smile and a little wink. I finally spot Max and Lisa in what looks to be an engaging conversation. I decide I might as well get the pleasantries over with. I have to be careful not to act as if she is my arch rival…even though she is. As I start to walk over, Keeva catches my elbow and says, "Before you head over there I want you to know that I took a few minutes to work the room when we came in."

"OK, but what does that have to do with me?"

"Well, darling, it appears that several people in this room either were invited by Adaris or invited themselves so they can see him. To your right is a young lady who attends church with Adaris' mother. At three o'clock is Dr. Clark, who just so happens to have treated Adaris in the past three months for some back issues. She is here "just in case…" But she just so happens to be wearing a very sexy pantsuit. And I believe you and Johnnie are acquainted. She is talking with Tiffany, who looks like she is about to spit nails. I have—"

I grab Keeva's arm and whisper, "Did you just tell me that Adaris' baby momma, his architect, his doctor, and his Bible study partner are here?"

"I said his *mom's* Bible study partner is here. I would hazard a guess that there are a few more of his fans lurking as well. Didn't you tell me that he said he had five 'associates' before he met you?"

I squeeze her arm even tighter, then close my eyes and start swaying.

"Jackie, don't you pass out on me! I do not want to have to pick your big ass up off the floor. Take deep breaths girl!"

I take a few deep breaths and count from ten down to one. My body starts to sway again and then I feel a small but painful pinch on my arm. Before I can let out a yelp I hear-

"Jackie, get your shit together girl! Your competition in this room is steep. You got some stunners in here, but you are the number one stunner. You have about three hours to get through and then he is yours. You know they are watching you, so straighten up! Keep your friends close and your enemies closer! Even if they have no idea what is going on with you and Adaris they are going through the process of elimination right now. Even baby momma's wheels are churning. Now, I am going to let you go and pour you a glass of wine, let Ms. Thang over there pour some tea and find out who else is choosing up in here."

I had been pinched and chastised and now I was coming back to life. I leaned over Keeva again and say, "What the hell is choosing Keeva?"

"You remember the song by the Isley Brother's called Choosy Lover?"

"Yeah girl, that's one of my jams."

"Well there are a whole lot of hoes up in here trying to choose your man. It's time for us to play a little chess so you can get your King!" she said as she stomps away to get my wine or my tea or whatever she is doing.

I take a few more deep breaths, then fall down in one of the cushy leather chairs and decide to do what I came for, enjoy the game. My girls are doing the detective work, and they will let me know what my next move should be. While I sit there gathering my thoughts, I can't decide if I should be pissed, insulted, hurt, or all three. All these women being here is not a coincidence. Surely Adaris knows by now that I met Lisa and he knows Johnnie wants him. Did he invite them to make me jealous and show me that he isn't sitting around twiddling his thumbs? Didn't he think about how I would feel?

My thoughts are interrupted by a smallish older woman with salt-and-pepper hair swept back into an elegant bun. She has Adaris' coloring and eyes, and she is wearing a number 14 jersey. I know this has to be Adaris' mom. As soon as she walks in, Lisa goes over and gives her a little side hug. Adaris' mother smiles at Lisa, then goes to the food table to fix a plate and heads directly to Ms. Bible study.

I could tell Max and Keeva to stop the five point bulletin and the epic investigation because it's easy to tell who Adaris' admirers are, as they start flocking to Mrs. Singleton in a matter of minutes, hoping to win some brownie points. Keeva and Max are at the bar talking quietly, probably comparing notes before they come back to me. The girls join me and Keeva hands me another glass of wine.

"Here girl. I wanted to get you something a little stronger but you are already dizzy."

"And I brought you a plate of food, girl. You need something on your stomach with the wine," says Max.

"Ok, spill it girls. Tell me what I am up against so we can get this over with and I can watch the game."

"The game in here is going to be much more exciting," says Max. "Let's see, I just met the doctor, Lauren Clark. She recently treated Adaris for his back. I need to talk to him about doctor-patient confidentiality, because she sure is easy about telling his business. And then I met Jazzmine, with a "Z", bka Jazz. She is a haberdasher who is fitting Adaris and some other players after the game for tailor made suits. And I had the pleasure of meeting Lisa. Did you know she was Adaris' high school sweetheart? Now, ask me what I said when she asked who I am here to see. Come on Jackie, ask me!"

I massage my temple and take a big gulp of my Pinot. "Who did you say you came to see, Max and what is a haberdasher?"

"I told her I am here to see Adaris! She asked how I know him, and I told her we met about six months ago and spent a wonderful weekend together. And a haberdasher is a fancy name for a seamstress," Max says, batting her eyelashes.

I lean over to Max and whisper, "Max, did you really tell her that?"

"Hell yeah, I told her that and it's the truth. I did meet him six months ago and we did spend the weekend together. The heifer didn't ask if anyone else was with us. The look on her face was priceless. Now she is trying to figure out who I am in Adaris' life. I love outwitting simple women. She can ask Adaris all she wants, I know he won't say a word."

Keeva says, "I had a similar conversation with church girl. This is her first professional football game. She told me she attends church with Ms. Singleton and she met Adaris when he attended church with his mom a few weeks ago. She asked me who I am here to see, I told her Adaris. I told her we also met at church."

"Keeva, you are such a liar. You are going to burn in hell!" I chuckle.

"I am not! I did meet him at church. Well, technically I met him in the church fellowship hall. And then she asked me how long I have known him. I smiled and said about eight months. I told her we have seen each other in the park and at BB King's, and that he has even been over to my house!"

"Keevaaaa...I can't believe you said that!"

"I told the truth, but I embellished it a little bit. I think I knocked her out of the running. So that's two down. Who's left now, just the haber...I mean the seamstress and the woman responsible for his dream house?"

"No Keeva, you and Max missed his momma."

Keeva and Max both look around frantically and say at the same time, "Where is she girl?"

"Figure it out yourselves, Starsky and Hutch. The game is about to start."

At halftime the score is ten to seven, with Tennessee leading. Chris ran for a touchdown, so Max was pretty excited and got a little loud. I noticed that the doctor gave her a funny look, so I lean over to Max and say, "You are blowing your cover, girl. The doctor is going to think you are changing teams."

During halftime, Keeva and Max step out to walk around the stadium. I decide to run to the restroom, where I bump into Adaris' mother. As I walk into the bathroom, she comes out of a stall and smiles at me.

"Aren't you Jackie Donovan, AJ's basketball coach?"

"Yes ma'am I am, and you must be AJ's grandmother. I have heard some stories about your fried chicken...It is nice to meet you."

"My name is Katherine Singleton. Glad to know my grandson is talking about me," she says with an arched eyebrow. "I thought a lot of your father, young lady. I can't wait to see what you do with those boys this year. How is Ella doing? I haven't spoken to her in a while."

"She is doing well, Ms. Singleton, just staying busy."

"Please tell her I said hello. My son and his team are playing well today, aren't they?"

"Yes ma'am, they are. It's nice to get to cheer on my home team."

"I'm glad you are here, Jackie. There is nothing like seeing the season opener."

"Yes ma'am, I am thankful I got an invite."

"Well, some were invited and some invited themselves. Enjoy the rest of the game, dear," she says while walking out of the restroom."

"You too, Ms. Singleton."

I finish up in the bathroom and return to the box, and sit there thinking about what Ms. Singleton said to me. Does she know Adaris and I have been out a few times? And her comment about being invited, what was that about? The paranoia continues to set in.

Max and Keeva are back. Keeva is talking with Johnnie in the corner. I decide to walk over and say hello to Johnnie, since it's been a while since our last encounter. I find them engaged in a lively conversation, with Keeva telling Johnnie about moving her business marketing into the 21st century.

"Sorry to interrupt, ladies, but I wanted to say hello to Johnnie."

"Hey Jackie. I see you are still in the mix, girl. Congratulations cousin. I haven't seen you at the construction site lately and I was wondering how things were going."

"Things are going well, Johnnie. I like how you incorporated my ideas into the floor plan."

"It looks like the game is about to start back up ladies," Keeva breaks in. "Johnnie, here is my card. Let's try to get together next week to discuss getting you more exposure to all this new money moving into Nashville."

"I look forward to it Keeva. Don't be a stranger Jackie."

As Johnnie slinks back to her seat, I ask Keeva to get me another Pinot. I have one more half to get through, why not do it in the comfort of my own drunkenness. Meanwhile, Max is still working the room. She joins us just as the second half kicks off.

"Keeva, don't give this heifer any more wine."

The only person according to Starsky and my calculations who may have any idea why you are here other than Johnnie is Adaris' mother."

"His mother! Oh Lord, do you think she knows I tried to jump Adaris bones in my mommas pantry and that I stopped AJ's panty raid!"

"Take a sip of Pinot, Jack, 'cause it's your last for the evening."

"What did you find out?" It looks like you have left a few episodes out girl. What pantry and what panty raid?" said Keeva as she finished off my wine.

"It's not important right now. Tell me what you think Hutch."

"I prefer Thelma and Louise but didn't they end up dying-"

"Yeah girl and I would prefer two of the girls from *Set it Off*, that movie was the bomb, but they die too don't they?" said Max.

"Or what about the girl in *Dead Presidents*?" screeched Keeva.

"No," interrupted Max, "How about Rock a bye baby! You remember the chick on *New Jack City* who ended up on Soul Food!"

"Enough Siskel and Ebert I need some damn answers!" I yell.

Keeva looks around and says in a conspiratorial whisper, "The only thing they really know is that you are AJ's basketball coach, and Lisa is going around telling people that word is that you are a stuck-up bitch who won't talk to anyone. I suggest you keep it that way. The only two people who have a clue are Johnnie and Tiffany. Johnnie hasn't seen you in a while so she thinks she has a chance. Tiffany knows but her alliance is clear. My guess is we will hook up with her after the game."

"This shit is rich. Someone needs to write a book on you, girl. Now you sit over there and sober up. Hutch and I need to figure out who's zooming who up in this piece! You have about an hour to get yourself together before Adaris sends for you. And believe me, he will. He wants to get you away from these females as soon as he can so he can start doing damage control. Now you sit back in the cat bird seat and relax while I get you some milk," says Max as she walks away.

"No milk Max, after all this wine it will really make me sick.

Keeva and Max let out a whoop of laughter that was so loud that it scared me.

"Keeva you should consider adding reality TV to KeMarketing and the first episode should be shot right here," said Max.

Thankfully Adaris has a great game. He has three receptions and runs for over 100 yards. The Trailblazers end up beating the Giants 24 to 17. After the game I feel like I was on the field blocking. My shoulders are stiff, my back hurts, and my head is swimming. All because I was afraid to do anything but sit in my chair. Tiffany has been a small ray of sunshine. She sent me a text during the game to say hello and that she'll see me later. It is good to know that she too has drawn her line in the sand and that she has my back. The room is starting to clear out and I get a ding on my cell phone. I look down and see a message to Max, Tiffany, and me: *"Hey ladies. Early dinner set up 4 u in Hutton Room 212. Shelley, World, Amos and I will join u in a few hrs. Need to shower, do fitting, and interviews. Sweetness, Keeva is welcome to join us.*

As I finish reading the text I look across the room and see Keeva and Max smiling smugly. Tiffany gives me a sly wink as we head out the door. I grab one more glass of Pinot and take it to the head 'cause I have no idea how

Adaris will act and I need a liquid buffer. Our little posse heads to the elevator. As we step out on the first floor, I see AJ, Noah, and Junebug walking toward us.

"Hey Coach Jackie, hey Tiffany! I didn't know you were here. Did you see my dad? He really showed out, didn't he? We're about to head down to the locker room to see him and some other players!"

Thank God Keeva and Max are standing on either side of me because AJ has just scared the shit out of me! I hadn't thought about him being at the game.

"Hey guys. It's good to see you. The game was great wasn't it?" I figure I can get his mind off who I came to watch if I keep the conversation on the game.

"Yeah Coach, it was the bomb. Check out the jerseys Mr. Singleton got us. Scoop and some of the boys are going to be hating," says Junebug.

"Junebug, you may not want to tell the rest of the team you were here or Mr. Singleton may need to come up with eleven more tickets, right AJ?"

"That's a great idea, and maybe you can come with us to the next game too!"

"Yeah and bring your friends," Noah says with a big grin.

"How old are you young man?" Keeva asks, grinning right back at him.

"I'm 14 but I'm really mature for my age," says Noah, panning his eyes up and down her body."

"I may be small but I can whip your little a—" Keeva stops short, remembering I'm their coach.

"AJ, why don't you work on getting your teammates tickets first, and then we can see, ok?"

"That's cool Coach. We gotta run. Dad's waiting on us. He just sent me a text and said to hurry up because he has an important meeting in about an hour!"

"I wonder what that meeting is about AJ," says Max, pinching me on the arm.

As the boys walk away, Keeva says, "No more drinking for you, you little lush. You may be tall but you can't hold your liquor worth a damn. Let's get to the hotel so we can freshen up."

Keeva's limo drops us at the hotel and we walk up to the room. Before we get to the door, it's opened by a young lady who appears to be a waitress. She ushers us into the sitting area, where a spread of spinach, crab, and queso dips, chips, crackers, and an assortment of breads are spread out on the table. There is also a fruit tray laid out beside a fruit dip. To the right of the table is a mobile bar, where a man is mixing drinks. Ms. Door opener turns to us and says, "Mr. Singleton has asked me to tell you to please help yourself to hors d'oeuvres and drinks. He and the others should arrive within the hour. Dinner will be served once the men arrive." With that she leaves the room and we dig into the spread. Keep in mind I haven't eaten anything since breakfast. Max had brought me a plate at the game but I was so tense I couldn't eat it. I feel like I am in a safe place here with Tiffany, Max, and Keeva, so I decide to put something in my stomach, along with some more Pinot. Now I know why Aunt Lu likes to get drunk. It helps dull the nerves and the pain of rejection. It also gave me courage that I know I will need in about 60 minutes.

I do the obligatory press conference with some of the other players as quickly as I can, so I can meet Shelley and Chris and head over to the hotel. I brought the Rover so we can ride together. Amos Hunter, our star center, is going to join us for dinner. Chris and his team are staying at the Opryland Hotel, but he checked out this morning and reserved a room at the Hutton. He wants to spend as much time as possible with Max before leaving town. I'll drop him at the airport tomorrow morning so he can fly commercial back to New York.

As we get in the car, Shelley leans over and says, "I got a text from Tiffany. She said the team box was very interesting. You got anything you want to share with us before we walk into the lion's den, Dair?"

World chimes in, "I got a text from Max too. She said that Keeva was about to film a reality show about all the guests you had in the box. What the hell is that about dude?"

"I guess I better practice my story on you before I get to Jackie."

"Practice as in practice your lie, or as in try to get the story straight because Max will be able to tell if I am helping you lie. I swear that girl can see right through my ass," says Chris.

"There is no need to lie man, believe it or not. I knew when I moved back home that more people would be asking me for tickets to the games. I went to church with Mom two weeks ago and the piano player, the pastor, and the head deacon were all jockeying for tickets. I honestly didn't have any more to give so at least I didn't have to lie to them. AJ, Noah, and one of their friends wanted tickets in the stands so they could smell, hear, and feel the sounds of football. Lisa said she wanted to come because she didn't want her babies to be by themselves, but of course she wanted to be in the club box because it's been so hot. I promised Skip Fulton passes to the box three months ago, but he couldn't make it so he sent his daughter Johnnie in his place."

"Is that it man? That doesn't sound so bad," World says.

"No, that's not all. Dr. Carter was supposed to be on the field during the game but the doctor she was subbing for showed up, so he sent her up to the box. Mom wanted to invite a new lady from the church, and Jazzmine was there to fit some of the guys for custom suits after the game. Of course she wanted to sit in the box so she could make some contacts. Mom always sits in the box because she doesn't like to sit out in the sun. And then there is Jackie."

"Yeah, my babies' best friend who I asked you to invite to the game and put in the box," says World.

"Yeah, Jackie..." Adaris says, rubbing his head. "The only woman I want to deal with besides my own mother but can't, at least not in public because everyone knows her damn daddy and—"

"And everyone knows you!" says Shelley. "And pretty soon everyone will know she is AJ's coach."

"And now Jackie probably thinks I invited all these women to the game so I could throw it in her face."

"Let me ask you something, man. How do these women look?" Shelley asks me.

"They are all pretty women, but none as gorgeous as Jackie. She is not only pretty but she is sexy, smart, generous, and she cares about my kid."

"Sounds like she really sucks man. The good thing is you have five other women who can easily replace her sorry ass," World says, laughing.

"At least that is what she probably thinks," Shelley says, shaking his head. "But the question behind the question is, how would you feel if five men were at Jackie's basketball game and had some type of affiliation with her?"

"Unless it was someone from her family, I'd be mad as hell and ready to kick ass and take names later. Why do you think I have you three joining me for dinner? I know you would rather be alone somewhere with your ladies. I don't know if Jackie will give me a big kiss or kick me in the nuts! Thanks for taking pity on me."

"Well, I know my baby is going to kiss me and tell me I played a good game, even though you all beat our asses," says World.

"And my baby is going to open her arms to me as well. So that just leaves you and Amos."

"And that scares me. Amos is a loose cannon. I invited him because I thought it might be nice for him and Keeva to meet, but he was one of the guys talking about Jackie in the locker room. I may end up kicking his ass if he says anything crazy to Jackie. If he figures out that I defended Jackie in that locker room because I do like her, he is going to blackmail me to keep his mouth shut. I am hoping he will be so enamored by Keeva that he won't get caught up with Jackie."

"The only time Amos ever keeps his mouth shut is when he is asleep. I take that back, he snores," says Shelley.

As we wait for the guys, we turn on some music and really get comfortable. We have eaten our fill and are listening to Earth, Wind, and Fire. And of course we're sipping more wine. I have mellowed out again, but it is just the calm before the storm. I know I really have no reason to be upset with Adaris, but in the back of my mind I feel like he was trying to prove something to me.

Just as we're getting warmed up to "Let's Groove" and I'm into a one woman dance, the door swing opens and it was like Morris Chestnut, Boris Kodjoe, Idris Elba, and some huge Shaq look-alike comes walking through the door. I stop dancing and watch in awe as all four men troop in and start singing, "Gonna tell you what you can do with my love, alright. Gotta let you know girl your looking good, your out of sight alright," in some of the worst voices I had ever heard. Thankfully they are so fine that they are almost forgiven for jacking up one of my favorite songs. Keeva, who is closest to the IPOD, turns off the music and then the fun begins!

Chris and Shelley go to Max and Tiffany for hugs and kisses. Out of the corner of my eye I see the big guy walk over to Keeva, and I just stand there staring at Adaris. He is standing by the door and leaning on the wall, looking like he is hesitant to come any further. I just keep looking at him. It has been a while and I want to soak him in. He has on what appears to be a Tom Ford black suit with a crisp white shirt that is open at the collar. He has on some black Salvatore Farragamo square toed shoes. His head looks cleanly shaven and he has on glasses that frame his beautiful brown eyes. Actually, I want to tear his clothes off and I feel my mouth start to water, then I snap out of it and remember I am supposed to be pissed! I squint my eyes and work them up and down his body several times, and when I get to his face again he gives me a tentative smile. I lean forward to take a better look and see that he has gotten his braces off! Now his smile is simply radiant, and he starts walking toward me slowly. Slow like in the Spike Lee movies when they are walking but not really moving, or maybe it was the Pinot...

As we step off the elevator on the second floor, we hear what sounds like Earth Wind and Fire's "Let's Groove" belting from my room. "Sounds like I might just be making it rain after all," says Amos.

"Not on my watch you mother—"

"Chill guys. The ladies are just unwinding after the game," says Shelley.

"It will be in your best interest if Jackie is unwinding," World adds with a grin.

"I know you aren't talking about that fine ass Jackie Donovan, are you?" Amos yells.

"He is, and I would recommend that you keep your distance from her, if you get my drift Amos," says World.

"I knew there was something going on that day you got your panties in a wad," says Amos.

"And they are going to stay in a wad, so I suggest you keep your damn mouth shut Hunt!" I growl.

I open the door not knowing what to expect. The first person I see is Jackie, singing into a wine glass like it's a microphone. Her hair is in these curls around her head, which make her look like a beautiful lion. I just pray she won't act like one when she sees me. As World and Shelley head over to their ladies and Amos moves in on Keeva, who looks like she is frightened by the sheer size of him, I lean against the door and watch Jackie belt out: "Let this groove get you to move, it's alright, alright."

I have to lean against the wall to keep from keeling over. It has been almost two months since I have seen her and I know if I keep moving toward her it will be more X-rated than the face sucking that's going on with Max and Chris.

After what seems like an eternity I start walking toward Jackie. When I get about five inches away, I stop in front of her and say, "Hi." *Brilliant Dair.*

"Hi back. I see you got your braces off."

"Yeah, about two weeks ago. You changed your hair?"

"Yeah, I wanted something different. You look nice in your suit."

"Thanks, you look tall in those sandals."

"Yeah, I like towering over people."

As soon as she says that, a dam bursts and I yank her into my arms.

Before I know it, Adaris has wrapped his arms around me and is holding me as tight as he can with the wineglass wedged between us. We stay like that for a minute until I remember again that I'm supposed to be pissed. Adaris bends down to kiss me, but I turn my head and push against his rock hard chest. He loosens his hold on me, but just a little.

"Sweetness, what's wrong?" Adaris whispers in my ear.

"Let's see, what's wrong. I had the pleasure of seeing your other five today, then I met your mom, got tipsy, and then ran into your son. Other than that it's been a great day. Great game by the way!"

"Damn the game! What the hell did you just say?" Adaris grabs the wine glass and throws it on the floor, then tries to pull me closer.

"You heard me! Five other women. Hell, who knows, maybe there were more If Starsky and Hutch would have continued Operation Who's Zooming Who. And put me down Adaris. That caveman crap is not going to work today!"

"I am going to give you one more time to explain what one through five is and tell me who Starsky and Hutch are or I am really going to intimidate you," Adaris growled in my ear.

"You have a degree in Engineering. Figure it out smart ass! My words were so harsh that it threw Adaris off guard. I slip out of his grasp and start stomping away from him. I forget that his legs are much longer than mine and he catches up to me in a few steps.

"Do you want to talk about this in front of your friends or in private?" Adaris growls, since we now seem to have an audience.

I swing around, throw my hand on my baby-making hips, and scream, "My friends already met all of them so what difference does it make?"

Before I can get the last word out of my mouth, Adaris picks me up like a sack of potatoes.

"Put me down Adaris Singleton!"

Adaris turns around and says to the others, "You guys go ahead and start dinner without us. Jackie and I have some things to discuss." Then he stomps off to the bedroom with me beating on his back and yelling, "Put me down!" He has the nerve to give me a few love taps on my airborne ass.

"They won't be coming back anytime soon," Keeva says, looking at Amos still in awe because of his sheer size.

"Well, Amos is a growing boy and boys have to eat. Come over here and sit by Amos."

"First of all, please stop talking in third person, Amos!"

"I like you already. Do I need to sling you over my back the way Dair just did your girl?" says Amos with a leer.

"I wouldn't try that shit if I were you, Mr. Bone Crusher. Jackie has been drinking and her reflexes are off. My reflexes are just fine, and I know Karate, Jujitsu, and Tae Bo," says Keeva with a huff.

"Well I know Tackle and Tackle trumps all that shit. Come on girl, let's get some dinner and let me get to know you better."

Adaris carries me into the bedroom.

"Sweetness, I am not going to let you down until you can calmly tell me what is bothering you," he says while standing in the middle of the floor, still rubbing my butt.

"Stop rubbing my ass Adaris! I just spent the most uncomfortable four hours of my life, drank more wine than I have since my freshman year in college, and now you are acting like you had no idea what—I mean who—I was going to encounter today. Do you care that little for me Adaris?"

"Baby, I care more than I want to admit, and if you will just give me a minute to explain I will—"

"Explain! Explain! You told me a few months ago that you had five other women, and today you invite me to the game so we would all be in the same room. What the hell is so damn funny?"

"Baby, please stop pounding my back. I have been getting tackled a lot the last few hours and I am a little sore. And I am laughing because you are so damn funny when you're angry," Adaris says while swinging me to the floor.

That did it—before I can run to the bathroom, I bend over and throw up the five glasses of Pinot Grigio, my breakfast, and the dip all over Adaris' Salvatore Ferragamos.

"Oh Jackie! Baby...damn, you did have a jacked up day, didn't you," he says, bending down to pick me up again. This time he cradles me like a baby and takes me to the bathroom.

"Do you feel better now?"

"Other than the fact that I just ruined your $500 shoes and am totally mortified yes, I am just fine. Now put me down, find me a toothbrush, and then please get out," I whisper.

"Let me go change. There's an extra toothbrush in the cabinet. Why don't you clean up get in the bed, and I'll check on you in a few minutes," Adaris says with a big but kind grin. "Damn I have missed your goofy ass, Jackie!"

I wash my face, brush my teeth, and slip into Adaris' bed. I am exhausted from the events of the day and the bed feels simply delicious. I snuggle up on his pillow, sniff his scent, and almost immediately slip into a dreamless sleep.

After I change, I go back into the other room where the rest of the party is eating a meal of prime rib, lobster tails, twice-baked potatoes, asparagus, and rolls.

"Damn dog, did you throw it down like that? You come out wearing different clothes and your girl stays in the room? Amos needs a lesson on putting it down!"

"Shut up Hunt! Jackie is a little under the weather so she's lying down. I just came out to grab a quick bite."

"Is she ok, Adaris?" Max asks and starts to get up from the table.

Chris grabs her and says, "Sit down baby. Adaris has got her. I only have you 14 more hours. I need you to stay close."

"Do we need to do anything for her Adaris? I know she had too much to drink," says Keeva.

"How many glasses did she drink?" I ask.

Max leans forward and says, "Let's see, she had one on the ride to the game and one when we got to the skybox."

"She also had a glass right after halftime," says Keeva.

"I saw her drink a glass right before we left the box," says Tiffany.

Keeva finishes the count, "And she had at least one when we got back here. I guess that makes five glasses of wine. How ironic don't you think Adaris?"

"Oh boy. We'll, she'll be just fine after a little nap. Hurry up and finish eating so I can have some alone time with her after she sobers up."

"If you are paying, Amos is staying," says Amos.

"How about you eat your plate and Jackie's—she won't be eating any time soon—and then join me for a ride in my limo," Keeva says to Amos.

Amos replies, "Are you asking Amos out, Keeva?"

"Hell no! Keeva is trying to keep Amos' friends from killing him by taking him off their hands."

"I like you more already, Keeva. Amos will join you on the ride. Do I need to get some ones?"

"My stripper days are over, and you would need much better than one dollar bills. This body has a $10 minimum, boo."

While we finish up our dessert and after-dinner drinks, I go check on Jackie. She has thrown the covers off and is sprawled on the bed. I must admit, she looks damn sexy with those curls all over her head, but I'm not about to seduce her while she is drunk and sick. She also looks very uncomfortable lying there fully dressed. I make a quick decision and go back into the other room.

"Sorry to interrupt everyone's dessert, but I need to have a quick meeting of the minds. First, can we all please agree that whatever happens between these walls stays between these walls?"

Amos looks up from his dessert and says, "This must be pretty important to get me to stop eating man. What's up?"

"And since he has just finished your dessert and is about to move on to Jackie's I would think he could take a pause for the cause," said Keeva rolling her eyes.

Max, who is sitting in World's lap and feeding him dessert, says, "That depends on if what you're planning is legal or not. You know that as an attorney I have rules that I am bound to."

World leans over and kisses Max, then he says, "She can keep a secret and yes, it stays in this room cause the shit we have been doing under this table needs to be kept secret! What's up man?"

Everyone is tuned into Adaris now.

"Jackie doesn't feel very well. I need to move her to the guest bedroom and get someone from housecleaning to do some cleaning up. I also need you ladies to get her undressed and into something more comfortable for the night. Keeva, can you call Ms. Ella and tell her Jackie is staying with you? I hate to be dishonest, but I'm going to let Jackie explain to her mom after she sobers up. Max, what time does your flight leave tomorrow?"

"Not until 2:00. Why?"

"Here are the keys to my car. Do you know how to drive in the United States?"

Max's eyes narrow and before she can respond, World jumps in. "Let me handle this one, baby! Yes, she knows how to drive in the States you dummy! She is a U.S. citizen. I asked her the same question myself about two months ago," he says with a laugh.

"Sorry Max. I need you to take World to the airport in the morning since his flight leaves at 9:00. If Jackie isn't feeling any better, can one of you take Max to the airport?" I ask Tiffany and Keeva. "We have practice tomorrow at noon."

"I will make sure Max catches her flight," says Keeva. "What do you plan to change Jackie into? Max's clothes are too small."

"She can put on one of my t-shirts. I will have the hotel launder her clothes so they're ready in the morning. Amos, I need you to make sure Keeva gets home safely. Can you handle that?"

"It will be my pleasure, dawg," says Amos as Keeva rolls her eyes.

"Do you need me or Tiff to do anything Dair?" Shelley asks.

"Tiffany, I may need you and Keeva to check on Jackie after I leave for practice if she is not feeling any better. And Shelley, I may need you to call me tomorrow if you don't see me at the stadium by 11:00."

"Just send me a text in the morning and let me know what I need to do. My schedule is flexible," says Tiffany.

"Ok, then I am going to move Jackie to the other room now. Max and Keeva, can you get her changed? Tiffany, could you call the maid service and ask them to come clean the floor and bring fresh bedding? Amos, Shelley, and World, you supervise the women!"

That comment goes over like a ton of bricks, but laughter quickly follows and the United Negros work in harmony. I move Jackie, the ladies change her into one of my shirts, and everyone leaves the hotel suite much more quietly than they came in.

I wake with a start and I can't move. I feel like I'm being crushed by a big tree. As I lie there blinking and try to get my bearings, I realize that the tree is Adaris' arms. Somehow I have ended up lying across his big chest with his arms wrapped tightly around me. I'm in a strange bed in a strange room, and I can't open my eyes too wide because my head hurts so much. It's even too painful to think. Adaris must sense me moving because he bends down and whispers, "Its ok, sweetness. You are here with me. And I've got some aspirin and ginger ale for that hangover."

"What time is it and where am I?"

"Let's see, it's about 10:00 on Sunday evening and we're in the guest bedroom of my hotel suite. Open your mouth and take these aspirin."

"Why am I here and why are you giving me aspirin?"

"It's a long story baby. Please just trust me and take these. I will explain everything in a few hours when you'll be feeling much better."

Adaris rolls me over and puts two aspirin in my mouth followed, by a glass of ginger ale. "Drink this slowly. You don't have anything in your stomach."

When he says those words, it all came back to me in vivid detail. The game, the wine, the women, the, oh my God, the throw-up!

"Adaris, I—"

"Jackie, please be quiet baby. This is the most peace I have had in almost two months. Can we please just go back to sleep and talk in a few hours. I am exhausted from the game. I just want to hold you and go to sleep."

"Promise me we will talk?"

"Yes, I promise. Now good night." And with that he kisses me softly on my crusty lips, gathers me closer, settles my head on his chest, and we both go back to sleep.

I wake up again and look up at Adaris. He is just sitting there looking at me.

"What time is it now?"

"It's 2:00 in the morning. I figured you would be up soon. You've been stirring around for the last 30 minutes."

"Where is everyone Adaris? The last thing I remember is a room full of people."

"Max and World are in a room on the third floor. Amos took Keeva home hours ago in the limo, and Tiffany and Shelley went home."

"My mom! I bet she is worried to death about me."

"Keeva called your mom and told her you were a little under the weather and that you were spending the night with her. You can tell her whatever you want to," he says, then bends down to give me a kiss on my temple and rubs his big hand on my stomach. "How are your head and your stomach?"

"Much better. My head still hurts a little bit but I'm better. You played a big game today, how are you feeling?"

254

"I feel better than I have in a long time," he says, kissing me again.

"Whoa playa! Before you start anything we need to talk. What happened today?"

"You know how things sometimes just spiral out of control? I know it may have looked bad up in the box, but I did not set it up the way you think I did."

"How do you think I think you set it up, Adaris?"

"I know it looked like I was trying to show you I'm dating different women, but it isn't like that." Adaris looks deeply into my eyes and explains all the circumstances that brought the five other women to the box. It all makes sense but I'm still wary, so I ask him, "Is there anyone else I need to know about?"

He smiles and says, "Those are all I know of. No wait, my mom was there. Did you meet her?"

"Yes, I met your mother. She is very nice. I had a feeling that she knew more about what was going on than I did."

"Oh, my mother knew what was going on."

"Then maybe you should tell me. Are all of those women interested in you Adaris?"

"I knew I would eventually walk into the Lions' Den," he says, then bends down to kiss me again.

"I am not going to lie, Jackie. Johnnie has told me a few times that she is interested and Lisa has some vision that she and I can work things out, but—"

"But what, Adaris? Surely you and Lisa spend time together since you have a child together. How do you feel about her?"

"At one time I really did want to make things work. I thought that once I went pro and could provide a good income for my family that she would come back. But then she got married and stopped spending time with AJ, and I realized that I didn't want anything from her but for her to love my son and for us to get along for his sake."

"As for the others, Jackie, I could be ugly as hell, dumb as a rock, and have seven baby mommas, and I would still have women falling for me. You know that's part of the aura of being a professional ball player. But I don't want any of them, I promise you that."

"So what makes them think you are interested? Women like them don't stick around unless they think they will get something in return. As far as they know, you are fair game."

"If I weren't so crazy about you I probably would be seeing a few of them. I told you Jackie, I am not innocent by any means, but I have matured enough to know that a piece of tail every now and then is not going to satisfy me long term. I am willing to wait for what I want and I think it will be worth it. But I am going to be perfectly honest, I don't like watching you from a distance while I want you mentally, spiritually, and physically. It's torture. That's why I was ready to move heaven and earth to make sure I saw you tonight. I trust World, Shelley, and Amos and I know you feel the same about your girls."

"Thanks for being honest with me Adaris. I have a lot of self-confidence, but those women are gorgeous, smart, have great careers, and they would drop any man for you. I am pretty secure, but I was so tense in that box that I only talked to Max, Keeva, your mom, and the bartender the entire time. Between worrying about you out on that field and trying not to start choking some of those women I was a nervous wreck! I was not myself and I hated it. Any other day I would have worked the room. And I am so afraid that caring about you is going to change who I am. I am doing things that are just not me!"

"We both are frustrated, baby. I want to tell the world how much I care about you, but at this point my relationship with my son and your position as a coach are more important than anything. I don't know what else to do other than try to sneak in some time when we can to see each other."

I look up at Adaris as he is talking and tears start streaming down my face. Adaris gathers me close and starts kissing away my tears.

"The first time I saw you cry was at your father's funeral. I swear it almost tore me apart. To think I am making you cry is doing the same thing. Jackie, this should be one of the best times of your life. You are doing what you love, and I don't want to upset your happiness."

"Oh Adaris! I think the tears are just the last thing left. I was so excited about seeing you on the field, and you played so well I wanted to yell and scream. And then I had to worry, will I see him after the game, especially when I saw all those women. And now we have only a few hours together before we part again for God knows how long."

"I hear you baby, but we have nine hours before I have to head to the stadium, so let's make the most of the time we have together."

"I can't sleep with you Adaris. I don't think I could take it."

"You have been sleeping with me for the past six hours sweetness. It's a little too late for that don't you think?" He gives me a sly grin.

I scowl and say, "You know I don't mean sleep with you in that sense. I want to make love with you so bad but I think if we do it'll just leave us more frustrated."

"Let's just let nature take it's course. I promise we won't do anything you don't want to do, ok?"

"OK, but what if I want to do everything?"

"Damn, I hope you do! Now be quiet and let me really kiss you."

Adaris pulls me up so our faces are inches apart. "This is where I most want to be, right here with you. Just relax and let me hold you." I put my hands around his neck and relax in his arms. He starts giving me small kisses that soon become deep, delicious kisses. Adaris slides his tongue in my mouth and licks from side to side. "I have missed you so much Jackie!" he whispers, and then slides me on top of him so I can feel his desire. "Do you feel what you do to me baby?" He grabs my butt and grinds me against his erection.

"Mmm...do that again."

He moves his lips to my neck and starts placing small kisses down my to my collar bone. "Do what again baby?"

"Kiss me right there," I say hoarsely as I bend his head to my breasts.

257

As Adaris nuzzles my breasts he eases his hands inside my panties and caresses my ample ass. He slides his thumb down the crack of my butt and squeezes me tighter between his legs. "Tell me what you want baby!"

I climb up his body and slide my arms under his shirt to rub his chest. "I want you so much, but..."

Adaris kisses me hard on the mouth and slides a hand around my back to unsnap my bra. Then he moves me up so my breasts are even with his mouth and takes one of my nipples in his mouth and sucks. His other hand finds the valley between my legs. "Your mind may say no but your body is telling me yes. You better make me stop now or I won't be able to.

I move my hands down to his stomach and then I stop.

"If you move your hands any further then you are in trouble..."

I slowly slide my hands from his stomach to his erection. "Where are the condoms?"

"I don't have any!"

"What?"

He gives my nipple a tiny bite and then sucks it to take the pain away. "I don't have any. I had no idea we would wind up this way. Just let me please you and we then can go to sleep."

Adaris moves his finger to the edge of my panties and dips his fingers into my wetness. "You are so wet. I knew you would be this way..." He dips another finger and then another, making the same motions with his lips on my breasts.

"Adaris, you aren't playing fair," I say as I grind against his fingers. "But it feels so good."

"Then tell me to stop," he says, moving his fingers faster.

"Don't stop. Oh, please don't stop!"

"I want you to come for me!"

At that instant I climax. It is so intense that I just lie there on top of him, trying to soak it in.

As we lie together, Adaris rubs my hair with one hand and strokes my butt with the other. I look up and smile. "Now what do we do about you?"

He kisses me lightly and says, "What we do about me is what I have been doing since we met. I am going to take a cold shower! He gingerly moves me off his erection, jumps off the bed, peels off his clothes, and walks to the bathroom stark naked.

"What are you trying to do to me Adaris!" I yell while eyeing his perfect physique.

"I don't need to answer that," Adaris says laughing.

After his shower, Adaris crawls into bed, spoons his arms and legs around me, kisses me on the neck, and we are both soon fast asleep.

I wake the next morning to Adaris kissing me softly on the lips. "I have to go over to the stadium sweetness. Keeva is taking Max to the airport. You can call her to come pick you up when you're ready, or you can wait for me to take you home this evening."

"I think I better let Keeva come pick me up. But I want to sleep a little longer."

"Stay as long as you want. Order room service if you feel up to it. Your clothes have been washed and are hanging in the bathroom. Text me what you decide to do. Now come here and tell me goodbye."

Adaris gathers me in his arms and gives me a gentle kiss on my head, grazes his lips over my eyes, down to my nose, and ends with a lingering kiss on the lips. He whispers, "Thank you for yesterday. I won't forget the beautiful night we had. Have a great day sweetness." Then he lays me gently against the pillows and walks out.

For the second time that morning I sleep like a baby.

A few hours later I wake with a start. I look over at the clock and see that it's a few minutes after one. I send Keeva a text to see if she can pick me up. She texts back that she just dropped Max off at the airport and will see me in about 30 minutes. I jump up to go take a quick shower. Adaris' scent is on the pillows and sheets and has permeated my skin. I hate to wash it off and I decide to take his t-shirt home with me. I walk into the bathroom and see my clothes from yesterday hanging in a dry-cleaning bag. I also see a bag sitting on the sink that contains a pair of blue jeans, panties, and an orange pullover shirt that matches my orange shoes. I swear that man can dress me better than I can dress myself. Adaris also made sure I have all the toiletries I need. I shower quickly, get dressed, and make a small deposit in Adaris' toiletry bag, along with a note. I am just finishing up when Keeva knocks on the door. I open the door and say, "What time was Max's flight?"

"She just called to tell me it has been delayed an hour, why?"

"Let's wait to talk when we get in your car so we can call Max. I don't have the energy to repeat myself and I have a lot of questions about yesterday." As we walk to the car I send Adaris a text letting him know that Keeva has picked me up and that I left him something in his toiletry bag. We jump in the car and Keeva calls Max on her Blue Tooth.

"Hallo Keeva. I hope this call means you have picked up our little drunk from the hotel," Max croons into the phone with her Crucian lilt.

"Yeah girl, I got her. She wants to talk to us at the same time, and since your flight is delayed I thought we might entertain you for a while."

I lean back on the seat and say, "I figure instead of repeating myself I might as well kill two birds with one stone. But before I start, can one of you tell me what happened between the game and the hotel. I'm a little fuzzy."

"We had a United Negros meeting and determined that over the course of about six hours you had about five glasses of wine, which left you more than slightly inebriated," laughs Keeva.

"And when we got to the hotel, you put on a concert that rivaled Fantasia from American Idol singing to Earth, Wind, and Fire, then you cussed out Adaris and then threw up all over him," says Max.

"Adaris called a meeting like he was President Obama or something and then put the United Negros into action to move your big ass to another room and change your clothes, then he booted us all the hell out so he could feel you up!" says Keeva.

"He did what?" I yell!

"I'm just kidding girl. But he does give orders rather well and we did get moving when he waved his magic wand. Now this is where you continue the story," says Max.

"I woke up I guess a few hours after you left and still felt pretty bad. Adaris gave me some aspirin and we went back to sleep. When I woke up the second time we sat and talked about the people at the game."

"So how did he explain himself out of that one, girl?" asks Keeva.

"He basically said it was an unfortunate coincidence. Johnnie came in place of her dad, the doctor was banished from the football field because she was a major distraction to the team, Lisa invited herself so she could 'watch over' the boys, Jazzmine was there to fit some of the guys for suits, and Hannah was a guest of his mother."

"But surely Adaris must have known they were coming for him, girl. Each lady we spoke to had a fantasy of being Mrs. Singleton," says Max.

"He knows some of them are interested, but he assured me that the feelings are not mutual. He is still very torn about our relationship but told me this morning that he misses me. Max, how do you do it?"

"Do what girl?"

"How can you spend time with Chris knowing you won't see him for weeks afterwards?"

"I enjoy the time we have together and I store up the memories until I see him again. I try not to put too much pressure on him because our relationship is new. He has been burned in the past and he is also busy playing football. I do my best to be a safe haven for him. But it aint easy. After I dropped him off this morning I cried like an infant."

"You mean like a baby," says Keeva.

Max ignores Keeva's correction. "So...once Adaris explained things to you, did you feel better about the situation and the direction of your relationship?"

"I felt somewhat better, but at this point I can't ask Adaris not to get involved with other women. I really really like him, but at this point that's all we have."

"So did you give him something to think about this morning?"

"What do you mean, Max?"

"What she means is did you throw it on him?" laughs Keeva.

"You know a lady never tells!" I say.

"Well, this lady will tell. I threw it on Chris, around Chris, under Chris, and over Chris. He won't forget me over the next few weeks," says Max with a bellow of laughter.

"I probably would have begged him to make love to me but we didn't have a condom!" I admit.

"You what? Well, that actually could be good. It could mean that he isn't thinking about having sex with anyone so he has no need to keep any protection," says Max.

"Or it could mean he used them all up," adds Keeva.

"Thanks, Keeva, that makes me feel much better. What we did was beautiful, and believe me it put me to sleep like a baby. And I'm glad we didn't go all the way. It would have made it even harder not to see him over the next few months. But I can't wait for when the time is right. The preview was quite impressive," I say with a grin.

I change the subject. "Now, tell us about Amos, Keeva."

"Amos Hunter, better known as bone crusher, is a gentle giant. He talks a big game but he is actually really nice."

"So are you interested in him?" asks Max.

"Amos is kind, really smart, and rich as hell, but he isn't my type. I plan to keep him on my team for now but I think the only thing in the cards for us is to be friends."

"So your type is ugly and poor Keeva? You would prefer a jobless, ride-the-bus scrub like the guy you went out with a few weeks ago?" Max taunts.

"Right now I prefer the type of man who is not ready to settle down. Amos may have been talking about making it rain, but if I gave a little bit of effort I could have him eating out of my hand, and he could definitely fall in love with me ladies," says Keeva.

"You have always been short but never short on self-confidence cousin. And I am proud of you for not giving him any candy. But you do know that most men love a challenge. Telling him no is going to have him on you like a duck on a Junebug."

"What the hell does a duck on a Junebug mean?" says Max.

"It means he will be on me like white on rice," Keeva tells her.

"Now I am really confused. You off-island Americans say some crazy stuff."

"It means he will be on, over, around, and in Keeva if she allows him to," I tell her.

"Oh, I got it now. Hey, they just called my flight ladies. I had a great time and I love you both. Jackie, go get some condoms, girl!"

I make it to the stadium by 11:00. Leaving Jackie in that warm bed was hella hard. She is so soft and curvy and she smells so good—I wish I could bottle her scent to keep with me. As soon as I walk into the locker room, Amos corners me.

"What's up man? Is everything good on your end?" he asks.

"It's all good man, what about for you?"

"Little momma is all that and a bag of chips. Amos wants a repeat."

"Amos, you can stop talking in code man. It's just you and me over here and I doubt anyone is paying that much attention. Now, tell me what's up."

"Keeva is a dime, man. When I first met her I thought she was too small, I could really hurt a little thing like her, but her personality is huge, man. She is gorgeous, smart, and funny, and she owns her own business."

"So did you ask her out man?"

"Yeah man, I asked her out three times on the limo drive home, and she told me no."

"You aren't going to give up are you?"

"I am going to slow walk her little ass down man. I got plans for little Miss Keeva Hudson-McGhee that she doesn't even know about."

"OK Hunt, just keep me posted. I may need some tips."

"I got you dude. And thanks for including me yesterday. I may have just met my wifey."

"No thanks needed man."

We watch some game footage, have a light workout, and then I spend some time with Dr. Clark and the trainer to work out the kinks in my back. By the time I return to the hotel at about 4:00, I am exhausted. I got a text from Jackie earlier telling me Keeva had picked her up and that she had left me something in my toiletry bag. As soon as I got the text I called the hotel and asked them not to change the linen in the guest bedroom. I planned to lie in the exact spot Jackie and I had lain in hours ago. I wanted to keep her scent in my mind while I replayed the details of our time together in that bed. It had taken all the willpower I had not to make love to Jackie last night. For a minute I thought protection be damned, I wanted her so bad. I couldn't get enough of her scent, her hair, and her flawless body. I could have touched her all night. I felt closer to her than I have to any woman in my life. And she was so responsive to my touch. That little taste had me wanting more, and sleeping with her would have made me want her all the time. I enter my room and go straight to the bathroom to find whatever Jackie had left. I open my toiletry bag, and sitting right on top are the yellow lace panties Jackie wore yesterday. I put them up to my nose and breathe in her intimate scent and smile. Then I see she also left a note. I take another sniff of her panties and read the note:

"Thank you for a beautiful time this morning. I took your shirt so I had to leave something for you. I hope you like the scent you left on me after our time together".

Yours, Jackie

I take the panties with me to the guest bedroom, drop down on the bed, and relive those few hours we had together.

Keeva takes me home and of course she has to come in and get something to eat. For someone so small she can sure put it away, which is one thing that she and Amos have in common. As we walk into the house I notice it is very quiet. We go into the great room and see my mom sitting in "the chair."

Oh man, do I have some stories about that chair, which is more commonly known to my brother Leo as the "your ass is grass chair." It has been passed on through three generations, has been reupholstered several times over, and is now a striking electric blue. As we walk into the room, Mom looks up at us and says, "We need to talk." Those three words usually came right before, "Wait until I tell your daddy." They also act like a truth serum, and I instantly started apologizing. "Mom, I am so sorry I just got home, but the Pinot, the football, the other women, and then Adaris—"

Keeva jumps in before I can finish. "And Aunt Ella, she was too drunk to come home and—"

"Ladies, will you hold up a minute. You are both grown. I trust you and you also don't have to check in with me, even though something tells me I'll need to hear about yesterday. But that's not what I need to talk to you about. I need to catch Jackie up on what is going on with her Aunt Lucy, but you are welcome to stay, Keeva."

"No thanks Aunt Ella, Lu has gotten on my last nerves. Jackie can call me later and give me the quick and dirty version," Keeva says, rushing out the door, clearly glad to escape.

As she walked out I whispered in her ear, "You stool pigeon!"

I sit down in the chair opposite mom and say, "What's going on with Aunt Lu now? Did anyone locate her yet?"

"She is here."

"She is here!" I yell, jumping up from my seat looking around frantically.

"Not here physically, but she is in town. Leo called me a few hours ago screaming that Lu had shown up at the Happy House talking crazy. I finally got him calmed down, and about 30 minutes later she called here."

265

"What did she say, Mom? Did she say, I'm sorry I didn't make it to the funeral. How have you been doing in the nine months since my brother died!"

"No honey, she did ask me how I am doing but not like she was really concerned. She told me she is in town to find out what's going on with that old house your grandmother left to her and your daddy. She thinks because your dad is dead it belongs to her."

"That bitch! She doesn't give a damn about your feelings or what we have been through, she only came back because she sees dollar signs. Did she get my letter?"

"I didn't ask her, and please watch your language young lady. Aunt Lu is an addict Jackie and she sometimes has no control over what she does. I am sure your dad's death pushed her over the edge."

"What are you going to do, Momma?"

"I don't know yet. Your dad and I fixed up that little house a few years ago and we have been renting it out. We have been putting half the rent in an account for Jordan to use for college, and the other half in an account so we could send Lu money from time to time, but she doesn't know about it. I could offer to buy her out or let her buy me out, but I am not giving her a damn thing. When your grandmother passed away Lu was in jail, and she has never contributed one penny to take care of the place. So just like she was not in a hurry to come home and see my husband, I am not in a hurry to resolve this issue."

"What if she tells you she wants what is rightfully hers?"

"She can do that, but after I deduct her share of the taxes, insurance, maintenance costs, and attorney fees, she won't have much left."

"So you are basically in the catbird seat, right?"

"Your father's will was airtight. If I do sell my share to Lu, half of the money will be put away for Leo. Your dad said the proceeds from the sale of the house should go to Leo if it were ever sold, but only when he is responsible enough to handle it or when he turns 40, whichever happens first. I want you and your sister to know what is going on so you won't be caught by surprise if Lu calls you."

"Mom, how do you always take the high road?"

266

"Most people don't know this but between your father and I he was the most passive when it came to money and his family. I have been known to pinch a penny and be more on guard. In this situation I need to protect my family, and that means you Serena, Leo, Micah, Jordan, and Keeva. I can do that and still long-handle-spoon Lu. She will eventually either settle on a compromise or self-destruct."

"So what should I say if she calls me?"

"Jackie, you know your daddy and I never censored what any of our children said, except to us. Didn't some rapper say, 'do what you like'?"

"'Ella, I do believe that daddy left you his coolness and his gonads. And yes, Tupac did say that in one of his early songs. "

Mom gets up from her chair and laughs, "I was cool before your daddy left, you all just didn't notice it. I have a few things to take care of now, so would you please call your brother. He has called twice since yesterday morning looking for you. He has some good news to share with you."

I pick up the phone and call Happy House.

"Happy House, this is Leo, how may I assist you."

"When did you get elevated to receptionist Leo? And what happened to my rude friend who usually answers the phone?"

"Hey, what's up sis? That was Red and he got to go home a few weeks ago. I'm on the phone 'cause the person closest to leaving always gets phone duty. Something about getting us reacquainted with the real world."

"Oh, that's nice, but I will miss talking with Red. Wait! What did you say?"

"Daddy used to say Rena is the prettiest, I am the slickest, and you are the smartest, but I aint sure about that now. I said, I am about to blow this joint girl!" Leo says, laughing.

"Wrong choice of words brother!" I laugh. "When are you getting out and what happens next?"

"I hope to get out in the next two weeks, provided I have a place to stay and have either a job or school lined up. I took a few college courses while I was locked up, and I think I want to take a stab at a technical college when I get out of here. ITT has a criminal justice program that I want to check out."

"Pump your breaks, bro. You're getting out in two weeks and you think you want to go to college to major in criminal justice. This shit is rich. My brother, the ex-criminal wants to learn more about criminals?"

"No stupid. I want to learn how to defend criminals. I actually have been thinking about becoming an attorney. I know that as an ex-con I may not be able to do that, but I want to advocate in some way for people in jail who don't belong there. I aint gonna lie, a lot of these idiots should be put in and the key be thrown away, but a lot of innocent people also get locked up every year and it destroys their lives. I tell you Jackie, it's genocide of our race. You got some of the smartest, most athletic, talented people in prison, and most because they made one bad decision. And you wonder why you can't find a man. All the beautiful ones, myself included, are put away like animals!"

"That's the Leo I know and love. I haven't heard you this passionate about anything since Cheryl broke your heart in eleventh grade! So what do we need to do to help you get out of Happy House and get in school?"

"Nothing."

"Nothing?"

"Yeah sis, for once in my life I want to do something without using daddy's name or even your name. Mom told me daddy put a little something back for me, but I want to see if I can do this on my own. Queesha said I can live with her until I get myself together. I can do that, but I really want a place of my own. It doesn't have to be anything fancy, but I don't want to get caught back up in slanging again so I need to be in an environment where I can focus on getting this degree. I am 31 years old Jackie and I have nothing to show for it. I finally understand why Ma and Dad were so disappointed in me. They did not raise me to act like Lu, but somehow I felt that because she was trifling I had to be that way too. And that's bullshit."

"I am so proud of you Leo. Thirty-one is not too old to start over. And I think you will be a great advocate, not just for criminals or ex-cons, but also for young people. Just let me know what I can do to support you."

"First let me get into school. Then I may be calling you to help me with my homework! Now let's move on and talk about Lu right quick. I know that shit is eating you up."

"I actually wanted to make sure you're ok about her being back in town, Leo. Mom told me she came over and got you riled up."

"She did sis. I think she loves the element of surprise. She walked in here, put on her mommy act for Bill, and convinced him she wanted to check on me. By the time I met her in the conference room she had taken off that face and put the "I need you to help me get what's mine" face on. She didn't ask me how I was doing, when I was getting out--she didn't even hug me. All she said was, "I know half of that house is mine and I need you to help me get it."

"That sounds like the Lu I know and love. Was she high, Leo?"

"She wasn't high. It was too early in the morning for that. She explained to me like we were special operatives what we need to do to get the house. She even had the nerve to tell me I can stay in the house once we get the Wilcox's out. That woman knows subterfuge better than Hitler!"

"Yeah, you're right; it's time for you to go."

"Time for me to go where?"

"To school. You are already using words like subterfuge. So what did you tell her?"

"I told her I wouldn't do a damn thing to help her. I told her that she is on the bottom of my list because of how she did Pops and Ma Ella. I also told her I didn't give a damn about that house and she better not mess with Ma Ella, or I was going to catch another case. And the last thing I told her before I pimped out of the room was that she needs to stop treating me like we are homies, that I am her son and she is the woman who birthed me. The reason why I let myself get so screwed up a few years ago was because I didn't understand that Pops and Ma Ella were raising me to be a good person. I let the fact that she was such a horrible mom convince me that I needed to be a bad person. I told her that life was short and that she needed to get her shit together and to stop using me as a pawn. And she is not to come by here or call me unless she plans to get clean and stop gaming on people. And Jackie, I swear when I walked out of that room I felt a weight lift off me. All the shame I felt about being her child and the guilt I felt about Pops and Ma Ella giving me a great life went away. Man, I wish Pops was still here so I could tell him I am sorry for those bad years. I did call Ma Ella right away and tell her how much I love her and how much I appreciate everything that she and Pops did for me. I told her I was not going to disappoint her or my family anymore and that I was going to go get mine, in a legal way."

"And what did Mom say, Leo?"

"She just started shouting, 'Thank you Lord' over and over again," Leo says, laughing. "For once she wasn't shouting, 'Lord, please help my child,' like she used to say when I was doing some crazy stuff. She was thanking God for me seeing the light. Jackie, I am not going to screw up this time."

"Leo, I am so proud of you. I know you are going to do some awesome things for our universe."

"I am Jackie. I told Rena, if things don't work here she can always fire Kyle and make me her assistant."

"What did Serena say to that bro?"

"She said she would do everything she could to help me be an attorney!"

"I love you bro. I gotta run. Keep me posted on when you get out. I have a big dinner waiting for you at the house."

"I want some beans, greens, and nothing lean, my sister!"

"You got it Attorney Donovan!"

Game Time

Today is our first season opener and my first game as a head coach. The team has been working hard and I know we are ready. The last few months have been a blur. Adaris and I have kept in touch by phone and text. We decided after our last encounter that staying away from each other is the best thing for now. I decide not to focus on the other women in his life that I know about. It won't make me feel any better and I have enough on my mind.

Aunt Lu has been calling and our conversations have been tense. She is in Nashville for one reason only and that is to claim a little piece of nothing. She has completely skated around the fact that her brother is gone, and Rena and I have decided to cut off all communication with her unless we can talk to each other with respect.

Leo got out of Happy House and was accepted into a technical college. He is staying with Queesha and things are working out well. He comes over about once a week to eat and catch up on things. Mom is so proud of him that she decided to help pay his tuition. He even found a job, working as a custodian at ITT. Whoever hired him is a genius! Between classes and his job he is on that campus from 8:00 in the morning to 8:00 at night. His parole officer is so pleased with Leo's progress that if he continues doing well, the officer will recommend that they reinstate his driver's license. He already has visions of grandeur about the type of car he will drive. Mom is secretly planning to give him an old car that she and dad kept in the garage in case one of their cars was down. Leo is proof that it is never too late to start over.

It has been ten months since Dad passed and I can see that my mom grows stronger each day. She still misses him but knows that his wish for her was that she be happy and enjoy life. I finally figured out where she has been sneaking off to each day around noon. She joined a group of wonderful women who support each other after the death of a spouse or child. I am proud of my mother. Although she has an undeniable faith in God, she knows that talking to people in similar situations will help her deal with losing her soul mate.

Hell, I could use some counseling myself. Over the course of a year I have retired, buried my father, started coaching, met a wonderful man, fallen in love, and now our relationship is very much in limbo. I decide the best therapy for me will be to sink myself into our basketball season and let God do his job. I am tired of trying to fix things myself, so as my dad would say, "I put it in God's hands" to work out my fate.

Max and Chris are working out the kinks in their long distance relationship. She is still adamant about staying on the island until she feels more comfortable about the relationship, but Chris is committed to making sure things work out. I have never seen Max happier in the ten years I've known her.

Keeva, on the other hand, is—well, she's Keeva. She and Amos have been hanging out from time to time. Some of her stories about the "bone crusher" are hilarious. Amos is convinced that Keeva is his woman, even though she insists she is a free agent. Free agent meaning she is free to see whom she damn well pleases when she damn well wants to. Keeva shared with me that one night Amos chased her around her house insisting that she commit to being only with him and having his babies. He even told her he wanted to name their first child Ashlee Lauren! After that Keeva started running like Sanya Richards-Ross, but Amos is pretty light on his feet and he did catch her…but only when she wanted him to.

Serena's business in Chicago is flourishing. She just hired her second full-time employee and she and Keeva are considering opening a branch here in Tennessee. I am so happy my family and friends are doing well. In a sense, everyone is finding their way in the universe. And me— well the proof will be in the pudding tonight. There has been a lot of talk in the *Tennessean* about the merit of having a woman coach for a boy's high school basketball team. In fact, the discussion has gotten quite heated in the paper, on several blogs, and even on Facebook. I try my best to tune it out, but Keeva insists on keeping me abreast of the more fascinating comments. A few days before our first game, Keeva calls me.

"Hello."

"Hey cousin. Since I am your pro bono PR person, I thought I'd let you know the latest debate about your premier as one of the first female boys' basketball coaches in Tennessee."

"Yeah, I figure why read the paper and blogs when my PR rep will do all that for me."

"And I usually charge $100 per hour for my services, but I will work for a home cooked meal. I must admit, some of the opinions are quite interesting. One man blogged that you have busted the glass ceiling wide open so that more women will coach not only basketball but football as well. He even said women are much better coaches because they knew how to appeal to men emotionally instead of physically."

"He must be gay, Keeva."

"Not sure about that, but his comments got a ton of responses. Another guy said the only reason you got the job is because you are so beautiful that you will be able to sway the referees! Girl, this stuff is unbelievable."

"Girl, even Coach Frazier felt he had to give me the scoop the other day. He said several of the coaches in our conference made a wager that I won't make it through ten games before I quit. What trips me out is that he thinks by telling me that he will make me rethink my decision. Keeva, it still amazes me that my own assistant coach doesn't support me."

"You should have fired him on his day off! Jackie, things haven't changed much and you know just as well as I do that most men think they are smarter, stronger, and more athletic than women. But you also know Principal Leevins thought long and hard before he offered you the position. Back when he hired Uncle Shorty, blacks weren't being hired to be the head of anything except the cafeteria or the janitorial team. He has always had unbelievable foresight into how things should be and he rarely makes mistakes."

"I hadn't thought about that Keeva. Leevins has always gone against the grain. I hope me taking this position will open up more opportunities for women. But I want them to be qualified and not just get a job to even up the playing field."

"So tell me cuz, how do you feel about the season starting?"

"I am so excited. We really have a great team Keeva. I've changed the line-up and I am doing a few things differently, but I think it will help us get through the season. My decisions won't be popular with some of the parents or the fans, but I can't worry about pleasing people. I need to do what's best for our team."

"What about Adaris?"

"We'll see what happens after both our seasons. I love him Keeva. I finally admitted it a few weeks ago when I realized I was sitting in my car looking at his damn picture on my cell phone. And I think he cares about me a lot too. It takes a strong man to put the needs of his child before his own. Most men would have said the hell with it, and his making the decision to put our relationship on hold makes me care about him even more. But if he decides our situation doesn't work for him, I will respect his decision to move on. Right now I need to stay focused on these young men. They are my top priority."

"I just hope he doesn't come to any games with Lisa."

"Lisa is AJ's mother. If they come to a game together I will deal with it. It's time for me to put my big girl panties on and realize that anything worth having takes time and work."

"Do I see some maturity, girl?"

"Ask me that after our first few games. I will either fly like a bird or sink like a ship."

With that Keeva starts an offbeat rendition of "I Believe I Can Fly" and I promptly hang up.

I've been getting calls from the local newspapers and even *USA Today*. I decide not to return most of the calls, because the more things get hyped, the harder you can fall. One call I do decide to return is from Tony Stint from the *Tennessean*. He was one of my dad's favorite reporters. Not that he isn't tough, but he is also fair and unbiased. I sit down with Tony in my office a day before the game. There is really no way to prepare for an interview, so I figure I will do what I have always been taught, to tell the truth, the whole truth, and nothing but the truth. Tony comes in and gets right down to business.

"Jackie, it's great to see you. It's been a while."

"You too Tony. I believe the last time we spoke was at dad's funeral?"

"That's right Jackie, and I have been following you since then. Tell me, how did it feel when Principal Leevins asked you to take the place of one of the most successful high school coaches in the United States, who just so happened to be your father?"

"I was taken completely by surprise. I had no idea he was even considering me for this opportunity. Dad, I mean Coach Donovan, always had a competent coaching staff and I assumed Principal Leevins would choose one of them."

"Some people are saying that you aren't qualified for the position, Jackie. That you used your dad's reputation to help you find a job after being ousted by your WNBA team."

"I don't think I am any less qualified than any other coach. I have played basketball all my life. I was all-state in high school, ranked in the top ten in my conference in rebounding, and was all-conference three out of four years in college. I played in the WNBA for six years and won the sixth-man trophy three out of those six. Based on my research, over 50 percent of high school coaches didn't play in college and fewer than 10 percent ever played pro, so exactly what more qualifications do I need, Tony?"

"Maybe I should rephrase that question. Most say that you are not qualified to coach young men."

"I am not sure how you would coach boys and girls differently. My father didn't teach me to play basketball any differently than he taught his boys for over 25 years. In fact, because I often couldn't beat the boys physically in a lot of cases, I had to play smarter."

"So, do you think that bringing a mental aspect to the game is going to set you apart from your father and other coaches?"

"Of course not. All great coaches know that sports are about 60 percent physical and 40 percent mental. Why do you think that some of the best teams lose and some of the Cinderella teams win? At some point in time, skill alone won't win a game. Sometimes its luck, it's a player that gets hot, a bad coaching decision or even a bad call from the referee that could turn the tide of a game instantly."

"What do you plan to do differently from your dad?"

"My coaching style is more subtle than my father's. He was an in-your-face coach and he was smooth and flashy, and he had an impeccable ability to read not only his players but his opponents. I admit I still have a bit of a learning curve so I won't be operating as instinctively as he did, at least not at first. But I promise, you will see an upbeat and exciting game. I want to keep people in the stands, and that will mean winning games."

"So what happens if you don't have a winning season?"

"This is my first game Tony! Give me a chance to play one before we start talking about that. But I will say, I come from a line of winners and losing is not an option."

"Many say that the SHS bulldogs are cursed, that their luck has run out. Thirteen state championship, but none in the last three years. What say you?"

"Well, Tony, I say those people who are talking have never won 13 championships. And there is no such thing as luck."

"Jackie, many people have said your dad was cocky and often made his own rules, which created enemies among his colleagues and the media. Did he pass that trait down to you?"

"Yeah, Dad could be cocky and he did make his own rules, Tony. But the rules he made were to give his players the best opportunity to succeed, not just on the court but in life. Anyone who knew my father knows he was one of the most compassionate, modest people in the world. If he created any enemies, that was their problem, not his. And said enemies would often call my dad for help with problem players on their team and for help getting kids into school. So let's just say that my dad taught his girls to be very self-assured. And like my dad, I plan to leave any controversy on the court."

"A lot of people are saying you have huge shoes to fill and that Principal Leevins may be setting you up to fail. What do you say about that?"

"I am honored that Principal Leevins chose me to do this job. Over 25 years ago he chose a brash young man who knew how to walk the talk and gave him a chance to coach. He is doing the same thing for me. If I fail, it's my fault."

"How do you feel about your first game starting in this very gym in less than 24 hours Jackie?"

"It's bittersweet, Tony. I wish I could sit behind my dad's bench and listen to him shouting out plays. But I know my dad is in heaven resting in the arms of the Lord, and I have been prepared for such a time as this. I will do my best to honor my father's winning legacy but I also want to make this my team. I feel like one of the most fortunate women in the world, along with my mother and my sister Serena. I had 28 years with one of the most awesome human beings on this earth. I am thankful for that."

"Thanks for giving me an interview, Jackie. I heard you weren't granting any others before the game. You could have been featured nationally. I am honored that you selected a lowly reporter such as I to speak with you."

"Tony, my dad admired and respected you. Most people were his buddies when he was winning but his enemies when he was losing. You were always objective, and my dad appreciated that. So do I."

"That means a lot to me Jackie. I miss your dad like hell. He taught me a lot about the game of basketball and the game of life. More than anything he taught me to be myself and not make compromises just to get ahead."

Tony and I shake hands, he wishes me luck, then I sit back down and think about what I will do to get through the next 24 hours.

Thank God this is a bye week because my body is tired and we're only halfway through the season. Ironically, I am having one of my best seasons, averaging over 100 yards a game. For someone so preoccupied, my focus on the field has been amazing. Maybe it's because I have a single-minded goal to just get through this season. A few years back there was no way I would have been counting the weeks until the end of the season, but the end of this one means so many things to me. It could be the beginning of a new career with ESPN, as well as a new home and more time with my son. But most of all I hope it will give Jackie and me a chance to start all over. After being away from her for two months I'm not sure we can pick up where we left off. I can remember that night after my first game so vividly I ache. I have decided that if Jackie is still interested after her season ends, we will figure out a way to be a couple while she also coaches AJ. He will be a junior next year and should be mature enough to handle it.

Lisa has been pestering me so much to spend some time together that I decided to meet her to prove to myself that there is no spark between us. Thank God I was right. Our ships passed years ago. She has matured into a wonderful woman but she isn't the one for me. We had a long talk and decided the best thing is for us to be friends. She even wished me well with the woman in my life...I almost passed out! I asked her to elaborate, and she said she didn't know many red-bloodied men who would turn down the chance to get with her, so I must be in love. Love...I had not taken the time to think about whether I'm in love. Hell, half the time I am around Jackie I don't know what is going on because my hormones and emotions are a wreck.

Just to test Lisa's theory, I decide to meet Johnnie one night to review some changes to my house. After listening to 99 reasons why we should mix business with pleasure while she lets me catch a glimpse of her left boob and a bit of a nipple, I have had enough—even before she spits in my ear. I feel nothing. A few years earlier the tit alone would have got me going, but not that night. The only tightening I feel is in my jaw when I damn near have to pry Johnnie off my lap. After that she narrows her eyes at me and says, "For a while I thought Jackie's appeal would dwindle, but apparently she put some sort of spell on you. I don't throw myself at men often. I don't need to," she says, looking at herself appreciatively. "I guess this is my cue to officially move on. We would have made a striking pair, Adaris."

"My private life is not up for discussion, and if you continue to pull this shit..." I leave the sentence unfinished, throw a Benjamin on the table, and get the hell out of dodge.

After testing myself with two out of the five women Jackie had been concerned about, I decide not to chance it with the other three. That is until Hannah corners me at church one Sunday. That day the church musicians are jamming so hard I feel like I'm at BB King's. After a stirring rendition of some music that sounded vaguely like a combination of "Turn this Mother Out" by M.C. Hammer and "Joy and Pain" by Maze, I have to take a leak. I leave mom and AJ in the pew and step out to the bathroom. When I come back out I literally run right into Hannah. It is like a planned fully body tackle. I grab her to keep her from falling and then she grabs me.

"Whoa Hannah! Sorry about that, I didn't see you standing there."

"I was actually on my way to get some Kleenex. The choir has got us all going and I suddenly got a little full."

"Full of what?"

"Full of the Holy Spirit. But since I ran into you I feel even fuller," Hannah says while trying to wrap her arms around me.

I quickly remove her arms and step back.

"It's good to see you again Hannah. I hope you are getting settled here in Tennessee."

"I am. Your mom has been so wonderful, and thanks again for the tickets to the game. I just love watching you play."

"Thanks...well, I better get back inside before my mother starts looking for me."

"Before you go I just want you to know that the Holy Spirit told me I would meet my husband here."

"Here as in right here in this spot?" I ask looking nervously around.

"No silly, right here in this church. Maybe we ran into each other for a reason—"

"Hannah, you could not have missed running into me since you were standing right outside the men's room. I need to go. God bless you." She's full of it alright!

Having a bye week means early practices and rest. My back spasms have been getting more pronounced and I'm doing my best to treat them with stretching and rest so I won't have to start taking muscle relaxants. This week will give me a chance to chill. It will also give me the chance to see AJ's first two basketball games. I am so excited about his debut as a varsity player but I have to play it cool and act like I'm not too hyped. On Monday I find AJ in his favorite room, the kitchen.

"What's up Pops?"

"You got it. What's up with you?"

"Not much. We just finished our last practice before the first game."

"How was it?" I can't sound too interested or he'll clam up on me. I have been trying for the last few months to get AJ to talk about Jackie without him knowing I wanted him to talk about Jackie.

"Today it was off the chain! Coach really mixed things up. And at the end she just let us freestyle."

"Uh...come again son. Freestyle?"

"She had some real strange combinations out there. It was cool to play with and against each other. And then the last 15 minutes of practice she put on some music and just let us run the court and do our thing. We did some dunks and alley oops, and Peaches even did a granny shot. It was crazy fun! And then we danced a little right before we did our final huddle. Pops, you should have seen Hector. He can really break dance!"

"You danced? Did Coach Jackie and Frazier dance too?" His words bring to mind the first time I saw Jackie dancing at the club and the last time when she was dancing and singing in my hotel room.

"Yeah Pops. Coach Jackie can put it down!"

"She can put it what?" I yell.

"Chill pop! Don't beef because you don't think our coach should be dancing. She is pretty serious most of the time. She finally chilled a little. You know Pop, Coach Jackie is actually really cool when she wants to be. Most of the guys have said she is like the ice queen. Really pretty but cold."

As AJ finished his soliloquy I breathe a huge sigh of relief and thank God AJ didn't notice that I got a little excited. "So the guys think your coach is fine?"

"She's cool; I mean, if we were old like you we would try to holler at her. But we made a pact not to look at her booty or anything like that. We decided to treat her like an older sister since she's too young to be like our moms."

She aint too young for me, but I don't dare say that to AJ so I change the subject.

"Are you ready to play, son?"

"Yeah pops, I am. I really didn't think I would get much playing time since this is my first year on varsity, but I think coach is going to give me a chance to prove I can hang with the upperclassman."

"Whether you play 2 minutes or 20, I want you to play your best and have a good attitude."

"I know, you don't have to keep telling me that. Just make sure you come tomorrow to see your boy throw down," AJ says with a shout of laughter as he barrels up the stairs.

"Oh, I plan to watch you and Coach Donovan both show out," I whisper to myself. And I hope she gets her package on time tomorrow.

Shoot the Lights Out

I come to my office a few hours earlier than usual just to pray, meditate, and relax. In the words of my dad, to 'get my mind right.' I adopted this routine when I was a freshman in college. Putting myself in a quiet place physically and mentally is the best thing for me before a game. Serena flew in for the week and she, my mom, Keeva, and Leo will be coming to the game. Even my mom's sister Leslie said she would come—if I would leave her a $3.00 ticket at will call! Serena and Mom picked out an outfit for me. I have no idea yet what they came up with, but I am sure it will be beautiful. After making sure the lineup for the game is set, which will likely start me off as one of the most unpopular coaches in the league, I leave a few notes for Sophia to handle before the game, and then head home to grab a shower and change my clothes.

When I walk into the house I notice a sense of serenity. Not an uncomfortable quiet but a definite peace. I stand at the door and take several deep breaths as memories wash over me. A few hours before my dad went to the gym before a game he would always take a short nap, listen to a little music, and sit quietly to collect his thoughts. He said that was his way of "getting in his comfort zone." As I got older, I found myself doing the same thing before each game.

I head up to my room and find several items on my bed. There is a beautiful gold pantsuit with a small purple SHS pin on the lapel. It is the same pin my dad always wore on his suit for every game. There is also a beautifully wrapped box that looks like an Ella or Serena creation. When I open it the first thing I notice is an envelope with what looks like Adaris' handwriting. The front of the envelope reads, "Open the box and then read the note." I throw the note on the bed and open the box. Inside are at least fifty packs of chewing gum in every brand imaginable. I see Trident, Orbitz, Bazooka, Hubba Bubba, Dentyne, Bubble Yum, Wrigley's, and Double Bubble. I let out a gleeful yelp! I am in chewing gum heaven. I dump all the gum onto my bed and see another box that I recognize instantly as a Jimmy Choo box. Inside is an exquisite pair of deep purple peep-toe patent leather pumps with a three-inch heel. They will go perfectly with my gold suit. I try them on and they fit perfectly! Then I read the note,

> *"Sweetness,*
>
> *I know you have been working hard to get ready for this special day. I saw these shoes and thought they would go well with your outfit. I*

also wanted you to have enough gum to last you for a while. One of your biggest fans will be rooting for you tonight and during the season. Dair'

P.S. Save me a piece of gum!"

Now I truly have everything I need for my first game. A great team, a loving and supportive family, a beautiful outfit, and a clear sign that Adaris has not forgotten about me!

It's about five minutes before game time and I have to give the team the pregame speech I have prepared. "Ok guys, let's huddle up." The team gathers around me and Coach Frazier, I take a deep breath, and then I begin.

"I want you guys to know before we walk out on the court that I am proud of you. There are many teams that wouldn't have recovered from all that you have been through, but you bore down, worked hard, and all of that has brought us to our first game. Tonight I am going to mix things up a bit. The team we are playing is quick and tall, but they are prone to get into foul trouble fast if they don't get control of the game from the jump ball. Our goal is to take control from the onset. Coach Frazier and I plan to make a lot of substitutions tonight so don't sleep on me. I want everyone to stay alert and make sure you know what offense and defense we are running at all times. Tonight's starting five are Popper and Baby Baby at the posts, AJ and Little Daddy at the wing, and Scoop at the point. Scoop, you are going to have to play big tonight and take care of the ball. Every one of their starters will have you by at least a head in height, and as the point I really need you to see the entire court. Now bring it in and show me some of that SHS Tennessee Pride!"

Hector says a prayer in a combination of English and Spanish. By the time he is done, the final buzzer to the girl's game had rung. Then the boys run out on the floor as "Sweet Georgia Brown" blasts from the speakers. As Coach Frazier and I walk out onto the floor, I say another quick prayer and then just take it all in. There is nothing like the smell of a gym, sweat intermingled with popcorn, and the fans' excitement was almost palpable. My primary focus is on watching the boys warm up, but I do a quick scan and see my mother, Serena, Keeva, Aunt Leslie, and Leo sitting in their usual spot about four rows up from the bench. I give them a quick smile and a wink. I can see some tears in my mother's eyes as she beams at me. I am sure she has mixed emotions about coming into the gym, as she is proud of her baby girl but she also really misses her husband.

I kept scanning and see some of the parents, Principal Leevins and his wife, Tony Stint from the *Tennessean,* and then I spot AJ's mother and his grandmother, Katherine. I breathe a quick sigh of relief. Adaris isn't sitting beside Lisa. I turn to check the score clock. Two minutes to game time! I kiss my index finger and point it to the sky. "It's game time, Daddy, and this one's for you! We're about to shoot the lights out!"

I pull up at the SHS gym about two minutes before the game is due to start. My mom has been sending me texts to let me know I am running late. I have just left the stadium, where Griffin gave me a heck of a massage. I needed it to get rid of the tension before the game tonight, because for some reason I am incredibly tense. Amos and Shelley both offered to come with me, but I told them I want to do this first one alone. There are two people I plan to watch like a hawk and I don't want any distractions. I buy my ticket and then walk up the stairs so I can sit on one of the bleachers near the top of the gym. I don't want to get close enough to make AJ or Jackie nervous, and I also don't want to take any attention away from the game with any fans asking for my autograph or giving me a play by play of my last game.

I take my seat about 30 seconds before the game starts and my eyes are drawn immediately to Jackie. She looks incredible. I had called her mom over the weekend to ask what Jackie was wearing to the game. Without a moment's pause she told me that she and Jackie's sister had purchased a gold suit for Jackie to commemorate her first game. Since the schools colors are old gold and dark purple, I knew just the thing to accompany the outfit. I told Ms. Ella to expect a package early Tuesday morning. Her response was a deep chuckle. I was praying Jackie will be wearing the shoes I sent her and she is. My eyes travel up her body like I am starving. I notice her hair is hanging to her shoulders in a bone straight style. She has cut her hair, and the way it frames her face make her even more beautiful, if that is possible.

About 30 seconds before Kerryn the announcer introduces the starting lineup, a chill runs down my spine. Adaris is here. I feel it with every bone of my being. I am supposed to have my game face on so I can't smile too hard, but I allow myself a tiny smirk. And now it's time to play a little basketball.

When the announcer calls the starting lineup, I am shocked to hear him call AJ's name! I had no idea that he is going to start tonight. I know Jackie is taking a huge chance starting him as a sophomore, but I also know she is putting the best five out there to handle this opponent. She has also started another sophomore, the kid the team calls Baby Baby. I lean back against the bleacher behind me, cross my arms, and get prepared for 32 minutes of excitement.

We win our first game by six points. We jump out in front of the other team quickly and set the pace for the game. Scoop does a great job of controlling the team, and Coach Frazier and I work well together in substituting and changing plays. I am proud of our first game but know we have a long way to go. Someone once told me the first game is always the hardest. I believe that, but I also know that I need to treat each game like it is my first. I congratulate the team and head to my office so they can hit the showers. When I walk through the door I stop abruptly. Adaris is standing by my desk looking at some pictures on my bookshelf. He turns around quickly and we just stare at each other for what feels like a lifetime.

"Close the door and lock it sweetness," he says with an intense look on his face.

Like a robot under his control, I close the door. "What are you doing here Adaris?"

"You couldn't keep me away. I had to see you and tell you how proud I was of you tonight. Your mom let me in. Now come here."

I walk over to him slowly and stand a hair's breadth away. Adaris grabs a piece of my hair and twirls it around his finger, then bends down to smell my hair. "You cut your hair," he whispers.

"I donated it to Locks of Love. I needed a change and—"

Before I can finish my sentence, Adaris grabs me and plasters his lips to my open mouth. He runs his tongue in circles, then sucks my bottom lip, and we kiss until we are both out of breath. He leans back against my desk and gathers me between his legs.

"Adaris, I have missed you so much. I knew the second you walked into that gym. I got so nervous but so calm at the same time."

"Be quiet for a while and let me touch you before someone comes banging on the door."

Adaris massages my shoulders, runs his arms down my back, and settles them on my bottom, easing me closer to him. I lay my head on his chest and he starts nibbling on my neck. He moves his lips up to my ear and says, "If I didn't think someone would come knocking at any minute I would spread you across this desk and have you for dinner. But I will settle for this." He bends down and kisses my nose, then softly sucks my lips with his tongue. "Now go put some lipstick on. Your people are on the way. I am taking AJ out to dinner and then I'm going to the hotel. I want you to join me in no less than three hours."

As he walks out the door I plop down in my chair and let out a huge sigh. As I sit there in a daze I hear my family coming down the hall. I reach down to get my purse so I can reapply my lipstick, and suddenly come up with an idea for our rendezvous.

I arrive at the hotel two and a half hours later. As I get out of my car, several people are staring at me. I have on a full length fur coat with my beautiful dark purple pumps. I go directly to Adaris' suite and knock on the door.

Adaris opens the door wearing a pair of lounging pants and nothing else, and we both stare in shock. I recover quickly and whisper, "I saved you a piece of gum."

"Damn it woman. What are you trying to do to me? What do you have on underneath that coat?" Adaris says as he takes a gulp of air.

"A little more than you have on under those pants," I say with a smile as I stare at the bulge in his pants. "I didn't get to thank you for the beautiful shoes and the gum. Are you going to let me come in or leave me here in the hall?"

"We need to have a quick huddle before you come in the door," Adaris says, leaning against the door jamb. "But first give me my gum." He bends down to kiss my lips and dip his tongue in my mouth. Before I know it, my gum has gone from my mouth to his. "Ummm, green apple."

"Hurry up with this talk, gum stealer. I look like an idiot standing out in the hallway."

Adaris blows a quick bubble and says, "Here's the deal, sweetness. Once you walk into this room I will not be responsible for my actions, nor will I stop doing what I plan to do. If you can't deal with that, you need to turn your fine ass around and walk back down the hallway."

"What exactly did you have planned?"

Adaris leans over and whispers hotly in my ear, "That's for me to know and you to find out." Then he runs his tongue around the rim of my ear.

"Oh God! If that's a preview of what's to come I am about to turn my fine ass around and run. Adaris, what are we doing? Sleeping together tonight is not going to make things any better. If anything it's going to make things worse. Why do we keep torturing each other like this?"

Adaris yanks me over the threshold and shuts the door. He backs me up and rests his hands on the door above my head, then leans over and nuzzles my neck. "Then let's watch a movie and cuddle. Tell me what you want baby, because if it were up to me I would dip it low and pick you up slow."

"I want you! All of you. Not just a shag every now and then when our hormones are raging. I want to be able to hold your hand out in public without worrying if someone will see us. I want to stay where you are without feeling guilty. I want to stop feeling so desperate that I have to steal looks at you during a game. I want to take those damn pants off you and see how fine you really are, I want—"

"Ok, my nature was going down until that last sentence," he says with a grimace. "I want all of those things too, Jackie. It seems like we have Groundhog Day every time we see each other. It is a repeat, but it also gets sweeter and sweeter. Right now I want to take that coat off you and make love to you until we are both so tired we can't move. But I cannot give you any of the things you want right now. My son started tonight Jackie, and he played damn well. Not because I am sleeping with his coach but because he is good enough. He's actually good enough to start as a sophomore!"

"You looked so damn sexy on that court tonight that I thought I was going to come unglued. Every man over the age of 18 was checking you out. I almost caught a case in the gym because no one knows, well other than your Mom, Serena, Keeva, Max, World, Amos, Shelley, Tiffany, and Johnnie. And I suspect my mother and even Leo know something. He asked me for some tickets to the next game tonight with this big ass grin on his face. Hell, everyone practically knows! I miss you so much that my teammates can't stand me. They can't figure out what is going on with me off the turf. Thank God Amos and Shelley are both in love. They know what I am going through—"

I grab Adaris' face and say, "Are you in love with me?"

Adaris drops his head to my chest and says, "Hook, line, and sinker. Hell your Mom, Keeva and Serena started talking about how bad I was in my face! Like I was a punk! And I couldn't do a damn thing about it because they are right."

"I'm in love with you too, Adaris. So what do we do now?"

"We wait until your season is over in February and then we figure it out. You cannot mess up this opportunity, and my son needs my support without worrying if I am banging his coach. And I do plan to bang you against the wall, in the bed, in the shower, and anywhere else I can. I know it will take me over the edge, but let me see what is under that coat before you leave me."

Adaris moves one of his hands from the door to open my coat. He unbuttons the first two buttons, looks me up and down and says, "You can take the L off of Lover cause it's over." I am wearing a dark blue bustier with matching boy panties. He leans down to kiss my nipples through my bra, places tiny kisses on my stomach, and then stoops down to kiss me through my panties. He pauses there for a while and takes a few deep breaths. He picks up my foot, kisses the toes that are sticking through the peep hole, and says, "Pretty." Then he works his way back up to my hips, slides my panties down, and picks my legs up one at a time to remove my panties. Then he buttons my coat, backs up, and says, "Lord have mercy. These are for my collection. You can have them back one day. Let me change clothes so I can walk you to your car. There is no way in hell you are going downstairs naked and alone." As he walks away he mumbles, "I must love her ass because I have more will power than a mother..."

I slump against the door with a dreamy smile on my face and watch Adaris' rock-hard butt as he walks away.

Later that evening I am still restless.

"Hello," Keeva says in a breathy whisper.

"Keeva, did I wake you up? It's Jackie."

"Let's see…it's 1:25 in the morning. What do you think?"

"Can you talk? Do you have company?"

"What's with the 20 questions? Since you woke me up it's me who should be asking what the hell you want girl? I figured you would be with Adaris tonight, the way he sneaked into your office after the game."

"That's why I called, Ke. I went to his hotel tonight to seduce him and he turned me down and sent me home."

"He what? Please don't tell me he's gay. He's too fine to be gay!"

"He is far from gay. I pulled out all the stops Keeva. I put on some pretty lingerie under my full-length fur with the shoes he bought me, and went over to his room."

"Ok, that sounds pretty good, then what?"

"I opened my big mouth and told him that I wanted more than a booty call. Then he said he loves me and I said I love him, and then he sent me home. Why did he do that Keeva?"

"Sounds to me like he did both of you a favor. As much as you both want each other physically, he is willing to wait for what you both want, which is a commitment. But you do realize that you need to stay away from him until you both are able to do that, because I bet you tested every last piece of his will power tonight, not to mention he probably went to bed very frustrated."

"Why do you think I am calling you girl. I am wide awake. All he did was kiss me in a few places and I am like a crack head. I need another hit."

"Cool your jets, Jackie. You only have three more months. You can make it. Damn, he said he loves you and he couldn't have been lying

289

because you didn't even give him any yet you big tease. Now stop the blah, blah, blah and the pity part shit. I gotta get some sleep, you paranoid freak!"

"But Keeva—"

Before she can hang up the phone I distinctly hear a familiar voice say, "Glad to see you cussing someone out besides me."

Hmmm...Amos was over there.

After Jackie leaves I take a cold shower. I can't sleep and I want to call Jackie, but instead I call World.

World answers the phone sleepily, "Hey babe."

"Babe? Well hello boo," I say with a laugh.

"Who the hell is this?"

"It's me you moron. Who were you expecting?"

"Sometimes Max calls me if she can't sleep, which means it's working."

"I almost hate to ask, but what's working?"

"I try to make sure that after every time I visit she misses me more and more, especially at night. I have been trying to get her to at least think about coming up here during the holidays. That is about as much of a commitment as I can get right now. Enough about my baby, what do you want?"

"AJ's first game was tonight. I am so proud of him. He played like a man among boys."

"And what about the coach? How did Jackie do?"

"Man, she coached so well that I had a hard on the whole game. I was so desperate to see her after the game I practically begged her mom to unlock her office so I could see her."

"Go ahead, I'm listening," Chris says around a big yawn.

"When she came to her office I told her I wanted to see her later tonight."

"Is this about to get X-rated, 'cause I may need to go pop some popcorn."

"Man, she came over in a full-length fur coat, peep toe pumps, and some crazy lingerie. She was looking good and smelling good and—"

"Get to Z man, I got practice in less than six hours!"

"I sent her home..."

"I'm up now! The woman you are crazy about comes to your place damn near naked with her toes hanging out and you send her home?"

"Before I sent her home I, well, I did a few things and then I told her I love her."

"You went to Z alright. Did she tell you she loves you back, or did you hear crickets?"

"She told me she loves me too, but she wants all of me not just a few stolen moments. And I realized she was right. If we become intimate I will just want more. But the fear we would make things hard for AJ and her career is more important right now. She means more to me than a little bump and grind."

"Wow man, I am proud of you. The toes alone would have done me in. If I could get Max to admit she loves me I would be on top of the world, no pun intended. I guess since you obviously called me for some advice here it is. Stop selling wolf tickets."

"What do you mean?"

"Stop putting yourself in the position where you can't control your hormones or your jimmy. It's November man. Both of your seasons will be over by March at the latest. Stay away from her man. At least until you can love her the way you both deserve. You have less than 120 days. Take that time to focus on one of the best seasons you have ever had and give your son the time he needs. If things are meant to be, you will have a lifetime with Jackie. And you can woo her without seeing her."

"How man?"

"I am about to start charging you for my time, short bus. Are you that slow? Write a poem, send a letter, send a text, leave a voicemail when you know she can't answer the phone, send some flowers. Shit, be creative!"

"Sounds like you are speaking from experience."

"Damn straight. Just call me Don Juan Casanova Billy Dee. My baby knows I am sprung. I am just impatiently waiting for her to realize she is bananas for your boy. You are halfway there, Dair. Just be patient. In the meantime get the guest bedroom ready in your big ass crib. And make sure you put me in the west wing, 'cause Max is loud and I am louder. My baby is about to call and I need to save my bedroom voice to whisper sweet nothings in her ear. Now get off my phone you big goofy punk."

I hear only a dial tone in my ear. World knows how to make an exit. I should have called Shelley.

November has come and gone and we are heading quickly towards Christmas. We have been playing two and three games per week and can boast a winning record, which I am proud of. The games we lost were barn burners. I told my boys I would rather lose by a few points or at the buzzer than get shot out of the gym. Our fans are following us closely, and so is the media. The articles range from calling me the Pat Summit of high school basketball to saying I'm only a puppet being used to draw the crowd. I know from experience not to pay much attention. Sophia has become not only my statistician but also my publicist. Anytime she sees false information in any of the papers, she calls Keeva for advice and then contacts the editor to ask for a correction. I tell her that her talents obviously lie in public relations. I hooked her up with Keeva, who promised her a summer internship—unpaid of course!

Most of the time I can't see Adaris at the games, but I know he is there. He has a way of making himself disappear right before and after the games. Of course during the game I am so preoccupied that I don't even notice the crowd. I know he does that to keep the focus on AJ and to keep me from getting nervous. But that changes at one of our home games. The gym is standing room only and it gets so bad that the referees have to call a time out twice to clear people off the sidelines, and security has to stop a few fights. As a result, I have to fight like hell to keep my team focused on the game. We play a heck of a game but lose by four points to Oakland High School, one of our biggest rivals. I am crushed but trying not to let it show. I am mentally and physically exhausted.

After the game I stop to speak with the Oakland coach for a minute and I feel him staring at me. I look up and see Adaris standing at the top of the bleachers with his legs spread apart and his arms folded across his chest. My heart stops. No matter how many times I see him it is like the first time. He is magnificent. As we stare at each other he takes his fist and rubs it against his chest and smiles at me. And then he walks away. The other coach sees me staring and says, "That was Dair Singleton wasn't it? His son is quite the player. He is going to be amazing by his senior year." I have to stop myself from telling Coach Wade that AJ's dad is pretty amazing right now and that he can speak sign language like a mother! He just told me great game and he loves me.

Adaris sends me a text after every game, congratulating me, encouraging me if we have a tough game, or telling me how beautiful I look. He even finds ways to surprise me from time to time. One day I walk into my office and find a bouquet of gorgeous orange and pink calla lilies with a note that says, *"These remind me of you. Long, shapely, and beautiful."* Another day I walk in and almost sit on an iPod. It has a sticky note on it that says, *"A few of your favorite songs. You also have an iTunes account set up to select 100 more of your favorites. Your mom has your user id and password. AS."* The playlist includes Earth Wind and Fire, Luther Vandross, Angela Winbush, The Commodores, and Will Downing songs. I know my mother is helping him pull off his little surprises but she never says a word. She just gives me these knowing little smiles like she has a secret. These little gifts and notes really help curb my incessant hunger to see him. I decide to get in on sending surprises, and every now and then I bake some cookies, cupcakes, or brownies and drop them off at his hotel. I have become friends with one of the valets, who makes sure my sweets make it to Adaris' room. Hey, he has to get a taste of my brown sugar somehow!

I am sitting in my office during sixth period about two weeks before Christmas, getting prepared for practice, when Scoop, Junebug, and Shaky knock on my door.

"Hey coach. You got a minute to holla at your boys?" asks Scoop.

"Sure guys, come in. What's up?"

"We heard that there are a lot of families that don't have food or money for Christmas," says Junebug.

"Where did you get that information, Junebug?"

"Hector told us the other day that a lot of the people in his hood won't be able to have Christmas and we want to help," says Shaky.

"So what do you three stooges propose?" I ask them, hiding my sense of surprise and pride.

"Who are the three stooges coach? Anyway we thought it would be cool to give a Christmas party with the girls' basketball team. We could charge four canned goods or $4.00 to get in. All of the proceeds will go to buy food and gifts for the families. AJ said he would ask his dad to help find a DJ. All we need is you to help us convince Principal Leevins to let us use the gym and help us convince some of the parents and teachers to chaperone," says Scoop.

"It sounds like you all have it covered, except for the gym, DJ, and chaperones. What date are you thinking of having this party?"

"Our last home game before Christmas is on December 20th. We figured we could have it here in the gym after the game," says Shaky.

"And then we can come back the next day, load up the food, and deliver it to the families," adds Junebug.

"And before you ask, Coach, we can get Mr. Peebles, the president of the booster club, to take the money at the door so he can divvy it up for the 20 families that need the help," says Shaky.

"Hey boys, you had me at hello. Since you three are the head teenagers in charge, I recommend that you write up a proposal to present to Principal Leevins. Take it to Mrs. Levi so she can proof it and help you correct any mistakes. This is going to take a lot of work. If Principal Leevins approves, you will still have to get the rest of the team and the girls' team involved pretty quick. I also suggest you include the cheerleaders because you are going to need a ton of help."

"Uh coach. What does you had me at hello mean?" said Shaky with a puzzled look on his face.

"I take it none of you have ever seen the movie Jerry McGuire have you?"

"No," they all said in unison.

"It's a cult classic and I would say all of you are ambassadors of quan."

"What?"

"Look it up on You Tube. Get your proposal ready so we can talk to Principal Leevins."

The boys prepare the proposal and Mrs. Levi helps them perfect it. Peaches, presents it with help from Sophia. Principal Leevins approves it and the preparations begin. I am secretly very proud that the guys have decided to give back to people who need help. That's what Christmas is all about. I even get suckered into helping chaperone the party. I warn the team that we better win the game before the party or their coach will be a very unhappy chaperone.

On December 20th we win our game by 15 points. I tell the guys maybe I should let them plan a party more often if it will help us blow our opponents out. I go to my office to change into casual attire so I can get my chaperone on. All I really want to do is go home, think about Adaris, and listen to music until I fall asleep. But that will not happen for another four hours.

I have been assigned to sit at the door and help Mr. Peebles collect money for the first two hours and then head into the gym to chaperone. The time flies by and when I walk into the gym I literally feel like I am in the twilight zone. Now I really know how my parents felt when they watched me and my friends dance. I am not much more than ten years removed from this crowd but it feels like 20. What happened to guys and girls dancing together? In one circle I see about 50 girls gyrating, while in another about 20 guys look as if they are break dancing, but what I mostly see is a bunch of kids standing around texting. Who are they texting? It looks like everyone they might know is in this gym! Then I remember they are texting their buddy standing right beside them because it is too difficult to lean over and talk. What a world, what a world…

As I stand there tapping my feet to Michael Jackson's "Don't Stop Till You Get Enough," I feel him. I used to think that people were crazy when they said they could feel someone's presence, but now I know it's true. I glance across the gym and Adaris is standing there with a snap back sitting low on his face, a pair of slouch jeans that hang low on his hips, a black sweatshirt, and black Timberlands on his feet. He would have blended in with the crowd were he not so tall. He is talking to Peaches' mother but looking directly at me. My heart skips a beat. Just knowing he is no more than 50 feet away makes me smile. As we stand there smiling at each other, the song changes to "The Wobble." All of a sudden, AJ, Peaches, and Popper are dragging me onto the dance floor and before I know it we are all Wobbling together. What the boys don't realize is that I have bill-making skills on the dance floor.

After AJ's game, Mom and I run to grab a bite, then I drop her off at home. AJ convinced me to hire a DJ for the Christmas party, and he also signed me up to help chaperone. Of course I had to put up some resistance but I was secretly glad he had signed me up. It gives me another opportunity to spend some time with Jackie. I walk into the gym and am immediately cornered by Ms. Grimes, Peaches' mother. As I sit there only half listening to her, I see Jackie across the room. She is bobbing her head to a Michael Jackson song. She has on a pair of dark jeans, a white blouse, and black riding boots, and she looks almost young enough to blend in with the kids. I sit there and smile at her. I have worn a hat so I can stare without being too obvious. That stupid song "The Wobble" comes on and I see AJ and two of his teammates drag Jackie onto the floor. Ms. Grimes even tries to get me out there, but I refuse. I am not too big on dancing and I want to watch the show. I watch Jackie dancing with the entire team. They, like me, are clearly under her spell. I love her ability to be serious on the court but to have fun off the court. Watching her move is better than any stripper at Magic City. They go from The Wobble to the Electric Slide, but when "Doing da Butt" comes on, Jackie thankfully takes her fine butt off the floor. I would have yanked her off myself if she had started that dance! I see her walk toward the gym exit and know that if I time it right I can head her off at the door. Being back in a high school is making me want to cop a feel under the damn bleachers. She stops a few times to talk to students and parents. Just as she comes around the corner by the bleachers, I grab her and gently push her under them. I quickly kiss her to keep her from screaming.

The boys drag me onto the floor to dance with them. I have a ball watching them dance and laugh—to see them so happy. I dance with them until "Doing da Butt" comes on, and decide it's time to make my exit. It wouldn't look very good for the coach to have her butt stuck up in the air, especially it being as big as mine is. As I walk off the floor I look to see if Adaris is still standing in his spot. I don't see him and my heart sinks. My chaperone duty is about up and I am ready to go home. My sister and her family are flying in tomorrow and I need to start my Christmas baking. I also promised the boys I will help deliver the canned goods and money to the needy families. Thankfully they decided to do it on Sunday after church so we can all have a full day's rest.

As I'm walking out of the gym, I stop a few times to speak to students, teachers, and parents. When I am almost out of the gym somebody suddenly grabs me and pushes me under the bleachers. Before I commence to giving them a beat down I feel some familiar arms around me and the juiciest lips I have ever tasted. I know this is truly a stolen moment and I am going to take advantage of it. I wrap my arms around Adaris' neck, jump up and wrap my legs around his hips, and give him a big wet kiss. If this is all I am going to get for a while, then Merry Christmas baby! He grabs my butt, walks me further under the bleachers, and we stay under there locked in each other's arms for several minutes. Before I know it, my hand is under Adaris' shirt and working its way down to unbutton his pants. He puts me down before I can get us in trouble, squeezes my butt, and whispers in my ear, "Merry Christmas sweetness! Now go on before we get caught. It appears there are a few people on the other end who have the same idea."

I grab his head give him another quick but scorching kiss, grab his butt for a squeeze and then float out of the gym, down the hallway, and out to my car. I always wondered what it would be like to neck under the bleachers. Now I know.

After I grab Jackie I kiss her like a mad man, and before I know it she damn near has me naked under the bleachers! I make her leave first. My body finally settles down, and after about five minutes I walk out from under the bleachers and out into the hall where AJ and a few of his buddies are talking. I walk up to them to say a quick goodbye and tell AJ I'll be back to pick him up after the party. AJ looks at me, reaches up and puts his arm around my shoulder, abruptly turns me around and quietly says, "Let me holler at you for a minute Pops." As we walk away from his friends, he leans toward me and asks, "Pops, have you been kissing Ms. Grimes?" He looks shell-shocked.

"What! Why do you ask that son?"

"Cause you have lipstick all over you ! Dang pops, you are so embarrassing. You are getting more play at this party than I am. Please go home. I will text you when it's time to come back and get me."

I quickly wipe my mouth, grin at AJ, and get the hell out of dodge wearing a sheepish grin and humming EU's most famous song.

Merry Christmas baby

On the Monday before Christmas the celebrations have begun. My sister and her family have arrived, and my mother had promised that we will continue all our Christmas traditions, even though my father isn't here. Christmas was my parents' favorite holiday, if somewhat begrudgingly on my father's part. My mother decorates every corner of the house and a few years ago she worked her way up to five trees with the encouragement of her friend Chanta. Daddy had a fit because he kept running into trees, and Ella agreed to stop at five. The five trees have been put up, I have finished baking, and we have done most of the cooking. We decided to have a celebration with just our immediate family this year and we have made a pact to remember all the wonderful times and not be sad. Just in case things get emotional, my mother has decided to forgo our huge extended family celebration...that is until December 26th , when about 50 extended family members will descend on us and spend the day playing Bid Whist, Spades, Tripoly, and munch on heavy horderves . We figured this way we can have the best of both worlds.

Adaris has a game on TV tonight and I am determined to watch it uninterrupted. As I settle into my chair down in the Shack, I hear Jordan, Leo, Micah, Keeva, and Serena coming down the steps. Serena, Keeva, and my mother are the only people who know about Adaris, so I figure the questions will soon begin.

"What's up sis? You about to watch Tennessee play? I don't remember you watching much football," says Leo.

"I like football just as well as anyone else."

"Oh yeah, I forgot that AJ's dad plays for Tennessee. You know any more of the players sis?"

"I know a few of them..."

"What about you Keeva? I heard you were working on a bid to do some marketing for them. I bet you know a few of them don't you?"

"Yeah Leo, I know a few of them. Why do you keep asking?" asks Keeva putting her hands on her hips.

"I want someone to hook me up with some tickets. Ma said she sold her and dad's tickets last year since they weren't going to the games. Sis, can't you ask AJ to get me some tickets?"

"Jackie should ask for them herself," Keeva whispers.

"What did you say cuz?"

I pipe in, "She said she can probably get you tickets quicker since she knows Amos Hunter, the center."

"Well, then hook your cousin up! See if you can get me some club tickets, it's getting cold out."

The banter settles down as the game gets going. Tennessee is playing at Green Bay, then will head down to Jacksonville. At least Adaris will be in a warmer climate for New Year's. I find myself wondering what he'll be doing for Christmas and New Year's Eve and if we will ever celebrate those two holidays together.

As the game progresses the crowd expands. Leo has invited a few of his friends over, Serena's closest friends stop by, and some of my childhood friends Angela Dom, Maurice, and Andrea join us at halftime. These visits are bittersweet. Our friends have always made their way over to our house for every holiday, to this very room. My dad was always right in the thick of things, talking shit to the guys and teasing our girlfriends. My mom was holding court with her friends upstairs.

I notice that Keeva is a little nervous during the game. I lean over and ask, "What's wrong Keeva. I can sense you're a little tense."

"Girl, I hate watching him play?"

"Who girl?"

"You know who. His big ass is always right in the thick of things and I get nervous when all those bodies start falling all over the place."

"Do you like Amos enough to be nervous? What's going on girl? You know I heard his voice the other night when we talked. I thought he had been banished after he chased you around the house a few weeks ago?"

"First of all, you should believe half of what you see and none of what you hear! I do like him Jackie, but I am not ready for the things he wants. Amos wants a wife who will quit her job, have five gigantic babies, and be a stay at home mom. I am not that girl, girl! He is traditional and I am, hell, I don't know what I am. And he is so big Jackie. I look like a kid around him. But he is so gentle with me. Do you know he asked me to go home with him and meet his mama? Girl, when he said that shit I told him, hell no! I am not ready to meet his big ass mama. And yes, I know she is big because I saw her picture. I asked him if we could just go out from time to time and be friends, and you know what he said to me Jackie?"

"I have no clue. What did he say?"

"He said he already has enough friends. He told me that he knows my biological clock is ticking and we need to get started on some kids asap! You see, I didn't want to tell you Jackie, I knew you would laugh."

"That is priceless, Keeva. You finally have met someone who keeps you on your toes. I love it," I say wiping the tears off my face. What I see is you having a fit because you are afraid your 350 pound giant is going to get hurt!"

"Shut up Jackie! I aint going to meet his big ass mama, I aint pushing five kids out of my vagina, and I aint giving up my business," Keeva hisses at me before stomping away.

I think the lady does protest too much. Thank God she is gone so I can watch the game in peace for a few minutes. I turn around and see Keeva standing in the back of the room chewing on her nails as she stares at the TV. I think I will soon be picking out two ugly bridesmaid dresses, one for Keeva and one for Max.

By the fourth quarter we have about twenty people down in the Shack. Most of the girls are in the back eating and talking, except Keeva and me. We haven't budged from our seats since halftime.

"Yo, sis, what in the hell has got your attention in this game? I haven't seen you like this since Pop's made you sit here years ago to explain the rules of football."

"I just like watching a good football game from time to time."

"You sure have been cheering a lot for numbers 52, 14, and 10. Now number 10 is married so it must be—"

"Leo, I think I heard Queesha come in. Why don't you run and get her, and check on mom while you are upstairs," says Serena.

As he jumps up, Serena looks at me with a sly smile.

Ella always gets up first on Christmas morning and soon after my nephew Jordan will join her. When my dad was living he would wake up next put on some music like the O'Jays or the Temptations and that would set the mood for a soulful Christmas. Serena, Micah, and I would be the last to get up. Why, because we were usually up the night before putting some toy or contraption together or entertaining some of our friends. Over the last few years with Leo being away on vacation we would put an empty chair out to remind us that he was not here but with us. This year the empty chair was beside mom. That was the chair my dad has slanted his body in for as long as I can remember. He didn't sit down with his butt first like most people. Because of a back injury when he was younger his back would hit the chair first and then his butt. For dad, Christmas was about family and being together, no matter what was under that tree. He reminded us that when he was young a brown paper bag full of nuts, an orange, apple and a candy cane made the best Christmas.

We heave a collective sigh that Leo is home at last, then we look around the room and agree that we are having a good Christmas despite missing Dad, who always made Christmas a time to be thankful. Leo breaks the sense of loss by saying, "If anyone is looking for a gift from me under the tree, you better look right here instead. I am the gift of Christmas past, present, and future. And you better have some extra stuff for me under the tree since I have missed Christmas for three years!" It was exactly what we needed.

Serena and I start performing our annual duty of passing out the gifts. As I start digging into my stack, I see tags that say to Jackie from Mom and Dad, from Jordan, from Serena. I also see a small box with no tag on it. My mom has been known to do that just to trick us up. I tear off the gift wrap and find a jewelry box. Not a ring box, more like a pin box. I open it and gasp. Inside is a platinum chain, and hanging from it is a small platinum "seven" surrounded by tiny diamonds. The chain is just long enough so the pendant sits in the V of my chest. I instantly know it is from Adaris. As I sit there trying not to cry, I realize that even though one of the most important people in my life is no longer with me, it's almost as if he willed the man who was quickly becoming so important to me into my life. Serena leans forward, picks up the necklace, and fastens it around my neck. She gives me a hug from the back and whispers, "It fits perfectly." I look up and see my mother smiling at me, and then she gives me a sly wink. My mom is the best elf in the world. Once again she had helped Adaris smuggle in a beautiful gift for me. I hope Adaris will like the gift I sent—Keeva got Amos to sneak it in his bag.

The downside to playing football is that it means spending major holidays like Thanksgiving, Christmas, and sometimes New Year's away from your family and friends. At least I'll have some time with my family on Christmas morning before the game and a flight to Jacksonville in the afternoon. I don't think I'll be able to break away to see Jackie. From what I hear, her entire family will be in and out of her mom's house, so I wouldn't want to barge in anyway. I hope she likes her necklace. I know it will bring on a lot of questions, but I figure she can handle it.

I am getting a little tired of being away from her. In fact, I am getting tired of a lot of things. My house is almost done, but it seems like the builder is slowing down. I am tired of this back and forth with ESPN. I want to make a deal that works for me and mine, not for my agent and attorney. And I am tired of trying to get AJ to talk about Jackie without him catching on. Frankly, I am just tired of being tired. This is supposed to be one of the best times of my life and here I am having a damn pity party.

My pity party continues on the flight to Jacksonville. I decide to pull out my iPod and listen to some music. I dig around and my hand brushes across something hard that I don't remember putting in my bag. I pull out what looks like a scrapbook. I open the cover and the first thing I see is a newspaper article from 14 years ago when I signed with Auburn. As I flip through the pages I see articles from my college days, on the pro draft where I went in the first round, about some of the fundraisers and charity events I have sponsored, and so on. There are team pictures and even some photos that I had taken with World and Shelley. The last few articles are from this year's season, and the last picture is of AJ in his basketball uniform. It is unbelievable how much he looks like me at that age. By the time I get to the final page I have put my sunglasses on to hide the tears. On that last page I find an envelope. I pull it out and read,

"Adaris, I thought you might like a reminder of how wonderful your career has been for the last 14 years. The last few pages are blank. You have a lot more memories to add to this book. Merry Christmas, Jackie"

As I sit there letting Jackie's amazing gift sink in, the last 14 years wash over me and tears roll down my face. My pity party has become a wave of gratitude and hope for my future. I realize that I need to enjoy the rest of my season and stop worrying about the house and the job with ESPN. Everything will work itself out. I thank God that I have these memories to remind me how blessed I am. My son is healthy. My mother is aging gracefully. I am going to retire on my own terms and timing. And I have the love of a beautiful young woman. I feel her love in each page of this scrapbook. As I am closing the scrapbook, Amos walks by and whispers, "I told her that scrapbook would make you cry like a little bitch. But don't worry, I cried too."

Win or Lose?

As I sit here and prepare for what may very well be the last game of the season or the beginning of the post-season—I realize that I am good enough. And my team is good enough. We have come this far, 32 games and 24 wins later, bigger, better, and badder. I owe most of it to the good Lord for helping me figure out how to coach 13 wily young men and one ornery assistant coach, but I also know that to whom much is given much is required. God did his part but he will rely on me and these young boys to do the rest. My dad is ok with God, and my family continues to heal but now I know I can live. I don't need to wonder the hows or whys. That is not to be revealed to me at this time. I just need to know that ok is enough, and it is perfect, it is peace.

Due to our team's modest success, the school has been getting calls from the local papers, a few national papers, and even *Sports Illustrated* and ESPN. Principal Leevins is a man of few words in most situations, and he has been keeping his mouth shut. My allegiance is with Tony Stint of the *Tennessean,* so I decide to sit down and chat with him again.

"Jackie, I know you don't have much time so I am going to get right down to business. Here we are with a 24-8 winning season. Most said you couldn't do it. What do you say about your season thus far?"

"Tony, we came back with five upperclassman and added several strong underclassmen to our squad, so I am not sure why the naysayers said we couldn't have another winning season."

"I have heard some complaints that you are underutilizing your upperclassmen and over utilizing your underclassmen, and that this has caused some friction on your team. What do you say Jackie?"

"I have taught my team that everyone has a role and those roles may change from game to game. I have also taught them that it doesn't matter to me what year they are, I will play the best person at the best time. We play as a team and by doing that, everyone wins. There is no friction about the starting lineup with this squad. I won't tolerate it."

"Principal Leevins hired you for one season. What happens if you lose tonight?"

"I don't plan on losing tonight, Tony. Even though people say we are the underdog. My guys are in great shape, they have been playing well, we have great support from our parents, booster club, students, and faculty, and Coach Frazier and I are ready to guide our team to another win so we can head to Murfreesboro for the state tournament."

"I heard there was a position waiting for you in Seattle with your old WNBA team. I also heard you were offered a head coaching job at a prominent school in Atlanta coaching girls next year. So do you think you will return as the head coach here next year, Jackie?"

"I am trying to take one game at a time, Tony. I have loved being home over the last year and it's been great to be part of a winning tradition. At this point I am not sure what I am going to do. And some of what you have heard is only rumors."

"So there is no truth to you getting other coaching offers?"

"Let's talk about my future after we finish with the sub-state and hopefully the state tournament. Right now I want to focus on these young men."

"Ok, Jackie, I'd like to finish by asking you a series of questions that require only brief answers. Who is the best shooter on your team?"

"It depends on the game, but stat-wise it would be Jordan McCullough or Little Daddy, who is a senior."

"Man-to-man defense or zone defense?"

"Man-to-man."

"Talking or yelling?"

"Both!"

"Some say you could end up meeting either Oakland High or Whites Creek High. Which one do you prefer?"

"Either."

"Who is your best defensive player?"

"AJ Singleton, who is a sophomore."

"What bothers you the most about your team?"

"Laziness."

"What are you pleased with."

"Great chemistry and teamwork."

"You can use more than one word on this one, Jackie. What will you tell your team tonight before the game?"

"What I tell them before every game. That I am proud of them and that I want them to play hard."

"Jackie, I and many thousands of others can't wait to watch you tonight. Good luck."

Tony is always great to talk to, but its nerve racking. Tonight we will play away at Pearl Cohn. If we win this game we go to round one of the state tournament. I am a little antsy and the boys are downright nervous. Several of them have popped into my office throughout the day just to say "What's up?" which is code for I am nervous as hell. The only one who admitted he's nervous is Shaky. My three amigas—Serena, Max, and Keeva—won't come into town until we advance to the state tournament. I take that back, Serena and Max aren't coming till then, Keeva is too nervous to come.

I have grown accustomed to catching a glimpse of Adaris at the games when he is in town. He has cut off almost all communication, though I get a text from time to time. He is finishing up his final season and I guess he figures neither of us need the distraction. I must admit that it does sting a little that he hasn't stayed in contact, but I am grateful to see him at the games. I wear the necklace he gave me constantly and find myself rubbing it when I get uptight or nervous.

I didn't share this with Tony, but I have been offered a position back in Seattle with my old team, as VP of player relations. I also received calls from high schools in Atlanta and Seattle wanting to talk to me about coaching positions. So far I have held all three at bay. I really want to find out first if Adaris and I have a chance, and I don't think either of us is interested in a long-distance relationship. I am also getting accustomed to being back in Tennessee. Nashville has become a great place to live, and I really don't miss the rainy Seattle winters.

Tonight is a pivotal game for AJ and his team. Although I'm not happy that our team lost in the playoffs, I am glad that I can go to the rest of AJ's games. I am now officially unofficially retired from football. I have to admit, it is bittersweet. I spent the last 12 years of my life playing football, preparing for football and talking about football. I am proud that I got out on my own terms and that I escaped major injury, though this season was pretty hard on me. I also had more receiving yards this season than I have since my fifth season, which will set me up to be considered for the Hall of Fame one day. My only regret is that I didn't get a Super Bowl victory.

Pro ball offered me the opportunity to break records, play on a few pro bowl teams and the chance to really help my family, as well as people in my community. I have enough money in the bank to last me several lifetimes if I decide not to work again, and I've even decided to buy AJ a car, though he doesn't know it yet. One of my teammates has a 2008 Honda Accord he wants to get rid of and I plan to surprise AJ with it at the end of his season. I will insist that he pay for the insurance and his gas—he has to have some skin in the game, right?

My house is finished. It is beautiful and spacious, but above all comfortable. AJ and I decided to wait until his season was over to move in. The move is another reason for AJ's car. He'll be able to drive himself to school, as living out in Arrington will put him further away.

I have not been out with anyone since the disaster with Johnnie. And I must be in love because I haven't been intimate with anyone since well before the day I met Jackie in the airport. Love can make you do some strange things. I have limited my contact with Jackie since the hotel scene—it's just easier to cope that way. On the other, hand being celibate is difficult. At AJ's games I make sure I sit in a place where I can watch both him and Jackie without being interrupted. I feel like a voyeur sometimes. AJ keeps me abreast of what is going on so I don't have to ask too many questions. The last big thing he shared is that there is a rumor that Jackie has been offered a position at some schools in Georgia and Washington. I literally had to hang onto the counter to keep myself from falling over. But AJ assured me that it is only a rumor so I relaxed a bit.

I still have not made up my mind about ESPN. We are getting closer, but I really feel I want to be back in Tennessee permanently. A big part of that is my desire to build a future with Jackie. At this point I have no idea where we stand, but I do know I will try to get her to stay in Tennessee with me! I just need to figure out a way to balance my relationship with her and my son, especially if she continues to coach him.

All of these thoughts are running through my head as I go pick up Amos. He invited himself to the game so he can be close to Keeva. Apparently he pissed her off earlier in the week with his caveman tactics. She is now giving him the silent treatment, which is apparently not that easy for her. Amos had told me that the last three things said to him involved her middle finger, both her arms, and a movement with her lips and her butt. Amos will be a good diversion to help keep me calm—at least until he starts getting on my nerves. I am more nervous for my son and Jackie than I have ever been before any of my own games.

As Coach Frazier and I head toward the locker room right before our game, I sense a different feeling in the air. As we get closer I realize I'm not hearing the customary laughter and blaring music. Sophia meets us outside the door and whispers, "Coach, they are awfully quiet tonight. Even Peaches isn't trying to flirt with me, which is unusual."

"I think they are just getting their minds right Sophia. Those Yoga classes we took must be working." I open the door, stop in the doorway, and look around the room. It suddenly hits me that over the last few months these boys have matured. I look around and see 13 young men sitting side by side with various forms of headphones in their ears. Some have their eyes open, others are closed, but they all look intense. Scoop opens his eyes and gives me a quick wink. With that wink comes the realization that he is a senior and this could very well be my last game with him and the other seniors, or even with all of these guys. Now I know why my dad would get depressed at the end of his season. You pour your heart and soul into these kids, sacrifice time with your family and hope and pray that something you said or did will leave a positive mark on their lives. One thing I have taught them is that there is always a calm before a storm. I have just walked into calm.

But now it's time to liven things up and get ready for 32 minutes of excitement. I strut to the center of the locker room in my eggplant Calvin Klein suit and of course my good luck Adaris pumps, put my hands on my ample hips, and break into a huge grin that belies my nervousness. I look over at Coach Frazier, look down at my watch, and ask him, "What time is it, Coach?"

"It's game time, Jackie!" he says, giving me one of his first genuine smiles of the season.

Then I look around at my team and I imagine I am the late great Malcolm X speaking at the New York Audubon room and I say, "It has been an honor to coach 13 wonderful young men this year. We beat the odds and shook off the haters. You were made fun of because you have a female coach. They called you punks and little bitches for staying with me when you could have transferred to another school. You put up with yoga and Zumba sessions, and above all, you dealt with losing a coach you admired and adored. But you rose to the top and I am so proud of you! You have accomplished more in one season than most teams do in a lifetime. Tonight's game against Pearl Cohn High is going to be tough. Tonight I want you to play the best game of your life!"

When I finish my rousing speech, Peaches jumps up and yells, "WHAT TIME IS IT?"

"IT'S GAME TIME!" the entire team yells together.

With my heart pumping, I walk out of the locker room and head down the hall. I reach down and grab my necklace, say a quick prayer of thanks to God, do a fist bump to my dad and enter the brightly lit gymnasium. It is indeed game time, and I know my dad is proud of me. The gym is packed and the air is crackling with excitement. I quickly do my pre-game scan to look for three people: my mom, Principal Leevins, and Adaris. I also see Leo, Keeva, and all of the parents of my players. The pep squad is rousing the crowd as the minutes tick off the clock. My eyes travel up to the top of the gym and land on Adaris and Amos. Amos is grinning, but Adaris has an intense look much like one I often see on his mini me, AJ.

It's the fourth quarter, and Kerryn the game announcer is working the crowd.

"This game has been a show stopper! The lead has volleyed back and forth like a tennis match. Both teams are playing darn near flawless and the referees are giving them just enough rope to hang themselves. As we start the fourth quarter the score is 67- 70, with SHS in the lead. Coach Jackie, the best looking coach in the state of Tennessee, is almost as

animated as our late, great, beloved Coach Shorty would be. It just so happens he was her father, and she has definitely got his genes!"

"Amos, will you please shut up! I don't want to hear another word about Keeva ignoring you. She is less than 50 feet away, so walk your big ass down the bleachers and talk to her. This game has got me nervous as hell, Jackie just ripped off her jacket which has me horny as hell, and you are aggravating the hell out of me!"

"Adaris man, calm down! I won't say another word about Keeva's mean ass the rest of the game. I am here for you dawg! AJ is playing a great game. Your girl is coaching a great game...and looking fine, by the way. So just chill!"

"Stop looking at my woman and focus on the one you are trying to get!"

"Guys, this game is ours to win! Just continue to focus on the full court man to man defense. AJ, you have got to stop number 11. He is keeping Pearl in the game! Little Daddy, I need you to shoot more so we can open up the middle to get the ball to Junebug and Popper. Keep your heads in the game and block out all the distractions!" As the boys run onto the court to start the final quarter, I take several calming breaths. There is nothing else for me to do but guide them through this last quarter.

Kerryn is back on the mic.

"For all of you folks who decided to stay home tonight and listen to this game on the radio, it was a dumb decision! We have two minutes left and the lead has swung back to the Firebirds. The score is now 78- 74 and neither team seems to be losing steam. Coach Donovan had a small fit over a questionable call, and Coach Brown, the Firebird's coach has just called a full timeout—guess he wants to get their final plays straight so they can hold the lead."

"Guys, we have two minutes left in this game and we are only down by four points. Keep up the intensity on the full court defense and know that you have some fouls to give. We have two full time outs left. If you get in trouble, use them but be smart about it! And don't worry about the referees. That's what Coach Frazier and I are here to do. You just concentrate on getting that ball in the basket and playing great defense!"

I jump up from the huddle and suddenly feel light headed. I guess the pressure and the overheated gym are getting to me. I sway a little and try to catch myself before I fall on my ass. I simultaneously give myself a pep talk and pray to the Lord: *"OK you punk, do not pass out and embarrass yourself and your team. Lord, give me the strength to make it through this game without fainting! Come on Jackie, get your game face on. You have thousands of people watching you. Get it together!* When I open my eyes, Sophia is standing by my side with a cup of something orange. I pray it is Gatorade and gulp it down gratefully. That's the quickest answer to a prayer I have ever seen!

This game is about to kill me. I am on pins and needles for my son and for Jackie. Only two minutes are left on the clock and we are down by four. AJ has three fouls and I wish I could use mental telepathy to tell him to stick it to the other team's number 23. I don't know what Jackie is saying to them in that huddle but I am staring so hard that I can see her spit coming out of her mouth. I suddenly see her sway as she gets up from the huddle and I jump up so I can run down to catch her. Thankfully Amos caught me just in time.

"Fall back dude! Where do you think you're going?" Amos says after almost tackling me. "She is ok man. You know how it is when you get hyped. Sometimes the air goes straight to your head. And what the hell were you going to do? Step on everyone's damn head to get to her? We would be fighting for sure then!"

"I'm good, man. It looks like Sophia brought her some Gatorade and Mrs. Donovan just moved a few bleachers closer. Damn, this is about to kill me. Now I know how mom must have felt when I was playing ball!"

"Yeah man. I can't wait to tell Shelley and World about this shit. You are gone!"

Jerryn (Kerryn's substitute announcer)

"Folks, pardon a slight modulation in the voice. My brother Kerryn's voice has officially tanked. He has given all that he's got and I am here to give you a play by play of the last 75 seconds of the game. Rest assured Kerryn is right beside me writing furiously on a piece of paper

making sure we don't miss a beat. Coach Donovan has just called the first of her last two timeouts. That will leave both teams with one full timeout. Samuel Shaky Hall, the Sixth man Sensation, just sunk a three-point shot to bring the score to 78-77, still in favor of the Firebirds. The Bulldogs are still trailing by one point, but we still have a lot of round ball left in the game. Chauncey Junebug Smith, just fouled out, but what a way to go. He stopped number 23, Timothy 'Hound' McCain, from scoring but has put him on the line for two free throws. The Firebirds are now in a bonus!

"Coach Jackie has called a timeout to make a substitution and try to freeze Hound out. Bass Baby Baby Smith, who is Junebug' s little big brother holding at 6"6 has just checked into the game. In the words of Keith Sweat, 'He may be young but is ready,' and Coach Donovan is going to need his size in the paint to keep up with Booker Watson, the Firebirds' star guard. The crowd is going crazy! They know this game is going down to the wire and that a bad call can cause a barn fire! Stay with me as we break back into the game!"

The referee tells me, "Coach you have a full and a 30-second timeout left, which one do you want?"

"I thought I had two full. I'll take 30 seconds. Thanks ref." I turn to the team to give them instructions. "Baby Baby, go check in for Junebug. Junebug, you played a phenomenal game. Guys, number 23 has two free throws. Rest on the first and block out on the second. Scoop, I want you and Shaky out on the perimeter of the three point line. I want everyone to crash the boards. Baby, if you can't get the ball to Shaky, find Scoop or AJ. One of them will get it up the floor. Stay in your full court man to man defense at all times! Play hard and remember we have one more time out. Don't use it unless you are about to lose a possession. We have 65 seconds left in this game. That's a long time guys. Stay strong!"

Jerryn is going crazy.

"Folks, we are down to 55 seconds and the score has changed hands again! For those of you just tuning in, Hound McCain hit one free throw which brings the score to 79-77 in favor of the Firebirds. The Bulldogs got the ball in quick and put it in the hands of Samuel "Shaky" Hall, who sank a three pointer and moved the score to 80-79, Bulldogs now leading. The ball is back with the Firebirds. They have 55 seconds to score. My guess is they will take time off the clock and then shoot a quick two-

point shot or try to draw the foul to put them in a one and one. Both teams still have one full timeout. Folks, I want you to stay with me for the next 55 seconds and hold on, this is going to be a bumpy ride!"

"The Firebirds throw the ball in to their point guard James Foster and he's advancing up the court. The Bulldogs have him trapped in the corner and Foster is attempting to pivot out of the trap. He gets the ball to the point guard, who dribbles past the half court line. AJ Singleton picks him up there and the guard keeps dribbling to kill some time. We are now at 46 seconds and counting. The Firebirds have just spread the court in a four corner play. Guard Lawrence Brown just threw the ball to Harris, who goes in for a slam dunk. Only 39 seconds left and the score is tied. Both coaches have thrown down their charts—I can imagine they are giving their boys the pep talks of their lives. It all boils down to these last 39 seconds!"

"The Bulldogs take the ball out and—OMG, number 12 of the Firebirds stole the ball! The Firebirds have the ball with 27 seconds left and the score is tied. Evans throws it to Hound, who shoots a three-point shot from 25 feet out! He banks it off the backboard and it's in! Only four seconds left and no more timeouts for the Bulldogs. Coach Donovan is almost out on the court yelling at her boys. The crowd is deafening! Coach Brown won't take his last final timeout, he doesn't want to give the Bulldogs a chance to figure out how to score. Now Nixon takes the ball out, throws it to Scoop, who takes four quick dribbles and throws the ball to Shaky. Shaky launches the ball at the buzzer but misses the shot! Folks, the Firebirds have just upset the Bulldogs and will move on to the first round of the state tournament!"

"It has been my brother Kerryn and my pleasure to be with you through these 32 minutes of crowd-shaking basketball. This game was fantastic! Stay tuned to WSINK for more news on the first round of the state tournament. Good night everybody!"

The last 60 seconds are a blur, and then I hear the final buzzer. My team has just lost by three points. Right now I am not only at a loss for words but I don't know whom to console first. Coach Frazier is standing beside me shaking. Scoop, Popper, and Peaches are in the middle of the floor with tears pouring down their cheeks. Hector is yelling something in Spanish. AJ is standing on the other side of Coach Frazier with a look of utter misery.

I know my job is not done yet. I have to get these guys back to the locker room with as much dignity and grace as possible. Then I need to find the words to convey just how proud and honored I am to coach them. With the help of Cry Baby Frazier and Sophia, I get my boys off the court into the locker room. Some sit crying, some are angry, and some still in shock. I gather my wits and make what feels like Martin Luther King's "I've been to the Mountaintop" speech. I look at my boys and from my heart say, "I have never been more proud of any group of people in my life. You just played the most exciting, soul-stirring, animated two halves of basketball I have ever seen. We didn't win this game, but you are winners to me. Thank you for giving me the opportunity to earn your trust as your coach, mentor, and friend. I thought I was coming into this to teach you a few things but you actually taught me. The main thing you taught me is that I can coach, and for that I am grateful. Now, I want you guys to jump in the shower, and then let's celebrate a wonderful record, an outstanding team, and a great season."

As I turn to walk out the door, Jordan "Little Daddy" jumps up and says, "Coach, before you leave we want to tell you something. The boys appointed me the spokesperson of our team. We have to admit we had a lot of doubts about you. We aint I mean haven't ever seen a woman that can coach like you. You know the game of basketball but you also know how to make it fun. At first some of us were pissed off because people were joning on us about having a female coach, but it eventually became cool. Not just because you are fine, I mean pretty, but because you are better than all of the rest of those punks, I mean coaches out there. We miss Coach Donovan, but some days it seems like he never left. You are so much like him that it trips us out sometimes, even down to the way you talk and laugh. Anyway, a really wise man once told us that we should tell people how we feel while they are living. My moms said there was a song about giving people their flowers while they are still alive. So we pitched in and brought you some flowers."

Sophia comes out of the bathroom with two dozen red roses. As she walks toward me, my boys start clapping, and then the floodgates open. I just stand there crying—I could not be more surprised. As I walk around the room giving each of them a hug and whispering words of praise, I wonder if this is it. Will this be my last time in a locker room with this team? And then I decide I will think about it tomorrow. Tonight I want to focus on helping my team deal with the bitter taste of defeat. I gather my roses in one arm and Sophia in the other, and we leave the locker room so the guys can shower.

As the crowd spills out of the gym, I sit on the bleachers like a balloon that has lost all of its air. I can't imagine how my son must be feeling right now. The saving grace is that he has two more chances to win a state championship. One day he also will realize that this loss helped teach him how to lose gracefully and to treasure the wins. Amos left me to go and find Keeva. I really want to see Jackie just to reassure myself that she is ok. As I sit there lost in thought I feel a shadow over me, and I look up to see Ms. Ella. She smiles at me gently and says, "We are about to go check on Jackie. I could use an escort." I jump up and loop my arm through Ms. Ella's, and we walk down the bleachers together. She looks at me and says, "This gym brings back a lot of great memories. Jackie's dad and I met here." We head to the locker room to find all of the parents, Principal Leevins, the cheerleaders, and the rest of Jackie's family waiting for the boys to come out. I see Amos and Keeva out of the corner of my eye. I guess Keeva is over being pissed at Amos because he has his big arms wrapped around her. Ms. Ella turns to me and says, "Jackie is just like her daddy. My guess is she is in that small coatroom about two doors down on your right getting herself together. She won't let anyone see the pain she is feeling. I will hold everyone off. Go on and check on her."

Before she gets the last words out of her mouth I am heading down the hall. I knock softly and then open the door. When I see Jackie's face, my heart breaks in two. She is sitting in a raggedy chair at a makeshift desk looking smaller than I have ever seen her. I bend down beside her and gather her to me.

"Hey Coach. How are you doing?"

"Sad, happy, proud, deflated...thinking there was something I could have done to change the outcome of that game."

"Shhh," I say, breathing into her hair. "You coached your ass off and your team played great. That game wasn't decided until the buzzer. I am so proud of you and I know the parents and the team are as well. You couldn't have coached the team any better. Now, I'm guessing you have about two minutes to get yourself together before Leo comes bursting in here. Your mom and Keeva know why I'm here, but I am sure he is wondering what is going on."

I pull out a handkerchief and gently wipe Jackie's face, and then I say, "Did I ever tell you you're the sexiest coach I have ever seen? You look good, you smell good, even after getting hot and sweaty, and you've got the damndest swagger I have ever seen."

"Careful pro bowler. Flattery will get you everywhere."

I rise up and bring Jackie with me, then put my arms around her. No more words are necessary. I am the balm for her pain. I stroke my hands up and down her back, then say, "It's time to put your game face back on, sweetness. Go out and take in all of the atta boys, compliments, and probably some criticism, but just remember that you coached your ass off and that your family, your team, and I are proud of you."

I lean down and give her a gentle kiss on the lips. Before I succumb and start to suck her face off, I gently brush my tongue across her mouth. Jackie says, "hmmm tastes like mangos and peaches. Did you steal a piece of my gum"?

"You bet your sweet onion I did. When I chew it, it reminds me of you," I say as I back out of the office.

Jackie takes one last breath and goes out to join her legion of players, fans, and haters.

After the team goes out for pizza, I head home to some much needed rest. Now that the season is over I need a few days off just to unwind. I have a lot to think about. Principal Leevins told me he wants to extend my contract at SHS to coach the boys' team indefinitely. I also have to respond to the offers from Seattle and Atlanta. I know if I stay at SHS that will likely put my relationship with Adaris on hold for two more years, and that those two years will probably put an end to our already tenuous relationship. I have a lot of patience, but I can't imagine two more years without Adaris. Going to Atlanta or Seattle would mean a long distance relationship, and I definitely don't want that. What I want is a chance to be courted and to court him back. I need to decide what to do in the next few days. Mom, Serena, Keeva, and Max all pitched in to buy me a ticket to go see Max in the Virgin Islands for a few days. I will have three days of Crucian rum, mangos, and Max. Three days to make some decisions about my future.

I really need to talk with my Mom and AJ. I walk into the kitchen to find my mom making several gallons of her famous tea. I plop down in one of the kitchen chairs, and she turns around and smiles at me. Believe me, there is nothing like seeing the love in your mother's eyes. That is the main reason I am glad Lisa moved home. AJ needs to see that look in his mother's eyes.

"Mom, do you have a few minutes to talk?"

"I always have a few minutes for you, baby. Have you gotten over AJ's game?"

"Mom, if that game was any indication of how I am going to be when he really starts competing, then I need to work on keeping my blood pressure under control. It almost killed me."

"Now you know how I used to feel watching you play. But I think you were also having some issues because of someone else. I saw you hop up when Coach Donovan swayed during that game. Thank goodness Amos was there to stop you from making a fool out of yourself," Mom says with a big grin.

"Yeah, I figured my gig was up with you a long time ago. But why didn't you say something to me, Ma?"

"Say what? Say she is a beautiful young lady who comes from a great family. Say she is smart and funny and really seems to care about my son and grandson. Say she appears to have a great relationship with God. Say I love the way she pampers you with special gifts, like that scrapbook you can't seem to put down and those sweets you keep eating. Say you are so sprung over this young lady that you are dizzy with excitement. Say it is wonderful to see you excited about someone again because it's been a long time coming. Ok, now I said it."

"Have I been that transparent?"

"Only to those who know you well," she says with a huge grin.

"So you don't have a problem with me not getting back together with Lisa. You know she has really been pushing for us to do that?"

"The time for Lisa to push for you to be together was sixteen years ago. She's a little too late now don't you think? And just because you have known someone for eighteen years doesn't mean that is the person you are supposed to be with. God will send you the person destined for you. It's not always wrapped up in a neat little package either. Sometimes you have to work a little and make adjustments for things to work out. I have no doubt that the two of you will do that."

And with that last remark Katherine turned around to her gallons of tea and started whistling, "going to the chapel and we're going to get married." For someone so quiet she sure could say a little but mean a lot.

AJ and I were hanging out after school and I decided I needed to have a dude to dude talk with him so I could see where his head was. I figured the best way to get him warmed up was to feed him first so we ran out to Prince's Chicken to grab a bite. I don't know how that boy can eat the hot chicken but if it was going to keep him mellow I would let him eat himself into submission. After AJ finished stuffing his face I started a conversation that quickly spiraled out of control.

"Son, how are you feeling about the game now that you have had a few days to think about it?"

"I haven't really thought about it much. You always told me to play my best all the time so I won't have any regrets. I didn't play a perfect game but I played my best. So I'm cool Pops. I hate it for the seniors, but I have two more years to win a state championship. Anyhow, they are going to be a'right."

"I'm proud of you son. You are really growing up. I know how much you hate losing, but it does make it a little better if you know you played your best. How did you like playing for Coach Donovan?"

"I aint gone lie Pops, I wasn't excited about playing for her at first. I know she had some ups in the WNBA but I wasn't sure if she could handle Scoop and Little Daddy. Those two are pretty crunk. But she slow walked all of us down and she had us doing stuff that really made us a better team. She was a lot like Coach D but really different. Why you ask Pop's?"

"I was just wondering if you were happy playing for her? "

"What's it to you dad? You don't have to play for her," AJ says with a smirk.

"Well son, I wanted to wait for your season to be over with before I talk to you. This has been on my mind for a while and I really want you to give me your honest opinion."

"Is this about you kissing Ms. Grimes at the Christmas party Pops? Or about all of the tens you had at that football game in the fall?"

"The tens? Oh, you mean all the women who came to my first game? That was awful man. Don't ever put yourself in that position...or at least not if the tens know about each other."

"Me and my boys were taking bets on who was going to have a smack down. And Granny was just sitting back in the cut with a smile on her face. So is that what you want to rap about Pops?"

"First let me say that I did not kiss Ms. Grimes. And I did not intentionally invite all of those women to the game. I actually only wanted one other woman besides your grandmother there, and that was—"

"It was mom! I just knew you would get back together. I could tell by the way she was looking at you, and one night you all went out on a date right? And she has been going out more often at night and coming back really late. I knew it—"

"Pump your brakes, son! I will always love your mother because she had you, but we are not getting back together. Can you just hold up a minute and let me tell you what— "

"So is it Hannah from church? She acts all holy and stuff but she is fine."

I lower my head and rub the back of my neck. Then I look at AJ and say, "No, not Hannah. The woman I wanted there was—"

"Johnnie, the PYT!"

"Why do you call her PYT?"

"Oh, I heard Coach Donovan mumble something about her one day. She is a pretty young thang, Dad. If I was a few years "older I would be asking her to design my house too. Dad, you may be old as hell, I mean heck, but you can sure pull them!"

"Adaris Junior, be quiet! I need to tell you something and you won't let me get a word in edgewise!"

"What is it dad. I am all ears," AJ says with a sly smile.

"You know, don't you?" I say, feeling a bit lightheaded.

"I was born at night Pops, not last night. Of course I know, but I am going to make you tell me so I can gloat for a few minutes."

"When I met Jackie I had no idea she would be coaching you. In fact, she didn't either at first . Once she decided to take the job we decided not to see each other out of respect for her position as your coach and your position as her player. I am glad we did that, but now that the season is over I want to try to find a happy medium for all of us, and I want your input. But first I want to know how you knew about us."

"Dad, I may be young but I aint stupid. Anyone looking would know that the two of you are crazy about each other. I knew when you were getting all dressed up and smelling all good you were seeing someone special. Then the day that we went over to play ball at Coach's house and you two played each other, it was like the movie *Love and Basketball* all over again. When you let her win I knew your nose was wide open. Also, the brownies and cookies you've been bringing home are identical to the stuff Coach would bring to practice. I also knew you and Coach were underneath the bleachers at the Christmas party acting like two horny teenagers. I just said that about Ms. Grimes to give you a hard time. Hey Dad, Coach Jackie is dope! I can see how you would be all in love and stuff. And I think it's cool, Dad. I have always wanted you to settle down with someone who would love you and take good care of you. I might even like to have a few more brothers and sisters one day. The two of you would make some cool looking kids."

"Wow...I guess all this time I thought I was keeping this a big secret, and here you and your grandmother were on to me. Now I'm wondering who else knows about it."

"When I get old I want to be just like you. You got swagger Pops."

"Thanks. I think. The big question now is how will it be if Jackie decides to coach your team next year. I don't want anyone to think you're getting playtime because your daddy dates your coach. I raised you to earn your playing time. That's why Jackie and I are at odds."

"Dad, anyone who knows the game of basketball can see that I got game. I aint flossing but I am pretty good. And I have done some research. A lot of people are coached by a parent. I am cool with it as long as you are."

"Parent!" Son, slow your roll. I can see a future with Jackie but I am not sure about walking down the aisle just yet...or am I? Hell, this whole conversation is just confusing me."

"Pops, what makes you think Coach Jackie is even going to stay at SHS? She has some better offers on the table. She may decide to split."

"Split? What are you, a throwback? That word came out even before my time."

"OK, she may decide to get ghost, how about that? Why don't you just take one day at a time? You don't have to worry about sneaking out of the house to have your little rendezvous now. You can take her to a real nice place now, Pops. Just keep me posted on any turn of events so I can make adjustments, a'right? Oh, and Pops, believe me I have been taking notes. I got a love jones for someone in my backyard too."

"A love jones! What do you know about a love jones? And please tell me it's not with Ms. Grimes," I say.

"No dad, it's not Ms. Grimes. It's Sophia."

"The young lady who keeps the books for the team?"

"She is the statistician and Coach D's publicist, but yes that's the one. I know Peaches is kind of feeling her so I have been just sitting back in the cut."

"How did that happen?"

"Well, it's a long story but at the basketball camp in Lexington I realized how cool she was after a little incident in the girl's dorm."

"A little incident?"

"Never mind, that's not important Pops."

"Does Sophia like Peaches?"

"Come on now Pop. She likes me! But we can't figure out a way to make it work without making Peaches feel bad. So I feel you Pops on the Coach D tip. But I think you need to focus on Coach Jackie and not worry about my love life. I got this Pops."

"Maybe I need you to give me some advice."

"What you said!" AJ yells as he jumps up from the table.

Twice in two days the idea of marriage has been mentioned...

"Max, I could really get used to hanging out here in St. Croix. It's good for my blood pressure, my body, and my self-esteem."

"I know girl. You are fresh meat around here. The Crucian men haven't seen anything as fine as you since, well, since me."

"Girl, you are a trip. I can't thank you all enough for giving me this trip, it's exactly what I needed to get my mind right. And I must be pretty special if you took two days off to entertain me."

"You are special—I just wish I could get you down here more often. It's your last night, Jack, and we haven't talked much about Adaris or the team. Do you know what you're going to do?"

"Max, I know this coaching job could have been a disaster, but I really enjoyed it. I felt like God was guiding me the whole way through. And the boys actually liked playing for me. To be honest, staying on would be a no brainer if not for AJ. If I coach the team again I will probably give up any chance I have to be with Adaris. But if I take the job in Atlanta it won't be any better, and don't even mention Seattle."

"Don't you Americans say absence makes the heart go softer? Atlanta is just four hours away, and now that Adaris has retired he can come see you."

"It's 'the heart grow fonder,' Max, and Adaris just built a new house after being on the road for 12 years. Driving back and forth to Atlanta would get old pretty fast."

"That man is crazy about you. Chris and I talk about you two all the time. He was going nuts the last two days because he couldn't find you.

I finally told Chris to tell him you are here with me. What broad does not carry her cell phone in this day and age?"

"The broad who needs to get away from the phone. Maybe there is hope for us if Adaris is going nuts with me being out of touch. I don't know what to say to him, Max. The last time I saw him was over a week ago, after our game, and we didn't really get a chance to talk. I'm sure he has heard I have other offers. I am so confused, Max. I really want to stay in Tennessee for so many reasons, but AJ is going to be playing ball for the next two years, and he is so good that I don't want him to play anywhere else. So if it's me or him that gets sacrificed, I guess it's me!"

"I suggest you talk to Adaris before you make any major decisions, Jackie. Things may have changed in the last few months. Stop running away–run to him instead and see what happens. This aint no high school, check the box if you want to be my boo crap. This is the rest of your life. God brought you home for a reason, Jack, and I think it's to fulfill your destiny."

"I am so afraid he is going to reject me again. And I wish you could take some of your own advice, Max. Then maybe we would both have a chance to be happy."

"My situation is different from yours, Jack. It's...it's just complicated. Now, I am going to call my man and tell him to tell your man your ass will be home tomorrow. It's time for you to fart or get off the pot."

"It's shit or get off the pot, Max!" I say, laughing at my wonderful friend.

I finally get the nerve to call Jackie, and her phone keeps rolling straight to voicemail. After the third call I decide to text her. I send something simple, like, "Hey, how are you?" just to feel her out. I typically get a text back within a few hours, so when I don't hear anything, I start to get worried. I don't want to sound like a punk and call her mom or Keeva, so I do the next best thing, I call World. I knew he could find out from Max where Jackie has been hiding since the game.

"Speak!"

"Is that how you answer the phone now World?"

"No, sometimes I say, hello chump! What's up?"

"I'm just calling to see if you're bored since you got put out of the playoffs?"

"Oh, you got jokes, don't you? Actually I'm on my way to St. Croix, where you should have been for the last three days 'cause your girl is there. I suppose you are calling me 'cause you miss her."

"I knew you would know where Jackie is. She isn't answering her phone and I was starting to get worried."

"Maybe she isn't answering her phone because she doesn't want to talk to your sorry ass! A lady can only be turned down so many times before she decides to go another route."

"Turned down? What the hell are you talking about, World? I am trying to get her Turnt up!   I am trying to find her so I can talk to her about our future. The last thing I want to do is turn her down...unless I turn her upside down, if you get my drift."

"Stop being nasty for a minute. I want to know how you plan to get your girl? Hell, at this point I need some advice myself. I have done everything short of retiring from football, like your decrepit ass."

"Let me see if I can get Jackie first, then I will see if I feel qualified to give you some advice. When did you say she is coming home?"

"I don't have her ETA man, I aint no flight attendant. If you were on your JOB you would have all that info and wouldn't be coming to me. All I know is tomorrow afternoon she arrives in Nashville and I arrive in St. Croix. Now get off my phone!" World yells and then clicks off his phone.

As I sit there with the phone stuck to my ear I suddenly realize I'm about to play the biggest game of my life and I wonder if I will win or lose.

I get back in town on a cold Wednesday evening. As I walk through the airport I get a little deja vu, almost as if I will run into Adaris like I did more than a year ago. I can't believe it's been over a year since Dad passed away. The time has somehow gone so fast but also so slow. Another year gone, and here I am by myself again. I am lonely, like a huge chunk is missing from my life. I guess I could throw caution to the wind and not accept any of the job offers, and then pray that Adaris is as much in love with me as I am with him and that he pops the question. But I wasn't raised to live my life based on what if's and maybes. And what if I put all my cards on the table and things don't work out. Then I not only would be by myself again but jobless.

Actually, I'm not uncomfortable being alone, but I am ready to be settled. Not *to* settle, but *to be* settled, especially now that I have experienced a man who loves the Lord, loves his mother, and has made sacrifices to raise his son to be a great young man. He also happens to be handsome, caring, fine, and smart. It also doesn't hurt that he is wealthy. My daddy always said Rena and I need to marry for love and money. For the first time my heart went pitter patter when someone walked into the room. But even more I knew when the pitters puttered our relationship would sustain because our foundation was built on friendship.

As I walk through the airport pondering these thoughts, I'm also looking around to see if I can catch a glimpse of Adaris, even though I have no reason to think he'll be there. I laugh as I think about our first meeting. I grab my suitcase from the baggage carousel and roll it to the curb. Keeva is waiting on me in a brand new Jaguar XK. I put my bag in the trunk and jump in.

"Hey girl! You look two shades darker and well rested. I knew I should have gone with you. Did you have a good time?"

"I did have a good time. We went to the beach, drank too much rum, and just hung out. When did you get this beauty?"

"Girl, I had a dream the other night about Uncle Shorty and Aunt Ella. Uncle Shorty looked just wonderful, and so young. He told me he was happy to see me. When I woke up I pulled out my dream book and played the number 729. You know, that's the number you play when you dream about talking to the dead. But you know I boxed it to increase my chances."

"Uh, no Keeva, only you and grandma have dream books. So did the number fall?"

"Did it fall? Girl, it fell alright. It fell so damn hard that $10,000 later I took the Benz to the Jag dealership and traded it in, along with some of my winnings. Do you like?"

"Girl I love it! When I grow up I want to be just like you."

Jackie is due back in town this evening. I decide to give her a night to settle in before I call her. It is killing me not to call her mom or Keeva to ask if I can pick her up from the airport. Then I realize I have gone this far so I can wait another 12 hours. The next morning I go for a long run to calm my nerves. I have been planning things the last few days to make sure everything is set for the time I finally see Jackie. At about 10:00 am I send her a text:

"Jackie, I really need your help. I am out of town and I need someone to let Ros, my interior decorator, in to finish a few more things before AJ and I move in. Do you mind letting her in? I left a key in the power outlet on the front porch. Please let me know if you can meet her there at 2:00 pm."

Lord, please forgive me for telling that little white lie, but I needed a way to get her into my house so I can talk to her without interruptions. I sit there for about 15 minutes sweating bullets. It's worse than waiting for a new team to call and tell you they want to offer you a contract. And then I hear the ding!

"Good morning. Yes, I can meet Ros at the house. Why am I meeting her?"

Damn, I would be an awful thief. I forgot to tell her why I need her to meet Ros. Let's see...

"I need you to look at the wall in the study. I don't like the color and I need you to help choose something different."

"What color is on the wall now?"

Ugh...I don't know what color is on the wall! I just picked all the colors Jackie told me to. Let's see, she said warm colors...

"It's some type of baby boo boo brown. I don't really like it. Can you help Ros pick a different color? I trust your judgment."

"Sure, I hope you like neon pink! LOL"

Funny. I know when she sees that wall in the study it's going to blow her away. I've got about three hours to finish getting things ready at the house.

I wonder why Adaris wants me to meet the interior decorator. I haven't been to the house since it was framed. I must admit, I am looking forward to seeing the end result. I decide to hit the gym for a few hours and then head out to meet the decorator. I was so hoping I would get a chance to see Adaris. I guess I just have to wait for him to come back from his trip.

After my workout I head to the shower, only to be told the water valve is broken. If I had known that I wouldn't have worked out for so long. Now I have to meet Ros smelling jacked up to be damned and looking a hot mess. Thank God it's just her. I will try to pick out this new paint color quickly, then run back home and get my funky butt in the shower. What the hell was I thinking trying high yoga! It is 110 degrees in that damn room and everyone is sweating like pigs. I got so hot I couldn't even do the downward dog! I can't believe I let the gym manager talk me into doing that crap—I think he was just trying to look at my booty. I plop my hat on my head and pull on my sweats so I can get to the house on time.

I pull into Adaris' driveway, and I slam on the brakes. I just can't believe the transformation—the house is absolutely gorgeous! It ended up a Mediterranean design with a full walk-out basement. It's finished in peanut butter stucco, the lower half is detailed with chocolate and taupe stones that give it an earthy look, and the roof is chocolate tile. I feel like I have stepped into a foreign country. I pull around the circular cobblestone drive, and don't see any cars out front. I must have beaten the interior decorator here. I decide to run in and wipe some of the funk off my underarms before she gets here, but first I want to find the study so I can check out this ugly color. I find the key and open the door, and I immediately feel at home. The foyer boasts a huge chandelier and medium brown hardwood floors that are polished to a high shine. To the right is the dining room, painted in a beautiful terra cotta, with blue and taupe as accent colors. It is furnished with a round cherry table that comfortably seats eight. There is also a china hutch and buffet, perfect for entertaining. The centerpiece on the table is a blend of oranges, browns, and blues—in fact, it looks a lot like an arrangement my mother or sister could have put together.

I slip off my shoes and follow the foyer into the study. I enter the room and my mouth drops open. This room is anything but ugly! The walls are a beautiful chocolate brown, with a crown molding at least six inches deep that's painted a high gloss cream. There are bookshelves on three of the walls that hold framed pictures, trophies, and awards. There is a huge desk in the center of the room that has a chair on each end so it can be used by two people. But what has left me open mouthed is the poem Adaris has had drawn on the center wall. It is my favorite poem, "Our Deepest Fear" by Marianne Williamson. I stand in the middle of the room reading the poem aloud.

"Our deepest fear is not that we are inadequate. Our deepest fear is that we are powerful beyond measure. It is our light, not our darkness, that most frightens us. We ask ourselves, Who am I to be brilliant, gorgeous, talented, fabulous? Actually, who are you not to be? You are a child of God. Your playing small does not serve the world. There's nothing enlightened about shrinking so that other people won't feel insecure around you. We are meant to shine, as children do. We were born to make manifest the glory of God that is within us. It's not just in some of us; it's in everyone. And as we let our light shine, we unconsciously give other people permission to do the same. As we're liberated from our own fear, our presence automatically liberates others."

As I get to the end, Adaris walks into the room behind me and we read the last sentence in unison. I just stand there for a few minutes reflecting on what I just read, while tears run down my sweaty face. I finally turn to Adaris and whisper, "Did you do this for me?"

"I did this entire house for *us*. Just about every idea you came up with is in this house. I wanted to wait till it was fully finished before you saw it, and I enlisted Ms. Ella and Serena to help me with the decorating, since they know your tastes. What do you think?"

"What I have seen so far is gorgeous, and this room is incredible. The rest of the house will probably overwhelm me. But I thought you were out of town. Did you set me up?"

"I did set you up. I almost lost my mind when you went to St. Croix to see Max. I have been planning this for some time now. I am so eager to talk about us, Jackie, I just don't want to go another day without us having some decision about our future."

"I feel the same way. I went to visit Max so I could get my head together. I know you have heard rumors so I want to tell you what is really going on. I did get an offer from a high school in Seattle, and my old team offered me a position in the front office. And a few weeks ago I got another offer to coach a boys' team in Atlanta."

"And didn't Principal Leevins offer to extend your contract at SHS?"

"Yes, he did, Adaris. And that is the position I want, but I realize that if I take it we will have to put our relationship on hold for another two years, and that won't work for either one of us. I also don't think either of us would be crazy about a long-distance relationship. I can't ask you to stay on the road half the time and give up time with your family and in this beautiful new home. And if you add ESPN into the mix things get even more complicated. I love you Adaris. I have never felt even close to this with anyone else. And I feel like this is where I need to be for my career and for my family and—"

"And who says you can't have it all, Jackie? Didn't you just read that poem? Do you remember when we were playing 20 questions at dinner and you told me this is your favorite poem? That evening I went home and Googled it, and the words really spoke to me. You allow my light to shine, Jackie, and you make me want to be a better person. The main reason I left you alone—well, tried to leave you alone—this season is because you needed the time to heal from the death of your father. Coaching your dad's team was a way for you to come to terms with his death and to celebrate his legacy. But I also needed some time to really figure out what I want. When you literally fell into my life more than a year ago, I wasn't looking for a girlfriend or a wife, I just wanted to get away from the press and focus on my last year of football. But you know what God says about making plans, right? All my plans were shot to hell when I fell head over heels for you. I really believe your dad helped our good Lord orchestrate our meeting. We are just what the other needed, Jackie."

"Ok, we love each other. That was the easy part. But that doesn't change our situation Adaris!"

"What changes our situation is a little conversation I had with my son and Principal Leevins."

"What conversation are you talking about?"

"I sat down with AJ a little over a week ago, and after he gave me hell for about ten minutes, he finally admitted that he has known about the two of us for months," Adaris says with a bold laugh. "Can you believe he kept that from both of us for so long? And just so you know, he has given his blessing for us to be together. And he also said that he wouldn't have any problem playing for a parent—"

"He what? He knew all this time we were seeing each other! Oh Adaris, I am so embarrassed. There is no telling how many other people have known about us all this time. Did Principal Leevins know as well?"

"Principal Leevins, along with your father, wanted us to meet a while ago. Apparently they both thought we would be a great match. I hope you don't mind, but I did meet with him to discuss a potential conflict of interest in a coach parent-team member relationship—"

"You met with Principal Leevins! Now I am mortified. Do you think he thinks I was giving AJ preferential treatment because he is your son...wait, what did you say?"

"He said he has been dealing with such situations all his life and that you wouldn't be the first person to coach their child. He also said that if our situation were to drive you away from coaching the team, I would have to answer to him. The last thing he said is that he trusts your coaching ability and is sure that your continued winning record will shut most people up."

"But how do you feel about that Adaris? I don't want anything to interfere with your relationship with your son, or with me—"

Adaris walks over to me, takes my hand, and bends down on one knee. "What I was trying to say before you kept interrupting me is, Jackie Coretta Donovan, will you marry me? Will you be my wifey for life, booed up forever, my future baby's momma, my son's head coach and other momma, my partner, and my helper until death do us part?" And with that he pulls a blue Tiffany box out of his pocket, lifts a brilliant cut four carat ring in a Tiffany setting out of the box, and slips it on my finger. "This house was built for our family, Jackie. I have done my best to make it perfect for both of us."

I stand there with my mouth wide open for about ten seconds. Then I close my eyes, whisper a silent prayer of gratitude to God, and then look down at Adaris with tears running down my cheeks.

"I guess since you put it that way, I will have to say, most definitely yes. But can you do me a huge favor?"

"Anything sweetness."

"I would like you to let me take a shower, comb my hair, and come back clean, and then ask me again."

Adaris throws back his head and bellows. "I got one better for you. Since I made sure you couldn't take a shower at the gym so I could get you out here quickly, how about we take a tour of the house and end in the master bathroom? That way we can kill two birds with one stone."

I put my arms around Adaris and say, "What stone would that be, Mr. Singleton?"

"We can christen our new bathroom while you wash that funky smell off you, Mrs. Singleton to be. I love you and all, but you are a little rank," he says, giving me a wet kiss.

"Hey it's for better or worse. Right now you are dealing with worse."

"Sweetness, your worst is most people's best."

Adaris and I decide to have a short engagement. We are excited about consummating our marriage, but since we have waited over a year we figure another few months won't hurt...well, at least I feel that way. We decide to slip away and get married quietly, and then return home to the big reception my mom and Serena are busy planning. Serena, Max, Keeva, and Tiffany will be my honorary bridesmaids at the reception. Since they'll miss the actual wedding, they insist on coordinating their dresses and shoes for the reception. I decided to let them pick their own dresses, which are a beautiful old gold color, and told them I would surprise them with shoes from Nordstrom's—of course! Chris, Shelley, Amos, and AJ will be the groomsmen. Instead of tuxedos, Adaris decides to get them all custom suits made by Jazzmine.

We still don't know what the future will hold for our friends. Max and Keeva both have trust issues, which has made it difficult for them to have healthy relationships. While Chris and Max are working through their issues, Keeva is running as far away from Amos as she can. Leo continues to do well in school. Our engagement even has him thinking about settling down with Queesha. Leo says he wants to make dad proud by being a good husband and father. Aunt Lu returned to New York after she and my mom sold the property and split the profits. She still has not come to terms with the death of my father or her relationship with Leo. I guess every family has its issues.

When Adaris and I got engaged, AJ and I sat down and had a long talk. We decided to keep the business of basketball and our home lives separate. As AJ put it, it's kind of like the separation of church and state. I also suggested that he keep his budding relationship with Sophia in the same vein. Who knew a botched panty raid could lead to love?

Ella is adjusting to a new life without my dad. In fact, she recently reconnected with Johnny "Skip" Fulton, Johnnie's dad, at one of her group meetings. They are old friends, both are widowed, and they have a lot in common. I secretly have a good laugh at the thought that Johnnie might one day be my stepsister!

"This is Tony Stint, and I'm speaking with Coach Jackie Donovan, who just coached a great first season. Jackie promised me we would talk again when the season was over. So Jackie, how did you feel about losing in the sub-state to the Firebirds?"

"Tony, I was obviously disappointed that we didn't make it to the state tournament, but I knew my team played a great game. When you lose the way we lost, there's not much to say."

"Many people are wondering what will happen to your seniors. I believe you returned with five this year. Is it too early to ask if they received scholarships?"

"I knew you were going to ask me this question. Josh "Scoop" Stevens has been accepted to a great division II college in Winter Park, Florida called Rollins College. Leslie Peaches Grimes has elected to join the military. Lance "Popper" Nixson has decided to play football and will become a University of Tennessee Vol in the fall. Jordan "Little Daddy" McCullough has decided to go to Vanderbilt University on a full academic scholarship. Chauncey "Junebug" Smith is going to Middle Tennessee State University on a basketball scholarship. They all come from great families, did very well academically, stayed out of trouble, and they also happen to be great basketball players—in that order."

"Now the question we have all been wanting to ask, Jackie. What are your plans for next year? There have been rumors that you have been offered positions in Seattle, Atlanta, New York, and even St. Croix."

"St Croix, that's a new one for me! My dear friend Max would be happy to hear that. I have been offered a few positions and I was honored to be considered. But Tennessee is my home and this is where I want to be. Principal Leevins has offered me a permanent position as the boy's head basketball coach, and the county has offered me a new position as the athletic director. I can't give you much information about that yet, but I promise to have more for you soon."

"Have you accepted both positions Jackie?"

"I have, Tony, and I can't wait to start."

"Jackie, I noticed you are wearing a huge engagement ring and I have heard rumors about the giver of that ring. Would you like to fill people in on the truth of those rumors?"

"Well, I generally like to keep my private life private, but because I'm talking with you, I will say that I recently became engaged to Adaris Singleton and we plan to be married in the next few months."

"That would be the all-pro footballer Adaris "Dair" Singleton. His son AJ is one of your up and coming juniors, right?"

"Yes he is."

"So how do you plan to handle coaching your son for the next two years?"

"I am going to do what John Thompson, Earl Woods, Richard Williams, Coach Carter and many others have done. I will coach AJ just like I did this past season. When we are on the court he is my player. When we walk off the court he will be my step-son."

"Are you concerned that coaching AJ will create problems with some of the parents and players?"

"If you know anything about basketball you can see that AJ is a gifted player and athlete. He and the other players will be just as competitive next year as they were this past season. And the parents know if they have a problem they can come and discuss it with me, but the final decisions will always be mine."

"Looking back on the season, Jackie, what would you say was your biggest surprise?"

"My biggest surprise was how easy it was to make the transition from playing with women to coaching young men. Basketball is basically the same no matter where you go."

"Your dad taught you a lot about this game. What advice did you use the most during the last season?"

"He always told me to focus on the fundamentals of the game, developing kids and everything else would take care of itself. He also told me to keep the game fun and get to know your players."

"What will you do differently next year?"

"The team next year will be a little bigger and a lot faster. I plan to tailor our game to accommodate the change in height. Other than that I plan to focus on the fundamentals."

"Jackie, you had a whirlwind year. Your father passed away, you retired from playing basketball, you became one of the first women to successfully coach a boys' basketball team and you got engaged. Would you change any of these major events?"

"If I could bring my dad back I would for selfish reasons but he wouldn't want to come. He left a legacy with his children, students, and players. I received confirmation a few weeks ago that he is well with our Lord. I have no regrets about coming back to Tennessee. I came home to bury my father and help my family but in his death I was blessed to meet the man that God ordained for me. So, no, I wouldn't change a thing. I've got to run Tony. My fiancé is waiting on me."

With that last comment I get up and walk out of the SHS gym, recently named the Thomas Shorty Donovan Gymnasium with the purple and gold pendants swinging from the rafter and the gleaming hardwood floor that smelled faintly of sweat and popcorn into the arms of my destiny.

50073855R00188

Made in the USA
Charleston, SC
15 December 2015